As if she didn't have enough to worry about, now she was going to be eaten by a jaguar?

Carmen looked around the trailer. Shortly after they had moved in, she had been drawn to its colorful images of saints, mermaids, and dragons painted on the sides, peeling and discolored from the elements.

Rosa had straightened up some and fixed a spot to sleep on the couch in the front section.

"Mami, are you okay? You must be scared and lonely out here."

Rosa shook her head wearily. "I no help *solamente* I sit *aqui* la sitting duck loca, *sabes?*" She made a low, rumbling sound in her throat like a faulty electric razor.

"Oh, Mami, Don't worry. I have a plan. I am talking to someone who can help us. My friend Chia knows people in the...uhm, State Department that help if you can't afford lawyers. Here, just eat this, Mami. We gotta keep strong for Tomas. Promise me you'll stop worrying so much."

Carmen stepped outside the trailer into almost pitch blackness. On the flimsy step, she stopped to let her eyes adjust and thought she heard movement in the bushes. Then two bright, topaz spots grew larger, moving toward her from the middle of a fire thorn bush about ten feet away. Frozen to the steps, Carmen opened her mouth to scream but only a half gasp, half whimper emerged.

A sleek, spotted jaguar fixed its coppery-gold eyes on hers but did not move. The dogs in their pens were strangely silent. Carmen could smell the jaguar's musky, feral odor blending with another scent like very strong herbs. The dark trees swirled around them like inky plants caught in a tangle of currents deep on the ocean floor. Carmen wanted to run, but her legs were like wet sponges when she tried to move them. The animal surged forward then, and she just let go, slipping down on the steps, ready to be served up for its dinner.

When Carmen Luna's brother Tomas is abducted by Immigration (ICE) and taken to an unknown location, she knows her elementary magic will not be enough to free him. Forging a surprising friendship with Chia Yang, a Hmong girl, Carmen joins forces—and magic—with Chia in an effort to free Tomas and save her home from the evil realtor, Mr. Silver, who collaborates with ICE to steal the property and valuables of those who are deported. Together, Carmen and Chia must draw on the knowledge of their ancestors and the strengths of their separate cultures to save Tomas and battle the evil forces that threaten to destroy not only their families—but everyone on Earth.

KUDOS for *Carmen & Chia Mix Magic*

In *Carmen & Chia Mix Magic* by Dixie Salazar, Carmen is a 15-year-old girl, most of whose family is in the US illegally. In the neighborhood where Carmen and her family live is an evil realtor who profits from turning illegals over to the immigration services and then stealing all the family's valuable possessions once they are deported...*Carmen & Chia Mix Magic* gives us a revealing glimpse of what life is life for immigrants, legal or illegal, who leave behind everything they knew and loved and move to a new country, hoping to find a better life. Not only are they mostly made to feel unwelcome, they don't even speak the language of their new country and that, along with many other obstacles, makes it difficult for them to survive. It illustrates how important family can be at such a time, and what some people with do when their loved ones are threatened. It also illustrates how some unscrupulous people will use the problems of those less fortunate to make a profit at others' expense. I think the book is one that all young people should read. Maybe, if we have a better understanding of other people's problems and heartaches, we might learn to be more tolerant. – *Taylor Jones, Reviewer*

Carmen & Chis Mix Magic is a YA/educational novel about a family of illegal immigrants struggling to survive in a difficult situation. Their problems are compounded when they are targeted by a group of thugs who get rich by turning people over to the immigration control and then stealing their valuables when they are deported to their homelands. In this case, however, the thugs are after a magical plate that is in the possession of Carmen's family, though they are unaware of it...The book is well written, educational, and I recommend it to anyone who wants both a better understanding of the Spanish language and a glimpse of a world where culture and family are sometimes the only things you can call your own. – *Regan Murphy, Reviewer*

ACKNOWLEDGEMENTS

With special thanks to Sue Beevers, Bonnie Hearn, Geri Yang, Rosula Ramos, Jon Veinberg and the editors at Black Opal Books for their help and support. Also much thanks to Peter Everwine for permission to use the poem "Flowers are Falling" his translation from *WORKING THE SONG FIELDS, Poems of the Aztecs*, published by Eastern Washington University Press in 2009.

CARMEN

& CHIA

MIX MAGIC

DIXIE SALAZAR

A Black Opal Books Publication

Black Opal Books

BECAUSE SOME STORIES JUST HAVE TO BE TOLD

GENRE: YA/PARANORMAL THRILLER/FANTASY

CARMEN & CHIA MIX MAGIC
Copyright © 2014 by Dixie Salazar
Cover Design by Dixie Salazar
All cover art copyright © 2014
All Rights Reserved
Print ISBN: 978-1-626941-34-2

First Publication: MAY 2014

Published by Black Opal Books http://www.blackopalbooks.com

DEDICATION

To Zack, Heather and Zoe

GLOSSARY

A secreto encontramos cuando limpiamos la casa. Pero, donde esta Tomas?: A secret we find when we clean the house. But where is Tomas?

Abogada's: Lawyer's

Abrazos y besos: Hugs and kisses

Adios, le ver manana: Goodbye, I'll see you tomorrow

A falta de pan, las tortas son buenas: In the absence of bread, cakes are good.

Ahora: Now

Ahora mismo!: Right now!

Ahora somos chiflando en la loma: You are left whistling in the mountains now.

Ambulencia: Amublence

Amiga: Friend

Andale: Quickly

Aquel: That

Artifactos: Artifacts

AMULETOS, INCIENSO, VELAS: Amulets, Incense, Candles

A veces: Sometimes

Aquellos anos: Those assholes

Aqui: Here

Bien. Pero no queme al pescado: Fine. But don't burn the fish.

Bruja: Witch

Buenas dias, ninas: Good morning, children.

Buenas noches: Good night

Carbon: Goat

Carteristas de la corazon: Pickpockets of the heart

Cerrado, hombre: Shut up, man.

Chevere: Cool

Cholo: Gang banger

Chupar los faros: Time to suck the headlights/to bite the dust/to die

CH'ULEL SAK-NIK-NAL: Mayan for life essence, white flower thing

Cincuenta centavos: Fifty cents

Comida: Meal

Companeras: Companions

Comprehende?: Understand? (mispronunciation of the Spanish *comprende*.

Con mio: With me

Correspondencias: Letters

Crema: Cream

Curandera: Healer

Curandisma: Healing

Debemos: We must.

Deje a aves que anidan, en paz. En boca cerrada no entran moscas: Let nesting birds nest in peace. Flies don't enter a shut mouth.

Delicioso: Delicious

Dinero: Money

Disparate: Nonsense

Dolor de cabeza y estomago: Pain in my head and stomach

Donde: Where

Donde is Portilla Luna: Where is Portilla Luna?

Descubrir los Frijoles: Spill the beans

Dulcita: Sweetie

Duro—Arestro las sabanas que pienso: Hard—I am dragging the bed sheets.

El es inconstante: He is unpredictable, changeable, restless, skittish

El telefono, but no dinero for la abogada: The telephone, but no money for a lawyer.

Elegante para un polluelo: Smart for a spring chicken.

Ella hara volar su combre: She'll blow her top.

Empacando his tortas: Packing his cakes

Entiendes: You know? You understand?

Entonces: Then

Es Bueno: It's all right.

Es de nada: It was nothing.

Es hecha cocinandose: Is done cooking.

Es muy importante: It's very important.

Escuche, no palabras: Just listen, no words.

Espejo de Pelicula: Movie Mirror

Espere: Wait

Espiritos malos: Bad spirits

Este es la gota que desbordo el vaso. Usted es una muchacha desgradecida, recororsa, horrible. Pensar—en mi propia casa, en los alubios pinto—He estado mirando en todas partes.: This is the last straw. You are a disgraceful girl, horrible. To think—in my own house, in the pinto beans—I have been looking everywhere.

Este casa es frequentada, mija. Pero, the ghosts no molesta Rosa—old woman, pero ellos molestan jovenes como usted: This house is haunted, my daughter. But the ghosts don't bother Rosa—old woman—but they bother young people like you.

Estilo de vida: Style of life

Estoy bien. Pero participa usted en la brujeria durante las vacaciones de Septima: I am fine. But you take part in witchcraft during Septima's vacation?

Estrellas Gemelos Botanica: Twin Stars Botanica

Estupido: Stupid

Fuerzas mal: Evil forces

Gente pobre: Poor people

Gracias de los santos para las curenderas: Thanks to the saints for the healers.

Haberle visto las orejas al lobo: We have seen the wolf's ear.

Hara volar su cumbre: Will blow her top

Hasta manana: Until tomorrow

Hermana: Sister

ICE: Immigration and Custom Enforcement.

Ingles: English

La casa: The house

La musica: The music

Las cruzes mysticas: A long and healthy life line

La Frontera: The Frontier, the border between the US and Mexico

Las migras: Immigration Police.

Las migras estan pasado: The immigration police are gone.

Las turistas: The tourists

Leccion especial: Special lesson

Libros: Books

Limpias: Cleaning (used in the story to denote spiritual cleaning)

Lo siento: I'm sorry.

Los santos perdonenos: The saints pardon us.

Magia negra: Black Magic

Mal/Malo: Bad

Malcriados: Bad guys

Medicaciion por tranquilidad: Tranquilizers, medication for relaxation

Meso: Middle or in between

Mi cabeza: My head

Mi familia: My family

Mi querido: My darling/my love

Mija: Short for *Mi Hija* – my daughter or my child

Mira, cartas viejas: Look, old letters.

Mira, la nina!: Look, the child!

Mirada en la casa primero: Look in the house first.

Mire su boca: Watch your language

Mis blusas tiene mucho colores: My blouses have many colors.

Mis ojos suplementarios: My extra eyes

Motors Immaculada: Immaculate Motors

Muchachas: Girls

Muchachas jovenes: Young girls

Muchacho: Boy

Mucho mas: Much more

Mucho peligro: Much danger

Mujeres: Ladies

Muy bella: Very beautiful

Muy bueno—si, el corazon es muy importante—pero: Very good—yes, the heart is very important—but

Muy curiosa: Very curious

Muy extranjero: Very strange

Muy importante: Very important

Muy linda: Very pretty

Muy mal: Very bad

Muy mal cosas: Many bad things

Muy mal espirito: Very bad spirit

Nada: Nothing

Necessito: I need

Nina: Female child

Nino: Male child

Ningunas vacas, ningunos cuidado: No cows, no cares.

No es su falta: It's not your fault.

No hay carne, tengo miedo: There is no meat, I'm afraid.

No los necesito mas: I don't need them anymore.

No preocupar: Don't worry.

No se: I don't know.

No vi nada para bromear sobre: I saw nothing to joke about.

Offrenda: Offering

Orejas: Earlobes

Paganos: Pagans

Papels: Papers

Pachuca: A teenage girl who hangs around with gang members.

Para: For

Pero fino: But I am fine.

Pero, me hago little bit consado: But I need a little bit of rest.

Pescado afortunado: Lucky fish

Platica: Talk/chat (used in the story to denote talk/chat for healing purposes)

Por favor: Please.

Por su puesto: Yes, of course.

Puedo ayudarle: Can I help you?

Que es/Que es esto: What is this?

Que es incorrecto, poco cordero?: What is wrong, little lamb?

Que paso?: What happened?

Que piensa usted, pequena sista?: What do you think, little sister?

Que Sabes: Who knows?

Quiero encontrar...Busco a mi tia Portilla, por favor: I want to find...I'm looking for my Aunt Portilla, please.

Quiza: Perhaps

Rapido: Quick, fast

Sabes: You know

Seguro: For sure

Sentido sexton: Sixth sense

Septima y Teo no tienen mucho dinero ahora: Septima and Teo don't have much money now.

Si: Yes

Si, jefe: Yes, boss.

Si, se puede: Yes, we can.

Si usted permanence alli, usted esta in el peligro. Salga ahora: If you remain there, you are in danger. Get out now

Simpatico: Nice

Solo dejeme explicar: Just let me explain.

Solamente: Only

Soy: I am

Soy tan feliz solo encontrar mi hermana: I am so happy to be back with my sister.

Su armonica: Your harmonica

Su novio de anciano: Your old man

Su papa y yo vaya ayi to mira the washers: Your father and I went there to look at the washers.

Susto: A scare/soul loss

Tal vez—Si, creo tan: Perhaps—Yes, I believe

Tambien: Also

Telenovelas: Television series, similar to American soap operas

Telefono: Telephone

Teo, gracias de dios. Donde tiene Teo sido?: Teo, thank God. Where have you been, Teo?

Tengo que cerrar esta tienda ahora. Usted tendra que marcharse: I have to close this shop now. You will have to leave.

Tengo un dolor malo en mi...: I have a bad pain in my...

Tengo que dormer: I have to sleep.

Tienen novena: Your time/day will come

Tipo malo: Bad type

Tonto: Stupid

Tranquilidad: Tranquility

Tu sabes?: You know?

Una flor magnifico blooming purple light eternamente. Un signo, mija: Magnificent blooming purple flower light forever. A sign, my daughter.

Un otra Bueno: Another good

Un plato: A plate

Una pesadilla anoche: A nightmare last night

Uno, dos abrochan mi zapato. Tres, quarto, cierran la puerta: One, two, buckle my shoe. Three, four, shut the door.

Vamos: Go.

Vamanos: Let's go

Vaqueras: Cowgirls

Vida nuevo servicio: New life service

Vieja: Old woman

Voy a hasta manana: Until I see you tomorrow.
Y: And

Y no policia: And no police.

Y podria ser la ciatica: And it might be sciatica.

Yo: I

Zapatoes saltan: Vaulting shoes

CHAPTER 1

Four silver discs burned through the tinted glass, trained on the sobbing child and her mother.

Tonto's binoculars slid down from silver wrap around shades. "Ya sure it's them?"

"Yea, look just like Boss describe—Kid needs a smack with a two-by-four, shut her up." Sicko moved his black-rubber-gloved finger down the page of a notebook beside him. "And that's the address, all right."

"So what's next, Sicko?" Tonto growled.

"The beauty a this job is we don't gotta do nothing but make the phone calls and wait."

"So why we here then?"

"Make sure we got the right address, Tonto. Silver waitin for the call from us, then he call the ICE, then 'bouta week, they do their thing, pick up the woman and back she goes to Mexico—Silver got it all lined up to buy the house—we go in and make our haul—see that statue on the porch? Silver got his eye on that—had it checked out—it's real old and our inside person say they got lotta silver jewelry real old too and some real old Mexican pots 'n junk."

"So what happens to the kid? She's probably born here."

Sicko shrugged. "That's, like Silver says, *their* problem."

"Hey, ain't that other place on this street, too? The one with the old cars and stuff? Maybe we check it out long as we're in the neighborhood."

"Yea, think so—round the corner, 'bout two streets over. *Vamanos.*"

The van jumped away from the curb and sped up.

"Hey, look out!" Tonto screamed.

Sicko jerked the wheel and crunched the brakes, but not in time. All they saw was a flash of black and white, but they felt the sickening thump against the combined shriek of the tire and the terror-struck animal.

"Oh man, Sicko, I think you got a cat."

Sicko gunned the engine and swooped down the street, tires squealing. "We gotta scram. Silver gut us like fish if he finds out. We s'posed to be keeping low profile."

ح∕3ح∕3

Carmen Luna had just turned the corner when she saw the silver van streaking toward her, but it sped past with a blur of smoked glass and burning rubber. Then she saw the cat, a limp muff of fur slung in the gutter. Carmen caught her breath sharply and nudged it with her foot, but it didn't move. She knelt down, reaching for the still warm fur, then pulled back. There was nothing she could do for it now, except call animal control when she got home. Heart still pounding with fury, Carmen shakily made her way home.

They should have stopped to see if it was okay. Working in the fields, Carmen and her family had come across many a maimed creature and, always, her mother or father rescued the poor, broken beings and took them home to nurse. Carmen had once seen her mother bicycle the tiny, matchstick legs of a baby bird, fallen from a nest, to revive it, then take it home and feed it a drop of mescal. A few weeks later, when it was strong enough, they'd waved it back into the almond blossoms and watched it take to the sky.

Now Carmen could not stop thinking about the poor, black and white kitty—someone's pet, most likely. She hurried to make the phone call, hoping that whoever owned the cat wouldn't come upon it, especially since it had been thrown so cruelly into the gutter.

Occupied with her thoughts, Carmen didn't see it at first when she turned the corner, but she felt something cold snaking down her back. The smell of something rancid made her look up, then her whole body jerked. There was the silver van parked down the street and across from her house. Carmen stopped in her tracks. She was sure it was the same van with the darkened widows, and now it just sat there as if waiting for her. Maybe they saw her. All she could think to do was turn around and run. Flying over the sidewalk, her feet took on a life of their own, dragging her body along like a deflated balloon. Finally, lungs ready to pop, she stopped for breath behind Medrano's Market, a candy and beer stop along the bus route.

Panting, Carmen leaned against the back of the building. She knew that hit and run was a crime, but did that include animals? Angry voices from inside interrupted her thoughts. Carmen moved closer to the slightly ajar back door, and leaned inward. "*Mi hermana* es…es very sick, senor. We have to pay lot of dollars for the medicine. *Pero*…she do not want to sell her casa…"

"Well, what about all that stuff she had in the yard sale? She told me I could have it. I go over there to pick it up and some gang banger come to the door, says she change her mind. And she signed papers, you know, for the house."

"*No*! She wouldn't sign papers to sell," a younger voice chimed in. "You guys lied to her…we going to get a lawyer. You blood suckers better back off. And don't send any more people around to talk to my sister. She's a sick lady—"

"She signed those papers, and we got lawyers, too. This isn't over."

Carmen heard the front door slam and ran into a burnt metal smell, as she rounded the corner of the building. A shock of silver almost blinded her as a tall, iron-gray-haired man nearly mowed her down. His stiff hair and face that looked chiseled, as if out of ice, reminded her of one of her brother Tomas' evil action figures. Something round and metal tumbled around in his left hand—a measuring tape in a metal case, Carmen saw, looking more closely.

He whipped the tape out in Carmen's face with a jerk, almost smacking Carmen in the face, then laughed coldly when she jumped. "Careful who you stare at, lookie lou. There was a murder on this corner the other day—a girl about your age, too." His lips formed a smile, cold and hard as a zipper.

Shoving her hands in her pockets, Carmen frowned then turned on her heel and walked back the way she had come as slowly as she dared, her heart break-dancing against her chest. This route back now led her past the house where she'd seen the cat killed, but there was no sign of it now. Carmen let out a long, raggedy sigh. Her worries, that had before mostly involved her family's troubles, now widened out in a world suddenly become ominously dark and foreboding.

CHAPTER 2

*I*t was coming straight at her, squeezing out the light at the mouth of the tunnel, the icy breath of something—huge and looming—burning her nose and throat. Carmen's heart banged at her chest, as if trying to escape, and her ears roared. This is it, she thought, her legs slipping out from under her.

❧❧❧

Carmen sat up, shaking with the early morning cold and the aftermath of the dream she'd been having for weeks now. In the dirty gloom, she hurried to throw on her clothes and carry out junk to arrange on plastic sheets spread on the lawn.

A skeleton wearing a gummy felt sombrero crossed its cardboard legs on a pile of tires stacked like giant doughnuts. Ragged peacock feathers sprayed out from a dirty Pepsi bottle. Mexican ranchera cassettes dribbled strands of loose tape. Stale baby blankets and coveralls with worn out knees—all this and more—stretched across the front lawn like evicted household goods. Her aunt Septima had been up even earlier to do her own hair and make-up, which must be *"perfecto"* even for a yard sale. Carmen yawned and picked up a one armed Barbie with hair matted in clumps. Her felt-tip-marker bruises seemed to plead for rescue. *Too late for the battered-doll shelter for you,* Carmen thought, dropping her back into a box of brightly colored orphaned toys, most missing some essential part. A stuffed cat with one eye gouged out sprawled dingy and limp next to a scruffy pink feather boa. *Who would buy all this junk*, she asked herself?

Septima bustled with resolve and high hopes for hard cash to help them limp through a dismal winter. For weeks now, Septima had cast eagle eyes on anything of value that she could salvage for her sale, and Carmen had even seen her greedy eyes pounce on her silver bracelet, the only gift she had from her father.

Septima waved a page of sticky dots. "Help me price stuff, Carmen."

"I gotta help Mami finish going through stuff," Carmen said. She would rather haul bushels of bowling balls from the house than work under Septima's bossy glare.

Luckily, Uncle Teofilo interrupted, dropping a dusty box on the lawn at Septima's feet. "*Aqui es...*the box you wanted from the shed."

Just then a blue black crow, almost as large as Septima's head, swooped down from the umbrella tree and perched on the edge of the box. Pecking into its contents, it jerked backward then swept back up into the tree, trailing a pale blue ribbon behind. Carmen watched as it cawed to its mates, loudly triumphant over its crime, but no one else seemed to notice.

"Put *cincuenta centavos* on that junk." Septima jabbed a marker pen at Teofilo who knew better than to argue with the boss when she was in full bulldozer mode.

All he could manage was a muffled, sarcastic, "*Si, jefe*," too low for Septima to hear. Even though she was the boss, the balance of power hinged on her denying it.

Teofilo gestured at the huge box weighed down with hubcaps and oily, cut-rate tools. "Septima, where you want these?"

"Over by the box of candles," Septima answered with the impatient tone she alternated with annoyance, depending on whether Teofilo couldn't "decide anything for himself" or could "at least ask her opinion once in a while."

Carmen saw her chance and raced for the house. On the way, a bright, blue-green feather and some Day of the Dead ornaments, in a box of papers Teofilo had brought from the shed, caught her eye. Quick as a lizard, she scooped up the box and charged toward the porch, where she glanced over her shoulder toward Septima, who was calling out prices with a forced gaiety, buzzing around a large woman and her three daughters who piled from a dirty, brown van to listlessly poke into the wares.

In their bedroom, Carmen's mother slowly shifted piles of dingy clothes from the bed into a giant garbage bag. Rosa moved with the faded futility of so many Mexican women whom the blistering fields had depleted. Her speech was slow and wheezy, and the skin around her still-beautiful brown eyes sagged like a rose trampled in the mud. "*Tu hermano* called yet?"

"No, Mami, not yet." Carmen quickly stuffed the box into the closet behind a pile of worn sheets. She didn't know exactly why she wanted this box, but she was intrigued with the cut paper doilies, the rosary cards, and the spidery script of what looked like old letters. The turquoise blue feather went into her pocket as she tugged on the garbage bag, trying to heft it to her shoulder.

Rosa struggled to shift herself off the bed.

"Mami, just rest," Carmen said. "You look tired today. I'll help Tia Septima. Don't worry."

Ever since she and her mother had moved to Motors Immaculada, the used car business run by her aunt and uncle, Rosa had languished.

Carmen's father had died when she was very young and her brother Tomas was only four. Her father had been a coyote, helping smuggle illegals from Mexico, but Carmen had never been able to get the whole story about his death.

Her mother would only say, "Your father was a good man, not like some of them. He wanted to pay back those who had helped him," she would say, "but they tricked him. They used him."

Then she would clam up, and no amount of pleading would get her to say more. After Veloz died, Rosa had worked hard in the fields and then lucked into a job in a packing house, but she had gotten sick and then they had been evicted from their one-room apartment. Tomas had taken to disappearing for days at a time, infuriating Septima, who threatened to call the cops on him but never would have since Carmen's mother and Tomas were in the U.S. illegally. Carmen, however, was legal, having been born in the U.S. Ironically, she had heard gossip that Septima had married Teofilo to gain her own citizenship.

Carmen heard Septima calling her and hurried toward the door like a skinny, yard-sale Santa with the garbage bag slung on her back. Dumping the bag, she watched the last three years of her T-shirts, pullovers, and Dickies spill onto the lawn next to a pile of grimy tennis shoes and rubber flip flops. Her mother hoped to make some money to help pay Septima for letting them stay with her and maybe a little more for Christmas, which wasn't far off. Septima didn't ever say directly that Carmen and her mother were a burden, but little digs slipped out like her references to "Septima's boarding house" and "Someone's gotta work around here."

"What'd you want?" Carmen called to her aunt, who now nodded absently, her attention fixed on an old woman who had suddenly appeared in their yard, digging through a box of half-melted candles.

"Are you buying those?" Septima snapped at the darkly tanned, gray-haired woman in pigtails and a rumpled flannel shirt.

The woman dropped the half-burned candles, mumbled something under her breath, and moved on to a pile of lumpy stuffed animals. Septima moved a few paces closer to her and pretended to refold some clothes. Carmen thought she had seen the strange lady pushing a shopping cart sometimes, not far from school. *She's probably homeless*, thought Carmen, *and painfully aware that Septima doesn't want her here.* Carmen reached out to offer the woman a doughnut, but Septima pushed her roughly aside.

"If you're not buying, you better just move on. I don't want to have to make a phone call." This threat was one that both Septima and a street person would understand, for different reasons.

Suddenly the woman bent down in a half-crouching position and swung her body back and forth with her hands outstretched, a low growl issuing from her throat. With a sharp yowl, she jerked her hand back from the very spot where the box of letters had been. Carmen looked closely at the spot and saw that an object had dropped from the box she had snuck away. Moving closer, Carmen saw a carved wooden jaguar, painted with blue and purple dots in a swirling pattern, now somewhat faded.

Swarming the sun, a mass of clouds parted and a golden nimbus haloed the old lady's form. From seemingly nowhere, she waved a white scarf back and forth as the sun burst around her. As Carmen watched, mesmerized, the scarf began to change colors from white to pale blue to pink to lavender. Dropping the scarf at Carmen's feet, the old lady jerked back suddenly.

"Bid me," the old lady said, her eyes fastened darkly on Carmen.

Carmen stared at the woman's hands. "What bit you? Where?" She retrieved the jaguar and now held it in her open palm, as if it might have been the culprit.

With a catty grin, the woman hid her hands behind her back and said, "You be keffell."

She spoke in the muffled voice of a deaf mute. Carmen wondered what she meant. Was she also crazy? When her eyes locked onto Carmen's, however, she seemed to be looking deep inside, as if she could see behind the public mask into the darker crevices of Carmen's soul.

Septima's mouth was moving, but the bass of a boom box thumped over her words. Suddenly, Carmen felt a presence behind her, then warm hands wrapped around her eyes. "Guess who, *perequita*?"

"Tomas!" Carmen cried, twirling around into a hug.

She loved it when her older brother called her little bird. Tomas grinned. The shadow of a mustache brushed his lip above blindingly white teeth and eyes black as a jaguar's, his middle name.

"Mami's been so worried, T. She's not doing too good."

Tomas frowned. "Had stuff to take care of."

Suddenly Tomas bent down, scooped up the purple scarf the old lady had dropped, and handed it to her as she bobbed in a mincing little toe-heel dance around them. "Dropped this— should be more careful with things of value."

"Si. Pupple moon," the old lady answered cryptically.

But before Carmen could wonder more about this strange conversation, Tomas, who had been staring at the old lady, turned to say something to Carmen and stopped cold with a look of horror. "Don't move, Carmen! Stay still!"

Carmen felt a soft tickling on her shoulder and cut her eyes toward it, where she saw a large, shiny black spider. Her heart leaped and her body wanted to follow, but an icy terror froze her to the spot.

CHAPTER 3

Working in the fields with her mother, Carmen had encountered all kinds of bugs, snakes, and even a scorpion once, but her mother, who was fearful of everything, had instilled a particular fear in Carmen of black widows. And when they had visited Mexico, her cousins had filled her with stories of ghosts, *espiritos malos*, and an evil bruja shapeshifter who took the form of a black widow spider that swung silently through the darkness, bit little children in their sleep, and turned them into flies for its dinner.

Maybe the spider had already bitten her, Carmen thought. Or it might do so if she jumped or tried to knock it off. Sharp, bright spots swam around Carmen's eyes and she felt herself sinking down, ready for the poison to surge through her, when she saw a flash of purple.

The old lady had snapped the purple scarf at the spider and knocked it away. Now Carmen broke into a sweat as she sank down to her knees with tears of relief and her heart slowed to a weak canter. Tomas was talking to the old lady, and Carmen rose to thank her but, right before Carmen's eyes, she disappeared.

Loud music was still crashing from the boom box and now Septima strode toward them with her eyes snapping fire as a chopped-off bike skidded to a stop next to them.

"Come on, T-Man. We gotta get with Angel."

It was Fernando, a skinny cholo in a Raiders T-shirt, baggy pants, and home-inked tattoos on his arms, a thunderbolt through the numeral 13 on his neck. He pulled at a skinny braid at the nape of his neck, curling like a rat's tail from his shaved head.

Carmen had seen him hanging around school sometimes, selling stuff out of a paper bag to some of the older boys.

Tomas shuffled his feet, turning away from Fernando. "Tell Mami I'm gonna bring her some cash, Carmelita. I gotta be gone for couple more days. Then I can—"

Before Tomas could finish his sentence, a slim Asian girl, who looked familiar to Carmen, crossed the lawn to where they were all grouped. Her straight, black hair, with a pink streak down one side, shone in the morning light, and her soft brown eyes smiled shyly at Tomas.

The shadow of a silly, guilty grin slipped over Tomas' face. "Yo, Chia! Whas' up?"

"Hey, where'd you go? I waited for you after school a bunch of times—and I almost got beat up, too." Chia made a sour face.

Tomas said something, but Carmen couldn't hear him because the dogs had set up a howl, barking furiously at a black dog as big as a small pony that was nosing the fence between them. But the dog only turned and ambled languidly away when Septima lunged toward it with a stick.

"What's with the stick? That mutt ain't gonna hurt you," said Oso, the neighbor from across the street, who must have been drawn out by the racket. He and Septima had a running feud that seemed to require very little from either of them to maintain. Oso had told Septima that he'd have to turn her in if she had any more yard sales that month. But now, as Fernando flipped his cigarette into the yard, Septima ignored Oso and charged over to Fernando, her glasses practically steaming. "Andale! Get this gang-banger *sucio* outta my yard! And where you been, Tomas? Tu mama has been worried sick."

Carmen could almost see smoke pouring from Septima's nostrils. Anger was her hobby. She stormed through her days— Septima against the world. First, her eyes behind the gold-rimmed glasses would bulge to the size of quarters with sharp black dots in the center, where a spark of fire shot out. Then she would let loose with a stream of rat-a-tat-tat Spanish, her index finger chopping at the air.

Carmen was the only one positioned now to see the tendrils of smoke curling up from the box of Septima's used bras, camisoles, and panty hose. She inched toward the box, hoping to snuff out the slow-stoking fire before anyone saw, when she heard a voice behind her.

"De ode gwey mae-a set fie-a to er undea-weh-a." It was the homeless woman, her hands cupped around her mouth, eyes jitterbugging.

Carmen threw a puzzled look at Tomas, who grinned, "I think she said 'the old gray mare set fire to her underwear.'"

Fernando stuck his chin out in defiance but said nothing, glaring at Tomas who tried to reason with Septima. "We're going, don't worry. I just want to see Mami for a minute. Ferni's not here to make no trouble."

Oso was shaking his head as he watched the scene. Carmen heard him mutter something about the cops as he headed back across the street.

"*Santa Maria y todos los santos!*" Septima screamed pointing to the box Carmen had dumped on the lawn.

Chia also let out a horrifying scream. Carmen motioned for her to help, but she stood rooted to the spot, pale and shaking.

"Fire," she said, trembling.

As Carmen stomped on her smoking bras, Septima lunged toward Fernando. Before Tomas could block her, she twisted Fernando's ear, causing him to cry out in pain then shove his bike at her, knocking her smack on her butt. Her howling brought Teofilo running from the garage where he had been talking with customers.

"What the hell?" Teofilo didn't, however, move to help her since Septima had a history of clawing anyone who ventured too close when she went into one of her fits.

From the corner of her eye, Carmen saw her mother step out of the door onto the porch. Her face was a mixture of joy and confusion at seeing first Tomas and then Septima screaming on the lawn.

What happened next, however, overshadowed all of their private dramas. A cop car cruised by slowly then pulled over to the curb across the street. Two cops emerged, heading straight for Motors Immaculada. Fernando streaked off first, dropping his bike and hopping over the fence of the next-door neighbors.

With both cops in pursuit of Fernando, Tomas, who had edged quietly behind Carmen, now hissed in her ear, "I'm gonna run for the back yard. Watch my back, okay?"

Carmen knew that Tomas wasn't legal, but he had gone through the ninth grade with no questions asked, and she wasn't quite sure why he now seemed so worried. It appeared that the cops were after Fernando, but there wasn't time now to discuss it. Dropping Septima's scorched bra, she followed Tomas as he ducked through the maze of used cars parked in the front lot. With her back turned away from Tomas, facing the street, she glanced back and saw her mother start to run toward them at the same time as two men in dark blue shirts emerged from an unmarked, white van and yelled something she couldn't make out. On their backs was the word "ICE." Her mother went as white as stone and crept swiftly back to the house. The men had not seen her, however, as they were bent on following Tomas, who had disappeared into the maze of broken-down cars, tool sheds, dog pens, and RVs jumbled behind the house.

One of the men motioned to Carmen and then turned back to the yard sale. "Nobody move. You better have papers." He repeated the same words in Spanish, while the other man stayed in pursuit of Tomas.

Moving Carmen forward with his hand on her shoulder, the ICE man clamped his other hand on the gun at his waist. Septima looked as if she wanted to spit, but Carmen could see cold, hard fear behind the angry mask she struggled to suppress. "We all have papers, I assure you." Septima spit her words out like ice cubes.

While the man took down all their names, Carmen snuck looks at the back lot where the dogs were barking wildly. Strangely, the huge black crow that had pecked into the box earlier was now sitting on one end of the fence with another equally large crow parked at the other end, as if on guard duty. The other ICE man yelled over the fence, "Check the house. Make sure no one else is in there."

Carmen's stomach sank.

CHAPTER 4

Rosa was used to making herself invisible. She had spent her life in the fields, one of the ghostly ones who pick the lettuce, the spinach, the grapes that load the tables to fill the stomachs of those who never saw the stooped workers in their fields, even as they slid by in their air conditioned SUVs. Rosa knew this time, however, she had to disappear quickly, and she had to make it good. She looked around the house in a panic, her heart chattering like a wild bird.

❧❦❧

Carmen noticed that Chia had now dropped to her knees on the lawn. Their eyes met, and Chia made no attempt to wipe away her fresh tears. What was this, Carmen wondered? Could Chia have a crush on her brother? But there wasn't time to wonder for long. Fear for her mother made Carmen's stomach churn. The doughnuts she'd wolfed down earlier knotted into a sour wad. She wanted to puke, to cry, but could do nothing but watch in silence as the ICE man moved toward the van, talked on his two way, then set to work, clicking at his computer. Carmen tried to think of a way to delay them, but the ICE man was now climbing out of the van and heading toward the house.

Adding to the confusion, a nearby car horn went off with a blaring repetition that jangled everyone's nerves even more. "Honk, honk, honk…" On and on it went.

Septima began to pray loudly as Teofilo stood helplessly by. Suddenly, the other ICE man appeared, pushing Tomas in front of him, with Tomas' hands cuffed behind him.

Chia covered her mouth in horror. Carmen froze, and Septima began a loud, keening rant that was half wail, half prayer. "Where are you taking him? He's just a kid. He goes to school. *Dios de mio, dios.* He's a good kid. You can't just haul him off like a criminal."

Carmen was surprised at Septima's sudden defense of Tomas, but Septima's fierceness could just as easily be turned for you as against you, especially when it came to family.

"I'll get in touch," Tomas said.

But the tall ICE man shoved him swiftly into the van, saying, "Shut up, kid. You think we give you wet backs calling cards or something."

By now the car horn had stopped, the silence a frozen net that trapped them on the lawn.

The door to the house opened then, and the other ICE man appeared alone. Carmen's heart stopped in its tracks again, this time in relief.

The second ICE man climbed into the van, and just like that, Tomas was gone.

Then the two policemen emerged from the tangle of bushes next door, with a glowering Fernando prodded before them, his hands also cuffed behind him. In silence, everyone watched them shove him into the back seat before the police car pulled away from the curb.

Septima's anger seemed to have dissolved into a puddle of helplessness. "Let's all pray," she said finally. "Come on, everyone, *debemos*."

Carmen felt Septima's hard, icy hands close around hers, pulling her down into a circle on the sparse grass where the leftover yard sale items were strewn. Even Chia joined the circle, which now consisted of only the four of them.

It seemed like Septima would keep them there praying in the middle of their pain, sorrow, and scattered junk forever, but finally she rose. "Tu mama," she said under her breath. "At least *las migras* didn't get her. *Gracias de Dios.*" Septima crossed herself and then snapped at Teofilo, "Pack up this stuff. This is what comes from raising these *ninos* like *paganos*. Carmen, let's go see about Rosa."

"Not my fault," Teofilo muttered and started to roll up one of the sheets of plastic, tumbling all of the items together.

"Not like that! Do I have to do everything myself?"

While Septima and Teofilo argued, Carmen looked at Chia, who had gotten to her feet but didn't seem to want to leave.

It was strange, thought Carmen, how in such a short time, she had come to feel that she knew Chia, someone she never would have talked to at school or even really noticed.

Chia was looking at her thoughtfully. "Uh, what is *las migras?*" she asked.

"Immigration. Tomas wasn't a legal citizen. We never thought they'd—I can't believe this. I—don't know what to do. Maybe I should get your phone number, Chia?" The words came out all mushy and liquid and Carmen realized she was crying. "So we can keep in touch. You're a friend of Tomas, I guess..."

Chia nodded through her own snuffles.

Carmen tore off the back page from a stack of *Time* magazines marked ten cents each and looked around for a pen. Chia pulled a pencil from a little woven purse that hung around her neck, embroidered with a large plumed bird perched on the head of a spotted cat. She wrote the number down and handed it to Carmen. "Please call me and let me know if you hear anything. Please."

"Sure," Carmen managed to mumble. Her mind couldn't seem to fix on the new reality of Tomas' seizure. She felt numbness, a kind of denial that could be morphed into a false sense of hope.

Septima was getting louder, little baby snorts mixed with her words—bad sign of a fit coming on. Carmen wanted to ask her aunt if there was anything they could do to find out where Tomas might have been taken, but fixing Septima's attention on herself could fix her anger there, also. "I'm going to look for Mami," she said half to herself and half to Septima. Then she turned to Chia. "Wanna come with me inside?"

The house smelled like boiled chicken. Someone, probably Rosa, had set a pan of neck bones and vegetables simmering on the stove. It was strangely silent inside, and Carmen saw that her mother's bedroom was empty. "Mamiiiiiiiii," Carmen called through the house. "Mami."

They heard a rustling sound in the kitchen that seemed to be coming from behind the walls. "Mami, are you here? *Las migras estan pasado.*"

Suddenly, the wall next to them opened, and Rosa appeared, as if she had transported herself out of the air. Chia jumped in alarm. Behind what looked like a flat, narrow ironing board compartment was a deeper space between the walls of the kitchen and the adjoining bedroom, a space, luckily, just big enough for a small adult such as Rosa to crouch.

"Mami, how did you find—"

"*A—a—secreto—encontramos cuando limpiamos—clean la casa. Pero, donde esta Tomas?*"

Carmen put her arms around her mother, leaking tears despite herself. "*Lo siento*, Mami. The ICE took him away. Maybe we can...*lo siento*, Mami."

Rosa slid into a moaning heap on the floor. Carmen wished that she could have thought fast enough to have made up a lie, but now the damage was done. And Mami would have to know sooner or later.

Chia helped Carmen get Rosa into the bedroom, Rosa praying shakily between her tears as they eased her onto the bed. "Ayyyyyy Tomas! No, no, no! Why they take? *Por favor, Madre de Maria—haciendo de las suyas.*"

"What do you mean, 'up to their tricks,' Mami?"

But Rosa was crying so hard now that she didn't seem to hear Carmen.

Carmen dug into the top drawer of a flimsy cardboard cabinet next to their bed and found her mother's pills. "Can you get me some water in the kitchen?" she asked Chia.

When Chia returned, Carmen tipped out the last two of her mother's *medicaciion por tranquilidad* and coaxed her to take them.

When finally Rosa was calm enough to sleep, Carmen and Chia tiptoed out. Septima was on the phone, and from what Carmen could gather, she was making calls to try and find someone who could advise them about what to do next. Cupping the phone, she motioned to Carmen, "Rosa is okay?"

Carmen nodded. "I gave her a tranquillizer and she's resting now. She hid behind the ironing board. Can you imagine?"

"*Ave Maria.*" Septima turned back to her phone call. "No...no...no, I can't hold...*es muy importante...*"

Chia nervously rubbed her palms together. Finally Carmen said, "Let's go ask Tio Teofilo where they take people when they deport them."

Chia grabbed Carmen's arm and stopped her. "Okay. But, *las migras* is immigration. So what is ICE? I'm confused."

"I'm not sure I can explain it, but we call them *las migras* which means basically, immigration, I think—so it can mean those who immigrate here or the ones who patrol the borders and try to catch them. ICE stands for Immigration and Customs Enforcement and, ever since 9/11, they are supposed to be fighting terrorists, and all illegals have gotten thrown into the mix. At least that's what I heard the grownups say."

Chia frowned. "Okay. I think I get it. Either way, it's bad for FOBs." To Carmen's puzzled look she explained, "Fresh off the boat.

"'Fraid so." Carmen nodded grimly as they headed toward Teofilo who was filling and stacking boxes still in the yard, most likely according to Septima's orders.

Huge and shaggy as a buffalo, it was a mystery how Septima had managed to capture Teofilo's heart and tame him. Some had speculated that she had asked a bruja to cast a spell over him, but Carmen knew that Septima discounted spells and such as going against the church.

"Tio, where do you think they took Tomas?" Carmen choked the words up through her tightened throat.

Teofilo shook his thick mane, his large, misty eyes sagging. "No *se*. Maybe they take him someplace on la frontera. Or...sometimes they go to that place downtown...Homeland Security. They can throw you in jail if you got a record, but Tomas never been in no trouble...*entiendes*? Or maybe he was in some trouble we don't know about. Need to get a lawyer. But that takes *dinero*. We barely been paying the mortgage on this place." Teofilo waved his huge paws at the overgrown half acre of Motors Immaculado—a name he and Septima had chosen, hoping to bring in more business from the faithful who needed transportation. The land had been his father's, who had worked hard and saved up enough money to open a car repair shop and then added a small used car lot and eventually built up a semi-respectable business before he had died, leaving it all to Teofilo whose fatal flaw was plain laziness, overcome only by Septima's continual prodding. "And tu mama...well, she got her own troubles already."

"Teo. Teo!"

It was Septima's voice he jerked back from as if he'd been slapped, but he quickly hurried to her service.

Carmen and Chia locked eyes. "Let's go," whispered Chia. "I gotta be home by noon to help with the cooking. "

"Go? Where do you mean?"

"Homeland Security. I know where it is. My brother showed me when we were downtown. He works at Zacky Farms and they were—you know, talking on a break once that a Hmong man who had his visa run out was sent there for questioning, and nobody knew what happened to him. My brother said the place has a bad spirit. We'll ask them to give us information about Tomas."

Carmen was shocked that Chia was so ready to take action. She had never talked much with a Hmong girl before, but her impression of them was of shy, quiet backwardness. They kept to their own at school and seemed suspicious and wary of almost all other races. It certainly seemed like Chia had a connection to Tomas. *Could she be a girlfriend?*

Carmen had seen so little of her brother the last six months that she hardly knew what he thought or felt these days. However, he was the link between her and Chia now, and Carmen felt right then that fate had drawn them together. Something about Chia's sharp cheekbones, with the soft, slanted features, and feathery brows reminded Carmen of pictures she had seen of native Mesoamerican Indians, her ancestors, and she felt a surprising kinship. *Meso, meso,* she chanted to herself and felt strangely comforted by the word she'd just learned that year in History.

"Okay, *chica,* let's go. I'll tell Septima that I'm going to walk over to Walgreens to get Mami some more medicine. How we gonna get there, though?"

"You'll see," Chia said, smiling mysteriously.

Septima was still on the phone when Carmen slipped back into the house, so she decided to talk to Teofilo instead. She found him behind the house where the RVs and some old trailers were parked, sitting on an oil can leaned against a shed, the smell of alcohol wafting around him. Not wanting to interrupt his stolen nap, Carmen hesitated. Then something white beside the bushes caught her eye. Leaning closer, she saw a small nest of cigarette butts. But Teofio didn't smoke. No one in the family did. Septima outlawed both cigarettes and alcohol, although Teofilo snuck behind her back for his drinking. Behind her, Teofilo grunted and Carmen turned.

"Don't tell Septima, okay? Just grabbing a little snooze, Carmelita. El jefe had me up at five you know."

"Don't worry. I won't snitch. I'm just gonna walk over with Chia to Walgreens and get Mami's pills. Be back in 'bout an hour."

That was a piece of luck, she thought as she raced back outside to see what was up Chia's sleeve.

CHAPTER 5

There was Chia sitting on Fernando's chopped off bike, retrieved from the bushes where he'd slung it when he took off running from the cops.

"Check this out—it's a Mongoose. Hop up and hang on, *miga*, I'll hike you on my handlebars."

Chia was mispronouncing *amiga*, but Carmen said nothing, climbed onto the front bar, and held on tightly.

The cold December sun climbed the blue ladder of sky and dropped behind a cloud as they started on their way. The wind bit into their cheeks as Chia churned the pedals. After about four blocks, Chia was huffing so hard, they had to stop and rest.

"Something's wrong," Chia said, a puzzled unease in her brown eyes. "This bike feels like it really is a mongoose—a wild one—keeps jerking to the left and then the right." Carmen offered to switch places, but Chia just shook her head, regained her breath, and took off again.

Every so often, Carmen could feel the bike buck and the handlebars shimmy. Chia would have to bear down with all her might to keep control. Finally she stopped and motioned Carmen off. They stood on the curb and watched as the bike shivered quietly in the gutter. Carmen felt a chill. "Hey, maybe it's got a bad spell on it, Chia. You think we should just ditch it?"

But Chia narrowed her eyes and yanked hard on the Mongoose. "No. It's all we've got right now, and if we're gonna give up on a stupid bike, then how we ever going to help Tomas?"

"I have an idea," Carmen took Chia's hand in her own and placed both on the handlebars. "Now let's pour our thoughts together. Think power, Chia, flowing through us together. Wait, I saw a video at school about Cesar Chavez where the farm workers used to chant, '*Si, se puede*' when they were standing up to the farmers. Let's try it."

They placed all four of their hands on the handlebars and chanted, "*Si, se puede*," together, but the bike still shook.

Chia looked at the bike then back at Carmen. "Hmongs believe that evil spirits must be satisfied with a sacrifice."

Carmen bit her lip quizzically. "What kind of sacrifice? Blood...or?"

"Well, sometimes it's a chicken or a pig or even a cow. But a Mongoose would probably like a rat or even a worm, I suppose."

"*Guano*! Where we gonna get those, Chia?" Carmen asked, exasperated.

"First, what's guano mean?"

"It's bat or bird poo. When Tomas and I used to get into trouble for cussing, we made up our own cuss words."

Chia reached into the embroidered purse around her neck and pulled out a baggie filled with gummy worms. "I was saving this for later, but let's try it," she said, tucking it up under the bicycle seat. They put their hands back on the Mongoose and chanted, "*Si se puede*," again. And this time they could feel a hum coiling through the Mongoose. Suddenly, it gave a huge jerk then lay silent.

Carmen grinned widely. "All right!"

They hopped back on the Mongoose and took off. It was a good three miles to downtown from Carmen's street, and finally, after about ten blocks, Chia stopped and let Carmen take over the pedaling. When they came to an incline leading up to the railroad tracks, Carmen had to hop off and Chia walked the bike over. Chia was panting, her face freckled with sweat, but slowly, surely, they made their way downtown. At one busy intersection, Chia had to punch into high gear to get across the cross walk before the traffic belched forward.

When she saw a cop cruiser headed toward them, Carmen's stomach sank, since she knew that hiking on a bike wasn't allowed.

Chia tried to speed up, but the cop cruiser pulled up next to them and kept pace. Carmen's heart pounded. The cops had obviously seen them and now slowed in front and turned on the red light. One of them put his arm out the window and hollered, "Pull over girls, *now*!"

Chia put on the brake and hopped halfway off, still balancing Carmen on the front bar.

The cops had now stepped from the car, big and hairy like two grizzly bears in uniforms. "You girls not supposed to be hiking, you know. And it's dangerous down here in this part of town."

Carmen opened her mouth but her brain slammed shut, and she heard Chia's voice instead. "We're on our way to church."

"Don't try and lie to us. We going to have to write you up for hiking," one of the bears growled.

"Let's just haul 'em in, Ogre. Call their parents to come down to the station." The bear closest to them lowered his shades and drilled them with his steely eyes as he jangled the handcuffs.

"It's Hmong Ancestor's Day and we are going to a special celebration. It's only a block away," Chia chirped brightly.

The bears cocked their eyes at each other. "You gotta be kiddin'—Ogre, you ever hear of that?"

The one called Ogre ambled closer to the girls, his leather parts squeaking as he glared down at them. But Chia didn't flinch, and Carmen held her breath.

"All the FOBs comin' in now, who knows? Let's just take 'em in and then we'll check it out."

Chia was still half on and half off the bike, and to Carmen's surprise, instead of climbing off, she now balanced the bike straight as if to take off.

At that moment, the radio crackled and both bears turned and raced back to the car. "You girls go on home—pronto!"

They slammed the doors as the cruiser sped away to join other sirens now wailing in the distance.

"Guano! That was close." Chia's voice now shook.

"Hmong Ancestor's Day? Is there—"

"Nope. Just buying some time, and looks like we got a bargain today."

"You're too much, *chica*."

They both nearly fell off the bike laughing. Chia took as many side streets as she could to avoid the busy, downtown traffic, but they were in a part of town now where they had to turn onto some busy streets. Several cars honked at them, as if to say, *You don't belong here.* Finally, Chia stopped the bike in front of a closed-up-looking, cinder-block building with no name on it. "That's it—the one Toua told me about—the one he said to stay away from cuz it has a curse on it."

"What do you mean, a curse?"

Chia looked a bit embarrassed. "Hmongs believe that everything has a spirit—trees, wind, houses, rocks."

"A spirit, like a soul?"

Chia considered. "Kind of. But people have souls and things have spirits."

"So bicycles have a spirit?"

"Sure. This bicycle has a bad spirit because Fernando was using it to help him do bad stuff, you know."

"Yea. He's a *tipo malo*. I never did like Tomas to hang with him, but T got so worried about money, maybe he thought Fernando could help him somehow. But what about this place here? What do we do now?" Carmen was looking at the building that presented back nothing but a closed rock face.

"Let's go knock on the door," Chia said boldly.

Carmen was terrified, but Chia's apparent bravery made her feel stronger, and she swallowed the fear that shook her insides like the rumble before an earthquake. Together they stepped forward and knocked on the door.

They knocked until their knuckles were sore before an older man with glasses and a badly fitting security guard's uniform opened the door partially.

He looked surprised to see them. "You must have the wrong place. Go on now. Kids don't belong down here."

He had started to close the door, but Carmen stepped forward quickly. "We're looking for my brother. The ICE grabbed him today. All we want to know is where they are going to take him." The words tumbled out in a rush.

The man frowned down at them. "How did you know to come here, anyway?"

Every molecule of Carmen's body wanted to flee, but when she snuck a look at Chia, she saw a jaw set hard as a hammer urging her forward. "A friend told us the ICE take people here." She gulped, then continued. "The ICE man used a computer so we just want to know if you can look on it and tell us where they took Tomas. His name is T-O-M-A-S J-A-G-U-A-R L-U-N-A." She spelled the name slowly, as her eyes filled with tears, despite her efforts to hold them back.

"Sorry. Rules is rules. Can't help you. Now go on home. Tell your folks to get a good lawyer." The door slammed smartly in her face.

They stood on the sidewalk, the ring of finality still in their ears.

Chia frowned then dropped to the curb and cupped her chin. "Let me think," she muttered.

Carmen wondered what there was to think about but didn't say so. No one spoke. A few minutes passed and then suddenly, the door re-opened, and a Southeast Asian man came out pushing a broom. He motioned to Chia and spoke in Hmong.

Chia grinned slyly at Carmen. "He's a janitor and he overheard us. He says for us to go around to that door on the side, and he'll let us in. It's a Hmong tradition to help each other if you're from the same clan, which it seems like we are. He said he'd ask Lupita to help us out. She owes him a favor—she's down here putting in some overtime, and she's got a soft spot for puppies and kids."

"Put on your best puppy face," Carmen whispered to Chia as they rushed for the side door, Carmen dragging the bike with her and shoving it hurriedly in some bushes beside the building.

Just as he had said, the janitor opened the door and very shortly, they found themselves in the small waiting area of an office sparsely furnished with one padded bench against the wall before a long table with a row of computers. At one of them sat a very large Mexican woman with her hair coiled up into a feathery bun nested on top of her head. Carmen looked up over a huge, empty fish bowl and wondered if the fish had also been deported, but she put on her sweetest lost, milk-carton smile.

The woman tried to look stern. "Now, let's be quick here girls. I got lotta work to do today. You lucky that Mr. Yang got a soft spot for kids. What's your brother's full name?"

Carmen spelled the name again and watched while Lupita tapped keys on the computer with dark nails flitting like hard, black fish. Lupita looked at them over her little half glasses. "Have a seat girls. This could take a few minutes." Gold sparks flashed from her teeth when she spoke.

Carmen's nerves flared, igniting her heart with fear. She thought about Tomas, wondered where he was and if he was hurt. Had they taken the handcuffs off? Chia looked sick.

Carmen looked up to the wall behind Lupita where she could have sworn she had seen a clock when they first entered, but now there was none. She didn't dare ask Chia about it. From somewhere in the building came an angry, mechanical buzzing and it seemed best not to talk.

Luptia had a coughing fit and then went back to clicking. Just as she stood up, the phone rang. "Unnnh huh?" she said into it. "I can't do nothing about it now. You just gonna have to wait till I get done here. What? Call me back in ten, okay? And tell Butch ta take that five offa the table and get me some more you know what. Well, just tell him I said. Now let me get on here." She snapped the phone down.

Lupita clicked away some more then stood up, tugging at her panty hose. Dark, twisty, reptilian shapes chased across the long skirt that swelled over her ample hips. "You sure you spelled his name right?"

"He's my brother. Yes, I'm sure." Anxiety made Carmen's voice squeak.

"Well, he sure ain't in the system. I checked every which a way. His name does not come up. I got a bunch of Lunas, but no Tomas at all. When they took him in?"

"Today. Should we come back and check on Monday maybe?" Carmen asked desperately.

"Look here, girl. I'm not s'posed to be helping you even now, and if you come back on Monday, you ain't even gonna get in that door. Now, I checked everything I could. He just not in there," she said with finality.

As they turned to go, Lupita said behind them, "Have some candy, girls." She pointed to a tray of jellybeans on her desk. "And tell your parents to get a lawyer."

"No candy, but thanks for—" Carmen gasped. The jellybeans were moving on the tray, and as she watched, horrified, they began to elongate and grow tiny horns, like a mass of multi-colored tomato worms, hissing and writhing.

Carmen looked at Chia who was also staring at the squirming candy and backing slowly away. Carmen then looked to see if Lupita saw what they did, but Lupita also had sprouted two fleshy horns on her forehead. Her mouth was moving, but no words were coming out, just sprays of spit, as her features began to slide slowly down, leaving a blank where her face had been. Carmen opened her mouth to scream but only a faint squeak came out. She felt Chia tugging on her but could not move. Lupita slid forward now, slinking over the counter, and Carmen realized that Lupita could fasten onto her with the row of suckers that had sprang all up and down her arms just like the tomato worm that had once stuck on Carmen's thigh in the fields where she had been helping her mother harvest tomatoes.

Tiny beads of sweat peppered Carmen's face, and somewhere far away, she could hear Chia calling and pulling on her, but she could not move. Her legs had planted themselves firmly in the floor, heavy as tree trunks. A heavy tiredness sank into her bones, and all Carmen wanted to do was close her eyes and slide down to the floor to sleep.

"I'm tired, Chia, so tired...let me be," she said, but she couldn't hear her own words clearly, as if she was under water, moving her mouth soundlessly.

Trying to move her legs was like walking in thick mud that sucked at her feet. This must be what Mami felt like, thought Carmen. The blank face was right in front of her own now, moist with dribbles of spit. Two long, suckered arms reached toward her.

Frantically, Carmen struggled for breath, fighting to keep her eyes open. *Meso*, she thought to herself, and then said the word out loud again and again, "*Meso, meso, meso...*" and then everything went blank.

છઉઉ

Outside the building, the sun glared off the sidewalk in sharp contrast to the chill air. They stood in silence until finally Chia said, "Are you all right?"

"What happened? Where is—How did we get out here?" Carmen's head felt like a balloon ready to pop and her legs still felt spongy. Maybe she didn't have the guts to be part of this, she thought. Maybe, as she feared, she was like her mother.

"I don't know. Lupita was coming after you. I tried to help, but you were under some kind of spell, and I couldn't budge you. Then you started chanting something over and over. And then everything went completely dark and I heard somebody say something about the power going off and now here we are."

"Was I seeing things or did Luptia change into some kind of animal—her face—did you see it?"

"Yea, I saw." Chia's own face had drained of color. "Let's get out of here. I wonder what time it is. I got to get home." Her voice was trembling.

Shakily, Carmen moved toward the bushes to retrieve the Mongoose. "Hey, did you see a clock on the wall when we went in?"

"Yea. There was one right behind Lupita's desk."

Carmen frowned. "Well, it flew off somewhere then because it disappeared. I looked up to see what time it was, while we were waiting for Lupita, and it was gone."

"Time flies when you're having a panic attack." Chia's grin faded quickly into a frown and she sucked in her breath. "There was a clock and it disappeared. And Lupita's still in there—this is all too spooky. I think we're into something scary and big. We've got to scram."

Suddenly Carmen grabbed Chia's arm. "Don't move, Chia! And don't look behind you."

"What is it?" But Chia did look and saw a snake the size of a fat man's belt stretched out, sunning itself on the sidewalk behind her, its metallic scales shimmering with the same shapes that had been on Lupita's skirt.

Before Carmen could say another word, Chia whirled and, with the toe of her sneaker, flipped the snake up into the air, where it spun in a circle like a whirling lasso, and then vanished.

Carmen ran to the curb, bent over, and heaved into the gutter. When she was done, she sat down, her head spinning dizzily. All of the day's horror had spilled upward from her gut and now left her empty. She felt Chia's arm on her shoulder then and turned and sobbed into Chia's quilted jacket.

"Come on, Carmen, let's get out of here."

Chia helped Carmen up, and they climbed on the Mongoose and sped away as fast as Chia's skinny legs would take them.

CHAPTER 6

Tomas opened his eyes then snapped them shut against the piercing lights. Slowly, he tried again, and this time tried to lift his head, which felt as heavy as a bowling ball. His wrists burned and, when he reached to rub them, he jerked back painfully. One of them was still cuffed, now around the leg of an iron bed, if you could call it that, more like an iron gate from a fence wired to four metal posts. Tomas' head pounded and, adding to his discomfort, were loud, jarring noises that seemed to circle above him like dirty water around a drain.

"Ah ha I see that our guest is awake. I hope you are finding your accommodations to your liking." The man's head nearly scraped the top frame of the door and he shone from his silver hair to his belt buckle as if dipped in metallic paint. Even his eyelashes and eyebrows glistened silver white. His eyelids were the pale pink of earthworms.

When Tomas tried to speak, his lips, thick and heavy as bags of sand, got in his way.

"Where am I? What are you going to do with me? I think I have a right to a lawyer."

"Ha, not in this nightmare. I am Silver, and your attendant is Dr. Sicko, psycho—you can pronounce it many ways. Doesn't matter. We are in charge of your health or your illness, your comfort or your discomfort, your future or your eternal reward. You decide."

"I could decide better if you'd unhook me from this bed. And let's get down to it. What do you want?"

"I told you that already. But you are insisting on memory lapses, which means another of my memory cocktails." From the top of a cardboard box beside the bed, he reached for a small, plastic cup.

"If your cocktails aren't working, what makes you think more of them will do the trick?"

"Mescallic mushrooms always work. It just takes finding the right dose. Didn't your aunt teach you about these native tonics?"

Tomas' head felt as if it would split open. "Can't you at least turn down that noise?"

"I am insulted, *chico*. We have chosen this music especially for you. If you listen carefully, you can hear car alarms, heavy metal polka sung by your favorite, I'm sure, Barry Manilow, and other delightful sounds. Listen, there's a train wreck. If you don't want to hear Dr. Sicko's psycho mix, then tell us where your people have hidden the artifact."

Tomas blinked and swallowed, his throat dry and scratchy. "Can I get some plain water? I think it might help me remember."

Silver pulled a soda bottle filled with clear liquid out of the box beside the bed, held it to Tomas' lips, and dribbled it in slowly, waiting each time Tomas greedily sipped.

Tomas drank half the bottle then let his head fall backward. "Yea, now I remember," he said and smiled slyly.

"I thought your memory could be persuaded to return."

"I remember that I don't know anything about any artifact. And I haven't seen my tia in a long time—years."

Silver's face darkened like a tarnished plate. "Okay. You want to get down to it? Dr. Sicko and his assistant Tonto saw you on his rounds the other day at your aunt's place. Lying will only make things worse."

"All right, I saw her, but I don't know anything about an artifact. You saw where she lives. If she had a valuable artifact, would she live like that?"

Silver clucked like a demonic chicken. "Silver can wait a
while longer, but not much. Think about it, *chico*, and think
about your family. We have information I haven't told you, and
it will be better for you *and* your family if you tell us the truth.
So, here's some more of our special, truth cocktail."

When he reached Tomas' lips with the cup, Tomas suddenly whipped his head from side to side, splattering its contents
over them both.

Silver slapped Tomas furiously then bellowed over his
shoulder," Sicko, get in here and bring your needle."

CHAPTER 7

A fter she had dropped Chia a block away from her house, Carmen rode the Mongoose home alone and hid it in some huge dusty oleander bushes beside the house.

It seemed to be more behaved for the time being. As she and Chia had drawn closer to their neighborhood, Carmen's tongue had begun to itch, which usually meant trouble lurking nearby.

Now as she approached the porch, a burnt metallic smell in the air reminded her of a horrible medicine her Aunt Yoruba in Mexico had rubbed on her warts. The walls of Aunt Yoruba's small adobe hut had been lined with bottles of cloudy liquids on shelves. The rafters dripped with herbs drying upside down. Aunt Yoruba had called herself a *curandera* and had remedies for everything from dandruff to sties.

A buzz of voices from inside the house brought Carmen back to the present and the porch. An unfamiliar, large, square car was parked in front of Motors Immaculado. No one they knew drove a car like that, Carmen thought, as she opened the front door.

Septima was sitting on the couch, leaning forward intently, talking to a man dressed in a brown suit and a red tie. *An ugly combination*, Carmen thought. He had a pointed, urn-like head with ears big as handles, and when his mouth formed itself into the imitation of a smile, the two long teeth beside his front ones and his small, black eyes combined in a crafty, rodent-like way. On the couch beside Septima, at the third point of a triangle, sat Teofilo with the usual bored/slow expression that his face fell into naturally. The metallic, medicinal smell scorched the air as Carmen, feeling slightly nauseous, passed them on the way to her bedroom. Carmen heard the man say in an oily slick voice, "I understand your hesitation, but it can't hurt to let me run up some figures."

"We have business here. Carmen. Uh—I'll be in there in a minute to talk to you. Make sure you have clean clothes for church tomorrow, and don't interrupt us."

Septima's voice wavered in a way that meant she was doing her best to restrain a simmering fury.

Rosa was not in their bedroom, and Carmen's bones seemed to melt as she sank down onto the rickety bed they shared. Her entire body softened as the tears she'd been holding back slid out onto the scratchy, wool army blanket that left rashes on her cheeks. Once she had climbed into the trunk of a car to hide with Rosa at Cherry Auction where her mother had been selling oranges, grapefruit, and lemons from Septima's trees and had thought *la migra* was about to raid.

Carmen had begun to thrash and scratch at the inside of the trunk, fighting for air. She still had nightmares about that smothery feeling. Her chest tightened, just as it had then, and her breath came shallow, hot, and quick. As Carmen sat up on the bed, kicked off her shoes, and shrugged off her jacket, a bright turquoise blue feather eddied down from her pocket and sank to the floor. Its colors shone like oil rainbowed on water. Then she remembered the box in the closet.

Just as Carmen was about to drag the box out, Septima opened the bedroom door without knocking, her way of flexing her power.

"Where's Mami?" Carmen asked, jumping up and rushing to the doorway, hoping to block Septima's view of the closet where the pirated box peeked out.

"She got scared when our visitor appeared, and I think she hid in one of the trailers out back. She wants to lay low for now." Septima craned her neck, frowning suspiciously at Carmen.

"Has Mami had anything to eat? I can take her something. I'm kinda hungry, anyway. And you said this morning you were gonna make burritos for tonight. You know how much Mami likes your burritos, Tia Septima." Carmen shot the words out like puffs from an air gun. "And who is that man who was here? Is he from Sears? Cuz Mami is scared of Sears. I don't know why."

"Slow down, Carmen. He's Mr. Briggs, a realtor." Septima then added with a sneer, "Mr. Briggs. Teofilo answered the phone today and told him it was okay to come over. I wouldn't have let him in the house myself. But that's Teofilo for you. Teo-fool-o. I'm not signing no papers, though."

"What papers?" Carmen was now following Septima into the kitchen, where her aunt was arranging burritos on a Melmac plate with a dollop of beans. "Here, take this to your mami. Don't worry about papers. Teo can't sell this place without my signature. I'm not afraid of jackals—jackals that want to light up cigarettes in my home. Imagine! Never mind. I won't sign if it's the last thing I do."

Carmen took the plate of food, thinking better of pointing out to Septima that the last thing she did could not be to not sign. Carmen was used to secretly laughing at Septima's contradictions.

"Rosa's in the Caravan—the one with the posters on it." The phone was ringing again, and Septima raced to answer it.

Carmen grabbed Teofilo's thrift store army jacket from a peg by the back door and headed out. The sky had deepened to a dark wave of grape, fanning out from the fringe of trees that brushed upward to the first ragged stars. She shivered in the purpley cold of early dusk and watched steam rise from the warm burritos.

Carmen knocked softly on the flimsy aluminum door of the trailer and called to her mother. "It's me, Carmen. Mami, open up."

The door rattled open and Rosa peeked out, her ghostly face swamped with shadows.

Carmen looked around the trailer. Shortly after they had moved in, she had been drawn to its colorful images of saints, mermaids, and dragons painted on the sides, peeling and discolored from the elements, but Septima had shooed her away, threatening her with, "El Diablo will get you good. And if he don't, Septima will."

Rosa had straightened up some and fixed a spot to sleep on the couch in the front section. The walls were covered with pictures of animals, cut from magazines, and colorful replicas of saints. Mixed in with these were images of Elvis, Madonna, and Cher, streamers, and sagging balloons that had long ago deflated. Feathers and cut paper wove through here and there. Dime store rugs with images of *The Virgin*, *The Last Supper*, and sinewy leopards scattered on the floors, frayed and grimy from years of disuse.

"Mami, are you okay? You must be scared and lonely out here."

A small electric heater glowed behind Rosa. It was attached to a long extension cord snaking from the house.

Rosa shook her head wearily. "Yo no stop think about Tomas. *Donde* they taken him, *Mjja*? Septima uhmmmm...*el telefono, but no dinero for la abogada.* I no help *solamente* I sit aqui la sitting duck loca, *sabes*?" She made a low, rumbling sound in her throat like a faulty electric razor.

"Oh, Mami, Don't worry. I have a plan. I am talking to someone who can help us. My friend Chia knows people in the...uhm, State Department that help if you can't afford lawyers. Here, just eat this, Mami. We gotta keep strong for Tomas. Promise me you'll stop worrying so much."

The bit about the State Department wasn't true, but with Tomas gone, Carmen felt the need to protect her mother had fallen on her shoulders.

After Carmen had settled her mother down and watched her eat some of the burritos, she had offered to sleep in the RV, but Rosa had said no. "*Este casa es frequentada, mija. Pero, the ghosts no molesta Rosa—old woman—pero ellos molestan jovenes como usted.*"

Carmen started to argue that ghosts didn't play favorites, but when she saw that Rosa was getting upset again, she gave it up.

She stepped outside the trailer into almost pitch blackness. On the flimsy step, she stopped to let her eyes adjust and thought she heard movement in the bushes. Then two bright, topaz spots grew larger, moving toward her from the middle of a fire thorn bush about ten feet away. Frozen to the steps, Carmen opened her mouth to scream but only a half gasp, half whimper emerged. A sleek, spotted jaguar fixed its coppery-gold eyes on hers but did not move. The dogs in their pens were strangely silent. Carmen could smell the jaguar's musky, feral odor blending with another smell like very strong herbs. The dark liquid trees swirled around them like inky plants caught in a tangle of current deep on the ocean floor. Carmen wanted to run, but her legs were like wet sponges when she tried to move them. The animal surged forward then, and she just let go, slipping down on the steps, ready to be served up for its dinner.

CHAPTER 8

Carmen opened her eyes and realized she was lying at the bottom of the RV steps, flat on her back, staring up at the stars, a strange stillness around her. There was no jaguar that she could see, and she wondered if she could have imagined it. But it had seemed so real. Her arm ached and, as she pulled herself up, her back stung from where the steps had scraped her in the fall. Now the dogs were barking furiously and she yelled for them to shush.

But the barking continued to spill into the dark like liquid sound poured into a broken vessel.

As her eyes grew accustomed to the darkness, her hearing seemed to sharpen also, and a rustling drew her attention to the bushes from where the jaguar had crept. There in the dirt, she saw two cigarette butts and she heard what was unmistakably a cough. A cigarette smoking jaguar with a nicotine cough? she wondered groggily, just before the hot flare of danger shot through her. Frantically, she looked around for a weapon. Man or jaguar, this time she couldn't afford to give in to fear and allow herself to pass out.

Carmen grabbed the only thing she could find nearby, the broken off handle of a child's wagon, and held it aloft. The bushes rustled again and the jaguar stood before her, baring its long, canine teeth, its eyes, the coldest yellow she'd ever seen.

Just as she was ready to strike it with the metal tongue of the wagon handle, the jaguar did a strange thing. It shook its head slowly back and forth. Its amber eyes zeroed in directly on Carmen. More coughing then erupted from the bushes and a dark figure lunged toward Carmen. But the jaguar leapt upward toward the shadowy form, and both fell back into the tangle of night-soaked brush and foliage that wove itself erratically around the back yard. All Carmen could see was the wild flaying of brush as the battle continued, with occasional grunts and growls.

Then everything exploded and both the jaguar's and the shadow's forms curved upward into the trees, lost in a splash of sudden moonlight and wild primitive cries. Everything was still then and Carmen found herself alone, more fascinated than afraid of the scene she had just witnessed. It had been like watching a movie, with herself as an extra. But it had been real, she was sure. Torn shrubbery and scuffle marks in the dirt were evidence of that. And there were the cigarettes, which she retrieved and stuffed into her pocket. The dogs had stopped barking, and the newly risen moon swooned in the dark tops of the trees, her only witness.

When Carmen opened the door to the house, it was dark, except for a sliver of light inched under Septima's door. She carried a cold burrito from the fridge to her room and ate it sitting on her bed. *The jaguar never meant to harm me*, she suddenly realized. It had come as an ally. And this time she had been ready to fight. Carmen smiled to herself. Then she remembered the box she had stowed in her closet earlier and dragged it out once again. More green-blue feathers puffed up from the bottom, opalescent peacock eyes watching as she sifted through the contents. Under the Day of the Dead skulls, cut paper, and ornaments, she found a stack of religious death cards which she set aside along with a slim, gray, cloth-bound book with the word, "*Correspondencias*" on the cover. There were some papers in Spanish that did not seem too important, and Carmen shuffled through these to a stack of letters tied up with a dingy lavender ribbon.

Most of the letters were addressed to Septima, and Carmen saw with disappointment that they were in Spanish. She could speak fairly well, but her reading of Spanish was poor, and these letters were in a spiky script it would have been difficult to decipher even in English. The next to the last letter, though, was addressed to Septima in English. It had a return address for Sister Dolores Theresa Valdez at the Holy Sisters of Mysterium Tremedum and dated about fifteen years earlier. Carmen's stomach fluttered as she opened the letter and began to read.

Dear Sister Septima,

I take the liberty of addressing you in so familiar a way because I have truly felt a spiritual connection to you since you began teaching the catechism classes at Saint Agnes, and I have had the great honor and pleasure of making your acquaintance. We are all delighted with your progress both in the spiritual realm and with your English, and in the spirit of helping, you continue that progress, I will write this in English. I also am flattered and pleased that you chose me as your spiritual advisor and confidant and trust that I have lived up to your expectations. In the short time you have been at your position, you have impressed us all with your piety and sincerity. We are all missing you greatly, and everyone sends love and blessings to you that you find comfort in the Lord and allow him to shoulder some part of the burden of the recent loss of your mother. We are saying a special rosary for you each evening.

However, I must also bring to your attention some distressing news of your sister Portilla. I hardly know how to broach the subject, and at the risk of spreading idle gossip, I must inform you that she is now traveling a path of blasphemy and perdition that threatens her mortal soul, otherwise I should never speak of it. She has begun treating members of the congregation for physical ailments such as gout, dyspepsia, migraine, and constipation, with herbs, which we can accept, but she is flirting with witchcraft. She dispenses potions for lost love, memory loss, mild depression, and (I blush to even mention it) impotence! That is bad enough, but it is said she is also selling spells, even when Father Refugio expressly forbade her to do so. I fear she is a bruja. She is calling herself a curandera, but she has that little trailer fitted up with candles and idolatrous wax statues right next to our beautiful virgin and all manner of heretical paraphernalia that is a disgrace to all that is holy and pure. You must try and reason with her as soon as you return. While the church is able to indulge those who seek physical cures from such sources, she must remember her sacred vows and keep the holy commandments and remember her confirmation promises and honor the church and its teachings first. The most grievous offense to date is Manuela Hertado who, as you know, is in the same position as you and has come to the states without the proper papers. He was advised by Portilla to contact your brother-in-law Veloz to help him. Then there was that other business that was never properly explained and for which grave questions still remain. You know what I am speaking of, I'm sure. At first I did not agree with the spy network you set up for your sister before you left, but now I see the peril that threatens to destroy not just Portilla herself but the sanctity of our entire religious community. She has even taken up residence in that old trailer of her sister Pepita's, the one that some say is haunted, the one Pepita had fixed up with idolatrous statues and all manner of blasphemy. I thought it had been disposed of after Pepita died. Anyway, I have spoken to Father Refugio, and he urged me to write this letter in hopes that you can take care of this matter when you return, and we

will have no need to take any further measures to
protect the flock.
      Go in the light and love of the Lord and the
Blessed Mother,
            Sister Dolores Theresa Valdez.

Carmen folded the letter back into its envelope and stared at the bamboo printed nylon curtains Septima had bought at the swap meet. A splashy red flower twined through the bamboo, and the colors reminded Carmen of Mr. Briggs or Briggshot as Septima had called him. It seemed strange to Carmen that he had appeared right after Tomas had been taken away, or maybe it wasn't so strange. And now it seemed there was someone who might be of help—Tia Portilla. Why had she never heard any mention of this aunt? What steps had Septima taken against her? Was Tia Portilla really a *curandera* or perhaps a *bruja*? Could she really cast spells? What was the "other business of grave concern"? How could she get in touch with Tia Portilla? One thing Carmen knew for sure was that Teofilo would have some of the answers to these questions.

Carmen would have to go to mass in the morning, that she knew already. But afterward, she'd try and get Teofilo alone somehow and ask some of the questions that whirled inside her head like soap bubbles circling a drain. Before she had dropped Chia a block away from her house, they had agreed to meet the next day at a Pho restaurant—noodle shop Chia had said—to discuss what to do about Tomas.

Carmen yawned and dropped her head, leaning against the bed. She felt tired but fearful of falling asleep and dreaming of Lupita and the tomato worms coming after her. But in spite of herself, she fell asleep and, instead, she dreamed of a nun with a mermaid's tail wriggling out of her habit, walking a pet snake on a leash. The dream was pleasant except for the loud growls that echoed from distant clouds like gigantic jungle animals.

CHAPTER 9

Saint Agnes church was very crowded the next morning. Usually Carmen sat beside Rosa, avoiding her aunt and uncle, but Rosa had not felt like going to church that morning, so Carmen ended up stuffed between Septima and Teofilo on the hard wooden bench. Teofilo sometimes dozed and snored during the sermon, which caused Septima to shank him with her sharp elbow. She also kept herself busy monitoring Carmen who liked to lose her thoughts in the stained glass, making up unholy stories about the transparent saints glowing in the windows in their jewel toned robes. Her favorite involved a saint's rock band, and Carmen amused herself giving each of them different rock identities—like Saint Frankie & the Firecrackers, a band of birds, rabbits, and squirrels who threw firecrackers at the audience. When Carmen felt Septima's eyes on her, she tried to replace her wandering expression with a more properly holy one.

They had gotten a late start since Septima couldn't find her silver and pearl rosary which she liked to flash around at church. Carmen had hidden it in a canister of pinto beans on the kitchen counter when she had found it on the bathroom floor. Now, Carmen giggled in secret to herself, watching Septima work her old wooden bead rosary between her fingers with distracted irritation. Playing tricks on Septima helped Carmen endure her aunt's bossy ways.

Now Carmen tried to fix her face into a pious mask, facing forward toward the service. Sitting directly in front of her was a lady with a beehive hairdo that swirled hypnotically, and Carmen found herself drawn into its spirals. As she blinked her eyes hard, trying to refocus, the now familiar metallic smell floated nearby. She snuck a look around, but no one else seemed to be bothered by the smell that was getting stronger and stronger to the point of making Carmen's eyes water. A faint buzzing sound wafted up from the beehive lady's hair just as a small, fierce honey bee worked its way to the surface of the swirl and dived directly at Carmen, who swatted the air frenziedly. Septima glared at Carmen with her index finger pressed to her lips. Carmen pointed to where the bee still hovered, but Septima squeezed Carmen's thigh roughly and glared harder.

The bee now whizzed around Carmen's head in nervous buzzing zeroes, but no one else seemed to see it. Carmen had been severely stung once when she and some other migrant girls had played at making sopa in an old stump at the edge of an orchard, and the bees had snagged in Carmen's braids, stinging her head repeatedly. Now, more and more bees began to pour from the oblivious owner's beehive hair, swarming into an angry cloud that darkened the domed ceiling of the church then siphoned down to the bald head of an old man in one of the front pews. Horrified, Carmen opened her mouth to scream, but as she did so, one of the bees flew directly in. Sputtering, choking, and coughing, Carmen jumped up, climbed over Teofilo at the end of the pew, and made her way out of the church. Outside on the church steps, Carmen coughed more, unable to clear her throat. When she finally got her breath, the heavy doors of the church opened, spilling out a red faced screaming child. Her hand was firmly clutched by the bee-hive lady, who now jerked the child and hissed that she had better stop it and behave.

The beehive woman had a thick Spanish accent and when she spoke, Carmen saw glints of silver flashing from her front teeth. The child, however, still screaming, would not be stilled.

"Cerrado" the woman said, but unable to calm the child, now sobbing a jerky beat, the lady snatched her up and made for their car.

Carmen had stopped coughing now, but as she turned to re-enter the church, she saw the bees swarming down from the steeple of the church, where they hung for one instant in what looked to Carmen like the shape of the letter "O" which just as quickly flashed into the sun and was gone. Carmen watched the spot where they had been with a warm feeling in her gut.

What was that all about? Carmen wondered, watching the beehive lady strap her still screaming child into her car seat. Carmen squinted and shivered as blinding sunlight struck the granite steps. No one else had seen the bees. That much she was sure of, but she couldn't shake the nagging feeling that something strange had entered the sanctity of the church and sent a message only to her.

"What was that all about?" Septima hissed fiercely at Carmen, echoing her own thoughts as she slipped back into their pew.

"I just got something caught in my throat," Carmen whispered, avoiding Septima's sharp eyes.

The rest of the service continued as usual, but when they stood to cross themselves, Carmen's eye was drawn to the place where the beehive lady and her child had sat. There lay a plastic, toy spider. Without knowing why, Carmen scooped it up and dropped it into her pocket.

After Mass, they all lit candles and offered petitions for Tomas.

In the car on the way home, Septima kept a running tirade against Carmen and Tomas' lack of religious upbringing and its contribution to their present state. Into one of the rare lulls, Carmen spoke. "Don't go blaming Mami, Tia. She's done the best she could. And...I have just joined the Little Sisters of St. Agnes Girl's Club, and some of their meetings are after school so I hope you'll be understanding if I'm not right home from school every day."

Septima's delight was cut short however by a report on Spanish radio about immigration. Carmen tried to listen also, but it was nothing new and she lapsed into silence in the back seat where she still shivered, even though the car heater was cranked up full blast. Septima did not like to be cold. As Carmen rubbed her hands together to warm them, she noticed a fine dusting like silvery talc that shone when she held them up to the window's light. Wiping them on her denim skirt left faint silver streaks across her thighs.

She would have to tell Chia about all this. There was no one else who wouldn't think she was just plain crazy. There was something spooky going on, thought Carmen, as her fingers involuntarily rolled the plastic spider round and round in her pocket.

❦❦❦

Teofilo seemed to be on the same avoid-Septima train as Carmen because he took off for his workshop as soon as they got back to the house. "Can I help you, Uncle Teo?" Carmen said hurrying after him, before Septima could snag her.

Teofilo looked surprised but shrugged. "Es okay *con mio*. You can organize my drill bits. Oso never puts nothing back where he gets it from."

The shed he called his workshop smelled like musty rags, oil, and grease ground into the dirt for centuries. Engine parts and tools mixed with boxes of shingles, stacks of old wood, and car seats waiting for re-upholstery. Swagged with spider webs and fishing lures, a slightly bent, fake silver Christmas tree leaned in the corner in its rusted stand.

Teofilo's closely set eyes appeared almost cross-eyed, emphasizing his big, floppy goofiness. At any moment he might shake his large, mangy head, like a water buffalo sluffing off droplets of water, in a great heave of impatience and labored grunts, signifying either yes or no, which were the bulk of his conversation.

"Uncle Teo, who is Tia Portilla?" Carmen blurted out, as she sorted the drill bits out by size to arrange in their case.

Teo's big shaggy head snapped upward from the car seat he was measuring for a new cover he would cut from fake alligator Naugahyde. His eyes shifted skittishly. "You better ask Septima 'bout her."

"I was going to, but I thought maybe I'd better tell you first. Tia Portilla called here yesterday when you guys were outside at the yard sale. I answered the phone, and she said to give you the message that she has an old car she wants to get rid of. Said it's a junker but maybe you'd want it because you could fix anything. I forgot all about it after everything that happened with Tomas. Why haven't we ever met her, Uncle Teofilo? She still live in the same place?"

Teofilo bit his lip. "Uhmmm, I don't know where she lives. She's loca," he said, making a screwing sign in his ear with his finger.

"She said to tell you that when you come over to look at the car to be careful. There's been lots of gang bangers around her place, tagging and stuff but that probably wouldn't scare you. 'That Teofilo, he's not scared of some puny taggers,' she said."

Carmen snuck a look at Teofilo and saw a faint grin creeping around his mouth.

"Didn't they have a shooting over by her place not long ago? I forgot. What's that street called? The one over by..." Carmen said casually.

"Tulare Street's getting bad, but I go over there all the time. You gotta know how to get around the gang bangers. They don't bother big guys like me."

Carmen did not add sarcastically that she had noticed that very thing when Fernando had come around at the yard sale. Instead, she said, "Well, here's your drill bits. I better go see about Mami, Uncle Teo. Oh yea, Portilla said for you not to tell Septima that you're coming over. She wants to deal only with you cuz Septima's always suspicious of her."

Teo looked puzzled for a second then said, "Septima thinks Portilla uses *magia negra*, so you stay away. But I'll go look at the car, *seguro*."

CHAPTER 10

When Carmen arrived at Pho #39 after lunch, she did not see Chia. She locked the Mongoose to a bike rack in front of the restaurant with a somewhat rusty chain and lock she had dug out of a box behind Teofilo's workshop. Carmen wondered if there really were thirty-eight other Pho restaurants like this one in town. She had seen lots of them, usually in second-rate strip malls or seedier areas of town. A picture of a chicken and a pig danced around the 39 on the sign above the door and the window was so grimy and steamed over that she could barely see inside. A man, squatting on the dirty sidewalk, trolled his blood-shot eyes toward Carmen then turned back to the brown bag he sucked from like a baby bottle.

When Chia finally appeared, she was leading a limping, quiet-eyed child about five years old. Black bangs cut straight across her forehead and Chia introduced her to Carmen as her sister, True.

True met Carmen's smile with silent scrutiny. Solemn and wide-eyed, she watched Carmen like a scientist studying an alien life form.

"Let's go inside." Chia waved toward the restaurant. "I have a cousin who works here and can bring us Thuc Uong, Thai iced tea." They sat down and Chia's cousin Mai came and swabbed their table with a big, wet towel, after stacking bowls of soup and noodle leavings onto a cart. Mai was a thin high-school-age girl in a black and pink Hello Kitty T-shirt and thick, black mascara that made her eyes look sleepy.

Mai brought Thai iced teas, syrupy sweet drinks made with tea, coconut milk, tapioca, and different flavors, stirred with ice. She exchanged a few words in Hmong with Chia and went back to busing tables.

"Mai told me that everyone is uptight today so we shouldn't stay too long. Rumors are flying around that somebody new has bought the building and might raise the rent. Everybody is nervous."

Carmen sipped her sweet, strawberry drink and waited for Chia to go on. But now an awkward space hovered between them, as if the night had separated them back into their former wary selves. Finally Chia said, "I had to bring True because I'm her babysitter, and I have to always keep her close by and make sure nothing happens to her. True has a kind of club foot. Show her True."

True didn't seem embarrassed by her foot at all. In fact, she stuck it out like a prized pet.

"Does it hurt?" Carmen couldn't think of anything else to say.

"No, but it's hard to walk very far. At least she won't have to take P.E. when she goes to school," Chia answered for True.

When True put her foot back, she slipped her hand out of her pocket and then opened it on the table, releasing two spotted lady bugs that made a run for it.

"Those are her pets," Chia explained. "She has two lady bugs, five roly poly bugs, a praying mantis, and a daddy long-legs. She also has a bird that fell out of the mulberry tree which she nursed back to health."

"How did she do that?"

"We don't know for sure. She said that she gave it a drop of whiskey and rubbed its belly."

"Awesome," Carmen said as True bounced her hand, with the ladybugs on top, up and down like a ladybug carnival ride.

Then Carmen couldn't hold back her news any longer. "Guess what? I think I've found someone who can help us find Tomas."

"Spit it out already, ese," Chia did a dead ringer impression of Muneca.

Grinning, Carmen continued. "Did you see that box I rescued from the yard sale? A box full of papers, Day of the Dead stuff, and old letters. Well, turns out I have an aunt, who is a *bruja*, I think. One letter was from one of the nuns at church who was spying on Tia Portilla and telling Septima that she was healing people and stuff. But get this, Tia Portilla helped some people who were illegals. Septima doesn't like her cuz she's into magic—she thinks it's the devil's work."

"So, is a bruja like a witch or something?"

Carmen shrugged. "Kind of, I think—whatever she is, she might be able to help us figure out how to get Tomas back and explain some of the spooky stuff that's been happening to us."

Chia made a loud slurping noise as she sucked at the dregs of her tea. "She sounds a lot like Hmong shamans. That's funny. I just thought of something. My uncle's a shaman. We got double magic, *chica*, if we can get ahold of it."

"Double magic. *Chevere*."

"*Chevere*? What's that mean?"

"Cool. Double magic's cool, but it might be hard to get with Portilla. She's banned from Septima's. I had to trick Teofilo, but I got her street at least—Tulare—over by Zacky Farms somewhere."

"Hey, I know where that is. My older brother got a job at Zacky Farms right out of high school. What's Portilla's last name? We can look in the phone book."

"Her name would be Portilla Estrella. Everyone jokes in our family that my mom went from being Estrella, a star, to a moon, Luna."

They asked Mai to bring them a phone book, and Chia looked up Portilla Estrella but didn't find anything.

"Wait. I have an idea," Carmen said, sliding the phone book over to herself. "She just might have a botanica, so I can look on Tulare for one."

"What's a botanica?" Chia asked, pulling out a pad of paper and a pencil to occupy True, who had put her bugs into a little box with air holes that she carried in her pocket.

True immediately began to fill the pad with fat bubble but-
terflies and a bird with a fan of feathers, all very intricate and
detailed, Carmen noticed, remembering that Chia was also
known at school for being a gifted artist.

"A botanica is a shop...sort of...that sells candles, herbs,
charms, and religious stuff and sometimes they mix up potions
for you, like if you are afraid of losing your boyfriend or something. Have you lost your boyfriend, Chia?" she asked slyly.

Chia blushed. "If you're asking about Tomas, no...uh...I'm
not allowed to have boyfriends. I think we got to be friends, you
know, before he stopped coming to school. He used to walk me
home every day after school, after Muneca said she was going to
beat my butt."

"What did Muneca have against you?"

"There was that art contest in Sanchez's class, and everybody voted for Muneca's drawing, but it was supposed to be of
someone you admired from your own culture. Then Pico shouted out after they voted that Brittany Spears was not in Muneca's
culture. Sanchez thought it was the Virgin Mary she drew because she had a crown on her head and was holding a baby.
When he disqualified her drawing, everybody voted for mine."

"Who was your picture of?"

"This lady our family knew in Laos who saved our lives
when we had to escape. She swam across the river, pulling a
bunch of us kids tied together with ropes around our waists. She
didn't know until she got all the way across whether we were
still alive or not."

"*Chevere*! That's some story."

Chia looked embarrassed. "Hey, did you find any botanicas?"

There were three botanicas listed: Botanica Mi Esperanzo
on Belmont, and the other two were both on Tulare: San Judas
and San Lorenzo's Eye of God.

"Bingo!" Carmen snapped her fingers. "It has to be one of
those two. All we have to do is get over there and ask for Portilla. When do we go?'

Chia was shaking her head. "It's going to be hard. Everyone is getting ready for Hmong New Years and my mom wants

me to help with the cooking and sewing. She's working on a special outfit for True. They want to try and find a husband for her. The American doctors want to operate on True's foot, but the family's against it. They think her foot is a curse, but if they can marry her off, she'll be taken care of by her husband and that will solve it."

True had stopped drawing and looked up with big sunflower eyes. Her fine brows came together in the center of her forehead like soft, curious caterpillars.

"Okay then, how 'bout this? Let's ditch school tomorrow—right after lunch. Think you could forge our moms' signatures?"

"I think so." Chia glanced at True, dug a candy bar from her pocket, and slid it across the table. "You keep this quiet. Okay, True?"

True nodded solemnly in agreement and then pushed the candy back to Chia. She said something in Hmong and Chia laughed.

"She says I don't have to give her candy. She won't tell."

"Sweet," Carmen said. "We're on."

Carmen held her hand up with all five fingers splayed open. "Give me your hand," she said.

Chia held hers up, touching fingertips with Carmen. Slowly, Carmen collapsed her fingers inward. Chia followed. Then Carmen pulled them out and threw her hands out and upward.

"Victorioso!" she called out.

"Check this out." Chia spit on her hand and nodded at Carmen to do the same. Then they shook hands. "Only boys can do that in my culture, but I'm not a Miao—a backward, uncivilized Hmong," she explained when Carmen looked puzzled. "I'm a modern girl. And if we're gonna help Tomas, we can't let old-fashioned rules stop us."

A shiny black head bobbed up between them just then, and True threw up her own hand, pudgy for one so slight. Carmen and Chia joined their hands to True's and they sang out again, this time all three together. "Victorioso!"

"And praise the ancestors," Chia added. "We might need them."

As they left the restaurant, Carmen smelled the metallic odor again just as a man brushed past them into the restaurant. Carmen thought he looked familiar. She looked closer then gasped.

"What is it?" Chia and True had already started home, but turned back to Carmen now.

"That man. He was at my aunt's house yesterday talking to them about selling the house and the business. Chia, there's something really weird about him. Septima said she'd never sign any papers to sell, but she seemed very scared. And I smelled this metallic odor, kind of like burning electrical wires, but with singed fur mixed in. I smelled it in church today, also. Oh yea, I almost forgot to tell you. There was a swarm of bees in church, and I'm the only one who saw them."

Carmen told Chia the whole story about the beehive lady and the child and then about the jaguar and the battle behind Motors Immaculada. When she was done, Chia's eyes had gone round as nickels. She shook her head slowly.

"You need to be super careful, Carmen. I don't know what we're into, but we need to talk to your aunt."

"Hey, you be careful too. You marched us right into the middle of enemy camp when we went downtown."

"Hey, look."

Carmen pointed to the Mongoose which was vibrating softly in its chains where she had locked it to the bike rack. Before either of them could even sneeze, True pulled away from Chia, kicked the Mongoose softly with her bad foot, and it stopped shaking.

"*Chevere*," Chia said, "We can't be too careful."

"You're right. We need to talk to Portilla. The sooner the better." Carmen waved to Chia and True and rolled smoothly out of the parking lot on the now tamed Mongoose.

CHAPTER 11

Carmen opened her eyes from a tumultuous dream full of dancing pigs, chickens, and cats in a strange country where she'd never been before, with whirring, multi-colored insects lit up like Christmas tree lights blinking on and off. They had circled her body brushing against her like dust devil specks. When Carmen had looked down at her body in the dream, she saw tufts of spotted fur and knew that she had been visited and absorbed by the jaguar again. Carmen sat up in bed, scratching where her haunches would have been. A shadow flitted across the window and, for a minute, Carmen thought she had seen a large crow, but it was the wrong color. Instead of black, it was a soft purple blur. Carmen rubbed her eyes sleepily then sighed. *Maybe I'm going coo coo*, she thought. But when she looked at the clock, she jumped from bed. No time to waste. She couldn't be late today.

What shall I wear to ditch school? she thought excitedly. She'd never ditched school, or even thought of it. In fact, Carmen liked school, though she kept this to herself. Her friends would think she was *la coo coo loca*.

She pulled out her warmest, wooly green sweater, her favorite color, and then slipped on her jeans and Converse high tops, to which she had sewn strips of fake leopard skin cloth she had found in Septima's sewing basket. Everyone else wore the latest, brand-name sneakers, but Carmen liked to have her own style. She needed to be warm today if they were going to go all the way over to Tulare Street, so she dug in the closet and found a knitted cap of Tomas' and one of Mami's knitted scarves. With a sigh, she worked her old, black, puffy jacket over the sweater. It was getting too small and the cuffs were frayed, but there was no money to buy anything new. As she folded her thick, black hair into a braid at the nape of her neck, her eyes fell onto a picture of her father on the dresser. She had his high cheekbones and almond-shaped eyes. Mami had told her that he had called her his little China doll when she was a baby because of her looks, and he had also teased Rosa, saying that she had snuck off with their neighbor Mr. Chong.

Septima was in the kitchen, flipping tortillas in the big iron skillet. Some days Septima would make her own, but today Carmen saw that she was enveloped in an angry cloud, almost visible, and using store-bought tortillas, a bad sign. This, coupled with banging noises from Teofilo's workshop this early in the morning, usually meant they had quarreled. Septima handed Carmen a tortilla and pointed to a stack of wieners to go inside. Carmen slid a ribbon of salsa inside her tortilla, wrapped up the wiener, made another one for her mother, and headed outside to the RV. Her mother was already up and dressed in sweats and the big, fuzzy moon boots she wore almost all winter, since her feet were always cold.

"Maybe you should go back in the house, Mami," Carmen said. Although it was somewhat warm inside the trailer with the electric heater on, she noticed that her mother's nose was red, and when she hugged her, her hands were icy. "This place is not good for you Mami. I don't want you to get sick. And it could be haunted, too."

"Pero no ghost scares me, *mija*. It's the living that give fear to me."

Carmen wanted to talk more about this, but it was getting late. She had also noted a slight wheeze in her mother's voice when she protested that she was still afraid of the ICE coming to get her. Rosa's fears and timidity had always bothered Carmen, to the point of making her angry at her mother. Sometimes Rosa would not even speak up when she was given the wrong change, and it wasn't from ignorance either. Rosa was very sharp with calculations.

Finally, Carmen left for school, vowing to broach the subject with Septima of getting Rosa out of the trailer when she got home. Septima could always make Rosa do things, even when she didn't want to. Carmen would just have to convince Septima that it was more dangerous for her mother to get sick than to risk deportation. And Carmen wasn't convinced that hiding in the trailer was all that safe anyway. If the ICE came, they would surely search everywhere, if they were determined to find someone.

At school, Carmen could hardly keep her mind on her lessons. In History, it was something about the Mayans, an ancient civilization full of mystery, myths, and sacred rituals. Mrs. Jiminez was big on learning about your own cultural past. She put them into groups to talk about a group project and, as luck would have it, Carmen was in Muneca's group with two other Mexican girls, Lupe and Juana, and a blond boy named Joey. He had white hair, a very red face covered with pimples, and mumbled when he did manage to say anything at all. This made his face grow even redder and his pimples look ready to burst all at once. They were supposed to discuss ideas for a project exploring the daily lives of the Mayans, but usually no one talked about the project.

"Did you see that ugly top that Hmong girl had on?" Muneca whispered to the girls, with her back turned to Joey, completely ignoring him. "It looks like it came from the swap meet."

"Or maybe Walmart," Juana said, making a gagging sign.

"Or—I know, behind the swap meet where they throw away stuff that don't sell," Lupe chimed in, tipping backward in her chair.

"That's mean," Carmen said without thinking.

"Moon pie says that cuz Tomas has got a Chia Pet. Chi, chia, chi, chi, chi, chia," Muneca sang in a snarly voice.

"How come you call her moon pie?" Juana asked.

"Look at her round face, ese. And Luna means moon, *estupido*."

"You bitches is wastin' my time," Joey spat. "I'm goin' to the can for a smoke."

But, jumping up to leave, he caught the edge of Lupe's outstretched foot and pulled her off her chair. Down she went with a loud smack, her chair skidding into the desk behind her.

"All right, group three, that's enough fooling around or you can all have detention." Calling across the room, Mrs. Jiminez stood up at her desk where she had been previously absorbed in her own paperwork.

"Measles did it! Not my fault!" Lupe sniveled as she struggled to pull herself up. "We was pimpen' our project."

"Okay. Enough. You are not to talk like that in my classroom." Mrs. Jiminez, who was quite tall, stood now, towering over them. "So what *is* your plan for the project?"

Carmen gulped. "Our plan is to uh…talk about the Olmecs and show how they set the stage for the Mayan culture. We're trying to figure out right now who's going to do what."

Mrs. Jiminez was visibly impressed. "At least one of you has it together. Finish up then, and Carmen report to me at the end of the period exactly who is doing what."

The relieved mask of Muneca's face quickly slipped enough to show the secret contempt beneath. Carmen ignored her and opened their textbook to assign each person in the group their section to research just before the bell rang. She gave herself the assignment to research Mayan death and resurrection myths.

As she headed toward the cafeteria where she was to meet Chia, Carmen brushed past Muneca and her friends who mad dogged her in hostile silence. It was supposed to make her cringe with fear, Carmen knew. But excitement now trumped fear.

Carmen had ridden the Mongoose to school that day and headed now to the bike rack where Chia was waiting. Chia climbed on, with Carmen balanced on the bar in front, and they were off. For now, the Mongoose seemed subdued.

When they reached the front of the school, there was a crowd of Mexican girls headed for the Taco Bell around the corner, all dressed in black hooded sweat shirts and low rider jeans with studded belts. Carmen had always thought it odd that kids who wanted to be rebellious dressed to conform. As they breezed by the crowd that had spilled out into the street, she thought she heard Muneca calling out "Chi, chi, chi, chiaaaaa!"

Tulare Street was about ten blocks away from the school, but the day was overcast and damp, causing the cold to trickle into their bones and the air that whooshed over them to sting their faces. Chia pumped hard, though, and they reached Tulare in a good twenty minutes, with only a few rests for stoplights. They had taken the back streets and came up from the other side opposite Zacky Farms. It seemed faster and safer that way. As they pedaled down Tulare, they headed farther and farther east, away from their school but found no botanicas. Chia stopped.

"Let's try that side of the street," she huffed, out of breath.

They passed car repair shops with angry toothed, mongrel dogs barking and snapping at the chain link fence that barely contained them; grimy second hand stores, sprayed with graffiti; and taco shops with names like Maria's Tacqueria, Tacos Tambien, and Zorro's Hamburgers and Donuts. As they came up to an intersection, Chia stopped at the light, and Carmen teetered on the bar. Her tongue had begun to itch horribly. Suddenly for no reason, she looked over her shoulder. Tucked into the middle crook of a small strip mall not facing the street, she glimpsed a sign that read San Judas Botanica. "There it is, Chia. Turn around." Carmen pointed over her shoulder.

There was nowhere to secure the Mongoose, so they leaned it up against the side of the peeling pink building, and Chia stayed near the door. Carmen peeked inside the small shop with the usual religious banners, statues, candles, and glass cases with an array of herbs, little bottles of potions, and a large altar set up on top of the display case, with plastic fruit, crystals, rocks, feathers, and twinkling Christmas lights strung about a cow skull painted bright pink. No one seemed to be about, so Carmen wandered through, taking it all in, still with an itching tongue but also a bit weak and light headed. Incense and herbs hung heavy in the air.

Suddenly, from between two bamboo mats hung in a doorway, painted with a mermaid on each side, stepped a large, barefoot woman dressed in a polyester mu mu draped with turquoise necklaces and a ring for every finger. Her mercenary smile quivered with flecks of gold between her teeth, where a lit cigarette played out curls of smoke.

"*Puedo ayudarle?*" she asked in a drowsy voice, her eyes locked onto Carmen. Sharp, black fingernails forked the cigarette, as she funneled a thin cloud of smoke into Carmen's face.

"*Si, senora,*" Carmen answered timidly, coughing, then stood straighter and dug into her Spanish vocabulary arsenal. "*Quiero encontrar...Busco a mi tia Portilla, por favor.*"

The woman began to rattle off jumbled Spanish, and Carmen had to work to follow her words. Finally with a frown, she said, "*Donde es Portilla Luna?*"

Almost immediately, her eyes narrowed to hard, black discs as her entire body stiffened and the ringed fingers moved in the air as if typing invisible script. "*Tengo que cerrar esta tienda ahora. Usted tendra que marcharse.*" She ended with a waving motion that Carmen could easily interpret as a signal for her to scram.

Outside, Chia was stamping her feet in the cold, dancing from one foot to the other. "What's going on?"

"I'm not sure. When I said Aunt Portilla's name, she asked me to leave. She said something about closing the shop now."

They stood on the sidewalk, unsure what to do next, the gray day circling them like a lazy, smoky cat. Suddenly Chia cried, "Look! Isn't that the old lady from the yard sale?"

She had the same pigtails, but now she was wearing a dingy old army coat. Underneath was a long skirt which came down to her toes, decorated with jaguars at full sprint, leaping over waterfalls.

A pink, feather boa, like the one from the yard sale, snaked around her neck as she paused at the stoplight on the corner about ten yards away.

Pushing the Mongoose, they raced toward her. Instead of crossing at the stoplight, she twirled and headed past them taking no notice of them. She then twirled again in a circle and headed back down the street from where they had just come.

Flipping the Mongoose around, they hurried after her, but in the middle of the block, she disappeared.

"She was just in front of us. Where'd she go?" Carmen asked Chia, who was peering into the dirty window of what appeared to be an abandoned storefront.

"I don't know, but this place looks like it used to be a botanica or something. Look."

Carmen joined her at the window and saw a large, empty showroom with tattered religious posters still on the walls and some worn, purple-fringed drapes hanging on a wall. With the side of her fist, Carmen cleared a circle in the window dust, and peering more closely inside, saw the fading letters, *AMULETOS, INCIENSO, VELAS*...the rest covered with a swish of white paint.

"It used to be a botanica. If this was Portilla's place, where could she have gone to?" With these words, the Mongoose gave a sudden jerk, slid out of her hands, and crashed to the sidewalk.

Chia looked at it then back to Carmen with a frown.

"It jumped out of my hands," Carmen said, picking it back up.

Now it was shivering, like it did before. But as they watched it shake, a yellow striped alley cat with a perfect black triangle on its forehead appeared before them, meowing furiously.

"It's pulling me to the right. I can hardly hold onto it," Carmen said as the cat rubbed around her leg then trotted off to the right, also.

It turned once and meowed again, even louder. Together, forcing the Mongoose forward, Carmen and Chia followed the cat about ten paces to where it stopped, sat down in the middle of the sidewalk, and proceeded to wash its face leisurely, as a huge black crow dropped down beside it and danced in a circle around the disdainful cat.

With a sudden ruffle of its feathers, the bird flew upward then gave a loud, shrieking caw.

Both girls looked up to where the bird had flown and saw a purple flag hanging from an upstairs window of the building next to the one they had just left. Red letters spelled out, *Estrel-las Gemelos Botanica.*

"This must really be it. The sign says Twin Stars Botanica." Carmen squealed. "But how do we get up there?"

As she said this, the face of a woman appeared at the window, looking down at them. Then the window opened. "I've been expecting you. Wait there, and I'll come down."

CHAPTER 12

It seemed like hours as they stood on the sidewalk waiting. Carmen's hands were numb with the cold, and she saw that Chia's nose was red and shiny. They were standing in front of a store with a sign on the window that said, *Twin Stars Thrift Store* which had not captured their attention before since it seemed to be a junk/thrift store like many others found in these rundown neighborhoods.

Chia stamped her feet from the cold. "You think that's her?"

"It's her," Carmen replied with a confidence that surprised even herself.

Suddenly, the door opened before them and Carmen gasped. It was a jaguar like the one that she had encountered in the back of Motors Immaculada the other night. But it stood on two feet, wore a long, denim skirt, and seemed to have the body of a stooped wisp of a woman, holding out tiny, gnarled hands, cupping two ceramic bowls. The jaguar spoke. "I thought it would take you longer to find me, but it's good you have come today—the moon is favorable. Come in, por favor." The jaguar waved a cane carved with animal eyes and wound about with feathers and strips of leather.

The jaguar stood aside and they passed into a shop crammed with shelves of dusty knick knacks, old dishes, magazines, toys, all manner of used goods, and rounders packed full of clothing worn well beyond its natural lifespan.

"I have made tea. I was hoping you would get here before it cooled too much. I don't like my tea *tibio*." The jaguar had passed through a beaded curtain that divided the room, and they were now in another world altogether—a jungle of patterns and bright colors.

Both girls could only stand and stare, taking in just sections at a time. Candles glowed softly from niches in the corners of the room. Billowing lengths of silky pastel cloth swagged across the ceiling and cascaded down the walls like chiffon waterfalls. Pictures of saints, Buddahs, dragons, dancing goddess figures, mermaids, jaguars, and faces that Carmen recognized as if from a dream covered almost every inch of the walls. In between these, chalked on the stucco, were drawings of birds, monkeys, peacocks, and tigers. Animal skulls fought for space with gilt-framed mirrors.

One wall was filled with shelves that housed shells, jars of feathers, sun-bleached animal bones, coiled pieces of wood, and jars and jars of seeds, herbs, and other mysterious dark substances. Carmen and Chia were each handed bowls of hot tea by the jaguar. Her jaguar head was now replaced with that of a thin-ish woman with braided snow white hair, but with a surprisingly smooth, barely wrinkled face and deeply set eyes, black as nuggets of night. She had a version of Septima's hooked nose and Rosa's high cheek bones, and she waved them over to a spot in a corner piled with pillows. On the floor next to the pillows lay a jaguar mask, finely crafted from what looked like real fur with rows of iridescent feathers framing the edges.

Just before she sat down, Chia suddenly clapped her hand over her mouth. "Uh oh, the Mongoose. It's outside. I forgot—"

"No tension. I have people who look out for me. I'll be right back." The old lady moved through the curtains with the agility of someone much younger. "Your mongoose is in the front corral." She winked. "It's a live one, but one of my helpers, Flora Linda, calmed it down. She's *mis ojos suplementarios*." Tia pointed two fingers toward her own eyes. "She guided you here with some help from Itz the cat and my pet crow, Caw

Caw. You may have seen Caw Caw before. I sent her to Immaculate Motors to keep an eye on you. She got her name for two reasons. One has to do with her shrill voice and the other, I bet you can guess—involves exactly what it sounds like."

Carmen looked puzzled, then Chia jabbed her and said, "Ca, ca, Carmen."

"Oh I get it."

They both giggled.

"She likes to anoint you with the blessings of her excess. *Mis blusas tiene mucho colores.* Now let me have a look at you." Tia scrunched her eyes at Carmen then turned to Chia. "And I have only met you in several of my dreams," she said, bowing before Chia, who smiled shyly.

"I am Chia Yang." she said, bowing in return, then lowering herself to a pillow on the floor.

Tia suddenly put out her hand and stroked Chia's head on the side, across the pink streak, then pulled back and stood staring at it, heedless of Chia's discomfort.

"My cousin talked me into it," Chia mumbled, which surprised Carmen who thought it had been Chia's idea—just to be different.

Abruptly, Tia turned back to Carmen. "You may call me Tia—short for Portilla and also because I am your tia, your mami's sister." She held out her arms. "Come give me a hug, *mija.* I have been calling you to me for a long time now. I'm sorry it is trouble that finally reunites us."

It was odd, Carmen thought. Seeing this stranger was like coming home after a long, dusty journey. Tia's face, her hug, even her smell—a mix of herbs, musk, eucalyptus and something sweet like baby powder—was familiar, recovered from some half-remembered place swaddled in the cobwebs of baby or even pre-baby memory.

"I'm sorry, I barely just remember you, Tia. Did you know me when I was a baby?"

"Si. A few times, before you were walking. But I was there at Tomas' birth. He had the cord wrapped around his neck three times. The midwife said he was dead. Perhaps he was, but I undid the cord and I breathed into his lungs and brought him from blue back to cinnamon. I knew he was *especial*, even then. And now, together, we will find him." She stopped and looked at Carmen as if to ask a question but didn't.

"So you know about Tomas?" Carmen said, amazed that Tia seemed to already know so much without their having to tell her a thing.

Tia nodded.

"We are all so worried, Tia. How can you help us find him?"

Suddenly the old woman looked very tired. "I have already begun to work on it. But I'll need your help, also. Are you ready to take a journey that may be full of trials and great danger?"

"We both are," Carmen said without hesitation. "Can I ask you...that is, Septima says..." Carmen didn't know how to put the question, so finally she just blurted out, "Are you a *bruja*, Tia? Is that why Septima fears you?"

Tia smiled mysteriously, then snapped her fingers and opened one palm. "What do you see?"

"Nothing," Carmen said, shrugging.

"And yet, my hand is full of creatures—millions—microscopic, *mija*!" She made a motion, as if tossing them into the air. "You can't always trust your eyes. And Septima has many fears. Months ago, I had a dream and I thought it was tu mama who would return to me, but I see—it was you. We have a shared purpose now. There is much that I have to pass on to you, and you'll come to the answer yourself in time. Now, put out your hands, *mija*."

Carmen did so, and Tia took hold of all ten of her fingertips. Carmen felt as if she was back in second grade, with the teacher checking to make sure she had washed properly after recess.

"Your hands are much wiser than you can know, *mija*. You have the ring of Solomon," she said, turning them over. "See that line in your palm. It means you could have mystic abilities. Also I see *las cruzes mysticas*—a long and healthy life line—many life adventures. But there is one shadow—an enemy perhaps. But now we have important business to take care of. Tomas is in grave danger, and I want to help all I can. But lately I have been plagued with both a physical and spiritual—a sickness of sorts. Sometimes I am frozen in place and can barely move to do the simplest things. The other day I went to feed Itz and I could not gather enough strength to open the can. I am either sleeping all the time or sometimes at night not at all. Horrible itching—and terrible thoughts come into my head—not like me."

"What terrible thoughts?" Carmen asked, before she could wonder if it might be a rude question.

But Tia didn't answer. Instead, her head dipped forward, her face frozen, eyes half closed and glazed over. A deep, droning seeped out of her mouth like the sound smoke would make if it could be heard. Carmen snuck a look at Chia whose eyes had widened but more in amazement than fear. It must be a trance, thought Carmen. She had read about such things.

As they watched Tia, not sure what they should do, a tiny insect buzzed around her mouth, smaller than a fly, in the shape of a cockroach, but purpley-blue, with wings.

Suddenly Tia's head popped up, and the insect disappeared. "Something mal…" She frowned and pressed her hand to her temples. "*Que es? Que es?* I can't get ahold—Another—something bad is exerting undue influence over me—as soon as I begin to work on ridding myself of this—*espirito malo,* I feel weakened again."

Carmen started to say something, but her aunt's head lowered again slowly and she began the same droning chant as before.

"My uncle, the shaman, makes that same sound sometimes," Chia whispered.

In the middle of the droning, they heard a loud *boom* from outside, then a series of pops, like a car backfiring, but Tia did not raise her head. Carmen wondered if this time she really *had* gone to sleep.

The minutes ticked by as her aunt sat perfectly rigid, and then once again, her head jerked, and she said, rocking back and forth, "*Un otra bueno*—not here today perhaps, but within a certain range. This one—helpful *tal vez*—*Si, creo tan,* but not so easy to recognize—many distractions can block…"

"What do you mean, Tia?" Carmen asked, despite fearing she would break the spell.

Tia looked startled. "What—what did I say? *A veces*—I mean, sometimes, I don't know what I've said."

Carmen repeated her words and they waited while Tia worked her lips in thought. "There is an *espiritu mal*—bad spirit—behind my illness, chicas, behind Tomas' disappearance, and it will most likely try to interfere with both of you as well. It would be best if you could stay here, but I know that can't be. Carmen, we need to start preparing you for your new purpose. Are you ready to make a prenda—a pledge—that binds you— more than a promesa? In this prenda, you will be dedicating yourself toward a *vida nuevo servicio*. Your old life will be but a shadow of this new one."

"Yes, I'm ready," Carmen said quickly without thought.

But Tia shook her head. "You are young and impulsive, and I can see that you're anxious to follow. Go home and think about this and also look for a sign. It'll come to you if this *estilo de vida* is for you. " Tia turned to Chia. "And you also must think very hard about being involved in all this. Would your family approve? What would they do if they found out you were here with me?"

Chia sat up very straight. "There are shamans in my family, and I'm not afraid."

"Si, but maybe they wouldn't like my kind of...powers. I am called a *bruja* by some. But it's more complicated. In time, you'll know who I am."

Chia's face showed the barest whisper of a smile. "I make decisions here." She thumped her chest softly over her heart. "But I'll think about it, like you said."

Tia was smiling now also. "*Muy bueno—si, el corazon es muy importante—pero*, don't forget—" She placed her index fingers on her ears, her eyes, and then her forehead. "The heart can be tricked—*carteristas de la corazon*—they know it is the weakest part."

"What is a carterista, Tia?" Carmen asked.

Tia grinned. "Pickpocket, caro, pickpocket of the heart. You are both very trusting, which is good, but be careful. Trust with open ears."

"I just met Chia this week, Tia, but I already know I can trust her. And you, also. I know it. Here—" Carmen pointed to her heart. "—and here." She pointed to her head.

"No! Don't drink the rest of it." Tia almost grabbed the tea bowl from Chia's hand as she raised it to her lips. "Let me see what's in the bottom. Both of you, por favor."

They handed over their bowls with the dregs of their tea.

Tia peered down into them, one after the other, then raised her head and smiled widely. "Your journeys are blessed, whatever you decide. Both of you. Carmen, it was decided long ago that you would be here today. And Chia, you belong with us, too. You appeared in my dreams, but not in human form—a Siamese cat, with a pink streak down its side. It can only be you."

Both girls looked solemnly at each other.

"Now, don't try to give me an answer about the prenda. Just talk to me, and tell me things, whatever comes into your mind to tell. Your greatest weapons are these." Tia pointed to her ears. "Most people forget to use them and they over-use this—" She pointed to her mouth, made a snapping motion with her hand, then reached behind her, pulled out a long, pewter-colored bone pipe that she seemed to snatch from the air, and handed it to Carmen.

It was wound round with leather strips and blue black feathers that hung down from one end. As Carmen turned it over in her hands, she saw tiny bones also wrapped in leather with a small spray of dried herbs. Carmen rolled it between her fingers and noticed two very pronounced holes, a snout at one end, and then four paws carved into the thin body of the pipe. It took shape as a sleek, snake bodied jaguar.

"Now, the jaguar listens," Tia said.

Carmen began to speak then, but the words seemed to dance from her mouth on their own. "There have been many strange happenings this past week after Tomas was taken away. I've noticed strong smells, like burned chemicals, metal, or strong medicine, with a licorice smell mixed in. And every time,

I have sensed danger." Carmen told about the yard sale and the homeless woman who she now realized was Flora Linda, about the jaguar behind Motors Immaculada, about the bees in the church, the trip downtown to Homeland Security, the missing clock, Lupita, and tomato worm jelly beans, the snake, the real estate man. She also recounted some of her dreams."

Tia said nothing when she was done, just took the pipe and handed it to Chia.

"I have little to add to what Carmen has said. But my uncle is a shaman, and he has also been talking at home about a bad feeling he is getting that he can't place—headaches, tiredness, and other symptoms that don't add up. Then, also, my neighbor who owns a small grocery store is having the rent raised because some big investor is talking to the owner, an Asian man whom we thought would not betray us. Everyone is very upset. And now my youngest sister True is ill."

Tia raised her palm. "How so?"

"Oh, pain and shivering, like chills. Mother is consulting the shaman, but he is so busy right now, blessing the houses before Hmong New Year, that he hasn't gotten by yet to see her. But she isn't getting any better."

"Has she been behaving in any way that is…different?"

"Well, she has been sleepwalking. But Mother says it's not so strange since it runs in our family. It's just that True hasn't done it before now."

Tia looked agitated. "What about the other things, caro?"

Chia looked startled. "What other—oh, just that we are getting ready for Hmong New Year, and everyone is very busy, but Pa our godmother has not been able to finish preparations since some of the utensils she needs are missing. She thinks she has just misplaced them, but everyone is looking everywhere and Pa is very upset. She likes to use certain ones."

Tia reached to take the pipe. "I think we should stop now. I know that you girls skipped school today. You can't do that again, you know. I will have my driver take you home now. He can drop you off a block before your homes. But you must promise not to miss school again."

Both of the girls' jaws dropped together. "I'm glad you're on our side, Tia." Carmen grinned. "Chia's gonna write us a note and forge our mothers' signatures. But we won't skip school any more. When should we come again?"

"I have some things to do, and I can only work in spurts now. Maybe two days from now. Chia, you have much powerful magic about you and your people, and Carmen, so do you. It's not a coincidence that you two have been brought together and that we are all joining forces. My powers have been slipping for some time now, but your coming here gives me great hope. You know that when magic is put together, it's not just doubled. It's like—" She blinked and shook her head. "—hard to explain, but the power is even greater than just double. There is a word for it...synergy en *Ingles...que sabes*?"

Carmen and Chia shook their heads.

"It means...let's say that Carmen has lost her keys on a sandy beach. If she searches by herself, her chances are small of finding them. But if Chia joins in the search, the chances are not just doubled. They are multiplied many fold because you can brainstorm and, when that happens, your brains spark off of each other, creating *mucho mas* possibilities. And the same is true with magic."

At that moment, a squat, dark-complexioned man appeared in the doorway, as if in response to a magical summons. He wore a Mickey Mouse sweatshirt with a leather vest over it, and his face looked as if someone had taken a spatula and smashed all his features inward, like a flattened pancake.

Tia waved her palm from him to both girls. "This is Choppo."

"So, you gotta job for me?"

He spoke with a thick, Spanish accent and a bit of a lisp. As Tia gave him directions to both of their homes, Carmen and Chia could not hide their amazement.

Tia just smiled mysteriously as Choppo said, "Get used to it, chicas. Tia can tell you what you are thinking before you even think it."

"What will you tell Septima, Carmelita?"

"I already told her that I had joined the Little Sisters of Saint Agnes and that I would need to go to classes after school. Chia and I have been makin' our own plans."

"*Perfecto.* I don't want you to lie. Today you are joining a new club—Little Sisters of Magdalena—my own middle name. And I am your new spiritual maestra. We'll begin lessons day after tomorrow. I'll send Choppo to pick you up from school. What about Chia?"

"I'll come when I can. Can I bring True?"

"*Si. Por su puesto.* Under normal circumstances, I would try to heal her, but right now I couldn't cure a flea with the hiccups."

Tia turned away from them in dismissal. Carmen wanted to ask her aunt about *brujas*, but when she opened her mouth, different words came out. "I don't mean to question your judgment, Tia, but two days from now—what about Tomas?"

"I understand your concern. But you must trust me."

"What about the sign you spoke of? What if I don't recognize the sign when it comes?"

"There will be no doubt. The sign will be absolutely clear. The dream you had is very significant, Carmen. I'll explain about that later."

"Isn't there something we can do in the meantime?"

"Two things. Trust me and have patience." Tia closed her eyes and began to shiver for only a few seconds, but when she opened them, she was smiling. "I have had a vision of Tomas, and he's not been harmed—yet. In my vision he was asleep."

"Asleep? Could that be a symbol for...we learned in English that—"

"No. He's not dead. He was clearly asleep and he opened his eyes and sent me a message without words, but I can't tell you what it was."

Carmen looked as if she was going to jump out of her skin. "Wouldn't Tomas want me to know?"

"Not for him to say. What he told me will very soon be revealed to you, but when the time is right. For now, patience, Carmen—and trust. Also, here. Take this."

Tia pulled a card from out of her skirts and handed it to Carmen. It was printed with bright feathers in the shape of a heart, with a jaguar eye in the middle. In the dark pupil was another circle with a phone number on it. "Only use this for emergencies, *mija*."

Carmen took the card, then snuck a glance at her aunt. "I'm wondering about the jaguar and the bees. What are the animals trying to tell us?"

"Good question, *mija*. What I can tell you right now is that they are our friends and they stand by ready to help us. I think you'll see more of them both." At that moment Caw Caw swooped down with a flash of feathers and a whoosh of air, perched on Tia's shoulder, and began to dance and squawk madly. When it was done, Tia spoke rapidly in Spanish to Choppo. All that Carmen could catch were the words, "…different streets and home…"

Tia motioned to Carmen and Chia and waved them to the door. "Caw Caw will go with you. She wants Choppo to take a different route this time, and I've learned to heed her directions. We can receive much from the animals if we learn to pay attention."

CHAPTER 13

They were standing outside the botanica now, and there, parked by the curb was a foreign looking, distorted, beetle-shaped car painted bright mustard yellow, with TAXI on the side.

"What kind of car is this?" Carmen asked Choppo as he lifted the Mongoose into the trunk and fastened the hatch down with a bungee cord.

"Carmenghia," Choppo said, wiping his hands on his pants.

Carmen snuck a look at Chia as they climbed into the back seat. "Get this, ese. If we owned this car, it would be Carmen and Chia's Carmenghia."

Chia giggled. "And we could stop at the Taqueria in Carmen and Chia's Carmenghia."

Choppo turned and shot a look over his shoulder at them. Carmen saw then that Choppo had one blue eye and one dark brown eye and one gold front tooth. He reminded Carmen of a clumsy gangster in a B movie.

"Take it easy, *chicas*. And don't you get diarrhea in my Carmenghia."

This sent both girls into fits of giggles until Chia suddenly called out, "Look, Car, look!"

There walking down the street was the homeless woman, twirling a purple parasol, the yellow striped cat following as if on an invisible leash.

"That's the one from the yard sale—the one who led us to
Tia. That must be Flora Linda. Why does she have an umbrella?
It's not even raining."

"Wait, look closer, Carmen."

Following the old lady down the street was a funnel of lavender rain that seemed to fall only above her and her umbrella.

Choppo chuckled. "Get used to the magic, chicas. Tia must
have sent Flora Linda on an errand."

Caw Caw began to screech at them in what seemed to be
loud, hilarious bird laughter.

☙☙☙

After Carmen had been dropped off by Choppo a block
from her house, she hurried up the steps, rehearsing the story of
her first day at religion class. But as soon as she entered the
house and saw Septima's face, she knew there was trouble. Septima must have found out about cutting school.

Never good at hiding her anger, Septima seldom even tried.
Her face was like a cobra's ready to strike. "Don't even start
with the lies." Then she launched into Spanish.

Carmen watched as, amazingly, Septima's lips turned into
two pink worms, squirming in bizarre, almost obscene gymnas-
tics.

"*Este es la gota que desbordo el vaso. Usted es una
muchacha desgradecida, recororsa, horrible. Pensar—en mi
propia casa, en los alubios pinto—He estado mirando en todas
partes.*"

These Spanish-speaking worms were more comical than
scary. Carmen opened her mouth to speak, to buy time or to spin
the lie about religion class. Then a picture came into her head of
Tia making the yapping motion with her hand. And she said
nothing, just waited and watched Septima's silly putty lips.

"And I told your mama what you did, but I'm going to
handle this. Rosa isn't up to dealing with you right now. It had
to be you. I know it was, so don't try and deny it."

Carmen's mind raced. '*What you did...it had to be you.*'
That didn't sound like someone who had skipped school. Then it

struck her. One word she had extracted from Septima's Spanish tirade was "pintos." The silver rosary! Septima must have found it in the canister of pinto beans and figured out who put it there.

"What are you saying, exactly, Aunt?"

A look of impatience and disgust mingled in her face. "This morning I found my rosary in the canister of frijoles pintos on the counter. You must have done it. Don't lie to me, Carmen."

Carmen could hardly keep the relief out of her face. She hung her head in what she hoped was a properly remorseful pose. "Okay, I won't lie. I did put your rosary there. It was supposed to be a joke, but then I forgot about it. I'm sorry. What can I do to make it up to you?"

Septima looked surprised, almost deflated, as if she had been expecting an argument, and having not gotten one, didn't know what to say. "Well, all right then. You can clean out the RVs out back. Start with the trailer Rosa was in. I had to bring her inside. She isn't well."

"What's wrong?" Carmen fought to keep her voice steady and not betray the annoyance she felt over Septima's blustering over the rosary when her mother's health was more important.

"Oh, *nada*. Rosa is not strong like me. She can't handle things the way I can. And now she wants more medication. I don't think she needs any more. The bottle's empty. Maybe she should learn to do without it." Septima stopped for a minute then frowned. "Didn't you get her pills refilled the other day?"

Since Carmen had said she was getting them as a cover for leaving to go off with Chia, she couldn't tell Septima the truth. "They weren't ready. I'll see about her medication tomorrow. And I'll get started on the trailer as soon as I see about Mami."

Carmen hurried into the bedroom where her mother was lying on the bed with her face to the wall. She turned to face Carmen. "*Mija, mija*, can you get me some more pills? *Tengo que dormer*, but I can't seem to. *Necessito* sleep."

"I'll get them tomorrow, Mami. Let me rub your back for a little while."

Carmen sat on the bed beside her mother and rubbed circles on her back, over the thin, flannel of her nightgown. She sang a song in Spanish, a lullaby that Rosa had sung to her years ago. In a few minutes, Rosa was sleeping.

I'll just have to spend more time with her, Carmen thought, then she put her fingers to her lips when Septima appeared in the doorway, holding up a bucket, a sponge, and a pair of rubber gloves.

Carmen tiptoed out of the room, taking the cleaning supplies from Septima, and headed out to the RVs. Dusk came fast these days, and the sky was spreading pastel scarves of twilight over the horizon. Carmen plugged in the extension cord and turned on the little fringed lamp in the main sitting room area. The place really was a mess—magazines scattered about, a pile of walnut shells in one corner, balled up Kleenex, tumblers and plates on the counters, and various items of clothing piled on chairs and the built-in couch.

As Carmen began to straighten up, her thoughts drifted toward her mother, who hadn't been well in a long time. Maybe Tia could help heal Mami. Maybe Mami had lost her soul, and Chia's uncle could help also. Carmen felt a little dizzy and sat down on the small couch. She heard a rustling sound and lifted her eyes. Quarter sized splashes of purple light danced on the ceiling above, spinning like lights from a disco ball. More rustling sounds came from the back of the trailer, and the lights began to strobe down the ceiling of the hallway.

Carmen sat straight up and was sure she could see a flickering light like that from a candle at the back end of the trailer. She moved cautiously down the hallway. Recent events had zapped her nerve, especially the encounter with Lupita at Homeland Security. Chills ran down her spine at the memory, but it also reminded her that she didn't want to be like Mami, who was no help to Tomas at all. Almost against her will, she felt herself guided down the hall.

The door to the tiny back bedroom was ajar, with the same purple light spilling out. Carmen pushed on the door, which gave inward easily, then she sucked in her breath. The most beautiful creature she had ever seen filled the center of the room, a bird of sorts, or half-bird, half-flower. But instead of feathers, lush, purple, spaghetti-thick hair frothed over its body.

As Carmen uttered a cry of delight, it spread its tail like a peacock's, and she could see that each tail feather had a real eye surrounded in the same long, purple silks. The cup in the center of its body had a scalloped edge. From the center of the cup, now rose a spherical shape covered with the same long, silken purple hair, which parted right in the middle where one large eye opened, blinking slowly.

"Who—what are you?" Carmen managed to ask in a whisper.

The creature didn't speak, but stepped forward a few inches, and Carmen could see that it had two disc-like feet that its long, curved tubular legs balanced on. Slowly, ballet-like, it lowered itself down, its purple silks streaming around in a soft puddle. Then it tipped its head of purple streamers forward, and Carmen could see that there was a space in front of the tail feathers shaped like a seat. Without any words spoken, she knew that she was being asked to sit there.

Carmen remembered then that, at first, Lupita had seemed helpful and benign. Her heart seized with fear. All she could do was shake her head and back away, but the floor tilted, and as fast as she backed away, she slid forward. The whole trailer was bucking and jerking. Carmen couldn't find her balance. As quickly as she got to her feet, she slipped again and fell. Then she couldn't get her breath. Her chest felt like it had been zipped up tight.

The room went washy. Carmen realized she was crying, sobbing like a little baby, lying on the floor that had stopped jerking now that she no longer struggled. As the purple flower bird bent over her, a soft purring sound wafted from its center. Carmen remembered what she had said to Lupita.

It couldn't hurt, she thought and said aloud, "Meso, meso, meso."

The bird threw back its head, closed its one huge eye, and gave a trilling sound—what Carmen thought to be laughter.

Then Carmen clapped her hand over her mouth—the test, of course, the test. This must be it. She couldn't fail it, she thought, as she climbed over the flower-bird's head, holding onto the cupped edge, and slid down into a warm, soft, womb-like enclosure, much roomier than it appeared at first.

A sense of warmth and security engulfed Carmen. She knew she had entered a space like her first home where nothing could harm her, and she fell fast asleep. It seemed like hours later when she opened her eyes to the sense of speed, rocketing forward like a spaceship, or what she imagined it must be like. But Carmen was nestled down, surrounded only by purple soft-ness. She felt a bit sore and squirmed, trying to shift her posi-tion.

"Hold still, *perequita.*"

The words came from behind her, and Carmen tried to twist her head around, but could only get so far, when two hands held her head firmly in place.

"Don't try to look at me now, Carmelita. I'm right behind you. There's plenty of room inside Parajoflor, but it's better if you don't look behind you right now. We are on a journey to-gether, so don't be afraid. Just relax and go back to sleep, Car-melita."

"But, Tomas, where have you been? We've been so wor-ried. I—"

"Shush. Have patience. Very soon, I'll tell you everything." Tomas put his arms around her then.

Carmen sighed and gave into sleep once more.

CHAPTER 14

Carmen sat up in a field of gently waving purple plants like none she'd ever seen before. Tall as corn, they had elongated bell shapes all up and down the stalks, each bell open at the top with long silks spilling out like corn silks, only purple.

A faint breeze kept them moving and swirling against a pale lavender sky. Carmen breathed deeply, inhaling a peppery, sweet vanilla smell, and felt something nudging her. It was Parajoflor who began to glide away. But she stopped and turned back, winking her one huge eye. Then she shook her long purple tendrils in the direction of a huge rock at the end of the field. The rock was glowing a deep indigo.

Parajoflor bent down in front of Carmen and leaned her head forward, exposing the pocket where Carmen had ridden before. This time Carmen jumped in without hesitation. They began to fly over the fields in a fast, hovering/floating motion as if they were swimming and flying at the same time. In the blink of an eye, Parajoflor stopped before the indigo rock and curtsied, indicating that Carmen was to climb down.

Moving closer to the indigo rock, Carmen saw that it glowed with a transparent, almost electrical blue. She reached out to touch it, but Parajoflor snapped her tendrils in the air around Carmen's hand, surprisingly taut, like thin, rubbery ropes, pulling her hand away from the rock. Parajoflor shook her head.

Carmen had thought of Parajoflor as a she, although she didn't know why. "Where am I? How did I get here? Where did Tomas go?"

Carmen felt impatient now, but Parajoflor released her hand then began a strange, toe-heel dance before the rock. She tapped each disc-foot twice then bowed her head and seemed to vibrate all over, making the purring noise Carmen had heard before. She then scratched four Xs in the purple powdery dust that settled around the rock, waited, then performed the dance again.

After the fourth time, Parajoflor rotated her head slowly in a circle, stopping four times on the circle. She then faced Carmen. The top of her head began to sink inward, and a bump the size of a golf ball formed, issuing forth hundreds of purple bubbles. One landed on Carmen's arm and she found that it was surprisingly resilient.

Lifting it upward, she saw writing all over the bubble and read the words aloud as Parajoflor jumped up and down excitedly. "*CH'ULEL SAK-NIK-NAL.*"

As soon as the words were out of Carmen's mouth, Parajoflor lowered herself to the ground in a deep bow before Carmen, her tendrils splayed out around her like loosened tassels. Slowly, Parajoflor raised her head again, watching Carmen expectantly.

When she began to purr again, Carmen repeated the words, "CH'ULEL SAK-NIK-NAL."

This was repeated twice more before Parajoflor seemed satisfied, which Carmen determined from the soft churring sound she made, something between a hum and a purr. Then Parajoflor turned in a circle four times, ending with her back to the rock.

The rock seemed to catch fire right behind her then, giving off blue, red, and silver sparks. To Carmen's shock, Parajoflor leaned into the fire slowly, until she had fallen completely backward and disappeared into it.

Peering into the spot where Parajoflor had been, Carmen saw a long, very deep pit that narrowed into a tunnel. She stood dumbfounded, wondering what she was to do now. She couldn't lose Parajoflor who was her only connection back to Earth and Tomas, and, apparently, also her ride. But what was she to do? Some minutes passed. Carmen scanned the landscape around her that, until now, she had been distracted from.

A faint purple fog had begun to drift and settle around what looked like purple sand dunes to her right, other large rock forms, and small mountains. To her left, stretched fields and fields of the purple stalks she and Parajoflor had flown-swum through.

Something brushed her hand then. Carmen started to knock it away in alarm but stopped when she saw it was another purple bubble with writing on it. "Zap the fear. Capture courage. Fall backward. CH'UEL SAK-NIK-NAL."

Not knowing what else to do, Carmen repeated the words again four times, which seemed to be the magic number. As soon as the last "NAL" was out of her mouth, another indigo fire sprang up where the tunnel was. Carmen knew what she was supposed to do now, but an icy fear overtook her. It seemed like hours that she stared into the indigo fire, when a dark hand reached up out of the fire toward her. Carmen jumped back, but then the hand formed a fist with index finger pointing at her and Septima's voice echoed from below.

"Don't run with those scissors. Give that pocket knife back to your brother. Put your knees together. Don't swallow your gum. Don't pick that scab. Don't get so close to the fire…"

The voice went on and on with a litany of warnings that began to jumble together into nonsense syllables.

"Don't swizerlug tu globbyglub. Don't ficklenob tu zeegerbits. Don't mimsy el focklebubbs. Don't zag the pooterpoos."

Despite her fear, Carmen began to laugh. The bubble on her arm slid right up to her lips and she swallowed it. Then repeating the words, "CH'UEL SAK-NIK-NAL," four times aloud, Carmen turned her back to the fire and backed slowly into it. When she felt it licking the backs of her legs, she began to tremble. She wanted to jerk away, but instead she leaned slowly back as she had seen Parajoflor do and, taking a deep breath then letting it go shakily, she fell fully backward.

Now she was freefalling on her back, the fire just a warm breeze lapping her face. Gradually, the speed of her fall slackened, until she was just drifting slowly down like a feather. Along the way, she caught glimpses of passageways and niches where variations of the purple stalks seemed to be growing. As her descent continued to slow, shadowy forms began to take shape around her. Carmen could see that she was going to come to rest on a quite large plateau suspended in the middle of the tunnel like a floating island.

Landing with a soft plunk, Carmen looked down and saw that she stood on a clear, see-through platform which was actually the covering for a large aquarium about the size of the swimming pool at her school, filled with lavender water and beautiful, twisted coral-like forms made from the indigo rock. One end of the aquarium was a deep, black purple and glowed as it pulsed. Then suddenly, Carmen felt two hands wrapped around her eyes.

"Perequita," someone whispered.

"Tomas!"

Carmen wriggled free of the hands, and there stood her brother beside her, dressed in a long purple robe over strange, dark layers of transparent cloaks. He was holding a feathered jaguar mask, much like Tia's but even more elaborate.

"Welcome to Om, Carmelita. *Que piensa usted, sista pequena?*"

A million questions fought for possession of her mouth, but in the end, she only opened and closed it like an astounded fish.

Tomas warbled a quick tune then like a bird's, and Parajoflor swooped down from a shadowy perch not far above them. A silvery purple ladder dropped down behind her, and Parajoflor led the way as the three of them climbed upward to another plateau. It was furnished like a small living space, with soft, beanbag-like chairs and purple transparent cubes scattered around, displaying purple bowls filled with bubbles and other assorted oddly shaped items.

Parajoflor took up and passed over to Carmen a transparent bowl of what looked like glass straws. Carmen looked at Tomas who nodded at her then took one himself and stretched it out until it was as long as a short garden hose, which he attached to a hole in the floor. Both Carmen and Parajoflor did the same.

"Dig in sis, enjoy the nectar of Om," Tomas said, sipping from the snaky straw.

Carmen sucked on the straw and a milky, sweet flavor passed through her mouth, mixed with another flavor she could not compare to anything she knew. But as she sipped, she felt herself growing pleasantly calm and at peace.

"Om's finest Sak nic nal nectar. You like?"

Carmen gasped. "Those are the magic words I used to get here. Tomas, how did you...where are...Okay, what is this place, and how did you get here?"

Tomas sat down and leaned back, propping his feet up. But as far as Carmen could see, nothing was there. Tomas appeared to be reclining on air. "Go ahead, Car, make yourself comfortable on an air-chair. If you move around, you'll feel warm spots. When you find one, just sit, lie, whatever you feel like. The air chair will mold itself to your body. One size fits all, ya know."

He smiled as she hesitantly moved around to a space near his. She leaned backward but couldn't let go completely. "Am I gonna fall right on my butt? And give you a good laugh?"

He rose and came over to her, placing his arm behind her. "Now, lean back and sit. If you are going to fall, I'll catch you. Trust me."

"Hmmm...I seem to recall a certain toilet filled with frogs and when the lid was raised—"

"That was Trickster Tomas. Here on Om, I have important work. There's no time for my kid's jokes anymore. Here's the deal, Carmen. Om is a parallel universe to the Earth. I have been coming here since I was twelve when Portilla began my apprenticeship to be a *curendero*. I'm getting valuable training here on Om where an advanced consciousness is at work. I found Tia first, but then she came to the school, picked me up, and told me about my birth and that she had always known that I had the magic in me—kind of like a *brujo*, but not bad. She had seen signs when I was a baby. And remember when I had that bad fever right before I turned twelve? Well, I had some visions. Everybody said it was the fever making me hallucinate, but when Portilla asked me if I had ever had waking dreams, I told her about those visions. There were animals, jaguars, and lions and others who talked to me. One lion, as tall as a house, took me in its mouth, spun me around, and communicated with me that I would be protected...and other dreams too."

Carmen, without realizing it, had leaned back and was now reclining in her air-chair. "I've been to see Tia also, Tomas," she said excitedly. "I've also had dreams, Tomas, where a jaguar sort of takes over my body. But it's not scary. It's kind of nice." Tomas jerked his head and stared, but Carmen hurried on. "And Tia is going to help us get you back. Oh yea, Chia and I are working together. You remember her?" she asked, watching Tomas' face for a reaction.

Tomas' expression didn't change, but Carmen thought she detected a slightly rosier glow creeping into his cheeks. "That's cool. That's what a *brujo* does—hooks up with the living energy of the universe. I got so much to tell you, Car. But we don't have a lot of time. I have to go to work soon. I belong to a corps of—I guess you could say shamans and helpers—who are work-ing here on Om to fight negative forces that affect both worlds. There are other shamans from different cultures, and we are working together. So it's cool you're working with Chia, be-cause the time for thinking and acting like we're all separate is over. We've got to—"

Carmen broke in. "Chia's been very worried about you, like all of us." A slight smile shadowed Tomas' face, but Carmen rushed on. "Did you break out of prison to get here? Are you—"

"I'm still in prison on Earth, Carmelita. See? We've both had to travel outside our bodies to come here to Om. I can only leave Earth for fourteen hours at a time—Earth time, that is. Time is different here—compacted. So you've only been gone from Earth for a few seconds."

Carmen frowned. "If I'm in both places at once, where am I on Earth right now?"

"Wherever you were when you left the Earth, but you prob-ably appear to be asleep or just resting."

"So if you're a *brujo*, why can't you use your powers to get out of the jail? And where is it anyway? Chia and I tried but couldn't find out where they took you. We went to Homeland Security and you weren't even in the computer."

"Truth is, Car, they had me blindfolded so I don't know where they took me, but it's about an hour away and it was mostly on the freeway and then they turned off onto some gravel. They have me locked in a room and guarded day and night. I don't hear any outside noises, only the ones they manufacture. And they give me some kind of drug that makes me sleepy all the time. The loud noises they pipe in interfere with my powers. Remember that car horn that went off when the ICE came and got me. That's how they were able to capture me—interference."

"Then how were you able to get here to Om?"

Like a dog shaking off water, Tomas shook his head, as if to clear it. "There's several ways to get to Om. Arrangements are made by someone on Om to send Parajaflor, in which case she finds an open portal and transports you. The other involves special powers that only those trained as *brujos* or shamans have access to. And there is at least one other way, but I can't tell you about that now. I can't use my powers on Earth right now because I am weakened there by the noises, the drugs, and by the black magic that someone is blocking me with. It's kinda like a battery charge. I have enough to get to Om, but not enough to break out of where I'm being held. But if it goes on much longer, I won't be able to make it to Om anymore. This is also affecting Tia right now. She's been getting weaker for some time now."

"So what do they want, Tomas? These bad people."

"We're still figuring it out. I'll fill you in as soon as we know more for sure."

Carmen sighed. It was almost too much to take in all at once. Finally, she said, "How can we find you, then?"

Tomas winked and fished around in his robes, pulling out a small, purple velvet bag. He pulled on the ends of a satin cord and out spilled what looked like a tooth, a molar, only made of a milky lavender stone about the size of a cherry tomato. "It's quartz, Carmen, and it has very special magical qualities, kind of like a small computer, only better. It's made of special piezoelectric quartz that stores and transmits information by radio like waves through the nervous system to the brain. The information can be stored for centuries then tapped into through subconscious means."

Carmen had taken the velvet nestled tooth and was staring at it as if it might reach up and bite her. "But what do I do with it?"

"First of all, never let it out of your sight. We're going to have you fitted for a BSC before you leave Om. We're not sure how, but this tooth is connected to an artifact that we need to help us counteract the black magic. We're not sure how it fits or where it is right now. Tia has some information that she'll share with you in time."

Carmen's eyes popped. "A BSC? That sounds scary. I keep thinking this is a dream, and I'll wake up laughing at all the crazy stuff."

"Not a dream, Carmen. Some serious stuff's going down and I need your help. A BSC is a body security storage cavity. We'll add another layer to the bottom of your foot that looks like skin where a coin/key can be stored. Don't worry, it won't hurt at all. We have new surgical laser techniques here on Om, and the coin/key will activate the tooth, which you must keep on your body at all times. We'll fit you up with a small, extremely strong magnet inserted under your scalp, and then the tooth will clamp to your skull magnetically. When you receive my signal, you touch a special mark, we'll tattoo on your foot, flip open the flap, remove the activation key, and you can use the tooth to communicate with me. It does other things, but you'll have to be trained. For now, we just need to be able to communicate."

"Why not just give me a cell phone, bro?"

"Cell phones can be blocked too easily by the bad spirit forces. And like I said, the BSC does other stuff too that you'll be trained to use."

"Okay, I'm trying to compute all this. What or who are these bad spirits?"

Tomas sighed. "That's not easy to answer. Tia says you've already encountered some of them—we think Silver's realtors work with the ICE who deport people to Mexico and then take their stuff. But there could be more involved. There is a bad spirit here on Om, too."

"Yea, they've been after Septima, and I've had some run-ins with them, too."

Tomas was grinning and rubbing his chin, something he did when he was either pleased, puzzled, or uncomfortable.

Carmen started to wonder if this was a huge joke, but then two women appeared, dressed in purple robes, holding out a pale lavender robe to her. They had risen up through the mist of the tunnel from somewhere below.

Carmen shrank away from them and turned back to Tomas. "Are you really my brother? How do I know you aren't some psycho clone who is going to cut out half of my brain and turn me into his personal rutabaga robot?"

"Okay. Ask me something only Tomas would know."

Carmen put her finger to her lips and thought what to ask, but nothing came to her. Then suddenly she remembered. "When you were just a kid, you found something you used to make your own game that you would play for hours. What was it you found and what was the name of the game?"

Tomas' grin stretched across his whole face. "Pitz! *Es claro*, Carmelita. I found some old chipped dice, and I rolled the dice, kept score on paper bags, and had dark and light pebble teams. It was real complicated, and I was the only one who knew the rules. I could play with up to four people or just myself—usually it was just me playing against another ghost team."

"Yea." Carmen also grinned at the memory. "I remember sometimes I woke up to the sound of those dice smacking against the wall. One time you let me play, but I was too little and I couldn't remember the rules. And you told me I was disqualified and I cried. Where did you get the name Pitz?"

Tomas shrugged. "*No se*. I just made it up. Used to see the owner's kids playing Sorry and Monopoly, and I wanted to play, too, but they wouldn't let us, and course, we never had money to buy any games. But, I can tell you this, Car, lots of things here on Om are modeled after ancient Mayan culture. And I've learned there was a sacred ballgame named Pitz the Mayans used to play that was kind of like the cosmic battle of the forces of good and evil. It involved human sacrifice, but we don't go for that on Om, which is dedicated to a new consciousness of peace. When there's more time, I'll explain more stuff to you, but right now, it's important that you get fitted up with your BSC devices, so we can communicate after you leave here. I'll explain more after the operation."

Carmen felt her heart leap at the word "operation," but Tomas hopped up from his air chair and stood before her. "Here, let me show you my BSC." Kneeling down, he turned over one foot and tapped a mark on his heel just larger than a freckle. It looked as if the bottom layer of his foot sprang open, and there Carmen could see what looked like a coin just smaller than a dime with a hole in the center. He handed Carmen the coin/key device and told her to rub the top of it against the tooth.

Immediately Carmen felt her scalp begin to tingle. "Hey, my head's tingling. Is that like a signal to me or something?"

Tomas just looked at her but said nothing.

Then a most unusual thing happened. Carmen knew that Tomas was answering her but without any words being used, like she could read his mind, which was telling her to ask the tooth her questions.

'Is this operation safe?' she asked silently. 'Is it permanent? Can I tell Chia about it when I get back?'

'Yes, it's completely safe. It's permanent unless you don't want it anymore. Yes, you can tell Chia. She's part of the team now, and I know we can trust her. We are sure. Our people are working with her people here on Om. She was chosen to work with us.'

Carmen smiled, amazed that they could communicate without words. She then decided to try asking Tomas a different kind of question—involving Chia.

Tomas broke out in a mischievous grin. 'That's personal and I'm not answering. You'll just have to figure it out for yourself. This telepathy can be sidetracked when you want to, little sister.'

A strange thing happened next. Tomas began to fade right before Carmen's eyes. His image broke up into tiny particles like sand slipping out of an hour glass and disappearing.

"Tomas," Carmen called out, her voice shaking with fear.

Little by little, Tomas' body reassembled before her. "I have to go, Carmen. I can't maintain the energy to keep myself here any longer. But you're in good hands." Then he was gone.

The two ladies stepped forward with the lavender robe. Carmen slipped both of her arms in and went with them willingly, both excited and happy and not at all scared, which surprised her. She was asked to lie on a table that looked like a big block of transparent Lucite, about the size of a twin bed only taller, with each lady standing on either side of her. One of them, who looked distinctly Asian, touched a spot on the cube. Carmen felt herself lowered down into what seemed like purple Jell-O.

"Don't worry, all you need to do is relax. You're now floating in Ch' ulel, life essence that continually renews the body and the soul. We can program this cube, called our di-pro-homeostasilator to diagnose, treat, or, in your case, plant maintenance elements. If the body can be kept in the proper balance—most diseases and maladies can be avoided."

Carmen wasn't sure where the words were coming from since the lavender-robed ladies never moved their lips.

"I think I'm supposed to get an implant in my foot and a magnet attached to the scalp to keep the crystal tooth safe." She felt the words going all slushy in her mouth as she slid down a soft hillside of warmth and peace. The last thing she saw was a very bright light lowering over her head.

CHAPTER 15

The pounding noise seemed to come from far away, as Carmen sat up and looked around bewilderedly. Had she had a dream? If Om had really happened, how had she gotten back to Earth? She didn't remember talking to Tomas again or getting back on Parajoflor or any journey back. But here she was sitting on the scratchy carpet of the back bedroom of the trailer with no sign of Parajoflor or the revolving lights, only the smell of Pine Sol and burned wax.

Gradually, it dawned on Carmen that the pounding was someone at the door. She leaped up, stumbled briefly with dizziness, and ran to the door where Septima's angry, red face filled the little, tinny window.

"Carmen, why is this door locked? And why haven't you answered me? I've been banging here forever!"

The gray, dusky sky was melting into darker shades of purpley charcoal. It looked to be about seven o'clock. Carmen wondered if several days had passed, but surely Septima would have come looking for her before now, if that were the case. Then she remembered that time on Om didn't match Earth time. She must have been gone from Earth for about five minutes, and now she had to answer Septima's wild cat eyes and snarley questions.

"I...uh...don't know why—how that door got locked. I think I fell asleep. I'm sorry, Aunt Septima. I'll make it up to you, I promise. I couldn't sleep last night because I've been so worried about Tomas, so I'm tired, really..."

But strangely distracted, Septima didn't seem that interested in her answers, busily scratching her head, her stomach, and a red spot on her arm. "Look, forget the trailer for now. I need you to go to Walgreens and get me some lotion for this itching." Septima raised her sweater, revealing little camps of recently clawed red welts on her stomach. She shoved a ten dollar bill at Carmen. "And bring back the change. It shouldn't be more than about four or five dollars. Teo can't go because he's got work to do."

Carmen took the money, started to ask more questions, then remembered Tia's advice, and clamped her mouth shut.

Inside, the house was colder than usual, and Carmen shivered. Teofilo did not look up from the dining room table where he poured over papers. Something was up. Carmen could feel it.

"Did we hear from Gabino yet?" Septima's voice was raspy and wheezing, her eyes ringed with dark circles as she flopped exhaustedly into an arm chair beside another pile of papers that she shuffled through.

Teofilo didn't even look up to answer her. "No. No one has called."

"I'll get my coat," Carmen said, making her way into her bedroom.

"Carmentita." Rosa was sitting on the edge of the bed with her Bible open and her lips moving. "Bless me, anoche when I said the rosary for Tomas, tenido mucho dolor, pero—" She paused as if listening. "*Entonces*, I hear someone singing. *Si*, I did," she added as if to ward off Carmen's doubt. Her large, brown eyes widened like sunflowers. "*Muy bello*...like angel's songs wing from heaven. *Entonces*, I kind of fall asleep, but only little, and I could see beautiful sunset through el window— sky like una flor magnifico blooming purple light eternamente. *Un signo, mija*...a sign, I know it."

Rosa's cheeks burned with two bright pink spots.

"Si, Mama, *es bueno*. I've had a...um, a dream about Tomas, and I think he's all right. And I think he'll be coming back to us very soon. But right now, I have to go to the pharmecia for

Septima. How have you been sleeping, Mami? It's better for you if you don't keep taking those pills so much. I don't think I'll get you anymore? Okay?"

Rosa was nodding her head in agreement. "*Si, mija. No los necesito mas.* Get me my knitting, *mija.* I want to work on that gora *para* Tomas. I make him a cap of purple, just like the sunset I see today."

Carmen's heart soared as she started down the walkway to the drug store. There was every reason now to feel hopeful, and Mami looked better than she had in a long time. Could her dream/vision be just a coincidence? Then Carmen remembered Om and the BSC chip. She had to know for sure, she thought, ducking back into Teofilo's workshop and flipping on the light. First, she slipped off her high top, then her sock, then examined her foot in the dirty yellow light. There was a tiny mark like a baby asterisk and she touched it lightly. Nothing. She touched again, this time pressing harder, and a flap the thickness of cardboard lifted up. There, lodged in its own slim compartment like a shallow cocoon, she found the key/coin and closed it inside her sweaty palm while her fingers worked circles through her scalp. She found the spot where the crystal tooth was attached and carefully removed it. Placing the coin next to the tooth, she rubbed gently. Nothing. She rubbed again and again, but still nothing happened. Her stomach sank. Maybe she had left out a step. She tried to remember Tomas' instructions, but she had followed them exactly, she thought. Then she heard a faint rustle behind her and whirled around to Teofilo's fishy stare.

"What you doing in here, Carmen? Septima's waiting for her medicine. She's in no mood to be kept waiting. *Ella hara volar su cumbre.*"

Carmen stifled a grin after a vision came to her of the top of Septima's head flying off. "She'll blow her top" was Teo's favorite expression to describe Septima's anger.

Carmen had tucked the coin and tooth quickly behind her back. "Okay. Okay. I was just trying to get a pebble out of my shoe. I'll get going."

As Carmen left, she looked back once to see Teofilo staring at her suspiciously. It was now almost completely dark as she started back down the sidewalk. This time, though, her eyes locked onto something white sticking out from under a cracked flowerpot beside the walkway. She stopped and quickly slid the key back into the BSC and the tooth back to its spot on her scalp. Then she reached down, picked up a white card, and read, *SILVER/BRIGGS DIVERSIFIED DEVELOPMENT GROUP – Residential, Commercial Realty Services. We buy properties in any condition. Also estate acquisitions and appraisals. Speed- Service- Experience.* Then in smaller letters below that: *Free prequalification, Back child support OK, Liens & Foreclosures OK, Bad credit OK.* Then only a phone number was listed, with no address.

As she tucked the card into her pocket, she noticed a cigarette butt tossed not far from where the card had been. Reaching into her pocket, she pulled out one of the butts she had found behind the house when she'd faced the jaguar and, sure enough, it was the same brand, Camel. Carmen held the card and the cigarettes in her hand, pondering, as she made her way to the drug store.

Septima had complained about the realtor who had been smoking the other day. If it was Mr. Briggs with the jaguar that night, why would he have been hiding behind the house? What had he wanted? Could this have something to do with what she had overhead on Friday at the store when the tall, silver-haired man had threatened her? She reached behind her head and felt the place where the tooth nestled. What had gone wrong with the BSC?

Carmen decided she needed to talk to Tia right away. Tia would know how all these events were connected. She couldn't wait until Wednesday, she thought as she turned into the parking lot at Walgreens.

When Carmen got home, Septima grabbed the lotion and her change and said not to disturb Rosa who had turned in early. Carmen could sleep on the couch in Septima's sewing room, she said, swishing her feet in a pan of Epsom salts, uncapping the cream the pharmacist had recommended. The sound of angry hammering echoed from Teofilo's workshop.

Carmen realized she was starving and asked Septima if there was anything to eat.

"*Ai ai ai, no se*," Septima said wearily. Then, "*Vamos.* See what you can find. This is not a restaurant, you know."

Carmen hurried into the kitchen before Septima could sink any deeper into a tirade.

She rooted in the fridge, found half of a tamale and a couple slices of leathery baloney, and poured out a glass of milk. At the kitchen sink, she felt a sudden twinge of sympathy for Septima, who was rubbing lotion on her belly, with her feet soaking in the dishpan, her varicose veins on display from under rolled-up pant legs.

Carmen carried the baloney and milk to the doorway of the living room where food wasn't allowed. "Mami looks good today. I didn't even get her pills cuz she said she didn't want them. She had an awesome dream about Tomas and I think—"

"Si, she told me. Look, Carmen." Septima's face hardened and then drooped almost sadly. "I'm glad she's so hopeful, but I been talking to people and—" She paused, clawed at her neck, then continued. "Things don't look so good. Oso's brother, Rudy, the one who has that taco truck, he was grabbed yesterday on his way home, and the family is going crazy. He has that heart condition, and they don't think he had his pills with him when the ICE got him, and you know they don't care. I talked to Gabino Garza who did all that legal work for the church and he said he'd look into Tomas' situation. But he hasn't called back. I called the office today, and they gave me the run around."

Carmen's mind whirled. "What happened to Rudy's taco truck?"

"Tsch!" Septima made a disgusted sound. "Confiscacion!" she said, her nostrils flaring. "They love to sack the *gente pobre* that got a little something to plunder. I hear their houses are full of Mexican *artefactos*. People are saying that Rudy had some old stuff from Mexico he went around bragging about. Here, rub some of this *crema* on my neck."

Carmen saw more red welts on the back of Septima's neck, streaked even redder from where she had scratched. "This looks bad, Tia Septima, maybe you should go to the doctor," she said, rubbing in the cream.

"*Si,* when there's time, I will. There's too much to do right now. This cream should help."

Carmen wanted to ask questions about Mr. Briggs, the realtor, but she knew that Septima was of the adults-only school when it came to sharing information with children and she still saw Carmen as a child. So instead, she said, "Can I call Chia? I need to ask her about something for school."

Septima sighed. "*Si, si, si,*" she said irritably, "Just don't stay on too long. Gabino might be trying to call."

Carmen went into the sewing room where Teofilo had his desk and the extension phone. Glad that she had memorized Chia's phone number, she dialed it now. After a few rings, a boy's voice answered and Carmen asked to speak to Chia.

"Who's this?" the boy said.

"A friend from school," Carmen answered and then waited nervously on the line, hearing the boy calling Chia in the background.

When Chia finally picked up, Carmen tried to keep her voice low. "Chia, it's me, Carmen. I can't talk long cuz Septima's waiting for a phone call, but we gotta meet and talk somehow. A buncha stuff has happened."

Chia was silent for a few moments, then she said, "I don't know, Carmen. I'd have to sneak out and if I get caught, then they'll really be watching me. And you'd have to sneak out, too. I think it's too risky. Can you tell me real quick?"

"Okay. Uh…" Carmen didn't know where to start. As briefly as she could, she told Chia about going to Om, seeing Tomas, the crystal tooth, and the operation.

"Wow! That's awesome, Carmen." Chia gave a low whistle. "You went to Om."

Carmen was relieved. She had worried that Chia either wouldn't believe her or would say it was just a dream or something. "Thanks for not telling me I'm full of guano, Chia. Even I wondered at first if it wasn't a dream, but I've got the tooth to prove it."

"Well, we Hmongs already believe in spirits and stuff, so it don't sound that crazy to me. But this is bad timing," Chia said. "Everything's all about Hmong New Year here. And we'll have relatives coming to town soon."

Carmen told her about finding the realtor's card and the cigarette butts. "Look, I think either Mr. Silver or Mr. Briggs is mixed up in all this somehow, or maybe both. We need to talk to Tia right away. Tomas said he's being kept about an hour away. We gotta move faster, Chia. Can you at least go to Tia's tomorrow after school? I'm going to call her next and see if she'll send Choppo for us."

Chia was silent, then she yelled something in Hmong to someone in the background. "Okay, Carmen. I gotta go. I'll have to bring True, but hey, if you went to Om and fell into a fire pit and got a tooth planted in your skull, I can figure out a way."

They said goodbye just as Septima yelled from the living room, "Carmen, get off that phone! I told you to make it *rapido*."

Carmen hung up the phone and wondered how she was going to call Tia. She pulled Tia's card out of her jacket pocket and held it in her palm, frowning. From the living room, she could hear the choppy murmur of Septima's and Teofilo's voices, Septima's occasionally rising in angry Spanish. As Carmen strained to catch and understand what they were saying, she became aware of a tapping noise just beyond the desk. It was coming from the window. She moved closer then and heard her name half whispered and half growled.

Carmen lifted the shade, but all she could see was the black night snug against the window, then, "It's me, Choppo. Open the window."

Carmen climbed on the desk, unlocked the window, and pushed upward. It took half a dozen tries before the window finally scraped open. Choppo stood between the shrubs in the dry leaves and accumulated debris no one had bothered to rake.

"Tia sent me," he hissed. His gold teeth glinted in the stray light from the street. "She needs to see you pronto. I'll come for you tomorrow right after school, okay?"

"Awesome!" Carmen hissed back. "This is so...so crazy. I was just now trying to figure out how to call Tia, since Septima said I had to get off the phone."

Choppo grinned. "I told you she's got the *sentido sexto*...sixth sense. And she said for you to also bring the letters to Septima that you found." They both jerked, hearing a noise behind Carmen.

Choppo jumped away from the window. "*Adios, le ver manana.*"

But the noise had only been Teofilo slamming the bedroom door. Carmen tugged the window shut and slid off the desk. As she did so, a pile of papers scattered to the floor. As she scooped them together, the letters SBDD jumped out at her from one of them. It was a letter from Silver/Briggs Diversified Development, she saw, and it was directed at Teofilo but all in Spanish. Carmen struggled to translate it, but could only pick out a few words here and there—something about Immaculate Motors and something to do with "*estimacion.*" Estimation? *Isn't that like an appraisal*, she wondered? Carefully, she folded the letter and buried it in her backpack to show Tia the next day, just as Septima's voice hollered out from the living room.

"Get to bed, Carmen. Put out that light, *ahora mismo!*"

Carmen had heard it often enough to know that "Right now" was not to be argued with.

She decided that the next day she'd wear the same clothes she had worn that day. Maybe just change her top in the morning. But it was so cold in the house now that she slipped off her Converse high tops, leaving her socks on and looked around for something else to wrap up in. Teofilo's big flannel shirt was draped over the chair, and shrugging, she slipped it on over her T-shirt. It smelled of gasoline and beer, but it was better than nothing, she thought, hugging herself for warmth.

She barely had time to ask herself if the house was so cold because money was tight, before the heavy log of sleep rolled over her and smothered her thoughts.

CHAPTER 16

Carmen woke Tuesday morning from a tumultuous dream where she had lost her house key and went from thrift store to thrift store, searching for it through bins of stuffed animals and shelves of dishes that slid back and forth. Furious clerks kept yelling at her and one, who blew smoke directly in Carmen's face, even accused her of shop-lifting and threatened to call the cops. Carmen sat outside the thrift store on the street and sobbed, terrified of what Mami would say. She decided to go home and tell Mami herself, then took off, wandering in a dark, scary part of town. A talking chicken told her to follow and it would lead her to safety. But it kept darting down dangerous alleyways and filthy, narrow, twisting streets with Carmen barely able to follow.

When she rubbed the sleep from her eyes and checked the clock, Carmen saw that she only had a few minutes to get ready for school. A note in the kitchen from Septima said she had taken Mami to early Mass. There was no sign of Teofilo.

Carmen stuffed the letters into her backpack, grabbed a clean T-shirt and a cold tamale from the fridge, unwrapped it, and charged off for school. She had planned to walk to school with Chia, but as it was, she was ten minutes late for her first class and spent the morning barely able to keep her mind on her lessons, anxiously awaiting lunch when she could talk to Chia.

Outside the cafeteria, Carmen waited in a frail patch of winter sunlight, her stomach growling. There wasn't much to eat at home these days, and Carmen had not had time to pack a lunch, nor had there been any lunch money left for her.

"Why so frowny?" Chia asked, rounding the corner. "Let's go over by the trees. Hey, where's your lunch?"

Carmen's hunger overtook her pride as she sighed heavily. "We don't have much food at home anymore. I think Septima's got big money problems. And I found a letter from those real estate sharks on Teofilo's desk last night. We can take it to Tia's cuz it's in Spanish, which I can't read that well. But it looks like it's about appraising the value of the property. I think Teo wants to sell off and go to Mexico."

Chia just raised her eyebrows. "Here, have some of my lunch. My mom always packs way more than I can eat. It's just sticky rice and spring rolls, but there's plenty," she said, scooping the food out of tin foil packets she pulled from a paper bag.

"Thanks." Carmen found herself devouring the food, thinking that nothing had tasted so good to her ever before. "This is good stuff, and there's some heat in that rice, chica!"

Chia laughed. "Yea, both our people like their chilies, don't they?"

Carmen told more of the story about Om then, and Chia just kept shaking her head in amazement until the part about Tomas saying that Chia had been chosen to work with them.

A silly, bright red grin crept over Chia's face.

"Hey, chica, speaking of hot stuff, what about you and Tomas, eh?"

The blush on Chia's face deepened. "Oh come on. Can't we be friends without..."

Their school lunch hour was short, since they ate in three shifts, and the bell rang before either of them could say more. "We're meeting Choppo by the front gate. Don't be late."

"It's a date, sistah. I can't wait!" Chia shouted back over her shoulder as she headed off to class.

After school, Carmen sailed down the halls through the throng of escaping students. But as she turned the corner at the end of a now deserted hallway, she ran smack into the path of

Muneca and the Moreno sisters. They all grinned wickedly, and Muneca said, "What's your rush, Moon Pie face? Did you lose your little chi chia pet?"

All three girls linked arms, mad dogging around Carmen. Lil' Hueso Moreno gave Carmen's shoulder a fast shove. Lil' Sucio Moreno spit lugies in both her palms and rubbed them into Carmen's hair.

"We just want to be your best amigas, Moon Pie," Muneca said with a dirty grin, while Hueso stepped behind Carmen and yanked her arms behind her back roughly.

Soucio took hold of Carmen's backpack and as Carmen watched in horror, unzipped it and began pulling out the contents.

"*Mira, cartas viejas,*" she said, pulling out the bundle of letters.

Before Carmen could stop herself, she yelled, "No! Leave those alone!"

"Ooooh, love letters, maybe. From *su novio de anciano*— the old man you hook up with in the cemetery." Muneca was making smooching noises. "Here, make these smaller. *Sabes?*" Muneca handed the letters to Hueso who began slowly to tear them into strips.

"No!" Carmen screamed again, trying wildly to wriggle free.

Wishing that Tomas had given her something for protection, Carmen then felt her legs turning to the same old mush as she closed her eyes and waited for the blows she expected to follow.

The first one came in the stomach and Carmen doubled over, almost losing her breath. She waited then, her heart pounding, but instead, a loud clanging rang down the hall not far from where they stood. Carmen opened her eyes just as Hueso gasped and dropped her arms. All three girls took off. Carmen jumped up when she saw Chia motioning to her, towing True behind.

"Look what they did to my letters," Carmen spluttered through her tears, as she and Chia scrambled to gather the scraps Hueso had torn and stuff them all back into her backpack.

"Are you okay?" Chia asked.

"Wow, talk about saved by the bell," Carmen panted, behind Chia and True as all three raced for the front of the school, hoping to see Choppo's cab waiting for them.

Chia swished a knowing look over her shoulder, as they ran.

"Oh wait, don't tell me. That was you? Did you set off that alarm?"

"Did you see Muneca?" Chia yelled back. "Jumped like a jack rabbit."

Carmen laughed, gasping. "Scared the chonies off her."

Out of breath, they stopped briefly at the gate. There was no sign of Muneca and her gang. Chia had scooped True into her arms and run with her. Now she could hardly catch her breath.

Carmen couldn't stop grinning. "Just a good thing you didn't get caught, Chia. They expel you for setting off the fire alarms, you know."

"Nobody saw me. The kids were all watching for you to get your butt beat by Muneca. I don't know where all the teachers went."

They heard a honking Choppo edging his way through the snarl of waiting cars in front of the school. Both girls jumped into the taxi eagerly, Chia pushing True in before herself.

"It's lucky True has morning session," Chia said as she buckled her into the back seat. Carmen sat up front with Choppo and just caught a glimpse of Muneca and the Moreno sisters, staring at them open mouthed just beyond the gate, as the taxi sped away.

"Muneca wrote a bad check-a so they put her in the pokey in Zapateca," Carmen sang out the window.

Chia giggled. "Hueso, Hueso, dirty face-o, hurled her cookies all over the place-o, dropped her chonies, and lost the race-o."

They fell into spasms of laughter. Even True wrinkled up her doll's face with laughing.

At Tia's, Choppo pulled into the alleyway and let them out. "Stand by that door there," he said, pointing to a wrought iron security door just inside the chain link fence.

"How do we get in there?" Carmen asked.

The fence was at least six feet tall, with no gate. But Choppo was already gone. He hadn't talked much and seemed to be in a huge hurry. Also, Carmen thought she had smelled beer. They stood behind the fence staring at each other.

Finally, Carmen said, "What do we do now?"

Chia looked baffled. "Wait, maybe?"

After standing in silence for a few minutes, Carmen said, "What excuse did you give your parents?"

"I said that I was going to take True to my cousin's house after school, and I called my cousin and told her to cover for me. I've covered for her when she's gone out with her boyfriend, so she owed me."

True's little nose was a red, plump cherry and she had begun to shake quietly from the cold. "I don't get this. Where's Tia?" Carmen asked the chain link fence.

"I guess we could go around to the front," said Chia. "But what's up with Choppo dumping us out here?"

"I thought I smelled beer on him. And he had jawbreaker eyes—that's what Tomas used to call Teofilo's when he drank too much," Carmen said, dancing from one foot to the other to keep warm.

True gave a delighted squeal as a dainty, iridescent dragonfly, which had been perched on the fence at eye level, landed softly on her uplifted hand.

"Wow, it's not even the season for them," said Chia.

No one spoke as they were caught in the shimmer of the dragonfly's spell. But finally, it darted from True's hand back to a different spot on the fence. True raced there, with the girls following. Right below it, they saw a ragged hole.

"Here." Chia pulled on one side of the wires. "Help me pull."

Carmen pulled on the other and the fence came slowly apart to reveal a hole about the size of a large watermelon.

"I think we can fit True through," Chia said as they both hoisted her into the hole, careful not to scrape her on the jagged sides. And then True was staring at them, big-eyed, from the other side of the fence.

"You're a brave girl," Carmen said, but the words were no sooner out than a caramel colored dog slunk out from behind a pile of boxes and bared its sullen teeth, a growl boiling low in its throat, as it locked True in its cold, pink-rimmed stare.

True didn't even whimper, mesmerized by the dog's greedy teeth. Even though they weren't touching, Carmen could feel Chia trembling.

"Don't move, True. Don't move," Chia whispered, as still as a rock herself.

As time jerked to a terrified halt, they all froze in their own boots, the dog growling low and menacingly.

Carmen's stomach lurched. She remembered once in the fields when she had disobeyed and wandered away from Mami down a row of newly erupted cotton bolls, then turned down another row where a pack of wild dogs waited at the end to "tear her into bite-sized pieces," as she'd been warned. She'd gone stone still and closed her eyes, waiting to be shredded, but when she'd opened them, peaches flew through the air instead, and the dogs turned tail and ran. Mami's face had drained white as a cotton boll, but when she saw that Carmen was safe, she threw the last peach at her before dissolving into tears. It made a good story later—how Mami had ruined the peaches she'd been given by the boss man that day.

And for weeks Tomas had teased Carmen. "Hey, Gaines-burger, why'd you make Mami waste all those peaches?"

Now Caw Caw was flying circles above them. She landed directly on True's shiny, little black head. The dog sucked its teeth back in, seemed to almost shrug, and ambled back behind the boxes where it lay down in a warm puddle of sunlight.

Before they could even blink, there stood Tia, lifting True up into her arms. "Carmentita, take off your shoes, throw them to me, and put on these shoes." Tia threw a pair of old, fraying sneakers over the fence. "Hurry. No time to waste. What's wrong with that Choppo tonto, anyway?" she muttered as Carmen obeyed, slipping off her own high tops.

"Okay. Now jump."

"Jump? What do you mean jump?" Carmen gave Tia her la coo, coo loca look. "How can I?"

"Over the fence, *mija*. Trust me, okay. Mira…Look, I've had a dream where I talked to Tomas. Andele. We've got a lot to do."

So Carmen backed up, took a short, running start, and bounced as hard as she could, expecting to land with a jar right where she was, but instead, she went flying right over the fence and would have landed on her butt, if Tia hadn't put True down quickly and reached out to break her fall, almost knocking them both over.

"Wow, that was fun!" Carmen squealed.

"Throw them to Chia now. But don't jump quite as hard as Carmen," Tia said as Carmen flung the tennis shoes back over the fence.

Chia already had her own shoes off, tied around her neck. She quickly laced the sneakers on and then bounced over the fence, with a joyful little whoop.

"Every task only requires the right tool," Tia said with a wink as Chia bounced little circles around Carmen, giggling.

"But they're so old and ugly, Tia," Carmen said.

Tia smiled. "In Mexico, *las turistas* flash their fancy, name brand camera bags—eye candy for the thieves."

"Oh, I get it," Carmen said. "Don't advertise your wealth."

Chia continued bouncing. "Teddy Bear, Teddy Bear, jump so high. Teddy Bear, Teddy Bear, touch the sky."

"Let me try 'em again," begged Carmen.

"We have work to do, *muchachas*. Don't forget Tomas! The *zapatos saltan* are only for work. *Vamanos*. Get your other shoes and follow me."

"What does it mean—*zapatos saltan*?" Carmen asked, slipping her own high tops back on. She then followed Tia from the parking lot to the back door of her shop into the sage smokey dimness.

"I guess you could say Vaulting Shoes," Tia explained.

Inside, they saw that everything seemed readied for them. Candles blazed in their niches, pillows were plopped down in a circle, and on the floor in the middle stood a small altar of purple feathers; pink, white, and purple crystals, wrapped bundles of smoking sage; and a photo of Tomas, looking very serious, propped against the back of a dark, onyx jaguar.

"Where did you get them?" Carmen persisted, unable to get the vaulting shoes out of her mind.

Chia grinned. "She got them at the Spring-A-Later Store."

Tia looked amazed. "How did you know about those? They're way before your time, senorita."

"It's just a joke," Chia explained to Carmen. "My cousin Pang's all into vintage stuff, and she kept talking about Spring-A-Laters till we went to this vintage shop and she got some leopard skin Spring-A-Laters. But the first time she wore them, she sprained her ankle, so her ma gave 'em to the thrift store."

Tia clapped her hands. "Okay. Let's get down to business. I have much to teach and many other tools to give you, but the rule is always the same. Only use the tool when there is no other choice. *Ahora.* Give me the letters, Carmen. They are *muy importante.* I can't believe you actually have them in your possession. I asked Septima for them long ago, but she said she had burned them."

Carmen's face fell. "I'm sorry, Tia. Muneca and her gang jumped me at school and they...uh, they..." Carmen couldn't bring herself to say the words. Instead, she pulled off and unzipped her backpack, pulling out the strips of the letters, which fluttered to the floor.

Tia, surprisingly, did not look upset. Instead, she gathered all the strips together and placed them in a large woven basket. "*Ai, chihuahua,* my work is never easy."

Carmen couldn't contain herself any longer. "Don't you want to hear about Om first?"

"All in due time, *mija.* And besides, I know quite a lot. Didn't Tomas tell you that he communicates with me through telepathy? Eventually, you'll be able to, also. He gave you the crystal tooth until you can be properly trained. Also, the tooth is important for other things that we'll talk about later."

"That's why I wanted to come here today. The BSC isn't working. I tried it out the other night, and nothing—*nada.*"

"Yes, there's been interference. Tomas is aware of it. There is great evil at work in all this, and we could all be in danger—

mucho peligro. That's why I am going into a trance right now—
to find out about the tooth—and get an update. So let's all sit
down. True can play with some of my carved animals over
there." Tia pointed to the corner of the room.

True quickly jumped up and then sat back down against the
wall, stroking the carved fur of a tiny wooden squirrel.

"Now—get relaxed—breathe deeply—in through the nose,
out through the mouth." Tia began to chant then and sway back
and forth. "Your eyelids are getting very heavy. You want to
close them—give in to the feelings of *tranquilidad*—just relax.
Let go of all tension."

Tia chanted more, a high pitched wailing song that droned
on and on, and all three of them sat still with their eyes closed.
Carmen opened hers once but quickly closed them again. Time
began to drag like an old record player, winding down as all
three lost themselves in its sway.

Carmen's eyes began to sting. She opened them to see Tia
shaking her sage bundles around the room, scattering smoke into
the corners. Then she scattered something that looked like sparkling dust. Carmen's heart gave a sudden hard thump, as if
someone had socked her in the chest. She heard a voice.

It was Tomas. "You have been doing good work, Carmen—gathering clues for me. Even though you couldn't hear
my words—some bits of information came through to me from
you. Our suspicions of the realtor, Silver, are correct. He is very
dangerous. It's just as we suspected. His company buys up
properties of Mexicans and other illegals and often they are deported either before or soon after. Then property and estate valuables get confiscated. But lately, there's something even darker. Tia is trying to find out more about that—maybe there's
something in Septima's letters. Tia needs to find out exactly
what Silver wants and who the shaman is who was chosen long
ago. She also needs to shore up her powers with this other
shaman who could help. I'm looking into getting your BSC
working again very soon. Until then, you must stay in close contact with Tia at all times and let her know everything that seems
important."

Carmen opened her eyes and sat up just as Chia did also. Tia was lying on a bright, multi-colored rug on the floor and appeared to be sleeping, but she began to talk in a low, drowsy voice. "Find...find the secret shaman who was chosen to help us...will increase my powers. Bad spell cast on Carmen...we must try to find out who...*muy mal*...using black magic..."

Suddenly Tia sat up and, as if sleepwalking, moved to the table where she had placed the basket with the scraps of Septima's letters. Astonished, Carmen saw her lift one of the letters, whole and restored from the basket and begin to read.

Carmen looked at Chia, both of their eyes wide with amazement. Chia smiled, her face pink and excited. True came over to the circle and sat down.

Chia waved her back to the corner. "Go play, True."

True frowned but did as she was told.

Tia was now smiling, also. "I have wonderful news. This second letter was sent not to Septima, but to Pepita, our sister who died many years ago—the one who first had the trailer that Portilla took over and now is at Immaculate Motors. The letter was from your father, answering a letter from Pepita about an artifact that she wants to get to him. Somehow it got in with these other letters of Septima's. This is what I have been seeking for many years. Septima must have found it in the trailer and removed it. I am just grateful she didn't destroy it. It tells of an artifact that has been in our family for centuries. In that part of the letter, the original ink was smeared some, but it is clear that this artifact goes back to Meso American times. There are still some unanswered questions about the artifact, however."

Carmen gave a little squeal. "Tia, tia, *meso*—that's the word I used to get away from Lupita at Homeland Security and I used it again on Om. There were other words also, strange ones that were sent to me on bubbles." But then she stopped. "Wait, how did the letters get put back together?"

"I restored the letters by chanting a spell that I learned in Mexico. I was taught this method of restoring matter many years ago. It can only be used in special circumstances, not just for any old repair. Those were magical words you used, Carmen. I have some for you to learn and to take with you today. Our magic is still closely related to our Mayan ancestors—ahead of their time, you know. Some of my magic comes from their teachings."

Carmen bounced on her heels, sitting up straighter, her face shining. "I'm doing a report in History about them, Tia. I need to go to the library and look up stuff."

"*No preocupar*. Don't worry. I will send some books home with you. Read as much as you can. I'll give you two spells today you can use when you are in danger. But we need to gather more from Chia, also. Do you know a shaman, Chia? We need to bring one in to work with us, as well as finding the hidden one."

Chia eagerly bobbed her head. "When we all closed our eyes just now, a shaman spoke to me, said for me to open my eyes and take notice—that he was nearby, and I was being a fool. He said that he would come to me in a dream very soon because he wants to work with us. But then he just laughed and laughed. And he was dressed in a long, bulky robe that looked too big for him. The robe was blues, greens, and purples—kind of like a dragon fly's wing." Chia stopped talking because Tia had closed her eyes and was shivering.

Tia rubbed her chin then fell to the ground, groaning. "Aiii, aiii," she cried out. Then she curled into a ball, refusing to let Carmen and Chia help her up when they rushed to her side.

"Are you okay, Tia? What can we do?" Carmen sputtered distraughtly.

Tia put her palm up to silence them but did not rise. She just lay on the floor, rocking back and forth like a roly poly bug. Instead, she began to chant, and the whole room shook in time to the groaning syllables.

At first Carmen had thought they were having an earthquake, but the shaking grew stronger, and now the candles flickered, the walls shimmied, and objects on shelves danced. The same purple lights that she had seen on the ceiling of the trailer splattered the walls and ceiling above, pulsing hypnotically.

In a split second, it all stopped and Tia sat up, her hand to her forehead. "*Mi cabeza, mi cabeza*," she muttered, squinting her eyes hard and looking at all three girls. "*Un plato!*"

"A plate?" Carmen shook her head. "What does that mean, Tia?"

"*Muy extranjero.* It's very strange. Usually I see pictures in my visions. Like an image of something, like a dog, *tu sabes*? But this time I saw a word—P-L-A-T-O. *Si*, a plate. That must be the artifact we are looking for. There are some very famous Mayan plates. One contains pictures of the beginning of the world. It could be one of those, perhaps. But it has great powers, and whoever has this plate in their possession could have access to those powers. This is a real breakthrough, *muchachas*."

Carmen blurted out the thought she'd been holding back for a while now. "Tia, I hope I can learn to use even half your magic. Do you think there's time for me to learn all I need to know?"

"First of all, we did it together. I've been working on this for a long time, and it wasn't until you found and brought me the letters that I was able to have this vision. And, yes, time is short, but soon you'll have to go to Om again, where time is compressed and some of your lessons can be speeded up."

Tia turned to Chia, took one of her hands, and began to rub it, as if rubbing in invisible cream, then dropped it after a final jerk. She went to her shelf then and rooted among the many pots and jars. Finally, finding what she was looking for, she began to mix up a concoction.

Turning, she held out a small baggie of herbs to Chia. "Make a tea of this. It will help you remember your dreams, Chia. Write them down as soon as you wake up." Now Tia turned to Carmen. "Here's some *libros* for you. Read as much as you can. This one is about herbs and spells and potions, like the one I just made up for Chia. There are several spells for protection. And here is a protection packet for each of you." She even handed True one.

"I'll keep True safe. That's my job as her older sister," Chia said.

"But you can't be with her at all times, and she's now been exposed to the same *fuerzas mal*—evil forces that we all have encountered. Here's some books on Mayan culture, Carmen. But there is something else, isn't there? Some unfinished business, before you leave me?"

Carmen began to shake her head then remembered. "Mama mia, Tia. I found this on Teofilo's desk. It's in Spanish, and my reading of Spanish is poor, but it's from Silver/Briggs Realtors." Carmen fished out the letter and handed it to Tia.

Tia read silently then turned to Carmen again. "It's just as I thought. They are trying to lure Teofilo into selling Immaculate Motors. But you need to be careful taking things from these people. Even a harmless looking letter could contain evil spells that could affect you. Don't let the enemy have physical contact with you if you can help it. And never, never take anything from them."

Carmen clapped her hand over her mouth and dug into her pockets. "I also have this, Tia. I found it last night when I couldn't get the BSC to work." She handed Tia the business card.

Tia pounced on it. "Aha! This is the culprit. This is what's blocking your BSC most likely. Someone knows how to use black magic, and when you touched the card, it cast a bad spell over you. Let me get my salt." Tia left the room then returned with a pan of water and a blue bowl with about an inch of salt in the middle. "Don't move, Carmen," she said, passing back and forth in front of her, throwing the salt in all directions. Then she told Carmen to sit perfectly still while she moved her hands, as if up and down an invisible wall around Carmen, stopping to throw what just looked like air away from Carmen.

"Now take off your shoe and get ready to transmit."

Carmen removed her sneaker, flipped open the flap on her foot, removed the coin/key, and rubbed it over the crystal tooth, while Chia and True watched in silent fascination.

"Do you feel anything?" she asked Carmen after a few moments.

Carmen's eyes popped. "The top of my head—it's tingling like it did on Om. It worked, Tia. It worked!"

"Close your eyes and see if you can contact Tomas."

Carmen did as Tia bid, but although her head continued to tingle, she heard nothing.

"*Nada*," she said, shrugging her empty palms.

"Carmen," Chia chirped suddenly. " Didn't you tell me you also picked up cigarettes you thought Silver or Briggs had left behind the house?"

"Yikes, yes. I forgot about those." Carmen dragged out the cigarettes, which Tia snatched up and dumped into a baggie.

"I'll have Choppo take these far off and get rid of them." Then Tia went through the same salt and water ritual as before.

Almost immediately, Carmen jumped up and down, chattering like a crazed squirrel. "It's Tomas. I hear him."

Tia put her finger to her lips. "Shhhh, *mija*. Remember, *escuche, no palabras*...just listen, no words. Remember, I connected you to him before in this receptive space, so try again as soon as you leave here, as a test."

Carmen closed her eyes and listened.

'*Great work, Carmentita. When we work together we can do a lot. That's what Om is all about—joining forces to make things better. I can't talk long right now because much is happening here on Om, and I'm running out of time. Learn as much as you can from Tia, and do your homework. And I'll send for you again soon. Right now, it's important to find out who the shaman is there on Earth. Work on that, and I'll try and find out more about the plate. I knew it was some kind of artifact we were looking for but now I have more to go on. Also, work on finding out where they are holding me. Being locked up on Earth keeps my own powers weakened, which is perhaps why our communications are not strong. So only contact me if it's an emergency. The enemy has very strong powers of interference, so we gotta increase our strength. Take care, little sister. I'll send messages when it's important. Wait, one more thing—your BSC needs some fine tuning. I can see now what is wrong, and I will contact our engineers here on Om to clear up some problems. Omites do things differently from Earthlings, and I'm afraid they forgot that. I'll be in contact about that soon.*'

Carmen felt very important as she relayed Tomas' message to the others. Although she listened carefully, Chia's foot had begun to tap nervously, and when Carmen was done, she said, "I think I better get True home now. It's getting close to dinner time."

"*Si*," Tia said. I'll call Choppo to take you home." Almost as fast as she said the words, a car horn honked out front.

"Can we take the vaulting shoes with us?" Carmen asked with a rabbity grin.

"No, no, I'll hide them somewhere in the alley. But don't worry. I'll speak to Choppo and he won't be dumping you there like that again." Tia looked tired, but before they reached the doorway, she called to them, "Wait, here's a number you can call for Choppo if you ever can't reach me." She gave Carmen the number on a slip of paper, along with two religious cards.

"What are these for?" Carmen asked, staring down at the cards, one of Santa Agnes and the other of Saint Anthony.

"They are known to give good protection against nosy tias and also for miracles," she said with a wink.

Carmen grinned. "Maybe tias named Septima, si? So we'll see you tomorrow after school for more lessons with Little Sisters of Magdalena?"

"*Voy a hasta manana.* I'll give you your magic words then. For now don't forget to drink your tea," Tia said, disappearing behind the curtains between the rooms.

When they climbed into the cab, Chia buckled True into the backseat as usual. Choppo was singing in Spanish, and Carmen saw that he still had jawbreaker eyes.

Carmen settled into the front seat as Chia said, "Will you show me your BSC again Carmen? That is so cool."

"Sure, when we get to your house," Carmen said. Silently, then, she stared out the window, her thoughts drifting back to the dog. "Chia, you know what? I wish I was as brave as you."

"I'm not that brave, Carmen. And you're plenty braver than you think you are."

Carmen told her the story of the pack of wild dogs in the field. "When I saw that dog today, it all came back to me like for real—the same old fear that makes me go all frozen." She shivered.

"But, Carmen, you should have been scared. You were little, and they were killers. What could you have done? How could you have stood up to those dogs? That would just have been stupid."

"I guess you're right. But Mami did stand up to them. I have to remember that. Even if she did throw a peach at me. I've always thought she threw the peach because she was mad at me for being scared and a coward."

"She threw that peach because she was relieved that you were okay. And the fields were dangerous, I bet. Anyone would have grown up scared. And you guys had no power."

"It's true. We had no power. All the people I knew were running scared cuz they could always be caught and sent back."

Chia was quiet for the next few minutes, then she said suddenly, "Carmen, remember at the yard sale when Septima's undies caught on fire? I got all panicked and really freaked out. That's because I have fears, too, and the thing I'm most afraid of is fire. I'll tell you why someday, but that day I was frozen with fear just like what you say happens to you. Everybody has at least one big fear, I think."

"Yea, Mami's is Sears. I don't know why. But I have lots, even lawnmowers. Tomas got hit with a rock that was thrown from one once and it took out a chunk of his thigh. Mami fainted and I had to take care of him and get help. Fear sucks."

True had begun to giggle so hard her little shoulders shook.

"What is it?" Chia asked. "What's so funny?"

But True couldn't answer, drowning in a sea of her own giggles.

CHAPTER 17

"Okay. Don't tell me." Chia snapped her head away from True. "I don't even want to know."

True continued laughing, her hand now over her crotch as if she might pee her pants.

Carmen couldn't stand anyone to tease her with not telling a secret. "Well, I want to know."

True whispered something to Chia, whose eyes bugged as she turned to Carmen. "Guess what? True said she talked to a mongoose back at Tia's—said she played hide and seek with it and every time it was about to catch her, she changed herself into a different animal, first a mouse, then a cat, and then a bird."

"Did she fall asleep, or did she just imagine it?" Carmen asked, but no one got a chance to answer.

At that moment, Choppo's song got even louder, as he pulled up to a curb, grinding the tires with a loud scrape against it.

"Ouch," said Carmen. "Hey, where are we anyway?" She could see the sign for Zacky Farms rising redly against the early evening sky, above the duplexes and smaller homes of this older, lower-priced neighborhood.

"Gotta make a quick stop."

Choppo seemed to have a mouthful of oatmeal, and Carmen and Chia exchanged somewhat alarmed looks.

"You're supposed to take us home," Carmen said.

But Choppo didn't hear. He'd ducked around to the other side of the cab and now crouched down, peering from behind the car through a pair of binoculars.

"I need to get home," Chia said, rolling down the window.

"Shhhh," Choppo hissed, as another car pulled up across the street in front of the house he'd been watching.

A woman of about forty with curly, reddish brown hair got out. She was short and somewhat thick about the middle, and when she saw the cab, her brows carved a fat V into her forehead. Lips pressed into a thin line, she marched across the street and lashed Choppo with her sharp, stinging Spanish. As the two began to argue, the woman rained blows down on Choppo's head with an orange, plastic purse.

"I gotta get home before it gets too late. What're we gonna do?"

"Let's go," Carmen said, opening the door and climbing out.

The woman was now across the street, still yelling at Choppo, who followed, first yelling, then pleading, *Solo dejeme explicar.*"

"Go explain to your other sluts," the woman threw over her shoulder as she struggled to unlock her door.

"We can walk from here." Carmen sighed. "It's only about eight blocks away. I think our cab's docked for a while. Wait 'til I tell Tia about this one."

So they walked until True complained about her foot and Chia had to pick her up. They came to a dry cleaner's, which was landscaped with a yard full of white, pointy rocks and thirsty-looking bushes, and sat down to rest on an overturned wading pool at the front of the alley that ran beside the shop. They'd only gone about three blocks, but no one got up to continue on.

"Let me see your BSC," Chia said.

Carmen reached to untie her shoes then sniffed, suddenly aware of a sharp, acrid smell like the same one she'd smelled around Briggs. But before Carmen could finish unlacing her shoe, a chicken suddenly appeared from behind a straggly bush in the alley, clucked its way over to them, and began to dance, hopping from one foot to the other.

Carmen opened her mouth but found herself speechless as the chicken minced over to True and bent to whisper in her ear. The chicken stopped, as if waiting for a response. True nodded her head up and down and then listened some more as it continued whispering. Amazed, they all watched as the chicken turned and mounted the sky, its feathers blazing as it transformed into a small explosion of feathers and gray smoke.

"What did it say, True?" Chia had taken hold of the lapels of True's quilted jacket as if she feared True might also sprout feathers and fly away.

"Just numbers," True said softly. "Bunch of numbers."

"Can you remember them? Tell me and I'll write them down," Carmen said excitedly as she grabbed a stick and scratched the numbers into the dirt of the alley as True recited them. "987429993282955."

Carmen's eyes popped. "Wow, how could she remember all that?"

"True has an amazing memory." Chia smiled and then pulled a pencil out of the little woven purse around her neck then and wrote the numbers down on a scrap of paper. "What do you suppose?" she asked, puzzling over them.

Carmen scratched her head and looked at the numbers. "Too many for a phone number. Hmmmm."

But a look of horror crossed True's face that stopped Carmen cold. A huge, black woman in a security guard's uniform had crossed the yard and now loomed over them.

"What y'all doin' here?" she said in a most unfriendly voice.

"Nothing, just tying my shoe," Carmen said.

"I know ever-body in this here hood and y'all don't belong here. Better be movin' on."

The woman was tall and heavyset. Her sunglasses flashed two blinding mirrors at them, hiding her eyes behind the blank, silvery discs. She nudged True with the steel toe of a heavy-duty work boot. "What y'all draggin' this little one 'round for? Get her on home or I gotta write you up."

"Excuse me. But we're not breaking any laws," Chia piped up, her voice steady and strong.

The mirrored glasses fairly smoked as the woman raised herself up and snorted, "Look here, don't gimme none of your lip. I bet you're FOB and I can get you put right back on the boat."

But Chia didn't back down. "What law exactly are we breaking?"

Carmen surprised herself by adding, "And who exactly are you? I don't see any badge. You're not a police woman."

The acrid smell Carmen had noticed before had gotten stronger, and now she could hardly breathe as it seemed to engulf the alleyway. All three girls began to cough, and True even gagged between each coughing spell. The woman began to laugh, and when she did, Carmen saw her teeth were lined with gold.

Slowly, finger by finger, the woman removed her thick, leather gloves. Carmen saw, with a fearful thump of her heart, that her fingers were weighted with heavy turquoise rings that looked eerily familiar. Folding the gloves carefully into a pocket, the woman backed up from them to block the alleyway completely. Out of nowhere rolled a boulder taller than either Carmen or Chia. With hands the size of catcher's mitts, the woman reached down and lifted the boulder like a tiny marble. If she threw it, any one of them could be crushed instantly.

"I got me a hankering to do some bowling," she said taking a bowler's stance at the mouth of the alley, swinging her arm back. But instead of throwing the boulder, she laughed again. "Set up that little pin for me there." She motioned to True. "I gotta pick me up a spare."

Carmen had started untying her shoe and bent over to reach down and slip it off, when the woman hollered, "Hold it right there, *muchacha*!"

But before anyone could speak, a loud, jangly rattle filled the space behind the woman Carmen had now recognized as the bruja from San Judas Botanica.

Suddenly, a loud, off-key song, accompanying the rattle of a shopping cart, cut through the stillness of their terror and halted just to the left of the *bruja*. Carmen could see Flora Linda, squinting at the scene like a spectator at a sports event. She was dressed in a long, billowy skirt, with a bullfighter's jacket and a purple visor shading her eyes.

"Who winnin?" she asked calmly.

The *bruja* laughed again, a laugh that had grown increasingly hideous. "It's a shut out, *vieja*. Ain't nobody winnin' here but me, so shut yer mouth and vamoose."

Flora Linda smiled sweetly, reached into a pocket that gaped from the side of her long, drapey skirts, and pulled out a tennis ball. "I yike to pway," she said then moved to the side of the big *bruja* and addressed Chia. "We pway pov pob, Shia."

Chia nodded. She knew that Flora Linda meant pov pob, the courting game of catch played by Hmongs. Flora Linda threw the ball around the side of the *bruja* to Chia, who caught it expertly then threw it back. More tennis balls appeared from Flora Linda's skirts, which she threw to the girls, bouncing them off the buildings along the alley. As if Flora Linda had turned on a ball machine, tennis balls went whizzing and flying every direction, some of them bouncing off the *bruja's* head and body. Flora Linda's pockets seemed to spit an endless supply of balls.

"Cut that out," the *bruja* protested, but the balls came more furiously than ever—a storm of them—so many hitting the *bruja* at once that she finally lost her balance and fell down, buried in a swamp of fluorescent green.

Motioning for them to follow, Flora Linda picked up her skirts and ran to the corner where Choppo's cab sat idling. The girls jumped inside and Choppo squealed off down the street. Carmen looked out the back window to see Flora Linda just crossing the street and vanishing into a row of oleanders.

"Did that big woman look familiar?" Carmen asked Chia when she had caught her breath.

Chia looked puzzled then sucked her lips in. "Yea. She did, but where—"

"Remember the San Judas Botanica? That was the *bruja* we saw there. I recognized her gold teeth and her rings."

"But she wasn't black."

"If she's a *bruja mal*, a bad brjua, she can be a shape shifter, can take on all kinds of disguises. But hey, amiga, you're really brave, you know? I wish I could be that—"

"Enough. I'm not brave at all." Chia looked almost angry. "I was just afraid for True. I have to keep her safe. We better make up our tea and drink it fast. And your BSC doesn't work so well if you have to take off your shoe and go through all those steps first."

"Yea." Carmen sighed. "I think that's what Tomas meant when he said it needs some adjusting. He said they're working on it."

They had pulled up at the end of the block from Chia's house. Choppo turned around in the seat, his face softened with contrition. "Uh, girls, I made a big mistake. Do you think you could please maybe not tell Tia about this? I gotta go on the wagon again."

Carmen explained to Chia that Choppo meant that he had to stop drinking. Choppo's jowls and his eyes drooped like a beaten down dog's. Carmen couldn't help feeling sorry for him. "Okay, Choppo. But this is your last chance."

"*Hasta manana*," True said, hopping from the cab after Chia.

All of them burst out laughing, even Choppo who said, "And her accent is *perfecto*."

"The kid's smart," Carmen said, leaning out the cab's window.

But Chia frowned and put her finger to her lips. "No, she's not that smart."

Carmen started to protest, but Chia said, "Just say goodbye for now. I'll explain about it later."

Carmen shrugged. "Bye, amigas. Can we walk to school together tomorrow?"

Chia nodded yes then whirled around and began talking swiftly in Hmong to a boy who had wandered up, whom Carmen guessed was her brother. Chia did not look happy, and Carmen thought she would try to call her before she went to bed.

CHAPTER 18

Carmen ran up the steps of the porch, anxious to study Tia's books and try to contact Tomas. Events seemed to be moving faster than she could keep up with. Her stomach tightened with urgency—the more time that passed, the more difficult it might be to find Tomas and the more chances for something dire—

She left this thought unfinished. In the front room, Rosa was rubbing lotion on Septima's face, kissed with furious red polka dot welts. She looked a fright, her hair snarled, her eyes sunken shadows. Carmen could not hold back a quick gasp. Telanovelas blared in the background where Teofilo slouched in his chair, swigging a beer, half-mast eyes dopily fixed on the TV where a strychnine blonde actress was plotting raving rendezvous of revenge.

Carmen pulled out the religious cards Tia had given her and waved them in front of Septima, ready to weave a tale of deception, but no one seemed interested.

Rosa cooed softly, urging Septima to lie back and rest. "*Aqui*, Carmen, why don't you give Septima one of your *simpatico* back rubs? I'll go fix us some *comida*."

Rosa stood up, looking brighter and more robust than usual, as if she and Septima had traded places.

Carmen pulled Septima's robe aside and began to rub her back up and down against the thermal T-shirt underneath. Septima groaned and sighed, her eyes shut, her lips pressed into a tight grimace. She began to mutter a low, growling Spanish, so Carmen just kept rubbing. Cooking smells came wafting out from the kitchen, and Carmen suddenly realized she was famished.

"Doesn't that smell good, Tia Septima? Hey, Mami, what's that you're cooking?'

Rosa stepped into the dining area between them, spatula held up like a flag. "*Pescado afortunado*, Carmentita! We got a lucky fish. I think it's a carp, *quiza*."

Carmen's fingers slid to a stop. "Where did you get the fish, Mami?" she called into the kitchen.

"Oh, some client of Teo's. Un *muchacho* bring right before you come home."

Carmen jumped up. "Be right back, Septima."

Something was fishy about this fish. It was just a feeling, but when she looked down into the skillet where Rosa was just flipping the fish over, she knew for sure. The fish was smiling. And two long, knife sharp incisor teeth hung out of its mouth. Now that she was closer, she also smelled the same acrid, burning licorice smell she'd come to recognize as a sign of danger.

"*Mira, mija.* The Lord provides." Rosa leaned toward Carmen in a whisper, "*Septima y Teo no tienen mucho dinero ahora.* Mmm...*delicioso, si?*"

Carmen had not taken her eyes off the fish and, just as Rosa said these words, it opened its mouth wide in a biting motion with the fang-like teeth striking.

Carmen didn't want to upset Mami, who had not seen what she had, but she knew something dire would happen if they ate this fish. "Let me finish this, Mami" she said. "You go see about Septima. I'm worried about her. She doesn't look good."

"*Bien. Pero no queme al pescado, mija.*"

"I won't burn the fish, Mami."

When she'd gone, Carmen looked around frantically, quickly grabbed an empty beer bottle of Teo's from the kitchen counter, and smashed it into the frying pan. Billows of noxious, blue smoke leaped toward the ceiling as Carmen ran from the kitchen.

"*Mija, que paso?*" Rosa's hands clapped against the sides of her head.

"*Lo siento*, Mami. I was going to add just a dash of salt and a bottle fell and broke in the pan. It's ruined now. Please, Mami, I am so sorry." Carmen felt terrible when she saw the disappointment in Rosa's eyes. "I'll go fix something else. Is there anything I can cook instead?"

Septima looked at them both wildly, started to say something, then dropped her head, and began frantically raking her fingers over her neck. The itching seemed to have completely distracted her.

"No…" Rosa's face looked like a popped balloon. "No *hay carne, tengo miedo.* But what is the smoke, *muy mal?*"

Both she and Septima began to cough. Teofilo had gone out of the house, probably to his workroom outside.

Carmen opened a window in the living room then ran back into the kitchen to open a window there. Her eyes almost popped. The smoke had begun to die down, but there was no sign of the fish. Rosa came up behind her. "What's going on, *mija?* What did you do with the fish?"

"I threw it out," Carmen said, realizing that the skillet also was missing.

"Well, you better get that skillet back. Septima *hara volar su cumbre.*" Rosa was shaking her head, looking increasingly upset. "And now all we have is beans."

Carmen rushed to the freezer, but there was nothing there but ice cube trays, a bag of frozen corn, and a plastic container of some freezer burned and unidentified leftovers. Rummaging through the refrigerator, she found jelly, mustard, a jar of salsa, ketchup, a bag of hardened french fries, a box of powdered donuts, an almost empty jar of peanut butter, and half a head of lettuce, browning on the edges. She yanked open the vegetable crisper and found an onion and a few curling carrots. The meat tray was empty.

Carmen sat back on her heals for a moment, thinking. Then she slid her hand to the back and pulled out a tin foil packet that yielded a block of cheddar cheese growing a beard of white hair which she carried to the sink and scraped clean. She then heated the tortillas on the griddle and grated cheese inside, rolling them up like fat fingers. Rosa sat at the table, her head hanging down into her cupped palms.

"I'll call Septima, Mami. Look. We have beans and quesedillas. Maybe it's not a good idea to eat fish you don't know about. It could have been bad. It smelled kind of funny, Mami," Carmen said, edging her way toward the living room afraid of what her aunt might have to say. But it was empty, and when Carmen went to Septima's door, it was closed.

Outside, there was no sign of Teofilo's car either, so Carmen returned to the kitchen and sat down with Rosa.

Rosa smiled weakly. "*A falta de pan, las tortas son buenas.*"

Carmen grinned, despite herself. "*Si*, for lack of bread the cakes are good. I wish this was cake. But we'll just have to make do."

Rosa shrugged. "Septima say to Teofilo they go Mexico to Christmas. I think is good idea. She thinks the doctors in Mexico help her. I pray for her. You pray, *mija*?"

Carmen sucked in her cheeks. Actually, she hadn't prayed in a long time, and she didn't want to lie to Rosa. "I'll try, Mami. I'll try."

After dinner, Carmen settled her mother with her knitting in front of the *telenovelas* and went to work on the dishes, when the phone rang.

Carmen grabbed it as quickly as she could, not wanting to disturb Septima. It was Chia.

Carmen told her about the fish, and Chia whistled into the phone. "If there's an evil curse put on you, isn't there some way Tia can get it removed?"

"She's stretched pretty thin right now, trying to find Tomas and remove the spell on herself, also. Who knows? Maybe it was some kind of protection that helped me to sense something was wrong with the fish. We just have to stay alert. Now tell me what that was all about with True. Why didn't you want me to say she was smart?"

"Because Hmongs believe that you should never brag about anyone in your family, especially the children because the evil dabs can overhear and try to steal their spirits if they have desirable qualities. So it's bad luck to say your child is smart. In order to trick the bad dabs, you would say, 'No this child is really pretty dumb.' But everyone knows this and knows what you really mean."

"I get it. Kinda like outjinxing a jinx."

"Um, kinda I guess. Look, I gotta go help with the sewing. Let's meet and walk to school tomorrow. Okay?"

"Sure. But what's a dab, Chia?"

"A dab is a spirit. But I gotta go for reals."

Carmen hung up the phone. She could hear Mami in the bedroom, humming softly to herself. At the doorway, Carmen watched Mami folding clothes. "For Tomas. I think he needs soon," Rosa said, smiling at Carmen.

It was good to see her in better sprits, thought Carmen, as she settled herself in a chair nearby with the books that Tia had given her. She flipped through them all then opened the one titled, *Curendera Secrets*, and began to read, very quickly losing herself in the pages of old and new rituals. When next she looked at the clock, it was after ten and Mami had fallen asleep on the bed, slumped over her knitting.

Carmen slipped the needles from her fingers and wrapped the yarn around itself, removed Mami's glasses, and folded them up on the nightstand. Rosa moaned softly as Carmen covered her with two raggedy quilts and a faded comforter.

Even though she didn't feel that sleepy, Carmen wanted a good night's rest, so she put her books away and curled up on the floor on an old twin mattress they kept there as a second bed. Tia had made Carmen a sachet packet of lavender wrapped in cheesecloth and netted in silk thread woven to catch dreams. Carmen held it to her nose now and breathed in full gulps of its fragrance. After a few deep breaths, she drifted down and slipped the moorings of time into a black pocket of calm.

Overhead, the sky splintered like a stained glass window, but when she blinked, it shifted and the patterns and colors danced like a sky-sized kaleidoscope. Each blink created new colors and over-lapping quilted scraps of vivid tints, refracting light like sunlight on water. *Am I awake*, she wondered, sinking

lower into herself, yawning into a deeper, hammocky stillness
that slowly inched up, filling her to the brim.

Just when she thought the sky could not get more beautiful
nor the serenity fill her more fully, a tiny gnat of discomfort
pricked her. Carmen sat bolt upright in the darkness, a distinct
unease engulfing her now. First her nose itched, then her scalp,
then the itch spread like a small wildfire. The room seemed
lighter than it should be and, as her attention fixed on a glow
behind the shades, she threw off the covers, jumped up, and
pulled them aside.

Through the moonless, thick night outside, a pinkish-gold
glow began to flicker and the sky sprang alive with small pin-
wheeling lights. *Fireflies*, she thought, *but in December*? As
quietly as she was able, she tiptoed to the front door, turned the
bolt, then the knob, and was outside, surrounded by pulsing
lights as if the stars had dropped to Earth and streaked around
her. Stepping off the porch, she took two quick strides into the
hushed night, not quite feeling, yet sensing a hovering of wings
brushing around her like a flock of invisible birds. But she had
no time to wonder. Car lights were approaching from down the
street, slowly at first, then faster.

Instinctively, Carmen stepped back into the shadows of the
bushes and trees. Her heart had also accelerated and now almost
braked with the car in front of their house. It was a big, white
van, the windows blank squares of unrevealing blackness.
Trapped and frozen in her cave of shadows, Carmen started to
shake with a blue-cold fear. What did they want and why were
they stopped in the street in front of Immaculate Motors?

The windows must be tinted, she thought just as one of
them slid noiselessly half way down. Carmen saw it first, like a
streak of fire, then heard a loud pop, pop, pop. Then the car was
squealing around the corner at the end of the street. At first she
was afraid to move. Maybe they were coming back. But the
night rolled on with a still and eerie sameness as if nothing out
of the ordinary had just taken place. Carefully, Carmen moved
toward the porch looking for signs of bullet holes. At first she
saw nothing, then she saw two holes gouged out of the stucco
beside the window that opened into Teofilo's study. She did not

see a third hole, but by now it was so cold, she could hardly
breathe.

Carefully, she opened the door, made sure to re-lock it with
the dead bolt and the house lock, and then crept back to bed,
amazed that no one else had been awakened by the gunfire. Her
mind whirled, but amazingly, she fell asleep almost immediately.

CHAPTER 19

Carmen woke to the telephone ringing, ringing, ringing. Mami was already up and the bed made. Carmen could hear voices in the other room as she threw on her clothes. Her head ached dully, and her neck and back felt stiff and sore. She must hurry and tell her aunt and uncle about the shots fired at the house last night. They'd want to call the police who would want to talk to her. She had seen no one and had no idea what make of car it was, except that it was a white van, probably with tinted windows. Could it be the same van that had hit the cat the other day?

In the kitchen, Mami stirred a pot at the stove, while Septima held the phone to her ear with a worried expression. "I see. Yes. Yes. You're sure she gave my name. Yes, I'm Septima Galopagord. Bien." Septima then launched into Spanish.

As Carmen moved toward the stove to see what Mami was cooking, she stopped cold. In the midst of Septima's stream of Spanish she heard Portilla's name.

Mami wiped her hands on her apron and motioned for Carmen to sit at the table where she served up a bowl of oatmeal. Carmen stirred in a half packet of sugar from a margarine tub full of them on the table—Teofilo's coffee shop pilferings. She decided to tell Septima about the shooting later because it would be better not to worry Mami, whose brightened demeanor seemed to have been squashed in the night. Mami's hair looked grayer today, her face drawn and gray, also. She even wore a gray sweat shirt, splattered with oily spots on the front.

Carmen reached out and tugged on her mother's apron. "What's the matter, Mami? You were so hopeful last night."

"I had *una pesadilla anoche*, and I dream *malcriados* they shoot at our casa." Mami frowned. "Entonces, I dream of Tomas." Her eyes filled with tears as she shook her head and turned back to wiping dishes.

Septima hung up the phone and charged out of the kitchen, but Carmen ran after her. "What's up, Tia Septima?"

Head down, Septima rubbed circles around her eyes. She sighed heavily. "Your Aunt Portilla whom you have never met is in the hospital. They think she has had a stroke. She told the hospital to notify me and your mother, but I can't go down there today. I have some very important business to take care of."

Carmen just caught herself before she gasped. "I—I—could go—"

"No!" Septima nearly shouted. "Maybe I'll go later today. I am going to the *abogada's* office this morning and sit there until he sees me. Then I have to go to the doctor's. This rash isn't getting any better. And I have to get some things ready for our trip to Mexico. Your mother told you about that, didn't she?"

"She did mention it." Carmen frowned. "When are you going?"

"We leave any day. I want to be there for Christmas. And I can get medicine cheaper there. You and your mother will have to take care of things for us here. *Sabes*?"

This did not seem like the time to mention the gun shots. And something else stopped Carmen, a feeling she couldn't quite place—a hunch that it was better for Septima not to know. So she just nodded, adding, "Si, Tia Septima."

Septima looked surprised at Carmen's Spanish then just said, while scraping her fingers at her neck, "You better head off to school, Carmentita. I'll take care of this business with Portilla either later today or tomorrow. I don't want to upset your mother." Her tone had softened somewhat, her splotched face part of a new, paler version of the old Septima.

೮೧೮೧

When Carmen met up with Chia at her house, her words tumbled out like puppies spilling all over themselves. She told about the strange lights, the gunshots, and then about Tia being in the hospital. "I had meant to tell Septima about the gunshots, but I don't think she would call the police now, anyway. She's too afraid of the ICE and she thinks they're all in cahoots. And she's getting ready to go to Mexico for Christmas, too—I don't think she wants her trip interfered with. And then I found out about Tia, so I thought you and I should just head to the hospital right now. It's the last day of school before vacation, so we would only miss the party. Hey, where's True?"

"She had a runny nose so Mom kept her home. They don't want anyone sick for Hmong New Year. Maybe we could call Choppo to give us a ride to the hospital."

"Good idea. Can we use your phone?"

"I'll do it. Wait here."

Chia whirled and was gone, leaving Carmen on the walkway, wondering why she wasn't invited to come into the house. It was another cold day, and although Carmen had bundled up in her old black coat, scarf, and gloves, she stood shivering and snuffling in the sharp morning chill. A boy and a girl zipped into puffy jackets stepped out of the house next door, releasing a burst of canned cartoon laughter. The boy's hair stood up in spikes and he stared sullenly at Carmen as he swigged from a Sprite can.

Just as Carmen was wondering if she should knock on the door to see what was taking so long, Choppo pulled up to the curb in his flame yellow car, but he didn't stop. Instead, he crept along the curb and stopped two houses down. Chia came out then and motioned for Carmen to follow her. Looking around, Chia climbed in the car after Carmen.

"I'd have lots of explaining to do if they saw me getting into this car," she said.

Carmen nodded. "Choppo, do you know how Tia is?"

"I dunno. She didn't want to go to the hospital, but last night she wasn't breathing right and she had bad pain. She called me, and when I got there, she was lying on the floor unable to move. So I called the *ambulencia*." He looked tired and wrinkled. "I been up all night."

Choppo let the girls out at the hospital. "I got to go take care of some stuff for Tia. Call me if you need me."

Chia and Carmen stood in front of the hospital, watching people enter and exit with a whoosh through the sliding front door.

Chia looked doubtful. "You think they'll let us see her?"

"Probably not. But maybe we can sneak in. Hey, it's cold out here. Let's go inside to the waiting room and think about this."

Inside the hospital, people bustled about, everyone looking as if they knew exactly where they were going. Carmen saw an information sign and asked where the waiting room was. She was directed down the hallway to the left. It was 8:45 and the waiting room was nearly empty, but the TV chattered down from its post in the top corner of the room, where a cartoon rabbit chased a chicken up a ladder. When they reached the top, the ladder swayed perilously in the air as the rabbit tumbled down the rungs, landing in a pile of rabbit fluff at the base. The chicken flapped off onto a cloud where it perched, laughing, as the ladder smashed down on the rabbit, poking its heads up between the rungs, circled by dizzy stars.

With no clear direction of what to do next, the girls sat down in adjacent chairs and watched the chicken swoop down, break out a cane and top hat, and begin a soft shoe dance for its captive rabbit audience. It stopped short and, using the cane for a microphone, launched into a comedy routine. "Why did the chicken cross the road twice?" The rabbit just shook its head mournfully. "It was a double crosser."

The chicken fell on the ground, holding its sides with laughter. Then the chicken hopped up and began firing jokes off, stand-up style. "Why did the rubber chicken cross the road? To stretch her legs. Why did the chicken cross the playground? To get to the other slide."

Suddenly the chicken stopped and looked directly at the screen. "Why did the magician's magic wand get lost in the mail?"

There was a long pause, during which the rabbit tried to squeeze between the rungs of the ladder. "I know. I know. Because he had the wrong zap code."

And then a whole wild, crazy new chase was on again.

Carmen looked at Chia and both of their mouths dropped at the same moment. "Guano! Why didn't I think of it before? Are you thinking what I am?"

Chia's mouth stretched across her face. "*Si, si, amiga!* Let's go tell Tia. And I think I know how we can get in the room. Put on your best cute and lost smile, *amiga*."

At that moment, a man poked his head into the waiting room. He wore a plaid cowboy shirt, jeans looped with a big clunky silver chain, purple Vans, and red-rimmed glasses. His hair stood up in spikes and, as he entered the room, Carmen noticed that he wore dark, burgundy polish on his nails. "Are you girls waiting for someone?" he asked, not unkindly.

"Actually, we're lost—Carmen's aunt is sick and we came to see her, and then we left to go to the bathroom, and now we can't find our way back."

Carmen nodded her head in agreement.

He scratched his chin. "What's her name? I'll find out what room she's in."

Carmen opened her eyes widely, hoping for more cute kid appeal. "Portilla Estrella."

"Sure thing, then." He typed in something on a computer then turned to them. "Just come on with Dave. This place is a maze once you lose your way."

They followed their new escort into the elevator and up to the third floor. "I'm a ward clerk, on a—" He mimed smoking a cigarette. "—break. Don't start that dirty habit, girls. Honest to Allah, it's a vice ya know—cuz it gets you in a vise, if you know what I mean. You girls playing hooky?"

Carmen didn't think Dave would turn them in. "It's the last day of school before vacation, and my tia is sick, so we got permission to see her."

"Sure you did. And I got permission to ride my motorcycle down the halls." He winked at them. "See that hall there. Go left, then straight. It's the last room on the right. 308C. Stay in school and don't do drugs, girls."

Carmen and Chia grinned sheepishly and followed Dave's directions. "Dave, Dave, lives in a cave, needs a shave—Dave, Dave, don't dance on my grave," Carmen sang in a whisper to Chia, who shot her a hush up look.

However, there were very few nurses around and the one they passed at the nurse's station on the way did not even look up from her paperwork.

In Room 308C, the curtain was pulled around one of the beds, and the other two were empty. The rings made a scraping noise as Carmen slid back the curtain. Tia was lying on her back, a sheet pulled up to her neck. She looked pale, lifeless, and very old, her thick gray braid curled at her neck.

Carmen's eyes filled as her legs buckled, causing her to jolt down beside her sleeping tia. Chia touched her shoulder softly.

"I think you should be alone with your tia, Carm. And I just got an idea. I'll be back." Before Carmen could protest, Chia was gone.

Carmen stroked Tia's forehead, and she began to move her lips. At first nothing came out, then Tia began to moan. As Carmen bent closer, she recognized the sound of her aunt's chanting. First the bed shivered, then it shook. Tia lay still, not moving. In the midst of the chanting, Carmen began to make out random words. "Tomas…plato pavon…pavon…pavon…" Suddenly the bed gave a hard buck and Tia's eyes flew open. "Carmentita, your BSC—take it out."

Fingers shaking, Carmen fumbled with her high tops, yanked off her sock, opened the latch, removed the BSC, then felt on her scalp until she found the tooth, and rubbed it. The top of Carmen's head buzzed and tingled as Tia motioned Carmen to bend even closer and take hold of her hand. Carmen heard Tomas' voice, but before she could open her mouth to speak, she heard her thoughts formed into words. "I know what the numbers mean, Tomas. Chia and I figured it out. The zip code is buried in the string of numbers and also the area code. If we can figure out the town, we can go there and find out where they keep people who are being held in custody. Then we will work out a plan to get you out, Tomas."

'*Carmen, good work, but Tia is trying to communicate with us now.*'

'*Yes,*' Tia said. '*I think you have been led astray. I was told in a dream last night here in the hospital that your first solutions would be false. The evil ones are hacking into our communication system and trying to sabotage it. Both chickens were trying to throw you off the track. Numbers are involved, but keep yourself open for the next clues. This time you'll be on the right track.*'

Tomas' voice took up where Tia's left off. '*You must come back to Om soon. The Omites developed the BSC using Om conditions and no one on Om wears shoes. It was a simple, but critical mistake. It is not practical for you to have to take your shoe off each time you need to use the BSC. We have updated the BSC and will fix this on your next visit. In the meantime, both Tia and I have much information to pass on to you. We need to find the plato because we think it can help us here on Om. And Tia has* bruja *knowledge—spells, remedies, healing—much wisdom. You will be infused with information today. I also have some basic information about Om to transmit. As soon as you hear a high pitched sound, you should hold tightly onto the tooth, find a place where you can lie down, and become a receiving vessel. This will take a number of sessions. I don't know for sure how many now, but we must begin as soon as possible. You'll know it's time when you smell the moon and hear a sound like a peacock's scream or the blast of a train whistle. All of the hairs on your body will stand straight up. We are coming closer to—*'

Carmen felt Tia jerk roughly and then her aunt opened her eyes. Tia was almost sitting up in the bed. "I know who the shaman is, Carmentita, and the plato—" The machine beside Tia's bed had begun to beep loudly and before Carmen could blink, the room was filled with white coats and green scrubs. "Her blood pressure is dropping. She's not breathing. Honey, you'll have to leave." A chubby, red faced nurse firmly pushed Carmen toward the door.

Carmen tried to peek back in the room, but a doctor with a pushed-in face, gold-rimmed glasses, and fishy lips said to move out of the way. She found herself being led down the hall by a young Filipino nurse, not much larger than herself.

"You know where waiting room is?" the nurse said with a thick accent.

"Yes. But will someone come get me when I can return?"

"Why you don't phone back and you be made known how she is. You really not supposed to be here outside the visiting hours and without adult either. Very sorry." The nurse did not sound sorry as she stood watching Carmen back away.

Carmen caught a whiff of night rain on pebbles with wet leaves and mystery mixed in. What was that smell? Of course— the moon! She must find a place to lie down. But where?

Then she remembered the chapel they had passed on their way to the elevators. It was a small room with rows of comfortably padded benches. Carmen lay down on one at the back of the room and closed her eyes as the fear and tension stepped into the background. She still clutched the tooth, and now she waited. The minutes hung frozen like a dark cloud above before Carmen heard the sound. At first it was a faraway drone that graduated to a high pitched whine like a cloud of locusts she'd heard in a movie once. Gradually, the sound increased until it was more like a factory whistle moving through space. Carmen closed her eyes and fell into a deep sleep, as if the world dropped away or she dropped away from the world.

CHAPTER 20

Chia cruised down the halls of each floor, looking into the rooms she passed on her way. Similar scenes met her on every floor—patients propped in beds, some tottering down the hallways in their flimsy hospital robes, nurses bustling about with trays or carts of medication. Stands with tubing and bags hanging down like transparent purses were wheeled by legions of men and women clad in aqua scrubs, scribbling furiously on clipboards, going about their duties, chirping the same falsely cheerful sing-song-y hospital talk. Finally, on the first floor, she heard and smelled, before she saw, and followed the faint sound of drumming and the smoky incense of a burning joss stick. In the room, a short, wiry Hmong man in a black silk jacket drummed to the flickering shadows cast on the sterile walls, the patient's family grouped solemnly around the scene.

"Chia, how strange to see you here."

Chia jumped before she recognized the short, stout Hmong girl who had come up behind her.

"Hi, Der. I'm visiting a friend here. Do you know the patient in this room?"

"It's my uncle Vue. The hospital give us permission to call the txiv neeb. They say Uncle Vue's liver bad, so we go home to wait for them to get a new one to plant in him. But my family want the txiv neeb to clear out the bad hospital spirits so they do not go home with us. Then we'll do another ceremony at home."

Der looked down shyly as if she might evaporate in the fog of so many words.

Chia fixed her expression between friendly interest and respect for the gravity of the occasion. "How much longer do you think it will be?"

"He almost done, I think?" Der's face was a question she was too shy to ask.

"My friend's aunt is very ill, and I was wondering if he might make a visit to her room next." Chia stepped aside to let Der enter the room.

Der paused. "I must go in now, but I can ask him if possible when he finish here. What room number?"

"Room 308 C." Chia gave a slight bow of thanks to Der.

Chia had to stop herself from running down the halls. Very pleased with herself, she stepped into the elevator and punched the button for the third floor impatiently, anxious to tell Carmen about their good fortune. At least she hoped the shaman would be able to come.

When the doors slid open, she ran smack into Carmen.

"Ow, that hurt." Carmen rubbed her shoulder, looking a little dazed still from her recent trance experience in the chapel. "Where's the fire?"

Chia shook her smacked arm and looked puzzled. "Fire? What fire?"

"Never mind. It's just an expression. I've been in the chapel meditating, sort of. They kicked me out of the room. Tia has taken a turn for the worse it seems. They were working on her." Tears welled up in Carmen's eyes. "I know I'm just a kid, but adults can be cold. Let's go call Choppo. Maybe if he comes down here, we can get more information." As she spoke, Carmen pushed the button for the first floor.

"Okay. But check this out. I met a *txiv neeb* downstairs and I think he can come up to Tia's room after he's finished where he is." Chia's face glowed in the dingy elevator light. "Remember, Tia said we should put the powers together."

Carmen knew she should be pleased, but instead, the ugly jealousy imp whispered, '*Once again Chia saves the day, while Carmen stands around twiddling her eyeballs.*' Carmen fought to keep the imp from hijacking her face, but she lost to the mutinous demon despite herself. She turned her head away, but it was too late.

"What's the matter Carmen? Did I say something wrong?"

"*No!*" It came out too loud. Carmen felt silly and childish, but the imp wouldn't let go. "It's just that I always hold back and you charge forward and things happen—"

"Yes, things happen when you *do* something instead of— Anyway, you get all the adventures it seems, while I come up with ideas. You go to Om, you get magical bees and spooky lights, and I—Look, I think I should just go home. It's your aunt who is sick. I don't know why I'm here. Anyway, Mom wanted me to stay home and help with the sewing."

Carmen wanted to tell Chia to stay, but the imp had frozen her vocal chords.

"What's wrong with this elevator?" Chia frowned and hammered the button angrily with her thumb just as the box went dark and began to shiver.

"You broke it," Carmen said, hoping to make Chia laugh.

"Why are the lights in here purple?"

Before Carmen could respond, the elevator began to rock and sway. Both girls were thrown against the carpeted wall. As they slid to the floor, Carmen reached out, grabbed Chia's hand, and began to chant. The words came to her as if funneled through her brain from some outside source.

"Get ready, Chia, for the ride of your life!"

Chia's face had paled but Carmen was grinning. The elevator had stopped bucking now but was filled with the buzzing whine of an unleashed speed boat cutting across time like a horizon-less lake. Gradually, Carmen began to feel woozy and saw the same dazed-rabbity look on Chia's face, criss-crossed with purple shadows and lights. And then everything went blank.

When the sound stopped, both girls sat up and looked at each other. "Do you think we should push the button?" Chia whispered.

Carmen looked at the button and, just as the thought of pushing it sprang from her mind, the doors swooshed open.

There before them spread a sea of purple billowing fields with Parajoflor waiting, all of her peacock eyes wide open. She curtsied low and then stood very still, as if listening to something far away. Before Carmen could climb in, she danced off, parting the purple field like a comb.

Carmen waved her hand at the landscape. "Welcome to Om, Chia."

Chia did not seem excited, however. Instead she began to twitch. "I feel itchy," Chia said.

And then a strange thing happened. When Chia began to scratch her neck, Carmen felt Chia's fingernails scratching Carmen's own neck.

"Chia, kiss your hand."

"What?"

"Just do it!"

Puzzled, Chia held up her hand as if to a prince and kissed it.

"I felt that on my hand!" Carmen jumped up and down, and when she did, she felt something behind her, brushing against her legs.

Chia gasped. "Car, you have a...a tail! And it's purple!"

"Guess what, chica, so do you!"

Chia reached behind herself and both of them stood holding their tails like newly sprouted garden hoses. "And look—what's that on your arms?"

They looked down and saw that a fine down of pin feathers covered their arms.

Before either could say another word, the purple Om crop crawled up to their feet like waves of an ocean tide. And then one huge wave crashed across the purple sea. It parted in front of them, depositing a canoe directly at their feet.

"What are we supposed to do?" Chia, who never whined, came close to it.

"Just follow me. While you were with the shaman in the hospital, I went into a trance in the chapel and received accelerated training from Tia. We are meant to navigate this canoe across the field of chulupurpla and find the lavender flower thing that will reveal something of great importance to us."

"Lavender flower thing?"

"That's what it's called. Look, I don't have all the information yet. It's like a giant jigsaw puzzle and I've only been given some of the puzzle pieces. In the hospital, I made contact with Om and I was given further instructions. White flower thing is what the Mayans called the soul. But trust me. If we can make it across this purple field, we will come to something...uh...important."

Chia was frowning. "Okay. But how are we to guide the boat? We don't even have oars."

Instead of answering, Carmen turned her back to Chia and climbed over the side of the canoe. Chia sucked in her breath sharply. Two wings had unfolded from Carmen's back and spread out like enormous fans.

"Wings," was all she could say, pointing at Carmen's new body foliage.

"Look, Chia at yours!"

Just as Chia felt a new weight pressing against her back bone, she twisted her head around and caught the curve of a large wing furled up over her head.

"Climb in. Nothing to do now, girlfriend, but flap!" Carmen sang.

As they flapped, the canoe lifted, gliding smoothly over the purple tops of the waves. It was like sailing and flying and canoeing all at once, and Carmen felt delicious exhilaration as they surged forward. Glancing over her shoulder, Carmen saw Chia's face set firmly and purposefully intent, with her new wings waving gracefully in the wind.

Little by little, the air grew colder. The sky, which had at first pooled with washy pastels, like an ever changing watercolor painting overhead, changed to a darker and darker indigo.

They saw the red spot, at first like a small drop of blood, blinking far in the distance. Up closer, it more closely resembled an angry fireball hooked in the sky. Suddenly, nine hairy, horned creatures, with tails that ended in a fork of fire, shot out of the fireball, streaking directly toward them.

"Carrrrrmen!" Chia's scream curdled the air.

CHAPTER 21

Some moments last a lifetime. When Chia saw the fiery tails shooting toward her, she froze with terror for her old enemy, fire. The terror all went back to her childhood, first from an auntie who told her a story one night before bedtime of the wise man Shoa, who lived in peace with his animal friends, a wild pig, a tiger, a dragon, a white bear, and thunder. All of the friends took turns going to the mountain top trying to scare each other. They howled, bellowed, stamped, and churned the sky black in turns, but no one showed any fear. When it was Shoa's turn, he sent them all into a windowless house and then piled up dry leaves and twigs in front.

He struck a flint against steel and cried out, "Now are you afraid?"

As flames licked the house, the animals threw themselves against the door, squealing and crying. By the time they escaped, the fire had singed each of them, turning pig's hair yellow, tiger's striped, and bear's black. Thunder and dragon fled and none of the friend's co-existed together again.

After the story, Chia and her terrified sisters huddled together in the bed unable to sleep. Hearing a strange noise during the night, Chia woke suddenly. Out of the blackness of the bedroom, she saw a single flame approaching. Chia let loose with a scalding scream. She sobbed and shook long after it was revealed that her older brother had snuck into their room with a hand held lighter to scare them.

Some months later, the trauma was re-lived after Chia's older sister, Moua had been badly burned on her arm, neck, and part of her face when the curtains had ignited from a candle set too close. Moua had been babysitting Chia, who was asleep in the bedroom.

Chia had heard Moua screaming and ran to Moua's room to see flames crawling up the sleeve of Moua's nightgown. Chia was only five, but she had run next door to the neighbor's, who called the fire department. Chia had tried to pour water on Moua, and fortunately, a neighbor had thrown a rug over her, dousing the fire. Everyone said she was a hero, but Chia had heard a nosy neighbor say that you should never throw water on a fire at first because it can make it worse. Chia had blamed herself for the scars on Moua's face and arms ever afterward.

In the few seconds it took for the horned creatures to reach them, Chia's hellish memories flashed through her, like a horrifying, sixty-second commercial for her greatest fears.

Then from behind her, Chia heard Carmen's voice, "Hold tight, Chia. We are about to go underground. Point your head downward, quickly. Flap your wings and kick back. Let go of the boat. Don't worry. They can't follow us now."

They were diving ever deeper into the purple sea of chulupurpla, like diving through a feather bed that never seemed to end. Fronds of chulupurpla brushed softly against them as they dove deeper and deeper. It was like diving into a lake of feathers with no bottom. But gradually, Carmen felt the sensation of shooting upward instead of down.

Carmen surfaced first, then Chia. They were now on the other side of the Sea of Chulupurpla and found that they could stand waist high in the purple featheriness, so Chia followed Carmen out of the silky sea onto the mushy purple bank.

Chia was blinking and sneezing, brushing tiny motes of purple fuzz from her face and arms. "Where are we?"

"Just over there is the crossroads to the Junction of Nine Paths." Carmen led them over an embankment and then pointed ahead into the distance where they could see the paths converging, surrounded by large rocks and boulders carved in the shapes of tigers and dragons.

"How do you know all this? How do you know where to go? How—"

Carmen pointed to her head. "It's all up here—part of my training when Tia and Tomas programmed me back on Earth at the hospital. You could say they downloaded me."

Chia grinned. "Are you a MAC or a P.C. now?"

Before Carmen could answer, a buzz-saw whining split the air and nine monster birds swooped out of nowhere, dive bombing them. Both girls hit the ground. Carmen could feel the hair on her neck raised by the cold air of the bird's attack. Then to her horror, they made another pass even lower this time, scooping Chia up and surging upward with her. All Carmen could see were Chia's arms and legs slapping the sky frantically. All she could hear was the disappearing echo of her screams.

Carmen leaped to her feet, shut her eyes as tight as she could, balling up her fists, and then sat down on her heels in a squat, her new tail and wings coiled close to her body. From this position Carmen bounced backward, landing back on her heels. She then opened her mouth and let the unfamiliar words pour forth. As the stream of ancient syllables tumbled out, Carmen's arms and legs began to ache horribly. Opening her eyes, she found she could turn her entire head all the way around and look behind herself. She was now in the body of an owl and wasted no time bounding up and into the air, soaring high over the theater of tree tops. Her keen yellow eyes could pick out the slightest movement below as the miles slipped away beneath her in minutes. Circling above the Junction of Nine Paths, Carmen picked out a tiny blur of pink and sailed down to the spot. There was Chia lying on the ground moaning, circled by the nine monster birds, their red eyes glowing like hot coals.

Carmen spread her wings and hovered just above them then dove straight downward. As she did so, the monster birds bared their fangs and a noxious smelling gas poured from their mouths. Carmen's muscles slackened, her head spun, and she found she had to retreat. Circling once again above, she sized up the situation. She could see one of the monster birds pecking at

Chia. There was no time to lose. Carmen remembered the BSC, now tucked into her feathers.

Almost immediately, she chanted, "Meso, meso, meso," and in response, the words came to her. "Go with the speed of light—charge!"

Once again she dove downward holding her breath through the fumes. Charging from one to the other, Carmen waved her BSC, emitting its own foul tasting fluid which she threw at the birds, moving around the circle at lightning speed. The last monster bird, however, had just enough time to grab Chia and swoop away once again.

Carmen swung herself in one flashing arc up into the sky and began to tumble in tight, super-hero fast somersaults, until the blur of her owl's body churned into a large billowy cloud. The monster bird carrying Chia could not out-fly the cloud and changed itself into a strong wind, with Chia tucked into its center, howling against the Carmen-cloud, which morphed now into a drop of water. Then the wind swiftly changed back into one of the flaming, hairy creatures, streaking toward the water with its fiery tail.

Swift as an arrow, the Carmen-water dropped down to the ground and soaked into the earth. Carmen could feel herself underground now, wondering what she should do next. Particles of Om dust, a purple, coffee-ground-like substance, cocooned her as she lay immobile, her mind empty of ideas.

As if from a great distance, she heard a muffled voice, "Carmen, Carmen. Where are you, Carmen?"

Carmen balled her fists up again and squeezed herself tightly into a knot. Then she pushed against the Om dust with all her might.

"Carmen! Look at you. You're covered with purple stuff."

Carmen was standing next to Chia now and they threw their arms around each other.

"Guess what, Carmen? The tables have turned, it seems. You have taken charge now and you saved *me*!"

"I did?"

"Yea. That thing couldn't hold onto me between the last two changes. Luckily, I fell into the chulu...whatever."

"And here you are on Om, *hermana*."

Suddenly everything went dark as a pair of hands laced around Carmen's eyes. "Tomas!"

She spun around and there stood her brother, this time dressed in a purple, jaguar-spotted body suit and vest, that looked made of bubble pack, and a helmet like half of a skull of translucent purple, with flying purple plumes. He was barefoot, with bunches of silver bangles around his ankles.

Tomas bowed before Chia. "Welcome to Om, Chia," he said through a crooked grin. Then he pointed to the spot where Carmen had surfaced and where now a single delicate tubular shape curled gracefully. "That's the lavender flower thing. It's an essence—we call them *not flowers* sometimes. We are very close to some powerful forces. That's why there is so much danger about. You made it grow there when you fell onto the ground as a drop of water which found the magical seed buried there. This is a very good sign. It means we have some extra protection for the rest of the rotation. We don't have days and nights here. We have rotations, and we don't think in terms of time passing during those intervals."

"Is it like when I draw or paint on Earth?" Chia asked, blushing ever so slightly.

"Yea, a lot like that. Sorry, I couldn't come to greet you or come to your aid since I've been called into active sky-painting duty. That's one of my jobs. We've got a lot to talk about, so let's get going. Follow me. I see that your new training kicked in just in time, Carmen," he threw over his shoulder as they trekked up a path that led through a winding, maze of purple plants, resembling undersea creatures. "You did very well, but you'll get more shape-shifting lessons later which should come in handy very soon."

"Yea, but it's sure good to see you. I was worried when Parajoflor took off and left us back there. Where'd she go anyway?"

Both girls had to jam to keep up with Tomas.

"It's chulupurpla harvest time and everyone works then. Our harvest is being interfered with this rotation. And the sky painters do double duty because they need to keep the skies painted since this serves the function of illumination, as well as beauty. But also Parajoflor had to take part in a special healing ceremony."

Carmen interrupted her brother, almost out of breath. "But shouldn't we be working on suppressing the dab? I thought things were getting worse here."

"The dab behaves kind of like a dormant volcano. Sometimes it erupts briefly or rumbles as if it will erupt fully and then we have to redouble all our efforts. The chanting and other ceremonies help, but if we had the plato, I think we could take care of the problem for good. But right now we can't afford to give up on our defensive efforts. Okay. Here we are." Tomas led them into a clearing where a double row of fountains, splashing a purple liquid, lined a pathway that led to another clearing, from which nine roads radiated outward like spokes of a half wheel. "Let's see how well your lessons went. You choose a road, Carmen. Your new enhanced intuition should give you the correct choice."

Carmen stood in the middle of the pathway and faced each road in turn. She was just about to tell Tomas that she had no idea which to choose when her foot jerked out and pointed toward the fifth road from the left. "That one," she said firmly.

Tomas tilted his chin and cocked his head like a parrot. "Are you sure, *perequita*?"

Carmen, who usually wallowed in indecision, surprised even herself. "I'm sure."

"*Muy bueno.* Good choice. Let's boogie. Hop on and I'll give you a ride."

All Carmen could see was Tomas patting the air behind him. "Hop on what? I don't see any ride."

Chia, however just jumped where Tomas pointed and, as she did so, landed on the rump of a great shaggy creature that materialized out of thin air.

"Air carriers," Tomas said, grinning as Chia wrapped her arms around his waist. "Part dolphin, part bird, and a special breed of Om horse—lots of shaggy air around a dolphin body with wings. They can fly, gallop, and swim both above and under water. We call them cabadejos. Watch this. Hang on Chia."

Tomas galloped across the sky until they came to a rainbow of colors that appeared to extend all the way to the ground. They slid down, with Chia's mouth open all the way. When they had landed back on the ground, the cabadejo reared up on its hind fin-legs and danced, Chia whooping with delight. Tomas shouted a command. The *cabadejo* got down on all fours, crawled over to Carmen, opened its wings, and hovered overhead like a huge, shaggy helicopter.

"Hop on, Carmen," Tomas called, as the cabadejo landed with a whoosh of air that stirred up purple Om dust.

"There's room for all three of us." Chia's voice sparkled.

Carmen got on behind Chia.

"Hold on, *chicas*. We're gonna swi-fly!"

Hugging low to the road, the cabadejo hovered and sped along, amazingly light and smooth. "It's programmed to move exactly six inches off the ground, so whatever bump in the road it comes to, there is an automatic adjustment. Now, don't worry, we're going underground here. We need to find one of the nine sacred spots, so we can talk without worrying about interference."

The ground opened like a mouth and swallowed them, but not for long. The cabadejo came to a halt in the middle of an underground grotto of sorts. Purple waterfalls spilled from ledges and niches throughout the interior. Patches of amethyst crystals were attached to the walls, ceiling, and floor, so that it sparkled and shone like the facets of a diamond. Crazy marvelous creatures with long, purple tentacles and rubbery hair like Parajaflor's, some spotted, others with elaborate patterned designs bumped and nosed up against glass windows set into the walls.

Tomas rubbed one palm with the fingers of his other hand and the cabadejo began to fade slowly, like a watercolor dissolving backward to a blank page.

Tomas waved his hand around. "Take an air chair, girls. Carmen, show Chia how it works."

Carmen demonstrated the air chair, and Chia followed, plopping down and not missing a beat.

"Okay. We got lotta stuff to cover. This is a first for Om. We've never pulled off bringing two guests to Om at the same time before. It's all because we've pulled together. We have some Hmongs and other Asians here on Om, working with us, along with other nationalities, too. And we've done lotsa amazing things by drawing on the different powers we all have and working together."

"Hmongs have a saying. 'One stick can't cook a meal or build a fence.' But where is everyone else?" Chia asked.

"We need everyone for the harvest of chulupurpla right now. And they're preparing for the ceremonies. You might get to meet some before you go. I'll only have a brief time with you before I have to go back to work. But everyone recognizes the importance of your work on Earth, and believe me, you've already helped us lots."

Chia's face lit up. "There's a Hmong folktale about nine evil dabs who are brothers and they try to ambush Yee Shee, a healer/magician. He changes into a bunch of animals. It ends in a battle of shape shifting. Can it be a coincidence that all this is pretty close to what we just went through?"

"Coincidences happen when you're ready for them. We're well aware of that fable, Chia. It helped us fight off the dabs who are on Om opposing us here. See, there's a dual battle taking place on both Earth and Om. We began to change you into creatures to help you fight back better when you first arrived, that's why the tail and feathers. That was just the start, but they acted more quickly than expected. All we know is that there is an important evil one on Earth and he or she is an official of some sort and part of a cabal of evil ones. We know that the Silver Real Estate Company is getting people deported so they can steal their valuables. So they must be connected to I.C.E. Tia had already notified us that they are searching for the plato. We think it might be an ancient Meso American, three-footed plate used by the Mayans to communicate with the spirit world. Since they want to buy Immaculate Motors, we suspect that possibly the plato is hidden there or information is stored there about the plato's whereabouts. We believe this plato could provide a portal to Om and also be an important tool to help us restrain the Ice Dab here on Om. But first, you will all have to put your powers together to help find me on Earth. This is your most important assignment yet. They pipe music into my cell all day and night to interfere with my powers and block me—horrible music."

Carmen frowned, turning to Tomas, "About those numbers—any more breakthroughs?"

"All I know is that your next hunch will be the correct one. We were all misled with the first two solutions. So pay attention."

Chia frowned again. "I'm sorry we messed up. Since the first chicken gave us the numbers, we naturally thought the second cartoon chicken was giving us the key to their meaning. Our bad."

"*No es su falta.* Actually, you did just right. In order to get it right, you had to fail the first two times. It's the way the evil ones seem to work. And in Mayan folk tales, they also use this same formula. You have to fail first in order to succeed. Carmen, we need to get that BSC taken care of and also you guys can get in on an important ceremony on Om. Two things are taking place—first, harvest, then the start of the new fires. When the end of the Earth solar calendar lines up with the end of an Om rotation, we have a special ceremony in which we light the fires to keep the worlds from ending. Even though we have other worries with the Ice Dab, this ritual must take place or things could get even worse."

Carmen heard a rumble and spun her head around.

"Don't worry. I've called up a cabadejo for each of us to take us to the fire ceremony. And, I know it's not New Year yet, but we are starting a ceremony today that will last into the solar New Year and Hmong New Year also. *Vaqueras,* jump on."

Tomas had hopped onto the cabadejo while he was talking, and now Carmen and Chia both did the same.

"Suave, Carmen. You did great. Now follow me," Tomas called over his shoulder, leading them from the grotto then up a trail cut into the crystal walls that circled up to the opening of the grotto. He held up his hand for a moment and they all halted. Tomas opened his palm, stroked it three times, cupped it to his ear, and listened. "It's safe, let's go."

CHAPTER 22

Instead of following the same path they had taken to the grotto, Tomas led them around a hillside to a wide plain, barren except for soft purple dust that powdered up as the cabadejos galloped across.

They stopped at the lip of a shallow, saucer-shaped crater. Carmen sneezed as some of the dust flew up. "Wow, that was fast, Tomas."

"It takes a few Earth hours to get here but time is different on Om. We should leave the cabadejos here. We'll need to walk in to the sacred circle." Tomas stroked his palm again nine times and the cabadejos dissolved. Then he reached inside his vest and drew out two flower things, which he pinned to first Carmen's and then Chia's shirts. "These are made to look like the lavender flower things, sacred to Om, representing one-ness."

"Hey," Chia piped up. "You're scratching your head, Carmen, and I don't feel it. We felt whatever the other one did before. Why was that, Tomas?"

"When we were shifting you to animal bodies at the same time, for speed, at that point, your senses blended. As for those new accessories—don't need them anymore." Tomas rubbed his palm again, and the tails and feathers were gone.

"Hey, I was starting to like the tail." Chia rubbed her bottom. "But the feathers were kinda itchy. No offense, T."

When they stepped up over the lip of purple land, Carmen saw piles and piles of purple chulupurpla strewn around the perimeter. A ring of red purple fires grouped at the center of the crater, surrounded a silvery dish about the size of a wading pool raised up on a crystal dais.

Grouped around each fire was a ring of drummers, who now pounded out hypnotic rhythms as other Omites, dressed in a wide array of purple garments joined in the rhythms, dancing and chanting.

People of all nationalities either danced, drummed, or swayed, and chanted, lost in a spell of somber celebration. They clustered in groups, through which tumbled small, puffy creatures covered with purple polka dots. One of them tumbled up to Tomas and the girls' feet.

"Meet Tikka," Tomas said. "From the Roly Poly clan. There are three main families of Omite creatures, the Roly Polys, The Chatterlings, and the Poke-a-Longs. They're sort of like Om pets, rolling around, having fun, playing tricks, and being silly. They remind us to think and see like children."

Tomas reached down and tickled Tikka's spongy belly. Tikka cooed, then curled up beside Carmen's toes, and nibbled softly, a feathery topknot bobbing.

Carmen gave a start and jumped. Then she too tickled Tikka's baby pot belly. She laughed. "Feels kind of like a nerf ball."

Another Roly Poly wrapped around Chia's ankle and nipped softly.

"Ooooh, that tickles," Chia said.

The creature began to make a chittering noise as it spun away from Chia into a fast purple blur, like a top, still making the ch, ch, ch sound.

Carmen grinned slyly. "Hey, Chia. It speaks Hmong."

Chia laughed. "Baby talk Hmong."

Catching up their hands, Tomas pulled both Carmen and Chia back to the rows of stacked chulupurpla. "This is the beginning of the ceremony. It's been going on for a while, but we are moving toward one of the main rituals where we give thanks to the spirits of our ancestors. See that dish like thing in the center?"

"Yea. What's that in the middle? Dust?" Chia asked.

"We've gathered the ashes of our many different ancestors. Each nationality chose one ancestor's ashes to place in the pot, and at the end of this part of the ceremony, we'll blend them all together. That will create a very powerful force to draw on for the harvest and for the lighting of the new fire and for the other work we must do. The nine fires around the center have all been lit consecutively, and when we are down to the last one, which should happen when you are both back on Earth, we'll have the culmination ritual. At that time, the new fire will be lit to take us into the next rotation. Look." Tomas pointed toward the crowd.

Out of the middle of the crowd an Indian chief rose, dressed in full ceremonial garb, with a feather headdress that fell like a waterfall to the ground. He began to speak in his native tongue.

Tomas rubbed his palm three times then and touched each of their fingertips. "Put them to your ears and you'll understand," he said.

Amazed, Carmen heard the chief's words. "'If the beasts were gone, man would die of a great loneliness of spirit.' Those are the words of my brother Chief Seattle. On Earth, people have grown farther and farther from nature, seeing it as separate from themselves, not as a living being with a soul. This separation from the stars, the animals, the hills, the lakes, and the plants is the source of all loneliness. As this split continues, men and women are themselves splitting apart, both within and from each other, searching for something outside themselves to complete them. And so they speed along the highways, past the lit up billboards urging them to fill those empty spaces with more things. The more the hole is filled, the emptier they become. Let us join now with each other, seeking the true circle of life—a new time of the spirit of love and oneness and connection with all living things, where we fold our energies and powers together and live in peace."

The chief tilted his head back then and opened his mouth wide to the skies. And where it yawned open, a lavender flower thing slowly unfurled. He spat it out and it took root beside the first fire. The chief spat beside each of the other eight fires, and eight more flower things sprang up. He then turned and bowed low to the crowd.

Tomas jumped to his feet as did others around the circle and began a circuit of the crowd with each person following the same ritual, where they rubbed their own palm three times, while the other person did the same, and then both palms were pressed together.

When Tomas rejoined the girls, he performed the same ritual with each of them.

"What does all this mean?" Chia asked, just before she went down, flat on her behind on the ground.

Tomas lunged to break her fall, too late. "Whoa, Chia, are you okay?"

Chia's eyes had gone washy. "I feel kinda weird, like my head is going to float off somewhere else."

"We better get you back to Earth then. Sometimes if you stay on Om too long, you can get Omsickness."

"Is that anything like homesickness?" Chia asked with a twinkling eye.

Tomas smiled. "Not really. It's more like sea sickness, but it makes you weak and spacey, and it can get worse, the longer you stay. I wanted to introduce you to some Omites, but there isn't time now. Quickly, come with me."

Tomas took both of their hands and led them through the crowd to the front where they could now see Parajoflor nestled down with her purple strings spread out around her, claw feet tucked under Indian style. Tomas sat down also and the two locked eyes as if in a psychic staring contest. Finally, Tomas rose, bowed slowly to Parajoflor, and said, "You better go now. Parajoflor is going to take you back, and during the journey, she'll implant a new BSC in each of your palms, where you can access it much easier. But don't lose that tooth, Carmen. It's important. I have only two more things to say. One: Beware of someone close to you—there is great danger at home. Two: Embrace someone close to you. A new identity is about to be revealed. Portilla will work with you on finding the plato and, as you know, she is working with the new shaman. She can fill you in on anything we didn't get to here. And she'll continue the important shape shifting lessons."

He rubbed his palm three times, touching his palm to Carmen and Chia's after they had done the same. As soon as they had done this, Tomas began fading as he had done before, and Carmen knew they had all stayed on Om as long as they dared.

Both girls climbed into Parajoflor's cushiony center and slipped into immediate, sweet oblivion.

CHAPTER 23

With a jolt, the elevator started back up, moving upward. Chia looked at Carmen and just shook her head. "Unbelievable! How long do you suppose we were gone? We better get back to Tia's room and see how she is."

The elevator doors swept open and they climbed out, blinking in the bright, false hospital light. The hospital clock said 8:40.

"Is that morning or night?" Chia asked.

"Morning I think. We should have only lost about five or ten minutes of Earth time. But let's hurry anyway."

At the third floor, they walked as fast as they could without running. Before they got to Tia's room, they heard the drumming. When they entered the room, Tia was sitting up in bed, her hand stretched out, holding the hand of a small girl who sat with her back to them. In the corner, the shaman from the other room, drummed from within a wreath of pungent smoke.

While Tia and the child were both chanting a low, monotonous tune, the candles between them and the shaman suddenly flickered. The child turned around, and with a gasp, both girls saw that it was True!

Tia patted True's hair. "When I heard her symptoms and that she had been sleepwalking, I suspected that True was the shaman in our midst, but I had to make sure."

The other shaman rose and pulled red string from his pocket, which he bit into two lengths and tied around Tia's wrists. Then speaking in Hmong, he removed some paper money from another pocket and, setting it in a metal dish on the floor, he threw a matchbook on top of it. The spirit money smoldered. To their amazement, the shaman drank the water in the bowl and sprayed it out into the room. He continued chanting. Standing before Tia, he spoke in Hmong some more, with True translating. He then bowed to Tia and both she and True bowed back.

Tia clapped her hands. "With everyone's help, I am much better. In fact, I feel years younger. True has helped me, and thank you Chia for bringing Mr. Yang to me. Are you related?"

"No, we are just from the same clan. I recognized him when I saw him in the room downstairs. He's a friend of my uncle's who is also a shaman. Chia bowed to the shaman and spoke in Hmong to him. "And now—" Chia was beaming at True. "We have a new shaman in our family, it seems. But how did you get here? Weren't you sick?"

True smiled mysteriously. "Uh huh, but different kind of sick. When I hear you talking to Carmen on the phone, I'm thinking I can help Tia. So after you left, I pretend to be asleep and then I call Choppo to come get me—I sneak out of the house and wait for him just like you did. Choppo bring me here and I work with the shaman, and Tia, she's better." True and Chia went to the shaman and spoke in Hmong. They all bowed to each other. True turned to everyone. "He has to go to do a blessing."

"Everyone thanked the twix neeb. Carmen said, "I'm sorry. We have no money to pay you..."

He spoke in Hmong again and Chia said, "He is not allowed to take money for his services. He says the bad spirit has been put off for now—he made a good bargain, but he doesn't think it's gone for good."

The fishy-lipped doctor came in and smiled broadly at everyone. "It seems that we have a miracle cure." He glanced at the shaman as he was leaving and raised his eyebrows slightly. "All the tests came back fine, and the good news is that we now believe there was no stroke. She was very dehydrated, which caused most of the problems, but we don't know what caused the blood pressure to drop. But at any rate, she can go home tomorrow. We want to keep her for observation one more night." The doctor stopped and looked at the children. "Are any of your parents coming to see about her? Will she have transportation tomorrow morning?"

"Um, yes." Carmen realized that she would have to take charge, so she fibbed a little. "My mother, her sister will be here soon. And we have a car to take her home."

Carmen paused, and Tia added, "Thank you doctor. I am feeling so much better. I would like to—I really think I'm ready to go home today."

The doctor gave a short laugh. "In a hurry to jump ship, I see, but I've ordered some meds for you tonight and we'll get you out of here in the morning." Briskly, he scribbled on the chart before he left.

Carmen could not contain herself any longer. "Guess what, Tia? Chia and I both just got back from Om. We saw Tomas there. And there was a ceremony and he talked about the plato that we need to find." Carmen and Chia both excitedly described their Om visit while Tia listened attentively. "I think they had a special healing ceremony for you on Om, Tia, and she was part of it—I mean Parajoflor—this awesome peacock kind of creature but with long purple things all over, and she gives us rides to Om. About the plato, though, Tia. Tomas thinks it could help them on Om. But where do we start to look for it?"

"Tomas and I think it may be hidden at Immaculate Motors, the reason that Silver wants to buy it so badly. You could start to look there." Tia shrugged.

Carmen told then about the shots fired at the house and Tia frowned. "Why don't you ask Septima?"

"Ask her about a plato?" Carmen couldn't hide her amazement. "Septima won't tell us anything, especially about stuff like that."

"Ah, but she may be more desperate now. Didn't you say she's having lots of *problemas*?"

"Yea, she's got an ugly rash and nothing seems to help. I suspect she's going to Mexico to get special medicine because it cheaper there. Maybe she thinks the doctors there can help her. Also, she's been very forgetful and confused about stuff. And I haven't even seen Teofilo for days. I think they were arguing over selling the business. Teofilo wants to sell—as usual, he doesn't think ahead—just get the money in his hot hand now."

Tia sighed heavily. "We have much to do. Finding the plato is important, *mija*. But we also need to find out where Tomas is being kept. Okay. We'll do this. I will do a *leccion especial* with all of you now. Two of you are now shamans in training and Chia is a shaman's assistant. Then you can go home to Immacuate Motors and start looking. I'll call you tomorrow after I get home, and we'll make more plans for finding Tomas. Now that we have True working with us, the extra power can maybe help us find him. Can you all sit down Indian style on the floor? Carmen, please light the candles."

They sat down, forming a circle, and everyone closed their eyes as Tia began to chant. Carmen's head swelled as light as a balloon. When she opened her eyes briefly, a faint purple glow filled the room. She heard a child's voice counting and the bed jerked as Tia suddenly swayed in it. "*Uno, dos abrochan mi zapato. Tres, quarto, cierran la puerta.*" She grinned foolishly, rocking back and forth on the bed.

"Look at Tia," Carmen whispered to Chia.

Chia's eyes opened then even wider like a goldfish. "Her hair—it's brown and she looks smaller in that bed."

"True-tie tootie, c'mere," Tia called in a sing song voice, as she flipped the covers playfully away.

True bounced over and they whispered and giggled together like schoolgirls. Carmen and Chia tossed mystified looks at each other.

"Hey, what's going on, True?" Chia demanded finally.

"Tell you in a minute." True went back to whispering. At last, she and Tia touched fingertips in a spider dance and True motioned them to the doorway.

"What's wrong with her? She's acting like she's eight years old," said Carmen still in a whisper.

"Our magic is very strong—maybe little too much. We make her well, but she is now like little girl. But not last too long. We better go now. She sleeps, it will help."

Tia nibbled on her long braid and a big smile broke loose, spreading into an enormous yawn.

"We're gonna go now, Tia." Carmen went to her aunt to give her a hug, followed by Chia and True.

At the doorway, they turned again and waved. Tia waved, humming her "Uno, dos, buckle my shoe," tune.

In Choppos's cab on the way back home, Chia kept staring at True as if she was a stranger. "Hey, True, how did you know Choppo's number?"

"Little chicken told me," True said. When Carmen and Chia's mouths almost came unhinged, she added, "Okay. Not chicken—bird come to me in my fake sleep and told the number."

"Holy jalapeno! Work on that plato tonight in your sleep, True. And work on those other numbers. Manana," Carmen called to them as she jumped from the cab and waved.

CHAPTER 24

Carmen nearly fell over her own feet as she raced up the steps of the porch. It was early afternoon now, and she hadn't eaten since breakfast. She wanted to talk to Septima and maybe convince her to help her look for the plato. At the door, she fumbled with her keys then stopped. Something was not right.

A burned metal smell drifted in the air. The door felt jammed, and when she shoved against it, something seemed to be blocking it. Pushing with all her weight, she managed to move aside what she now saw was the living room rug wadded up. The house was a mess, lamps and tables turned over, couch cushions on the floor, the batting torn into. Carmen sucked in her breath then slowly backed out the door. Robbed—they'd been robbed—and maybe the robbers were still inside.

Carmen jumped from the porch, raced across the street to Oso's, and pounded on his door. No one answered, but just as she turned, wondering if she should try another neighbor, Septima's car pulled up to the curb.

"We've been robbed!" Carmen hollered as Septima helped Rosa from the front seat.

Rosa's face drained of color and her hands fluttered to her chest like crippled birds. Septima's face had a scared, confused look that Carmen had never seen there before.

"I went to Oso's to call the police, but no one's home. Should I try that house nex—"

"Just hold on here." Septima had begun to mutter to herself in Spanish.

"They could still be inside," Carmen hissed under her breath to Septima, hoping that Mami hadn't heard.

Mami looked like she would topple over any minute.

Septima reopened the car door and helped Mami back inside. "You stay with Rosa. I'll go to the neighbors." But despite this, Septima didn't make a move. She stood in the street, rubbing her chin. "Where's that Teo? He was supposed to follow us," was all she said.

When Teofilo pulled up in his faded red truck a few minutes later, she was still standing there muttering to herself. "Teo, *gracias de dios. Donde tiene Teo sido*? Check out *la casa*. Robbers could still be inside."

Teofilo had the wooly, wild eyed look of a trapped beast. "Maybe we call la policia, *vieja*."

Septima seemed to regain some of her old fire. "No, no Teo. *Mirada en la casa primero*. Ach! Just forget it. I go myself!"

As she stamped toward the door, Teofilo grabbed a hammer from a pile of oily ropes and tools in the bed of the truck and ran to block her. "Calm down, *vieja*." Then, with hammer raised overhead, Teofilo shouted, "Stand back everybody. I'm going in."

Carmen almost burst out laughing. *Now Teofilo goes into SWAT mode*, she thought.

Only a few minutes later, he came to the door and waved them inside. "What a mess. *Aquellos anos*."

"Teo! *Mire su boca*! No need for that language."

They all stood in the living room surveying the scene when suddenly Septima yanked open the hall closet and pulled out her raincoat which still hung on the rack. She felt along the hem and released a huge sigh of relief. "Gracias de dos dios. My dinero is still here. And look...the TV, the computer—all aqui." She had crossed to Teofilo's study. "Everybody look around. See if anything is gone."

They set about, trying to restore some kind of order and to see what might be missing. It took the rest of the afternoon to straighten and inventory the household goods, but they could come up with nothing that was gone, except for some papers in Teofiolo's office. Septima's jewelry was even torn apart, but nothing was taken. They appeared to have come in through an unlatched window in the bathroom. Some of the cars Teo had been cleaning up in the back had been jimmied open and ransacked, as well as his work room and the trailers. Carmen could hear Teofilo cussing up a storm behind the house. She counted to five, and sure enough, Septima stormed out there and let fly salvos of angry Spanish that Teofilo returned. Septima, always so worried about appearances, was making it worse by trying to shut him up.

Her face, when she returned, was still an angry mask, but somewhat cracked. Teofilo just banged now and slammed instead of yelling. Septima kept shaking her head. "*Muy curiosa.*"

Carmen did not think it was curious at all. It fit with what Tomas had said about Silver Realtors or the evil ones. If they were looking for the plato, they had no need to steal a measly old TV or a computer that was out of date. The stereo which was broken already would be worthless as would Teofilo's old tools.

Finally they sat down to a meal of tamales that one of Teofilo's clients had given them and some warmed up beans. It tasted delicious to Carmen, and she ate as much as she dared with Septima's eagle eye on her plate. Septima talked about the trip to Mexico, which seemed to brighten her spirits. They would pack that night and leave in the morning in a borrowed van. She wanted to leave as early as possible to avoid having to spend more than one night on the road. They could stay in Sonora with some friends, but there was no money for motels. Chattering on, she seemed oblivious to Rosa's drowsiness and Carmen's halfhearted attention. Teofilo didn't bother to hide his own yawning, bleary-eyed disinterest.

"So, Tia Septima." Carmen finally got a word in edgewise. "Did you see Aunt Portilla today?"

Septima's eyes flicked at Carmen like a whip. "There was no time for that today. She's gotten along fine without us all this time. And, anyway, we had to go to the store and appointments with the *abogado* and the bank. How did you expect to get money for food and such while we are gone? Turn on the money faucet maybe?"

Carmen decided to zero in on what was most important right then. "So what did the *abogado* have to say?"

"He said that Tomas was taken downtown to Homeland Security to the detention center where they process illegals before deporting them. He thinks Tomas is in Mexico, and we will try to find out more when we are there. The *abogado* has an *oficina* in San Miguel and we can maybe find out more from them. Now, we have to get to packing so we can leave early manana." Septima's nails raked across an already inflamed patch on her upper shoulder and she scraped her chair back, almost knocking it over as she hurried from the kitchen.

"He's just putting us off again," Carmen said. "But anyway, I went to the hospital today to see Portilla, and she's okay now. They thought she had a stroke," Carmen slung at Septima's back, following her into the living room, waiting for the spin and the dropped jaw, which came sure as tock follows tick. Before Septima could speak, Carmen hurried on. "She thinks that the Silver Real Estate people are trying to get their hands on an old plato cuz they do that—they deport illegals and take their property. And why do they want this place so bad? It's not much value right now. You know anything about a plato, Tia? And if it's true, the robbery could be tied to that. We should call the police—"

Septima, frantically scratching, screamed, "*Disparate*! This is the very reason I did not want you messing with Portilla—crazy ideas. *Y no policia*. They work with the ICE. We'll find out more when we go to Mexico. Now, go talk to Teofilo, Carmen. He has things for you to do while we are gone. And, of course, you'll keep the house up, water the plants, and take care of Rosa. She has the money for food and a few things you might need. But don't go hog wild at the grocery store."

"What about the plato?"

"The only platos I know about are dirty ones in the sink." Septima made a shooing motion but her frown deepened.

Carmen went to check on her mother first. She was staring out the window, pale and quiet in the stuffed chair squeezed into a corner of their room. Rosa offered Carmen a weak, wrinkled leaf of a smile. "Septima will find out for us in Mexico what we need to know."

I doubt it, Carmen thought, but not wanting to squelch any of Rosa's hopes, she just pasted a smile on her face and went to find Teofilo. Maybe she could pry some bit of information from him.

CHAPTER 25

The sound of heavy rain woke Carmen from a jumble of vague travels on a bike trekking up and down an unfamiliar landscape. There was a ghost town where a circus was hiding out from a mean sheriff with an enormous, blue white handlebar mustache that hung down to his silver holsters. Carmen helped a midget hide in an old washtub, then held hands with twin contortionists dressed in matching gold satin costumes. They giggled and see-sawed Carmen between them as they tramped through an abandoned drive-in theater, before disappearing into the screen, leaving Carmen sitting in a pile of broken plates scattered across the ground.

Carmen lolled in the dream for a few moments then her mind drifted. Teofilo had been no help last night, as usual. He had asked her to take calls for him and get phone numbers of clients who might need work done. She must also set the garbage out by the curb every Friday. And stack the mail on his desk. And if anything *"muy importante"* came up, to call him at the number he'd scrawled on a piece of paper. He said they would know how to get ahold of him. She'd asked if he knew anything about an old plate or any old Mexican pottery or statues stored at Immacuate Motors.

"No-o," he'd said, making it two words. "Ask Septima. And don't loan Oso any of my tools. He never brings them back and then he says he never borrowed them." He had turned away from her and began pounding furiously on his work bench.

The next morning, the house was quiet, so Carmen threw back the covers and crept from bed, hoping that Septima and Teofilo had already left, which they had. She found two boxes clumsily wrapped in wrinkled Christmas paper and an adios note left on the kitchen table, with half a box of powdered donuts.

A twinge of guilt powdered her lips with the sugar from a donut, but there had been no money for any gifts for her tia and tio, much less for themselves. The next day would be Christmas Eve, and a sudden sadness large as a wooly mammoth snuck out of nowhere and pounced. When the tears trickled, she tried to push them back but then gave in and let them sweep her out to sea where she rocked into a rising swell of grief. She didn't care about the lack of gifts, but all the other losses—Papi, Tomas, their little rented house where they'd at least managed a small scraggly tree—piled together in a huge box tied up with the glossy bow of inconsolable sorrow. The cold dampness and gray, lusterless light coming in the windows didn't help.

Carmen was so wrapped up in this package of self-pity that at first she didn't feel the hand on her shoulder. "Carmentita, don't cry, *mija*." Mami was shivering in her thin gown, and her large, coltish eyes tugged at Carmen wistfully. "*Que es incorrecto, poco cordero?*"

"*Nada*, Mami, *nada*." Carmen tried to straighten her face but knew it was not cooperating. "It's just that it's Christmas, and we don't have a tree or any money for a Christmas dinner and then Tomas..." She felt the tears slipping, took a big gulp of air, and hiccuped.

For some reason Mami hiccupped, and they both hiccupped together.

Carmen found that she was laughing right through the tears and hiccups. "Mami, you're too much. Who ever heard of sympathy hiccups?"

"Pull your orejas, the..." she hiccupped again. "The...what are these?"

"Earlobes, Mami. Okay, together now—Pull."

They both pulled their ear lobes and waited. A full minute passed before they both hiccupped together again, which set them off to laughing once more.

"Remember, *mija*, when we made Christmas chains from colored paper? Is something here we could do that with?"

"Let me snoop around and see what I can find," Carmen said, realizing this was the perfect excuse to look for information about platos or other artifacts.

Rosa looked worried. "Maybe you should not snoop, *mija*."

"No worry, Mami. I won't snoop. I'll investigate."

Rosa hiccupped and they both laughed again.

They spent the day quietly, Rosa crocheting and watching her telenovelas and Carmen investigating. All she found was some more letters in Spanish, that she squirreled into her backpack to take to Tia's, and a box of musty things it looked like Septima had been saving for years—old broken rosaries, rust-corroded keys, baby shoes, death card notices, squashed hats with torn netting, a biscuit tin of old buttons, strips of leather, *Lives of the Saints* calendars from 1987 and 1990, a stack of postcards with hand painted pictures of the California Missions, sleeping peasants in sombreros book ends, and strangely enough, a set of false teeth. Carmen held up the teeth and made them hiccup, causing Mami to roll her eyes and cluck, "*Los santos perdonenos.*"

Septima had stocked the cupboards with some groceries, mostly Top Ramen, cans of beans, and cereal. For dinner Carmen boiled two eggs and dropped them in two steaming bowls of Top Ramen.

Rosa made hot cocoa, and they made a small fire in the fireplace with some logs that Septima had been saving. Snug in the warmth of the fire and the sweetness of the chocolate, Carmen closed her eyes and let herself slide into a warm sea of contentment. All the "if onlys" bubbled to the surface, but she shoved them back down.

Outside, the rain ticked on the sidewalks with the monotony of a clock.

"Hey, Mami, let's sing some Christmas songs—wait." Carmen clapped her hands. "I need to work on my Spanish, so you sing in Spanish and I'll follow."

Rosa smiled weakly and began to sing, but her voice wheezed and the song dribbled into a coughing fit. "*Mija*, I don't feel so good. *Tengo un dolor malo en mi...*" She rubbed her chest. "Y podria ser la ciatica. My hip, *mija*—the pain is—" Rosa winced. "And I have also a bad headache...*dolor de cabeza y estomago*...the stomach."

"Uh oh, maybe my cooking?"

"No, no, *mija*. *Muy dellicioso pero, yo...*not so good. *Lo siento*, Carmentita."

Rosa looked so troubled that Carmen hurried to reassure her mother that it was fine and she was tired herself.

"Why don't you call your *amigas manana, mija*? Chichal..."

"It's Chia, Mami. Isn't Chichal the stuff Septima hides from Teo?"

Rosa looked sheepish. "*Si*, corn liquor."

Carmen rolled her eyes. "She gets teased enough about the Chia Pets. But, sure, I'll call her tonight and see if she and True can come over. Now, I'm going to make you some tea and help you to bed."

"*No, no gracias, no te.*"

While Rosa prepared for bed, Carmen quickly dialed Tia's number.

Her aunt answered on the second ring. "Tia, *muy bien*. They let you come home. Are you okay?"

"*Si. Bueno.* Choppo took me to the store today, and I'm feeling stronger. I even did some spell work and meditation today, and I think I'm getting closer to finding the plato. I want to work with True some more. I have not been able to communicate very well with Tomas either. So, Saint Septima's left for Mexico?"

"This morning. I asked her about a plato, but she didn't know anything—at least she said she didn't. She and Teofilo had a huge fight before they left—one of the worst they've ever had—and she wouldn't let me call the police either about the break in."

"Just as well, mi Caramelo. We don't know who we can trust. I think the realtors are in ca...ca...how do you say?"

"Cahoots. Yea. I think so, too. I'm worried about Mami, though. She isn't feeling too good tonight. I wanted to sing Spanish Christmas songs with her. You know how she loves that, but she said her hip, her head, and her stomach are hurting. And she's got a bad cough and pain in her chest."

"If you can find chamomile tea, mix in some Yerba Buena and a touch of whiskey, if Septima has any. Try to get her to take that. And try to give her a limpia. Remember how I taught you. And make sure she keeps warm. I'll come over tomorrow to see her. Very soon we'll make a search party for the plato. It must be there if the realtors are so dead set on buying the place. Call Chia and try to get them to come over also. *Buenas noches y* drink some of that *te especial* I made for you. To help you work in your dreams. Right now all we have to help Find Tomas is those numbers."

Carmen made Rosa's tea and then brewed her own, using the herbs Tia had given her, and carried the two cups into the bedroom. "Look, Mami, I made tea for both of us. Please have a cup with me before you go to sleep."

After Carmen convinced her mother to drink the tea, she got her to bed, took the egg she had prepared, and held it above Rosa's body.

"What's that for?" Rosa asked in an almost whisper.

"For a limpia, Mami." Carmen tried to sound matter-of-fact.

Rosa looked puzzled. "How do you know this, *mija*?"

"Just relax, Mami. I'll tell you when I'm done." Starting at the top of her head, Carmen moved the egg over Rosa's body, front and back, slowly, chanting and singing softly. Just as Carmen had hoped, Rosa's lids fluttered then closed.

When Carmen was done, she tiptoed out of the room and called Chia to ask her to come over the next day. Chia said they could come for only a short while since relatives were visiting and the ceremonies for Hmong New Year were in full swing.

"Everyone's making a big fuss over True being a shaman," she said before she hung up.

Almost as soon as Carmen put the phone down, it rang again. Thinking it must be Chia still, she lifted the receiver, "Hola, sistah—"

There was only silence on the line.

"Chia, is that you?"

Silence.

Then a raspy, gutteral voice said, "*Si usted permanence alli, usted esta in el peligro. Salga ahora.*"

This was followed by a loud slamming sound and then another voice that sounded familiar. "Carmen, get out now. You're in danger."

And then the line went dead.

Shakily, Carmen hung up the phone. For a moment, she sat still, frozen to the chair, then she jumped up and ran to check all the doors and the windows. She double checked the bathroom window which Teofilo had secured with screws and window locks before they left for Mexico.

Finally, she sat cross legged before the fire and repeated, "*Meso, meso, meso. CH'ULEL SAK-NIK-NAL CH'ULEL SAK-NIK-NAL.*"

Carmen waved a lit sage bundle in a figure eight and then let her head fall forward. She began to feel light and dreamy. A wet pebble moon smell filled the room, and Carmen opened her eyes. The fire was flickering brilliant shades of purple. Her palm began to itch, and Carmen remembered then to remove her BSC and then the coin and stroke it three times.

Tomas spoke. '*We're getting closer, Sis. I think Tia is about to find the plato. And in the middle of our harvest ceremonies on Om, right after we lit the new fire, we had a volcito. It's the first one since the last ten rotations—kind of like a volcano erupting, but it comes from deep inside Om. It's a series of ice and fire storms that follow each other almost immediately. We all had to go underground for a while, and a some of our crop was destroyed. I haven't been able to stay on Om for very long because of weakness. How are things there?*'

'*Septima left for Mexico yesterday. We're having a storm here, too. Mami's sick again, and I just got a strange phone call. I thought I heard your voice, Tomas, telling me to get out because I'm in danger.*'

Tomas was silent for a moment. '*It wasn't me, Carmen. You and Mami need to get out of there, though. If Septima and Teo are gone, I don't like you two there alone. For tonight, I'll give you a protective spell to cast around the border of the house. Then I'll contact you tomorrow. So be alert for my signal. Okay, here's the spell. First you must take your BSC out, hold it in front of a mirror, and capture the moon there. Then circle the house three times, reflecting the moon toward the house, setting up a protective lunar shield. Go in the house and unlock all the doors. This is very important. You must show the evil ones that you are not afraid. If they come to the house tonight, they'll find they are unable to cross the protective barrier. If they try to cross, they'll experience excruciating pain. Good luck, periquita. We'll talk manana.*'

When Carmen opened her eyes, the fire had shrunk to white hot coals. She rose, worked the flap up on her palm, and took out the BSC. In the bathroom, she found a small hand mirror. When she stepped outside, the rain had stopped. Light from the newly risen moon washed over the lawn, glazing the tips of the wet grass to a silver sheen. She followed Tomas' instructions, captured the moon in her mirror, and flashed it toward the house. It took some climbing over fences and making her way through wet brush and shrubs, but she finally circled the grounds three times. Heading toward the house, she heard a rustle in the bushes and nearly jumped out of her skin. Heart slamming in her chest, she ran toward the porch then skidded down to her knee in the wet, mushy lawn. But she picked herself up. As she closed the door behind her, she had to fight not to lock it. Every molecule in her body wanted to slam the dead bolts home.

Carmen changed from her damp clothes into a flannel gown and lay stiffly on the pallet next to Mami's bed, finally drifting into a fitful, light sleep, from which she kept awakening. The wind shook the trees and somewhere a gate smacked back and forth. Once Carmen was sure she heard voices, but when she rose and peeked from behind the curtains, she saw nothing but moonlight and darkness.

When morning came, Carmen felt achy and unrested. Rosa, who had risen early all her life, was boiling water in the kitchen for tea, shivering in the morning chill.

Carmen tried to scold her back to bed, but even though she looked haggard and pale, Rosa would only go as far as the living room and Teo's chair.

"What is it you used to say about the cows, Mami?"

"*Ningunas vacas, ningunos cuidado,*" Rosa said half-heartedly.

"Si, Mami. No cows, no cares." Carmen wrapped a serape around Rosa's shoulders and made another healing tea for her then rolled up some heated tortillas with cheese inside. "Feliz Navidad, Mami," Carmen said, handing Rosa the plate, with the quesedilla and the last powdered sugar donut, but she barely touched her food and listlessly sipped the tea before dozing off in the chair again.

Carmen was just glad they had survived the night, and when the doorbell rang around 10:00, her heart went bouncing.

CHAPTER 26

There stood a jaguar on the doorstep, holding a sack of shiny presents, with Choppo right behind, lugging a box of groceries.

"Hey, let us in. This bird ain't getting any lighter," he growled.

"Bird, what bird?" Carmen said, hugging her aunt, the mask feathers tickling her nose.

"Surprise—Christmas *comida*. We have tamales and a turkey and yams and we'll make cookies."

"Mami, look we have Santa Jaguar."

Rosa straightened up in her chair with a look of alarm.

"Mami, I have a big surprise for you. Do you know who this is?" Carmen waved her hand at Tia, who had removed the mask.

Rosa clapped her hand over her mouth. "Portilla!" Excitedly, she began to babble in Spanish with her sister.

They all ended up in the kitchen, Carmen brewing tea for everyone, and Tia getting to work on the turkey, while Choppo peeled potatoes. When he was done, he pulled out his jack knife and a plug of wood and sat in the corner whittling to keep his "hands busy" which was, Carmen figured, also meant to keep his mind off of drink. When the meal was underway, Rosa, who had been settled in a chair in the corner, stood up and burst into tears.

"Mami, what is it?"

"*Soy tan feliz solo encontrar mi hermana.*"

Tia hugged Rosa so hard she almost fell over and did fall into a coughing fit.

Rosa's face was pale with dark circles around her eyes. "*Pero, me hago little bit consado* now."

"Here, I'll help you lie down. We'll work on a healing for you, *hermana pequena.*"

After Tia had fixed Rosa up in the bedroom, she returned to the kitchen, shaking her head. "I don't like the looks of it. She's so weak. I hope Chia can bring True over soon so we can work together on a healing ceremony."

Carmen tried to keep her face from falling. "I did the best I could."

"Actually, you helped a lot. Her voice sounds stronger. But this needs all of our powers together."

Carmen tried to soften her face, but it defied her.

"Come on now, *mija*. You must keep your own ego out of the healing, or you can affect the process."

Carmen knew she was right. "They're gonna try and come by, if they can get away from the relatives." Carmen paused. "Uh, Tia, what did you and Mami talk about earlier?"

"We both realized that Septima was the one who has kept us apart all these years. Your mami and I used to be very close years ago. Then life took us on different paths, but when Rosa came back to live with Septima after your papi died, I thought she didn't want to see me, and she thought the same about me. You can guess who gave us that idea."

"And they kept me from you too. But, Tia—something else. I talked to Tomas last night on the BSC, and he thinks Mami and I are in big danger here. He wants us to get out as soon as we can. I had to do a protection ritual and there was a strange phone call using Tomas' voice. But where can we go?" Carmen had been holding back her fear and worry and now they came out in a rush all her face.

Tia wrapped her arms around Carmen. "*No preocupese, bebe.* We'll make Rosa better. If you did the spell, that should help. And you'll come to my place tomorrow. I just have to get some things ready."

Carmen heard a racket on the porch then which turned out to be Chia and True singing, "Jingle Bells, Jingle Bells, magic spells, magic spells, open up the door."

Carmen was surprised to see both girls wearing lipstick, powder, and eye makeup. True looked like a sweetly painted confection and Chia looked several years older, her dark brown eyes larger, her features more defined.

"Can't stay too long. We put on our makeup already, but we still have to put our dresses on—takes a while—but since the family knows about True now, she's been studying with our uncle, the shaman."

"Look, Tia brought us a Christmas dinner and presents, too. But Mami's not well again and we're hoping to do a healing ceremony."

Tia had busied herself pulling objects out of a cloth bag decorated with feathers and beads: her pipe, bowls, jars of mysterious liquids, herbs, candles and a bag of corn.

She stopped. "I think Rosa has *susto*—her soul has been lost or stolen and we must do a soul retrieval for her. True, come sit by me." Tia patted a spot on the floor in front of the fire. "Carmen, you and Chia can start the cookie dough while True and I work out the curing spells."

Carmen suspected that Tia didn't want Chia to feel left out since she was the only one now who wasn't studying to be a shaman. While they stirred flour, sugar, and eggs in a bowl, Carmen told Chia about her conversation with Tomas. Choppo pulled out a harmonica and warbled out Mexican boleros and a clumsy Jingle Bells.

Chia took paper and scissors and cut out cookie patterns of a jaguar, a bird, a quarter moon, and one she said was a Roly Poly from Om. She made two other shapes, which she said were Hmong good luck symbols.

As the cookies filled the air with sugary warmth, they peeked around the door to see True and Tia mixing up something in a small, thick bowl Tia had taken from her bag. Tia was showing True how to measure the amounts of different oils.

Carmen jumped when she turned to see Rosa standing in the doorway to the living room, frowning.

She looked both perplexed and disturbed. "*Que es esto*? Carmen, ...what is going on *aqui*?"

"Mami, you look a little better. How are you feeling?"

"*Estoy bien. Pero participa usted en la brujeria durante las vacaciones de Septima*?"

"Rosa, calm yourself," Tia said from the living room floor. "We do nothing against the Lord. And this is not witchcraft. It is for a healing ceremony like the ones Pepita used to perform, remember?"

Rosa did not look completely convinced, but her frown eased up some. "Si, Pepita—a *curendera*. No harm, I guess." Rosa took a deep breath in. "I think your bird *es hecha cocinan-dose*."

"It certainly smells like it's done—time for us all to have a feast. Can you girls stay and eat?"

Chia shook her head sadly. "No, afraid not. We've been eating all day. Hmong New Year is one long party of food and music and visiting, and we have to go get our dresses on now."

"In that case, we'll open presents first because there might be some for you girls, also." Tia held up her hand when Carmen looked dismayed. "And don't worry about not having gifts. You both already gave me your gift at the hospital." Tia turned to Rosa. "This little one is a *curendera* also. She helped to heal me and I am much better."

They moved into the living room, and Tia handed around the presents, her face rosy as an excited child's.

Rosa opened hers first because they all insisted—a new wooly, velour robe which she promptly wrapped around herself with a wide smile.

Choppo held up a knitted wool cap and a pound of coffee. He laughed. "*Gracias*, my engine starter."

Carmen and Chia both received amulets of feathers and bone and True received a mortar and pestle.

Tia nodded. "For preparing the herbs."

True smiled and bowed, but Carmen detected a shadow of disappointment. After all, she was still a five year old.

But Tia must have seen it too because she said, "Put the handle of the pestle in your mouth and blow, *nina*."

True did so, and the lilting melody of a nightingale filled the room. True beamed and each time she blew on the pestle, a different string of notes filled the air, as if a flock of birds had swooped out of the trees stringing their songs around them.

Carmen bit her lip. "But there's nothing for you, Tia."

Choppo stood up. "*Que es esto*, then?" He took a box wrapped in a bandana from behind his back and held it forth to Tia who unwound the cloth and held up a beautifully carved wooden jaguar, painted with black and gold spots and a crimson mouth roaring in a wide yawn. "*Muy linda...muy linda*," Tia kept repeating.

"*Es de nada...*" Choppo's dark complexion turned a deep, purple red. "I keep my hands busy these days so they don't double cross me."

"We need *musica*." Tia clapped her hands. "*Su armonica*."

She tapped her feet as Choppo played a bouncy bolero and True joined in with her bird flute.

"Look, the Mexican chicken—hat dance." Carmen grabbed Chia and swung her around, sending her flying.

Abruptly, Choppo stopped playing. "*Escuche*—Listen."

A jingling noise was coming from the porch. And before anyone could open the door, Flora Linda poured in, dressed in a long, black velvet skirt with a sparkly pink jacket, multi-colored ski cap with flaps and a long tassel, the usual pink, feather boa flung around her neck, and a necklace of bells and blinking Christmas lights. Balancing a stack of gold and silver packages, without a word, she tossed her presents one by one until everyone had one.

"Oped, oped, oped," she mumbled in her croaky voice.

"Open yours first, Chia, cuz you guys have to go," Carmen said.

Chia fumbled with the wrapping paper, but when she opened the lid of the box inside, it was empty. She looked up, puzzled. "Um...there's nothing inside," she said hesitantly.

Carmen thought she heard a mewing noise, though, and sat up straighter, searching the room with curious eyes.

Flora Linda began to giggle, and the girls looked at Tia for an explanation, but she sat on the floor with her eyes half closed, as if in one of her trances.

True had opened her box now which was also empty but when she lifted the lid, a whoosh of air puffed out. "It's my power," she said, her eyes following an invisible draft that brushed the curtains and moved around the room.

Carmen had opened her box now, releasing the sound of flapping wings. "It's our power animals, *amigas*. We can call on them when we need extra help and to contact the spirits."

"So…mine is a cat?" Chia sounded unsure.

"And mine must be a bird," Carmen added . "And what is True's?"

True peered down into her box and then wrinkled her nose, as if something had landed there. "It's a dragonfly."

Tia opened her eyes. "Your power animals are important. They will always be there when you need them, but don't forget to honor them. I know you girls have to leave, but can you stay for just a few more minutes while we do a soul retrieval cere-mony for Rosa? True and Flora Linda have been working with me to mix our magic."

They agreed and Tia talked Rosa into lying down on the floor with her feet to the east as she sprinkled corn in a circle around her. True laid down her pestle and began to drum slowly and softly on a small drum Tia had taken from her bag. Carmen lit some incense and placed it at Rosa's head then waved a bun-dle of white sage over Rosa, moving from head to toe, then from all four corners of the room, and then from above her down to the middle of her navel. They all linked hands, sitting on the floor around Rosa, joining in on a chant led by Tia.

One by one, they called on their power animals to join the healing. Suddenly, True broke loose from the circle almost as if she had been yanked from above. Flora Linda had gotten down on the floor on all fours and was pawing the rug and snorting like a horse. True jumped on her back and Flora Linda began to buck, at first in steady jerks, then harder and more violent. True tapped out a rhythmic dance, shaking a rattle in one hand and a finger bell in the other. Earlier she and Tia had placed nearby a bowl of rice, a burning joss stick, and a bowl of water into which they had dropped the spirit money they had burned. True had drunk most of the ashes and then had dabbed some on each of them.

Now she hung on, her eyes closed in two dainty slits as Flora Linda twisted and bucked. When True's eyes flew open, a wild gurgle rose from her mouth. Tia jumped up and reached for True, just as she flew backward, hard and fast, off of Flora Linda's back. Tia placed True on the floor, where she lay limp, then stepped to the door and flung it open.

"Come home," she called out the door. "Rosa is waiting for you. We all are waiting. You have been gone so long. Come home to where we love you and wait for you."

She then turned and signaled to the girls to join her and they formed two lines at the doorway. Tia took her eagle feather and swept warm air into the room, even though it was still freezing cold outside. Just as the door slammed shut, Rosa sat up with a jerk.

"I'm hungry. *Donde es* the stinking bird done?" Rosa said in a loud voice, unlike any that Carmen had ever heard coming from her before.

CHAPTER 27

A fter Chia and True had left, Carmen remembered the presents from Septima and brought them in from the kitchen. "Open yours first, Mami," she said, handing Rosa the wrinkled package.

Rosa undid the paper, revealing a soap dish in the form of two praying hands, with the words *Jesus Cleanse Me* on the cuff. Rosa seemed pleased, but when Carmen opened hers, a paper weight with a plastic Virgin Mary inside, she knew that Septima had gotten them at the dollar store.

"*Yo* feel so *mal*. We no buy the gifts *para* Teo and Septima."

"We didn't get any gifts for them," Carmen corrected, then hurriedly added, "We can still give them gifts on the day of the Magi in January. You look much better, Mami. Tia thought you had *susto*—you know, soul loss?"

"*Si*. I know *susto*. Is possible."

"Tia says it can come from a fright. Did you have a fright, Mami?"

Rosa hesitated, started to speak, and then Carmen saw her eyes begin to glaze over. On a hunch, Carmen acted quickly.

"Mami, could it have something to do with Sears?"

Rosa's hands flew to her face and she began to sob. "It was so…so long. *Su papa y yo vaya ayi to mira the washers*. I wash the clothes in the tub. Teo say there was *credito a* Sears. *Pero*,

we fill up the *papels y la senorita,* she call on the telefono…"
Rosa began to babble in Spanish through her tears.

Carmen put her arms around her mother. "Please, Mami,
try in English."

Finally Rosa resumed. "Never do I forget." But she was
back to Spanish again.

Tia had now come into the room and began to translate Rosa's fumbling speech. "She says that after they filled out the papers, they got outside in the parking lot and she had to go back
to the store because she had to go to the bathroom really bad.
And your papi went to the car alone. When she came out, she
saw the ICE arresting your father and she froze. She went into
uh…she says like a statue…she was paralyzed for a long time in
the bushes beside Sears. The ICE later said Veloz had a gun and
they thought that he was going to use it, so they shot him. And
she was so scared, she did nothing. Finally, she called Septima
to come get her. She has always felt ashamed that she froze and
was not able to help your father."

Tia spoke Spanish to Rosa then, and she was finally able to
calm her. "Come, Rosa. You are stronger now. What happened
was not your fault. You couldn't have done anything to help
him. And by saving yourself, you were able to help your children. People should not have to make choices like that. I think
we should sit down and eat now before it's cold as i—"

Tia stopped herself, but Carmen caught on. "Cold as ice or
ice cream. We are not afraid of ice cream. And we are not afraid
of Sears anymore. Now let's eat."

Choppo came to the doorway of the kitchen. "Okay, *mujeres,* the bird's gonna fly the coop if we don't sit down to eat."

"Yes, and give thanks for being together."

Afterward, they all sprawled in the living room in post turkey torpor. Tia had not eaten any of the turkey or tamales, surprising Carmen with the news that she was a vegetarian. "I don't
eat anything con ojos—with eyes," she had said and then added,
with a wink, "Except potatoes of course."

Flora Linda fell asleep in Teo's big stuffed chair. She and
True had been exhausted by the soul retrieval. Choppo had taken
True and Chia home in the cab and returned. Sleepily, Carmen

watched as Flora Linda snored softly, then she stood up to look more closely. There seemed to be something floating out of Flora Linda's mouth, something transparent and filmy. To Carmen's amazement, shapes formed. A mother duck led a string of ducklings over a waterfall while transparent monkeys with party hats on swung out on streamers that morphed into multi colored snakes, dancing on the tips of their tails in swirling pirouettes.

"Whoa! Look at that. Tia, come here!"

From behind her Tia chuckled. "That's just Flora Linda's ghost dreams. You must have already noticed that she is quite magical. She came to me in one of my dreams years ago when she was much younger. Then I saw her begging on the street. I gave her some work at my shop and she's been working for me ever since. She was born deaf and her family was homeless. Every so often, she joins some of her people who live in homeless encampments around the city. I bailed her out of jail once."

Carmen couldn't help but ask. "What did she do?"

"A cop gave her a ticket for trespassing as she came out of a 7-11, and she threw it on the ground, so he arrested her for disturbing the peace and vagrancy."

"That's really stupid. But why?"

Flora Linda sat up, grinning, made some hand signs, and mimed pulling out a pistol from both pockets as she shot at the ground and hopped around in a goofy dance.

"I think she's saying they are power freaks, but she also signed a word that isn't very nice."

Carmen laughed. "I don't think you have to translate it."

Then Flora Linda entertained them with magic tricks, disappearing completely for her finale. Tia stood up. "It is important to relax and have fun. Much has been happening. Drink your dream tea tonight, Carmentita, so your upstairs mind can work on the plato. I will do the same, and tomorrow, we'll take this place apart."

"Oh, that reminds me, I have some more letters in Spanish that Septima had hidden away. I'll get 'em. Hold on." Carmen ran to the bedroom and pulled the letters out of her backpack.

When she handed them over, Tia smiled strangely. "Hmmm...*muy interesting, mija*. Some of these are from your father to your mother."

"But why did Septima have them then?"

Tia just shrugged. Carmen paused, but quickly her thoughts flew to Tomas and his warning. She wanted to ask if Tia thought they were safe for tonight and looked around for Mami, who had eaten heartily and then gotten up from the meal and disappeared. From the bedroom where she had gone to look for Mami, Carmen heard Tia calling her.

"Come, look out the kitchen window."

Carmen heard a pounding noise, like someone chopping wood, and there was Rosa splintering logs with an axe. "Wow, do you think our cure worked?"

"I was afraid I'd start talking baby talk in the hospital, our cure worked so well."

ᏊᎧᏊᎧ

Carmen slept fitfully in Septima's bed and woke up several times during the night. Once she was awakened by a banging noise in the backyard that finally stopped just when she had worked up the courage to go investigate. Also, it was too cold to go outside so she never made it out of bed, but that was the reason she slept longer than she intended the next morning. However, the minute she opened her eyes, the answer she had been hoping for was there.

Quickly, she grabbed paper and a pencil and began to scribble. She leaped up and ran to Mami's door, but her bed had been made and there was no sign of her. That was curious. Carmen looked for her in the back yard, the trailers, even Teofilo's workshop, but no Rosa. Trying not to become alarmed, she dialed Tia's number, but there was no answer.

As she sat on the edge of the couch, tapping her foot, trying to decide what to do, the doorbell rang in the uneasy silence. Yanking back the curtain of the door's window, she met a blast of silver light, just as an acrid smell wafted in. Carmen could see the tall man from Silver Associates on the porch, his head turned slightly away, holding papers in front of him like a weapon. His free hand flicked the end of a steel tape measure with a series of sinister clicks.

Opening the door only a slit, she said, "Yes?" in a hoarse voice.

"Can I speak to your mother?" Carmen saw a man who looked dipped in silver. Not just his eyebrows and hair, but even his eyes were the color of polished pewter, his skin washed out and bloodless with an oily shine as if someone had spent hours rubbing it to a sharp, pearly sheen.

Carmen had not yet unhooked the screen but did not take heart in its protective power. "My mother can't come to the door."

Silver laughed, the hideous shrill of sharpening a knife. "Of course, she can't. And you don't know where she is, do you?" His eyes fairly ripped through the flimsy screen between them. "Read these papers carefully, senorita. You and your mother have to vacate these premises today. If you're not out of here by five o'clock, we'll be back with the sheriff, all of your property will be put on the street and the locks changed."

"But we're not renters. W—we own this p—property," Carmen stammered.

"Not anymore. Weren't you told that this place was sold? The owner..." Silver scanned the paper dramatically. "Teofilo Galopagord signed the papers and agreed to vacate the property by this date."

He held a paper up to the screen and Carmen struggled to read through the mesh. It looked official.

Helpless tears surged, but Carmen fought to keep Silver from seeing them. "There must be a mistake. We're taking care of things here while Teofilo is in Mexico. He never said anything about any of this."

"You better find your mother and tell her right away." Silver laughed again, and this time Carmen realized there might be a connection between this and her mother's disappearance.

Carmen watched him carefully. "I think she went to the store. But she'll be home any minute."

Silver just smiled, pulled out a silver tipped cigarette, and lit it, blowing smoke through the screen. "Five o'clock. Don't bother to clean up. We'll take care of this...mess."

He turned on his heel and headed for the van parked at the curb. Carmen saw one of the smoky windows slide down but couldn't catch the words of the shadowy figure inside. She strained to see who it was, but the window slid up with a sinister whirr.

Silver had flung the papers down on the doormat, but Carmen didn't want to even touch them. Instead, she ran to the phone and dialed Tia's number. But it rang on endlessly in broken record phone space.

Carmen slammed down the phone. Then she remembered the BSC. Shakily, she rubbed her palm three times and pushed on the flap that sprang open. "Please, please, Tomas, answer—answer." She heard a very faint buzzing and then a far off whiffling noise like Frisbees whisking through a tunnel, then nothing.

Carmen ran to the bedroom and threw on her clothes, grabbed her coat, hat, and gloves, and started to race for the door, then stopped. *I better leave a note for Mami*, she thought, *just in case*. After she'd scribbled a message telling Rosa to stay inside with the doors locked and to keep calling Tia because there was an emergency, she checked up and down the street. No sign of Silver—or anyone, for that matter. The whole world seemed to have gone off the air at midnight.

All she could think of to do was to pull the Mongoose out of the shed and race to Chia and True's. She could have called them, but urgency and fear were shoving aside common sense.

At Chia's, she had to force herself not to pound on the door. As she stood on the step, panic set in again, and her knees went mushy. She realized she hadn't eaten anything yet that morning and her head started to spin. Finally, a very short Hmong woman dressed in a thick sweater and a long, printed skirt came to the door. But she did not seem happy to see Carmen. The woman said nothing, just stood at the door looking worried.

"I am a friend of Chia and True's. Are they here?" Her blank look said no English, so Carmen repeated Chia's name.

"Hmong New Year" the woman stammered out.

Carmen bowed to the woman and, not knowing what else to do, added a curtsey, then jumped on the bike and took off for the fairgrounds where Chia had said Hmong New Year was held. Halfway there, her head began to clear, and she realized that she should have probably gone by Tia's instead. It was too late, though, since she'd have to backtrack quite a ways. Carmen wanted to kick herself for going into a panic and not thinking things through. Chia wouldn't have been so impulsive, she knew. It was very cold. The wind ate through her jacket and burned her ears. At least she'd thought to grab her gloves and hat.

When she reached the fairgrounds, Carmen was astounded. The parking lots were full, and she could see throngs of people beyond the fence. Also, you needed to pay. She hadn't even thought of that. Carmen sat down on the curb, the Mongoose resting beside her. Groups of Hmongs dressed in their best clothes lined up at the gate with their tickets. It cost $10.00 and Carmen hadn't a cent on her. As the minutes ticked by, she felt the tears collecting, ready to gush forth. She had blown it.

Dropping her head to hide her tears, she suddenly remembered that Chia also had a BSC. If she couldn't reach Tomas, maybe she could reach Chia. Carmen sat up straighter, brushed her hand across her eyes and took a deep breath. With every breath in, she repeated, "*Meso, meso, meso.*" Then, "*Ch'uel sak-nik-nal. Ch'uel sak-nik-nal.* Chia, come to the gate. Emergency. Meet me at the gate."

Rubbing her palm three times, she opened the flap and took out the BSC. She waited and waited and despite herself, began to sob. Then she remembered her power animal, and taking more deep breaths, began to form the image of a bird in her mind. She saw its shiny feathers glinting in the sunlight and heard it caw as it flew to her and landed on her outstretched finger. She could almost feel its heart beating. Then in her mind's eye she saw Chia smiling at her and heard her lilting voice.

'*Carmen, what are you doing here?*'

"Carmen, can't you hear me?"

Her eyes flew open and there was Chia, standing just beyond the fence. "I was just playing pov pob when my ball started going haywire, all over the place. True told me she was getting a strong feeling that you were nearby. I pulled out my BSC and went behind the bathrooms and then I heard your voice telling me to come to the gate. I tried to answer you, but all I heard was the sound of water."

"That was me, crying like a baby..." And the words came out in a tumble, about Mami's disappearance, Silver, the papers, and not being able to reach Tia or Tomas. "I should have ridden over to Tia's. Instead, like a dodo, I came here and I don't even have any money."

Chia frowned. "Okay. Let's slow down." She bit her lip in thought. "Here's what we'll do. I'll go tell True that I have to leave. But wait right here. Okay?"

"Okay. But get some money so we can try to call Tia again from a pay phone."

After Chia left, Carmen dug in her pocket, found the scrap of a tissue, and tried to wipe her face and nose. Once again she was waiting, and again the dread crept in. Pushing her fears aside, she looked at the girls in their costumes—beautiful accordion fan skirts in reds and purples or straight kimono styles in blues and pinks. Bright patches of embroidery and coins swagged from their necks and waists like aprons. Their black, turban-like hats were criss-crossed with white and black-striped bands. Box hats of bright, woven colors were draped with red and white tassels. They all chattered happily in Hmong, laughing and teasing, despite the gloomy, overcast day.

Through the fence, Carmen saw booths offering souvenirs, snacks, and various wares for sale. Absorbed in the scene, Carmen did not at first notice the shadow that fell over her where she hunched on the ground near the fence.

However, feeling the darkness, Carmen looked up into the face of the *mal bruja* in her security guard's uniform.

"Hey, you. What're you doin' there? Scram, girlie!" Her mouth shot gold sparks of spit when she spoke.

Carmen made sure not to make eye contact with the *mal bruja* as she replied, "I am not breaking any laws."

"I'll just take you in and see about that. Where's your papers?"

Carmen rose slowly. Then, slick as a snake, she slipped through the crowd, ducked under the turnstile, and ran. Losing herself in the midst of the bright colors and jostling crowd, she ignored the shouts of the ticket taker at the gate. Afraid to look over her shoulder to see if the *bruja* had followed, she ran blindly through the crowds, past the stalls of carved animals, bars of fake silver and gold, jewelry, herbs, and glossy dresses in bright chartreuse, pink and red. Changing directions, she ducked between two stalls offering brightly colored balloons and blow up toys on wheels and a stall with CDs of Hmong music.

A thin Hmong boy with a Raider's jacket yelled at her, "Hey, Carmen. Wha's up?"

Carmen stopped and spun around. It was Dang from one of her classes at school. "Oh hi, Dang," Carmen chugged, out of breath. "Say, do you know where Chia is?"

"Sure. Hey, Xiong, come watch my stuff. Follow me." Dang led Carmen, winding through the tightly packed maze of people to an open space where girls in their long embroidered dresses tossed yellow tennis balls back and forth to boys in the courting game called pov pob.

"Thanks, Dang." Carmen smiled at Dang, who smiled back shyly.

Deep in conversation, Chia didn't hear them calling to her at first but when she spotted them, she rushed over. "Where's True? I sent her to tell you to wait for me at the gate, 'cuz I'd be a little delayed. Why haven't you answered the BSC?"

Carmen went pale. "Oh no. I thought I felt it, but I was running to get away from the *mal bruja* who was after me. Chia, we better go *now*!"

Dang looked from one to the other. "What's a BSC?"

"It's a new group, the Blood Shot Clowns," Chia lied. "They flash messages to their fans with mirror sunglasses. Catch ya later, Dang." She grabbed Carmen's hand and, together, they snaked their way back through the throngs.

"Chevere, quick thinking, Chia. But can you leave right now?" Carmen panted.

"I'm supposed to be part of a dance in a few minutes. I was going to tell my folks that I wasn't feeling well, but we can't wait any longer," Chia huffed as they ploughed forward, fighting the crowd.

"I know. True might be in danger," Carmen huffed back.

When they reached the front gates, there was no sign of True or the *bruja*. "Look, Chia. There's a silver van across the street. What do we do now?"

Chia scratched her head, her face blank. "If she's in there, we can't afford to wait. If the van takes off, we're sunk. Let's just go knock on the window."

Carmen's eyes bugged. "These people are dangerous. Tomas said we should not take chances."

"You have a better idea?"

A figure was exiting the van from the passenger's side. It was a big guy Carmen thought she had seen before. He looked around him, surveying the scene, then stood looking directly at the girls. Slowly, he pulled something dark out of his pocket and held it up in the air like a limp flag.

Chia gasped. "It's True's hat."

"How do you know it's hers?"

"Who else's would it be? They must have her in the van. Let's go."

Carmen felt a jackrabbit thump in her chest, her heart kicking as if to escape. She couldn't breathe and her legs went all rubbery. Watching Chia dodging cars as she raced across the street, Carmen looked down at her feet and saw two useless blobs, now heavy as blocks of cement when she tried to lift them.

CHAPTER 28

Tia sat up and looked around. The tent was still full of shadows, but gradually, they shifted and stretched into the forms of sleeping bodies as the first fingers of light straggled in. Choppo's snores rocked the flimsy walls, joined by other softer grunts in a duet of rhythms, a raucous snoring percussion section. Sometimes one of Choppo's snores would surge forth in a loud honk, only to fade off to the steady drumming of baby snores keeping the counter beat underneath. For a while Tia lay quietly in her sleeping bag, enjoying the mouth music, which she thought of as leakings from the soul.

As quietly as she could, Tia crept from her sleeping bag, easing her stiff limbs, stretching into the day. Already she could smell wisps of smoke from morning fires.

She had to be sure it was still there, still safe. Lifting her pillow, she brushed aside the boughs of evergreen and the velvet cloth and then dug into the soft dirt and gave a huge sigh of relief when her fingers scraped the surface of the wooden box. Carefully, she covered it back up with dirt and then the cloth and evergreen and finally rearranged her pillow back on top. She smiled to herself. There was much to do today, first of all, to get Carmen and Rosa out of the house and safe. And she needed to contact Tomas as soon as possible, if she could. There just hadn't been time the day before. And there was also the problem of the break in at her own place to deal with.

She opened the tent flap and stood looking at the strip of light banding the horizon, pale sliver peeking out from the slowly rising shade of the sky. Perhaps there might be sun today. Behind her she heard Choppo stirring, then Flora Linda.

"You want me to head out and try to call them now? Tell 'em we'll be by soon?" Choppo's voice was still ragged with sleep.

"Good idea. We'll get something together for breakfast while you do."

But Flora Linda had already hopped up—no need to dress. She slept in her long ruffled skirt, rubber boots, and army jacket. She twisted a pink scarf around her head turban fashion and stepped outside. The closest neighbors were grouped around an oil drum alive with fire. While their hands warmed, their dogs stretched and nipped at each other's tails.

"Get back here, Oasis," Connie, a short, wiry black woman called to her dog that had dragged its long chain over a pile of metal stacked ready for the recycler. "I ain't goin' over ta that place on G Street no more. Got half my stuff unloaded and they wouldn't take copper. Coulda' tole me before I dumped it out, ya know. Hey, watch my place. Okay? I'm goin' up on the hill for a while." She headed off, turned back around to Flora Linda, and pointed to Choppo and Tia. "You got visitors, baby?"

Flora Linda signed something in the air and then said in her gutteral voice, "Yeb. My fends."

"I'm Tia. This is Choppo. My botanica got broken into last night while I was there. I heard them downstairs in the shop tearin' stuff up. I stay upstairs, so I hid there until they left. Didn't take nothing much cuz I outfoxed them. Anyway, we're staying here with Flora Linda for a short while."

"Das cool," Connie had turned to head back up the hill when Tia stopped her.

"What are those white boxes across that field over there? They look like bee boxes, but whose are they?"

Connie grinned, nearly toothless. "They was left behind by some folks usta live nearby—got foreclosed on. One a the guys out here found 'em and he's been takin' care a them, gettin' the honey—Mexican fella usta be a bee keeper fore he come here to the U.S. We been getting' us some mighty fine honey. Well, I got to get along now." Connie turned and whistled to her dog.

Flora Linda did a little jig, tapping Tia's cane on the road. From this side of the encampment, the highway could be seen, not two hundred yards away down an embankment. The camp nestled in the space between the new freeway, the old, abandoned section of the freeway and an isolated, rarely used section of H Street, housing a few warehouses and worn industrial businesses. Hill Camp stretched along this corridor and up the hill, which gave it its name. Food scraps, rags, and broken household items were strewn between the lean-tos, tacked together shacks, tents, and strung up tarps.

"Wish we could help you clean up," Tia said, gazing around. "But we gotta eat something and get on the move."

"'S-okay. Cidy don gib no gabage pick up eddyway." Flora Linda had started a fire in her Weber and was warming tortillas on tinfoil. She threw a can of beans to Tia, which they opened and sat right on the grill. Tia understood Flora Linda's muffled words to mean that the city wouldn't pick up their garbage anyway, so it did no good to clean up.

Choppo returned looking distraught. "They ain't answering their phone, Tia."

"That's odd," Tia said as she finished the last of her tortilla. "Here, you eat something, Choppo, while I go do some trance work." Tia lit her sage bundle on the fire then retreated into the tent. First, she waved it in all four directions, circled the interior, propped it in a jar, and lay down on a mat, with her toes to the east. She chanted some secret Mayan words she hadn't even taught Carmen yet then invited the pictures onto the screen in her mind. Slowly, Tomas' face appeared and they spoke without words. *'Tia, you have done excellent work that will help us both. Things are tough right now on Om. You know about the ice storms. The Ice Dab has been rumbling and there is fear of another eruption, so they've had to redouble the chanting teams. Everything else had to go on hold. This has to be settled before they can go forward with the rotation ceremonies. I am hopeful that the plato can help us with that. But I am now too weak to travel to Om. But there are fires to put out everywhere. Carmen*

*and Chia are in great danger. True and Mami have been kid-
napped by Silver's men. Carmen has figured out that Silver
Realtors are hooked up with some of the ICE and they have been
trying to scare her and Septima away. I don't know all that's
going on because our communication is spotty. But you must get
Choppo to pick them up at the Fairgrounds where Hmong New
Year celebration is held. The van just left with True. You must
hurry. And also you need to find me…"*

All Tia could hear now was her own breathing and voices
coming from outside of the tent. She started to leap up, stopped
herself, took several deep breaths, and chanted, slowly and carefully, the words she had learned as a girl. Finally, she rose.
When she stepped to the doorway of the tent, scanning the horizon, she caught her breath. There, hovering in the sky was a
huge pillow of black specks swarming. *Bees—out of season.* She
smiled. *This can only be a good omen.*

CHAPTER 29

Carmen looked at Chia and saw an expression she had not seen there before. Chia's face looked as if it had been crumpled in someone's fist, as she sank to the curb.

She began to wail. "I have lost my sister. She was entrusted to me, and look what I've done. Why did I—I should have—"

Chia made the sound of a helpless kitten in excruciating pain. Carmen did not know what to do or say.

"Hey, you two. Get off the curb 'fore we gotta call the cops."

Carmen looked up to Choppos's grim face and then she saw Tia leaning from the window of the cab.

"Hop in," Tia said. "We need to hurry."

"How did you know where we were?" Carmen started for the cab, but she had to go back, pull Chia forward, and shove her into the back seat.

"Hurry, *mija*," Tia ordered. "I'll tell you on the way."

Carmen started to jump in then stopped. "Oops, I gotta get the Mongoose. It's across the street in the bushes."

"Never mind that," Tia snapped. "Just come on."

As soon as the door shut, the cab took off.

"I talked to Tomas," Tia continued, twisting her head around from the front seat where Caw Caw perched on her shoulder. "What is this about Silver?"

"He came to the house this morning, said Mami and I had to get out—that they own Immaculate Motors now. And Mami was gone when I got up. I'm sorry, Tia. I panicked and ran out of the house to find Chia and True. And now True is gone, too. Silver and his gang kidnapped her—they had her in a van, which just left. What are we gonna do? I know I should—"

Instead of answering, Tia turned back and talked to Choppo in Spanish.

Carmen waved frantically. "The van went that way."

Chia still had not said a word. Caw Caw began to shriek. Choppo pulled over to the curb, made a U-turn, and headed back the way they had come.

"What's this—no, no, not this way." Carmen's voice crackled like static on the radio.

"Calm yourself, *mija*," Tia said. "Caw Caw knows best. Right now you must trust me and follow my direction. Silver and the evil ones have Mami and True because they want something from us. Don't worry. They'll contact us. They broke into my place last night and tore everything—"

"So that's why your phone didn't work. But you're okay?"

"I did some fancy shape shifting and they didn't recognize me. I looked like a flea-bitten mutt." She winked. "I'm okay, but I heard them say something about getting the gold bars from Yang's. I'm sorry to ask a personal question, but does your family have lots of money, Chia?"

Chia frowned. "Um…Many Hmongs don't trust the banks so they hide gold bars in their homes. My parents have lots of doctor bills for True, and they still send money back to Laos, but my uncle who owns the restaurant—we think he might have some gold hidden. Is that why True—" Her voice caught, and she couldn't finish.

"Do not worry, Chia. We will get True back and Mami, too, Carmen. You need to be positive now. *Muy importante*. I think I know what they want. Look, here we are." Tia waved to Flora Linda who danced out to meet them.

They had to climb over a mountain of soiled, smelly clothes piled in front of the place where the road ended and the encampments began. When they climbed out, Choppo left to park the cab. "In a safe place," he said.

Tia led them to the campsite. "We're safe here for now. Let's go inside the tent. Flora Linda, can you make us some soup? We need to keep our strength up. Use those herbs drying on the fence *tambien, por favor.*"

Flora Linda moved quickly, placing a huge pot on the glowing coals, dumping in water, greens, and other vegetables she chopped on a plank of wood. She kept throwing in herbs, then flowers and something small, round, and black. Carmen didn't like the looks of it, but when they received their bowls of the strange soup, it was surprisingly tasty, even though it had some unusual flavors that Carmen couldn't place. It made her nose run, and Tia threw her a big, red handkerchief.

Chia at first said she couldn't eat, but Tia convinced her that the soup was good for their stomachs, minds, and souls.

Carmen marveled at the inside of the dwelling, which was part tent, strewn with sleeping bags, opening up into a room made of scrap wood covered with a blue tarp that created a milky, blue under-waterish glow, washing over the interior. Bamboo rugs covered the floor, and posters of Chinese dragons, tigers, birds, fish, and a huge, life-sized poster of Elvis filled the walls. The ceiling was covered with pictures of the Virgin Mary, various saints, Cher, Chief Seattle, Sponge Bob Square Pants, and an advertisement for Hmong New Year. The mats were arranged in a circle, with a ring of candles in the middle. Tia set about lighting the candles then her sage bundle, which she waved in the four directions. Chanting, she moved the smoke up and down, around each of their bodies, and asked them to sit. "Now, Carmen. Did you have any dreams last night?"

Carmen gasped. "I almost forgot. I did! I dreamed numbers. I wrote them down this morning. But—I left them at the house..."

Tia's face fell. "Okay. First let's do some trance work. And then we'll have to go back to the house. We need those numbers. They would be the third solution if we can figure out the code. Also, I have something incredible to show you before we go. Now, let's all chant together."

Tia began the chant and Carmen and Chia joined in. Carmen found that what she thought were unfamiliar words soon came out of her mouth naturally.

Suddenly, with no warning, the candles all went out at once and they could hear Tomas' voice. "They're blocking our messages and right now we don't have time to work on it. The Ice dab is coming out of hibertrance—Tia will explain that. You have to work fast. I can't help much now, but Tia has something that will help us on Om, we hope."

They heard the whistling sound of wind in a tunnel and then silence.

Carmen sat up. "Oh, no. We lost the connection."

Tia re-lit the candles which shot purple shadows against the blue walls. "Don't worry. It's time to show you my surprise."

Reaching into her straw bag that she carried with her everywhere, she pulled out another bag made of velvet and pulled on the drawstring closure. Out came another bag made of roughly woven hemp from which she pulled a silken bag out of which slipped a beautifully painted ceramic plate, with three feet on the bottom, which were rimmed in red.

"It's a Mayan offering plate, centuries old," she said as she tipped it toward them. In the flickering light, they could see spiral designs and scenes of scrolled animal and human forms. "It depicts the living cosmos and the struggles of mankind. The Mayans believed the soul was a smaller version of the universe. The outside of the plato is painted with water signs, lily pads, and shells for the Under and Otherworld—the eternal now—which they believed surrounds our world. Inside are the stories of the three layers of being that come from the Elsewhere and Elsewhen of the Otherworld. I have many stories to tell you about all this because it all relates to Om, which is very much like the Otherworld. This plato gives the owner a direct portal to Om. It also has special powers that can be used on Om to safeguard against the Ice Dab. We don't know if Silver knows this, but if he does, there could be very dire consequences. Tomas is very excited to know that I have found it."

Tia held the plate then to her heart and, closing her eyes, began to glide in small circles inside a circular path around the candles, whispering too softly for them to catch the words. When she stopped, she was smiling but said nothing.

Carmen opened her mouth several times then finally said, "But where did you find it Tia? And how?"

"Those letters you gave me yesterday. Remember? In the ones from your father, he talked about an ancient plato that had been in the family for centuries. He wrote to Pepita that he had tried to get the plato to me, but I was gone at that time. So he hid it at Immaculate Motors and he told Teo where he hid it. In another letter from Pepita to your father, she told your father that Teo wasn't to be trusted and that he should hide it somewhere else, and she suggested the attic. But the house doesn't have an attic, so Choppo and I went back after you had gone to sleep. I thought I remembered a crawl space above Teofilo's work space in the garage. You'd have to be looking for it to find it because it was covered by vines, but the latch was there, so we put up a ladder, and Choppo climbed up there, and sure enough, the box was right there inside. I thought it was better to take it to my place. Now I think they've been watching the house, and they followed us to my place. That's why they broke in. But luckily, I hid it well. I put it in an old Kotex box because I know that most men have an aversion to lady's products."

She grinned. "Then I did some fancy shape shifting, so that when they entered my upstairs rooms, I had taken the shape of a mangy dog asleep on the floor. And I barked and growled ferociously and scared them off."

"But Tia, if they thought that you had the plato, why did they come back to the house today and tell us we had to leave?"

Tia stopped and rubbed her chin. "When they didn't find it at my place, they must have figured we still had it at Immaculate Motors."

Carmen was troubled. "Papa must have been killed not long after he hid the plato the second time."

Tia hugged her. "Yes, and I suspect that Teo was tied into his death somehow. But right now Silver is getting desperate to find the plato, since we have been eluding him."

Chia, who had said very little so far, finally spoke. "So what do we do next?"

"The plato says we do nothing."

"But—how—how will that help? Shouldn't we—"

Tia re-wrapped the plate. "We must go back to the house, find Carmen's numbers, and then be patient and wait. We can't do everything at once. Silver should be contacting us soon. Let's go."

In the cab on the way to the house, Tia said, "Do you remember the creature at the top of the plato? That was the Cosmic Monster, a two headed snake-crocodile. At the center is First Father whose head is shaped like an ear of corn. First Lord and First Jaguar were born to First Mother after she visited the calabash tree where First Father's decapitated head spit into her hand."

Carmen made a twisty face. "Eeeew, Ick. Sounds kinda gory to me."

"Yes, the Mayans had some very blood thirsty customs, but they were part of their beliefs at the time—not just their religion, but how they saw their entire world. They provided chances for resurrection, they thought. We call ourselves more civilized now, but look at the wars and the killing and destruction one group of people brings down on another in our time. But Om is a chance to stop all this—a place where a new dawning of mankind can take place, no more hatred or wars. And this can spread out to the earth. The Ice Dab Tomas referred to is like the evil one in the Underworld. Tomas has told me that it is trying to suck the life force from Om and become powerful again and enslave the people. All of these years the people of Om, instead of destroying him, have kept him asleep in the Ice Mountain by chanting and saying special prayers. Now he is rising out of his hibertrance again because life on Om parallels that on Earth and there is much unrest and evil loose on Earth right now. Tomas and I both fear that Silver may have found out about Om, and we don't know what he might be planning. We also fear that if he gets the plato, he will travel to Om and we don't know what kind of damage he could do. He may only want the plato for its value as an artifact, but we can't be sure. He is so dead set on getting it, that we fear the worst. We need to safeguard Om because they value music, dance, art, poetry, love, humanity, and sharing over money, things, winning, and domination, which is what people like Silver value."

"My people would like that," Chia said. "The Hmongs have always been chased from one mountain to another. And we also value the arts and the earth. Hey, look, we're here."

They had now pulled up in front of Immaculate Motors, and from the outside, everything looked exactly the same.

"If they were watching the house before, maybe they still are," Carmen said. "Are you sure it's safe to take the plato back inside with us?"

Tia considered this. "I doubt that they would expect us to come back here now. Anyway, we won't stay long. Choppo, stay outside and honk the horn if you see anyone coming."

When they stepped onto the porch, Tia flung out her arms. "Don't touch those papers." she pointed to the ones still on the mat, left by Silver. Caw Caw swooped down, snagged some of them in her beak, and then flew off. One minute later, she landed again, snatched the rest of them, and flew off once more.

"They carried *muy mal espirito*—bad spirit. It's best not to make contact with those things."

Chia's eyes widened. "We Hmong believe the same thing." Then a troubled look crossed her face. "Uhmmm, Tia, I better get in touch with my family soon, I think. They'll be sick worried."

"Worried sick," Carmen corrected. "Won't they want you to come home?"

"I'm going to go home before dinnertime. Mai is covering for us until then. But we are having a big dinner at home tonight, and I'll have to tell them then that True is gone. I just don't want them to call the cops. If I tell them the ICE took her, they won't call anyone cuz they're more afraid of the ICE."

"But wasn't True born here?"

Chia's eyes glistened. "No. Our mother went back to Laos not knowing she was pregnant with True, and when she found out, it was too late. They wouldn't let her fly, so True was born in Laos. And then the family came back here again."

Both girls looked at Tia. "Can they de—send her back?" Carmen didn't even want to say the word "deport."

"It's hard when her whole family is here, but I don't know for sure. They've done some—" Tia had started to tell them how the ICE sometimes separated parents and their children, but seeing the girls' faces, she stopped. "Right now, though, let's get that paper with the numbers on it. Where did you leave it?"

They were standing grouped in the living room when they all jumped at the sound of sharp tapping on the door, but it was only Caw Caw returned from her seize-and-destroy mission.

"What about Caw Caw?" Carmen asked. "She touched the papers with her beak."

"Caw Caw knows how to purify after contact with *mal espirito. Andale, mija*, let's find those numbers."

Carmen raced to Septima's bedroom and there on the nightstand was her school tablet, lying open, and there were the numbers she had scrawled earlier that morning.

"Here they are." She read the numbers off. "36753705120378424."

Tia rubbed her chin. "Hmmmm…"

Carmen sniffed the air. "I don't like it here. Let's get out. I'll just grab—"

Shrill and sudden, the phone's ringing interrupted Carmen. Everyone just stared while it continued to sting the air.

Finally, Tia picked it up. "Hello." Then her face went pale gray.

CHAPTER 30

After the phone call, it had taken Tia quite some time to calm everyone. Carmen had even suggested calling the police, even though she knew in her heart that it was a foolish idea. They didn't know who they could trust.

Chia had wanted to do something but couldn't really come up with what that something should be. The unidentified voice on the phone had said that they had True and Rosa and would be in touch soon, but only if they kept quiet and didn't call the cops or anyone else. They were to leave Immaculate Motors and go to Tia's place. Then Rosa came on the line but only for a few words.

"Okay," Tia said. "We need to get out of here. Let's take the plato to my place and then let's do some trance work. Chia, do you want to go home now or later?"

"As long as it's before dinner, I'll be okay."

Everyone scanned up and down the street before entering the cab. The only thing different was a U-Haul truck parked at a house three down from Oso's place. But there was no sign of anyone around.

"Tia, what about your phone?" Carmen asked from inside the cab on the way to Tia's.

"Choppo fixed it this morning. They had pulled some wires loose is all."

When they entered Tia's, Carmen just shook her head. "What a mess. Shall we help you clean up, Tia?"

"Not right now. We can get this later. Right now we have to draw on the strength of the ancestors. Here."

She threw Carmen a kazoo and Chia a drum. She pulled a small mandolin from a shelf that, surprisingly, had not been disturbed and began to strum and sing. Choppo followed with his harmonica as Tia motioned them all into a circle. The song was one that Carmen had never heard before—a playful rhythm with Spanish words she tried to catch up with as Tia sang. Then Tia rose and, moving her head first right then left, began to dance while Choppo continued the tune.

The bells on the door jingled, and in came Flora Linda, carrying a small xylophone which she played quite well. Flora Linda then rose up on the tips of her toes, as feathers sprouted from the ends of her fingers. Raising her right knee high in the air, she flung the feathers into the air and threw back her head, on which had sprouted a richly ornamented head-dress. She began to leap and swoop around the room in an ecstatic, muscular dance. Slowing the rhythm, Tia began to sing a languid, soul-full song while Flora Linda swayed to the words, circling the room, as flower petals fell magically down on her from above:

> "Flowers are falling all about us.
> "Let there be dancing to the drums, my friends,
> "and celebrations among us. Our hearts grieve,
> "but the One…Don't you hear him?
> "He descends, he comes singing!
> "The flutes take up his song,
> "the flutes answer him."

They continued singing, playing, and dancing for what seemed like hours. Finally, Chia just stopped and ran from the room.

Carmen rose to follow, but Tia held onto her arm. "Let her go, *mija*. The dancing releases *muy mal cosas*."

"So just why are we doing this? I'm worried about Mami and True also and here we are having a sweet old time—"

"We can't do anything but wait until they contact us. And music is the portal to the divine, *mi querido*. When we play music together, we unleash powerful forces."

"But when I heard Mami's voice on the phone, I—she sounded so faint, so weak. And then there's True. What if they hurt them, Tia? I'm scared."

Tia looked stern. "Fear won't help them. The dancing was important. It showed the *mal espiritos* that we do not fear them."

Chia returned, looking somewhat greenish around the edges. "Sorry, I lost my soup," she said just as the phone rang.

Tia grabbed it up. "Hello, yes. Yes. I see. All right then." She scribbled something on a piece of paper. "Give us two minutes to discuss this, then call us back."

She hung up then turned to the group. "That was a man who called himself Dr. Sicko. He wants the gold bars that True's uncle keeps hidden in his house in exchange for True. He got our number from Silver, but it seems that he is working separately now. He didn't say anything about the plato. Maybe Silver doesn't know about the gold and the Dr. Sicko doesn't know about the plato. But we are supposed to bring the gold to this address." She handed them the paper. "What do you want to do?"

Chia did not hesitate. "I'll call my uncle right away. I know that—"

But the phone was ringing again and Tia snatched it up. "What? Your friends have already called us to make a deal for True. What's going on with your guys?" Tia jerked then turned back to them. "They hung up."

"Who—what did they?"

"That was Silver. He said they want the plato and the gold bars in exchange for True and Rosa."

"What about Tomas?"

"He doesn't seem to be a part of any of the deals."

"Well, they both can't have True. And how can we get them both back if we don't know for sure who has who?"

Tia sat down on the circular rug. "Let me think. Perhaps they are trying to double cross each other. Maybe we can use that."

Again, the phone rang.

It was Silver, talking so loudly that Tia could hold the phone out for everyone to hear.

"There has been some confusion here, but you can be sure that we do have True and Rosa. They aren't being held in the same place, but we will bring them both to that address Dr. Sicko gave you. Just be sure you bring the plate and $20,000 in gold bars and we'll hand them over. And make sure you don't bring anyone else with you—no police—nobody, or the deal's off. You have exactly one hour."

"What about Tomas?" Tia put the phone back up to her ear, listened grimly, then hung up. "They say that he is still in custody. They don't have him."

Chia was crying, and when Carmen put her arms around her, their tears ran together.

Tia's face was hard and waxy gray. "We have no choice but to go to your family and get the gold bars. Chia, do you think they really have that much?"

Chia snuffled then coughed, trying to catch her breath. "I think my uncle does. At least, that's the rumors I've heard."

"Carmen, you stay here in case they call again. Chia and I will go to her house."

Carmen walked Chia to the door, still hugging her. "It's going to be okay."

As Tia swung the door open, a floral scented breeze wafted in, followed by a glittery flash. Amazed, they all watched a silver red dragonfly land on Chia's head. Chia stood stock still.

Carmen grinned. "Isn't that True's power animal?"

"And this is not the season for dragonflies, is it?" Tia grinned back. "I think our baby shaman has learned a new trick."

Neither Chia nor the dragonfly moved an inch.

Tia continued. "She told me she was working on shape shifting but was running into some snags. But maybe our mixed magic helped." Tia also seemed afraid to move. "Let's try something. What is True's favorite food?"

"She loves sticky rice."

Carmen still stood stiffly beside Chia. "We sure don't have any of that."

"I have some in my bag, wrapped in tin foil." Chia pointed woodenly toward the colorfully woven bag hanging over her shoulder.

As Carmen moved to grab it, the dragon fly zoomed off.

Fumbling with the bag, Carmen pulled out the foil and opened it. As they waited with their breath held, the dragonfly circled the room then dove into the rice, followed by several more passes into the sticky, white pile.

They all clapped. Tia held out her hand and the dragonfly landed right on her middle knuckle. "Hmmm…something seems wrong."

"What if she doesn't know how to change back into herself?"

Chia's look of alarm made Carmen wish she hadn't spoken out loud.

Tia looked at the clock. "I could work on that, but we are running out of time. I think we should head to the address they gave us. I'm betting that they don't have True anymore. I'll go tell Choppo." Tia floated her hand toward Chia's. "Here, Chia, take your sister."

When Tia had closed the door, Chia gazed down at the dragonfly. "Do you really think this is True? What if it isn't? What if they still have her, and we don't bring the money?"

The dragonfly lifted up from her finger and began to zip back and forth in front of Chia's face, almost grazing her nose. Then it landed smack on her lips.

"It doesn't seem to like what you said, Chia."

When the phone rang again, Carmen had no choice but to answer it herself. "Hello."

"Did you get the gold bars?"

"We know you don't have True anymore."

"So what? We still have the old lady."

"All we can give you is the plato. True's uncle will not fork over gold for a Mexican lady he doesn't even know."

"Well, if you want her back alive, you'd better bring that plate to the address we gave you. *Comprehende*? And don't keep us waiting."

It took all of Carmen's strength not to cry. "Okay, okay. We'll bring the plate. Just give us time to get there. We're on our way."

CHAPTER 31

They were now in the cab, waiting for Choppo to finish studying a city map. The sky was shivering with gray, washy light edging toward night. Post-Christmas gloom hovered in the chill, dank air.

"This sucks. We just got the plato and now we have to turn it over to Silver." Carmen spat the name out. "What will this mean for Om? Aren't we failing our mission?"

"People are more important that plates, Carmen, you know that," Tia told her. "It will be all right. We will have to work harder. Also, I contacted Tomas when I was outside. There is a lull on Om right now with the Ice Dab. He suggests we give up the plato for now and then we can work on finding him with those numbers Carmen has. If we can free him, he can try to help us get the plato back. We've done a lot by putting our powers together. True is shape shifting, and you girls are also making great progress. I am better and so is Rosa. And I think we are close to getting Tomas back also. I have a feeling."

In the back seat, Carmen and Chia exchanged glances that said they were both beginning to wonder about Tia's "feelings."

"Okay, everybody. I know where this address is," Choppo said, "It's way over in the southeast part of town, kind of over where the encampments are, and it's not pretty—lots of druggies and gang bangers over there. Should we take reinforcements?

Flora Linda could round up some of her homeless friends to help
us."

"No," Tia snapped. "We'll follow instructions. We can't
risk messing this up. Contact your power animals, senoritas.
Let's go."

To their amazement, when Tia opened the door, the dragonfly was perched on Caw Caw's back. The bird was sitting on the
headrest of the front seat. Tia lifted Caw Caw first to her finger
then to her shoulder. "That's our True, *seguro*."

No one spoke on the way over, full of their own thoughts,
but the worries and fears hung over them like a toxic smog. Silently, they skimmed past the green squares of lawn and the neat
bungalows as they left the neighborhoods for the downtown
businesses. They crossed the railroad tracks into a tract of beaten
down houses, with straggling trees and fences ablaze with graffiti. Choppo slowed as a group of kids in baggy sweatshirts and
pants lunged at the car, flashing gang signs. One threw a rock
that bounced off the trunk with a heavy bonk.

Light disappeared fast this time of year and a blanket of
gray, wooly dusk wrapped around the sad businesses, which
were barely clinging to life. Then they were crossing another set
of tracks into the area that surrounded the encampments with
more forlorn buildings and industrial grime. Carmen recognized
the area from the day before.

"Now we're on Church Street," Choppo said, creeping
along the darkening roads. "Tell me when you see an address
number. We're looking for 6122."

"Nothing's marked," Carmen said, craning her neck.

Finally, Chia saw a gas station with a number, but it only
told them they were still blocks away. Suddenly, Church Street
ended and the last number they could find was 5900.

"It probably picks up again on the other side," Tia said.
"Turn right here and then make two more lefts and let's hope
that that's Church again."

"I ain't been to Church in a long time," said Choppo, but no
one was in the mood for a joke.

Sure enough, they were now back on Church Street, but
there were no houses and only some deserted and boarded up

buildings. Choppo stopped the cab. "It has to be here some-where cuz this street's a dead end."

They were idling in the middle of the street now. Carmen rolled down the window and a burning chemical smell drifted in. Just then car lights appeared from a dirt side road, that had not been visible before, and swung up to face them head on. Tia opened the door. "Keep the motor running."

CHAPTER 32

True sat parked on Caw Caw's back, angry at herself for her predicament. It reminded her of the time she had stuck her head between the slats of a chair, so easy going in, and then finding she couldn't get out. Chia and Moua had to take the chair apart while she screamed her head off.

She had thought herself pretty crafty telling Silver's men that she couldn't wait to use the toilet, and then when she'd seen that small slit of an open window, she'd had the idea to take another shot at shape shifting, and it had worked. Now here she was, with no idea how to change back. Things looked really different from behind a dragonfly's eyes—everything so large and colors more intense. She could see in all directions around her at once. That was awesome! In dragonfly land, Chia and Carmen's heads were the size of two blimps, leaned together talking. True strained to hear, but their voice were too low.

Tia placed Caw Caw and True on her straw bag and handed it to the girls who nestled it between them, holding on tightly. Tia was now standing on the road, outlined by car lights.

By now, True thought, the family would be missing them and starting to get alarmed. True wished she could do something to help but being a dragonfly was limiting. *Okay,* she thought, *you're supposed to help me, so help, you stup*—She stopped. It probably would not help to insult your power animal. But she had things to tell Tia and the girls, and now she couldn't. She knew that the man with the silver sunglasses got money to send people away and he told his men that they could get the plate and not hand over Rosa because what could an old woman and some kids do about it? Then they could still get the $5,000 from the ICE for her.

Something was happening now in the street. Both cars were face to face with headlights beamed toward each other, the space between the cars now a kind of stage where a nightmare drama was taking place. Tia was holding the wrapped up plate and talking to one of the bad men, the one called Tonto who had grabbed True when she had been looking for Carmen outside the gate at Hmong New Year and not paying attention to what was around her. He'd put something over her mouth that had made her sleep, and when she woke, she had been in that van and, she hated to admit, really scared. But she had kept her eyes closed up tight so the men would think she was still asleep and they would blab about their plans. If only she could tell Tia about their plans not to hand over Rosa. But now she saw that it was too late. Rosa had been hauled from the car, with her hands still tied up. True could see Rosa nodding, yes, to a question from Tia.

Then Tia handed the plate to Dr. Sicko, who unwrapped it, took a small bottle out of his pocket, dipped into it, and rubbed it on the plate. Then he carried it over to the front window of the van and handed it to the person inside.

True knew what would happen next. She had to do something. With her new telescopic vision, she scanned to her left, then right. She saw the white boxes beside the abandoned building. Pulling herself inward as tightly as she could, she followed the same steps she had before, and it worked! She was now in a new, fatter fuzzy brown body, with a large, striped abdomen and two smaller, delicate wings. Now she was a bee trapped in a car. With the loudest buzz she could manage, she flew at Chia's nose. Chia flapped her arms wildly and screamed then opened the car door.

True threw her new, buzzing body at the dark, empty space the opened door made and flashed through just before it slammed shut once again. Flying down to the hives, she danced

her message to the worker bees hanging groggily on the combs.
The cold made it hard for her to move, but she twisted, spun,
and looped the loop, transmitting her message to the other bees.

CHAPTER 33

Carmen and Chia watched the figures flutter in the headlight beams. Something was terribly wrong. To their horror, they saw Tia tugging on Rosa, who seemed frozen like a wild animal in the headlights. Dr. Sicko and Tonto were up in Tia's face, grabbing her arms as Dr. Sicko pulled Rosa away.

Carmen and Chia lunged to jump out of the cab, but Choppo barked, "You two stay put! I'll help Tia."

However, as soon as Choppo had climbed out, the back of the van opened. Two beefy young men jumped out, grabbed him, and threw him up against the cab.

Chia was the first to hop out, kicking at one of the men's shins, whom she could now see, were very big, young boys. As the boy dropped one of his arms, Choppo doubled over in pain, just as Carmen joined in, kicking the other one.

"Get the guns, you idiots," Silver yelled from the front seat of the van as the window slid down.

The boys let loose of Choppo to follow orders. The man who had been holding Mami also let go and turned toward the van. But he ran smack into Choppo's fist. He and Choppo rolled on the asphalt, throwing punches.

"Run, Mami," Carmen screamed.

But before she could do so, the two who had run to the van yelled, "Nobody move!" They were holding guns in front of them, and now everyone froze.

"Take the old lady and put her back in the van. And put that wet back in the trunk of his cab. Everybody else get back in the cab!" Silver yelled out the window of the van, without even leaving the front seat. "We got what we want. If you buttheads hadn't let the kid get away, we coulda had more. And, senoras, we got the papers on that car place—Galopagord signed 'em. But, tell you what we'll do, give you till tomorrow to get yer stuff out. See…we ain't all bad."

His laugh was grating as fingernails on a chalkboard. "Not her," he yelled when they reached for Tia. "We got unfinished business. Don't get cute—don't try any of your *bruja* crap. And don't think about calling the cops after we leave either. The old lady don't look too well to me. Her condition could get whole lot worse, you know?"

Carmen and Chia were back in the cab. Choppo was in the trunk, and Tia was standing just outside the van, facing Silver and his big, fat cigar, the tip an evil, red eye glowing in the dark as Rosa's sobs leaked from the vehicle.

Tia heard the buzzing before she saw anything. As she turned to look, a funnel of small bees swarmed through the misty glow of the headlight beams, hundreds of furious, fuzzy bodies attacking at once—an army of tiny stinging beasts.

"What the f—" Silver started.

Fast as a whip, Tia snapped her cane between the window glass and the frame, before he could slide it up.

Carmen and Chia were now beside her and all three of them pulled on the door against Silver's tug, before he could lock it.

"Help me, you stupid thugs," he cried to his men.

But as they piled back out of the van, their bodies were soon peppered with noisy, brown bullets. They fell down, screaming in searing pain, covered with red welts.

As Tia and the girls tugged on the door, the bees surged through the open window Silver had not been able to close. At the same moment, Silver gave a long, deafening howl, and the door fell open.

"Allergic, hospital—now—" was all he could manage to say before he crumpled helplessly onto the asphalt.

Carmen and Chia grabbed up the guns the men had dropped while trying to protect their faces from the storm of stinging bees, who, now that their work was done, were dropping dead onto the ground.

"I think we better call an ambulencia," Tia said as she ran to the van to release Rosa and settle her into the back seat of the cab.

"That'll take too long." Dr. Sicko stood up, scratching and rubbing himself. "We can get him there sooner."

"Not so fast," Carmen heard herself saying. She almost giggled, thinking of a B-rated cop show. "We want our plato back."

Silver was still on the ground, groaning. "I—can't—breathe."

"Go ahead, get him to the hospital," Tia said, as everyone turned toward the sound of Caw Caw screeching, perched on the trunk where loud thumping sounds echoed.

Carmen gave Chia her gun and ran to open the trunk, and Choppo climbed out, cussing and fuming.

His men had now thrown Silver into the back of the van, and before they knew what was happening, Dr. Sicko revved the van's engine and sped away.

There lying on the asphalt was Silver's tape measure, curled up like an abandoned silver slug.

"Tia! They still have the plato!" Chia cried, holding both guns limply, like a deflated cowgirl. "Let's go after them."

"Jump in, *vamanos*," Choppo was in the driver's seat, already restarting the engine.

"Espere—wait!" Tia held up her hand. "We need to see to Rosa right now. And we have to thank the remaining bees for their sacrifice first."

Carmen exchanged an exasperated look with Chia. "But Tia—"

"People are more important than—"

"But Tia, you said that if we had the plato it would help the people of Om and that it could be dangerous for the plato to fall into Silver's hands." Carmen stopped. Remembering Mami, she looked guiltily toward the cab.

"Yes, it may be true that Silver can create more trouble on Om. But we need to get our priorities in order also. We need to see to True and Rosa right now and we need to make getting Tomas back our priority also. Too much time has passed and I'm beginning to fear for his life. My hunch is that Silver only wants the plato for a valuable artifact. All he talked to us about was money. But there are others involved with him...If we get Tomas back, he can go to Om more and we can all work on getting the plato back. Now, Chia, give me those guns before someone gets hurt," Tia snapped. "Everyone back in the cab." Her voice was angry as she dropped the guns in the trunk. "Rosa, are you all right?" she asked, settling back into the front seat.

"*Si, soy*...mmmm...shake up." Rosa paddled her hands in the air. "*Pero fino.*"

Carmen by now had climbed in the cab beside Rosa, hugging her. "Mami, we were so worried. They didn't hurt you, did they?"

"No," Rosa said. "But the *nina*...she is okay? They...mmmm...say not to be funny, or...they...h—hurt *la nina. No vi nada para bromear sobre.*"

"No tension. She got away and she is safe." Tia grinned, turning from the front seat. "Rosa said she didn't see anything to joke about. Okay, now we will thank the bees. First, visualize your power animal. Then direct it to thank the bees for helping us. Then just be quiet and—" Tia made a shushing noise, gesturing with her index finger. "—listen."

Everyone sat silent in the cab, while the headlights streamed down the lonely country road, that no one seemed to use anymore, and the blackness of the night blossomed around them.

Carmen felt something heavy on her shoulder, but kept her eyes closed as she thanked the bees for helping save her mother and defending them against Silver and his men.

Then there was complete silence in the cab. All they could hear was the faint rustle of wind outside joined to their own steady breathing.

Carmen drifted into a bubble of pure purple stillness, as if she floated on a glassy sea. All worries sank like heavy rocks below.

A sweet honeysuckle scent began to fill the cab and then a tiny buzz, like the rumble of a distant vacuum cleaner headed their way.

Caw Caw was the first to break the silence, with a string of delighted caws filling the cab.

There on her head was a single honeybee, perched exactly where the dragonfly had been before.

Tia grinned. "Do you think this little bee might go for some sticky rice?"

"It's True!" Chia sang out. "But how did you know?"

"Two things. First, bees don't usually leave their hive in winter, and I had already thought of shape shifting myself, but she beat me to it. It was faster for the dragonfly to shift into a bee because that's a creature close to the same species."

"So can you help her shift back to herself, Tia?" Chia asked. "Because we need to get home as soon as possible."

"We'll go to my place. It'll be easier with my equipment handy. Then Choppo can take you back to your house in the cab. Then I'll take Carmen and Rosa back to the house to get their things. I think you'll have to move in with me for a while, *hermana*."

Rosa, who had not spoken much, frowned. "*Pero*, what about Motors Immaculada? We said to mmm...watch over...*para* Teo and Septima."

"Teo sold it, Mami, to those *muy mal* men who kidnapped you. He could have at least told us. And I wonder how he managed to sell it without Septima's signature."

Mami sighed heavily. "*Aquel* is Teo. *Ahora somos chiflando en la loma.*" She muttered more Spanish under her breath, just shaking her head.

Tia laughed. "She said you are left whistling in the mountains now. She seems to have an endless supply of those little sayings. I guess we are left whistling in the barrio."

But, again, no one was in the mood to laugh.

Choppo started the car and, as they sped along through the now darkened streets, Carmen's heart winced at the sight of the old mami who gave up to fate or the will of *Los Dios* so quickly and then sank like a fly giving into the web that held it. Carmen did not like the helpless feelings that rose up within her then.

CHAPTER 34

Tia had carried Caw Caw and the bee into her place, entering through the downstairs doorway. Chia had been afraid the bee would fly away, but Tia assured her that if it really was True, it would stay on Caw Caw's back. She had sent them all upstairs to straighten up the place while she shut herself, the bee, and Caw Caw into her rooms at the back, downstairs.

Shape shifting was an advanced business, she'd said, and right now, they needed to get True back as quickly as possible.

When Tia called to them, Chia nearly tumbled down the stairs, in her rush to get down. But when she threw back the beaded curtains, there was no sign of True. "What—what's going on? I don't see her."

Tia smiled like a crafty spider. "Look," was all she would say.

Carmen, right behind Chia, almost knocked her over, as they both surveyed the room.

Rosa had also entered now, and she was the one who pointed upward. "*Mira, la nina*!"

There was Caw Caw preening on the top shelf of the bookcase that nearly reached the ceiling, and there, squeezed into the narrow space was True, gazing down at them. "I'm hungry," she said softly. "How 'bout sticky rice with honey?"

cɔeɔ

Chia called Carmen later that night at Tia's to tell her that everyone was so relieved to see them that they didn't question their half-cooked story. Carmen didn't even bother to tell her the correct phrase was half-baked. They agreed to talk on the phone in the morning to plan their next move—first, to find Tomas, and then, to try and get the plato back.

Mami was complaining again of stomach pains, headaches, and tiredness and didn't want to go back to Motors Immaculada. Carmen suspected that the recent events had traumatized her and sent her back into her dark and fearful shell. Tia confirmed this when Carmen asked her about it.

Septima had farmed all the dogs out to friends before she left so, fortunately, they didn't have to worry about that.

Packing up their clothes and few possessions had not taken Carmen, Tia, and Choppo too long. They'd also taken whatever perishable food was still in the fridge since it would only go to waste. When they stopped at the grocery store for additional food, Carmen talked Tia into buying a tabloid magazine in Spanish, *Espejo de Pelicula*, hoping to cheer her mother up.

When they returned to Tia's place, Carmen and Choppo carried the groceries inside. They found Rosa bent forward, sweeping up the glassware broken by Silver's men when they had messed the place up. Rosa was breathing heavily, her face drained of color.

"Mami, stop. You don't need to do that. You need to rest and get your strength back. Here, give me the broom."

"Well, maybe is time for me to *chupar los faros*."

"What's that?" Carmen asked Tia who had just entered the room.

"Time to suck the headlights, she says. It means to bite the dust, to die."

"Cut it out, Mami. Tia, can we do another soul retrieval for her?"

"Sure, *mija*. But, Rosa, you have to take part. You can't be like a docked fish too lazy to jump back in the sea. The Aztecs believed that the first step of healing was to make a choice to be deserving of health. To live healthy and take responsibility for your own wellbeing. We can keep on with the *limpias*, but what will you keep on with?"

Rosa looked as if she had been slapped. Without another word, she turned and left the room.

Carmen frowned. "Maybe you were too hard on her, Tia."

"Maybe. At some point you stop adding salt to the soup," Tia said mysteriously, re-shelving some books scattered on the floor. She reached out toward Carmen, offering her Rosa's discarded broom.

ᘓᕲᘓᕲ

The next morning Flora Linda appeared with Connie, and the rest of the day was spent trying to restore order to Tia's rooms. Rosa remained in the back room, knitting or turning the pages of her magazine.

After the kitchen was cleaned up, Connie could be heard banging pans, chopping, scraping, and making other cooking sounds in the kitchen.

They sat down to a varied meal of cornbread, tortillas, spicy beans, macaroni and cheese, and a pot of slowly cooked greens picked that day from the encampments, where a small winter garden flourished. Carmen had to stop herself from gobbling up everything in sight. They finished the meal, fat and happy, all but Rosa. She claimed a lack of hunger and sat languidly rocking in her chair, staring moodily out the window or at her magazine. Tia kept Carmen too busy to comfort her mother.

Connie sipped from a Mountain Dew bottle, filled with a cloudy yellow liquid Carmen suspected was beer. While they ate, Connie told stories about the homeless man who juggled rats and the Siamese queen who painted her face, arms, and legs with nail polish. Why was she called the Siamese queen? She looked like a Siamese cat, of course and she wore a Burger King crown everywhere she went.

Connie didn't want to miss her football games, so she and Flora Linda took off as soon as dinner was finished. Choppo was off "making some money" in his cab.

"It's time for advanced lessons in shape shifting, Carmentita," Tia said. "We may need them soon. But first, we must contact Tomas."

She smudged the main room with sage and lit the candles. They lay on the floor with their feet toward the east, chanting together the ancient words Carmen had memorized. Carmen took out the BSC, rubbed it three times and waited. Into the stillness a loud, bass boomed up from the street.

Carmen sat up. "Tia, I can't concentrate with that racket outside."

"Put away your BSC, *mija*. I'll teach you how to reach Tomas without it. We are going into advanced lessons tonight. Bring me two of those quartz crystals from the shelf and lie down beside me with your feet touching mine." Tia held the quartz in her hand cupped to her ear. "Hold the quartz like this."

Carmen did as she was told.

"Now, allow yourself to follow everything I do." Tia's voice had grown lower and fuzzier, like Choppo's after too many beers.

Carmen began to drift as if floating on a warm, sun drenched body of water. Slowly, her toes began to tingle, and then the tingle moved up her legs, through her body until she felt a slight vibration in her ears. At that point, she heard a sound like wind riffling water, a soft, easy slap, slap, like the sea against a dock.

Then Tomas' voice came into the room, weak and strained. "Congratulations, Carmelita. You have advanced to a new level. You won't need the BSC anymore, except for a backup. I must be fast—things are bad again on Om. Several Omites have been frozen solid and the Ice Dab is erupting night and day. The chulupurpla crop is disappearing. Also, I have not been able travel to Om. My body is weakened from being held captive on Earth for so long and also from being drugged. I need you to find and release me soon. Work on those numbers..." Loud static. "...I'm sorry that we lost the plato, but I'm glad that Mami and True are safe. Be sure you cleanse yourselves from contact with the bad spirits. I don't know how much longer..." There was a long whistle and then he was gone.

Suddenly, Tia sat up and left the room in a hurry. Carmen felt groggy and weak. Tia returned with a bowl of water and a bowl of salt. "We must purify ourselves from contact with Silver."

Tia sat Carmen up. She moved her hands up and down the sides of Carmen's body then clamped tight onto her forehead. Next she moved around the room, throwing the salt in all directions, grabbing invisible particles from the air, and throwing them into the water. When she had cleansed the entire room, she took the pan of water and sat it on the back porch.

"I'll take care of this when we're done," she said when she had returned to the room.

"Now for some serious shape shifting. You are going to need this skill soon if we are going to rescue Tomas. Give me your quartz. I must charge it with energy. Use the words I taught you in our last session." Together, they held the quartz tightly in a pocket created when both palms were cupped around it, and Carmen felt it growing warmer and warmer, until she finally had to drop it on the rug, for fear of burning her palms. "Now tell the quartz what animal you want to change into. Let's try something simple like a sparrow. Here, take this clay and mold a bird from it."

Carmen set her quartz on the rug, took the clay and began to roll it in her hands. "My bird looks goofy, Tia."

Tia shook her head. "It's fine. Keep visualizing the bird in your mind as you mold the clay. Talk to the quartz and tell it what you want from it. Explain that you want to be turned back into yourself when you are done. That's the step True left out before. Now, take this mirror and hold it in front of your clay bird, while I light the candles. Picture yourself as a small, brown sparrow. Feel its feathers on your back, its sharp beak for pecking open seeds, slick tail feathers, little beebee black eyes and straw fine legs and claws. Imagine seeing everything in this room through the bird's eyes. When the candle has burned down completely, take your bird from out of this bowl of animal crackers and eat it. Then close your eyes and enter your bird fully."

Carmen followed Tia through each of the steps. As she watched the candle flicker in the mirror and slowly shrink, she took the bird animal cracker and ate it. Nothing happened, then very slowly she felt herself rising as if in an elevator. She slowly lifted out of herself and upward on a bank of air, winging high above the earth, looking down at the toy houses and trees, the cool air sliding over and around her, pushing her forward. Carmen soared and drifted for what seemed like forever before she heard a familiar voice whispering in her ear. "Time to re-enter, Carmen. Follow instructions carefully. Picture your crystal bathed in white light and fly into the heart of it, while you visualize the light changing back to its former color. Then picture yourself flying back out of the light. Take your time and allow each change to flow into the other."

Carmen opened her eyes and found that she was now crouched on the floor, gasping for breath. "Tia! That was awesome!"

"*Si, si*. Just remember that we do not use this power just for fun. Save it for times when it is really needed to achieve a purpose."

Just then a loud crash echoed from the other room. Leaping to her feet, Carmen helped Tia up. They found Rosa lying on the floor next to the rocking chair, groaning.

"Mami! Are you okay? What happened?"

"*Nada, nada*. I rock much *duro—Arestro las sabanas que pienso*."

"Si. You rocked too hard." Tia frowned and turned to Rosa. "But what do you mean you are 'dragging the bed sheets'? Do you mean you are depressed?"

"Si," Rosa said weakly.

"Rosa, tell me what troubles you. Tell me everything. We will have a *platica*. Here, come into the other room and sit."

When they had settled Rosa on some cushions, Tia brought tea for her and winked at Carmen. "That's my special brew. *Descubrir los Frijoles* Tea—spill the beans tea."

Rosa sipped the tea and as she did so, her large, wounded-fawn eyes filled with tears. The words spilled out in a gush of Spanish, some of which Carmen could barely catch.

When she was done, Tia was crying also. It was the first time Carmen had seen her aunt cry. "She says that she is not happy here in this country. When Silver's men had her, she overheard them talking about how all the illegals came here and stole jobs from Americans and got free services. And how they wanted to send them all back with a few bullets in their butts. She doesn't have a home anymore, she says. Septima did not make her feel welcome, and she does not want to be a burden to anyone any more. But she doesn't know what to do. She wanted you to learn English, but now you are losing your Spanish. And she can't even tell you how she feels since she can't explain herself so well in English and she doesn't want to worry you. She feels like she is far from home, drifting in a leaky boat that is sinking fast, with no familiar horizon in sight."

Carmen put her arms around her mother and rocked her slowly. "Mami, Mami," she cooed. "We'll find Tomas. We'll find a home again."

Rosa put on her smiley mask, and right then Carmen realized that this had to stop. "You don't have to smile for me, Mami. I want to know how you feel. We've both been protecting each other, and it's not working very well. Let's be honest."

"Okay." Rosa frowned. "The bad men of Silver—I not fight them too much. I want them to call the ICE…to de…"

Carmen stopped rocking. "You mean you wanted to be deported?"

Rosa shook her head sadly. "*Si. Pero*, I not leave you, *mija*."

Carmen didn't know what to say. "It's okay, Mami. I'm glad you told me. We'll find Tomas and then we'll—" Carmen sighed and added lamely, "—figure out where to go and what to do."

She looked helplessly down at her hands and then at the floor. Absentmindedly, she picked up Rosa's movie magazine, leafing through the pages.

Tia lit more candles. "You can help us, Rosa."

Rosa shook her head, her face drooping like a wounded hound dog.

Suddenly, Carmen gave a loud squeal and leapt about the room, waving the magazine in the air. "I know what the numbers mean. You did help us, Mami. I know what they mean!"

Tia was grinning from ear to ear. "Good work, Carmen. We are very close now to getting Tomas back. I'll have Choppo go pick up Chia and True and bring them back for some more lessons in shape shifting. It's good that you and Chia got lessons on Om. Now, we are all going to have to work together. And I have done some new research that I need to teach you all about—ground breaking stuff. I have discovered a very rare flea/tick mutation that causes paralysis, the Dermacenter Mutaflea. Its stings cause temporary paralysis and blackouts that last up to several hours. My source has adapted our shape shifting to include them and I think they can be very helpful to us. Their sting can cause death if untreated, but we will make an anonymous phone call to make sure that doesn't happen. I'm including Chia in these lessons because everyone will be needed to get Tomas back."

CHAPTER 35

The next morning was cold and damp, with a cellophane gray cast. The sun squinted like the eye of a sick dog layered with bluish phlegm. Nevertheless, Carmen's heart jumped up and down like a kid in a "bounce house" when she saw the cab pull up in front of Tia's with Chia and True.

"I was afraid you wouldn't get to come," she said.

"Our cousin Mai came over to pick us up and we switched to Choppo's cab around the corner." Chia winked. "We're supposed to spend the night tonight at Mai's—they think. I figured it would be safest to give ourselves plenty of time."

True closed both eyes in her own version of a wink.

"Can we all fit?" Carmen asked Tia.

"Of course. The skinny minnies go in back. Here, take this basket before you get in. Rosa made us burritos this morning before she left."

"You think she'll be okay with Flora Linda at the encampment?"

"No *problema*. Connie and Flora Linda will take care of her. *Buenos dias, ninas.*"

Chia and True wore bright woolen caps and their faces shone with excitement. Even Caw Caw bobbed and squawked on Tia's shoulder where she sat in the front seat.

"Look," Chia opened her palm, "I brought Caw Caw's favorite—gummy worms."

Caw Caw took one and gave an appreciative squawk.

"You know how to get to Mendota, Choppo?" Carmen asked, climbing into the back seat.

"Am I a cab driver or a choir director?"

Carmen rolled her eyes at Chia, who made a face, waved a hand in the air, then said quickly, "*Hermana*, how did you figure out what the numbers meant?"

"Remember that movie magazine we bought Mami? I was just glancing through it because I didn't know what to say to Mami—how to comfort her. There was a picture of some soap opera chick in a sun dress, showing her shoulder where she has numbers tattooed. It turns out they are the coordinates for all of the places where her kids were born, and holy telenovela, it clicked. I called the library and asked the reference desk to tell me where the coordinates for our numbers would be, and it turned out to be an address in Mendota, which is where we're headed right now. Also, the third solution is supposed to be the correct one." Carmen leaned forward. "What's the plan, Tia?"

Tia let her head roll back onto the seat while Caw Caw nestled down into her neck, ruffling her feathers. "Hold onto your donkeys, chicas. Right now I am full of tiredness—I am awake all night thinking about our operation today. And our special lessons also tired me. But we've gone over the most important things already. Now I need now to sleep some more."

They were out of town on the freeway now, passing small farms and ranch style homes with gravel driveways with two-ton pickups flashing by. Billboards hawking bail bondsmen, accident lawyers, and Happy Meals floated in the sloppy skies, darkened now to a smoky gray. Two huge, dark clouds parted, and the face of a man with silver hair and blue, razor-point eyes seared through the milky flow of almond orchards. Cupping a house in the palm of his hand, he flashed an evil, fake smile and a sign that read, *WE DO IT ALL.*

"Look, it's Silver! " Carmen called out.

True puckered her tiny nose. "A big, mean dab in the sky!"

Before Chia could snap her head around, they had sailed beyond Silver's face in the bloated clouds.

"Wonder what happened to him?" Chia asked, bending over True who was belted in the middle between herself and Carmen.

"He was hurt pretty bad from those bee stings," Carmen responded. "I hope he swells up to the size of an elephant's boil and pops!"

Chia frowned. "Remember, Tia said we should not use our powers for bad. She said it's better not to even wish ill on others. We should look for a way to get what we need by going around the evil, not by clashing head on. I just hope he doesn't get better *too* soon."

Carmen's face burned with shame. She knew Chia was right. Tia wouldn't like them to bring bad down on anyone else. But how, she wondered, were they going to get Tomas back without a fight—one they needed to win.

"So do you think everybody in the world can stop fighting? What about if somebody bad comes and breaks into your house or attacks your country? What do you do then?" Carmen asked, thinking she'd like to see Chia answer that one.

Chia took a while to answer. "It's okay to protect yourself, I think. But you don't go out and do those things first. If everybody did that—"

"What if Silver had hurt True or even—" Carmen sliced her finger across her throat.

"You know what, Carmen, I think Tia would say that you are thinking in the old way when you ask those questions. You have to start thinking in the new way."

"I don't think people can change," Carmen said flatly.

"Change to what?" True scrunched her face up, looking from Chia to Carmen. "I can change to a bee and lady bug. It's fun. You can fly or crawl or swim, and people don't be scared of you like they are of spiders."

From the front seat, Tia chuckled softly. "*Elegante para un polluelo*...um...smart for a spring chicken." she added for Chia and True's benefit.

"No, she's not that smart," Carmen sang out , grinning widely at Chia and True, who grinned back.

Caw Caw jerked as Tia sat up straight and announced, "Choppo, slow down. We should be getting close, I think."

"*Si*. But what are we looking for?"

"*No se*. Just that address I gave you." Tia gave a long, raggedy whistle. "Let's take this exit. I have a feeling. And I hear that look, *muchachas jovenes*."

"Did you hear their eyes rolling, Tia?" True asked with a mischievous smile.

"Enough out of you, True," Chia said as she and Carmen giggled to cover up their embarrassment. Quickly, Chia added, "Not much around here—just that car repair shop, and there's a closed up fruit stand—and what is that building there?"

"Let's park here on the shoulder, Choppo. Carmen, why don't you go see what the number of that place is?"

"Just, uh, knock on the door?" Carmen said, unable to hide her uneasiness.

"Look, the gas station is 5500," Chia said. "It has to be that building just after."

"Looks like a warehouse of some kind. But there don't seem to be nobody around." Choppo got out of the cab, hitching up his jeans. "Let me go see."

They watched him approach the building and knock on the solid, blank, metal door. Craning their necks, they could see him talking to someone standing just inside the shadowy doorway.

Presently, he was back, climbing into his seat. "Some big gorilla answered the door, and all I could see was a small room with a desk and another door that was closed. I said I was lost, but he wouldn't tell me what the number of the place was—kept askin' me what I was lookin' for. So I said I was looking for a friend's house.

"Could you tell what kind of place it is?"

"Nah. Just looked like the office of a warehouse. That guy at the door was packin' though, I can tell you that."

"Was it a packing house?" Chia asked, completely serious.

Everyone laughed, even True. "What are you laughing at, True?" Carmen asked, glad to have someone else looking foolish for a change. "You know what packing means?"

"You take a trip, you have to pack," True chirped, perplexed, when everyone laughed again.

"Or maybe he was *empacando his tortas*," Tia said. "We say 'packing' to mean gobbling up. But it really means carrying a gun, True."

"I know," Carmen squealed. "Let's shape shift right now and storm the building!"

Tia just looked at Carmen and said nothing.

"What was that look?" Chia whispered.

"The shrivel eye," Carmen whispered back. "Makes you want to shrivel up."

Tia ignored them. "See that old orange stand on the other side of the road. "Let's pull over there, eat our burritos, and watch the building for a while. We take our time. We don't want to be too hasty and blow our plan."

Caw Caw hopped up and down, shrieking her approval.

As they ate their burritos, they took turns scoping out the building through binoculars.

"*Na-da, na-da, na-da*," True sang after she'd watched for about five minutes.

"Hey," said Choppo. "The kid's picking up some Spanish,"

Carmen and Chia giggled. "Yea, she's packin' Spanish," Carmen said.

There followed a long stretch of silence, broken finally by Tia, "Did anyone have any dreams last night?"

Chia clapped her hands. "I almost forgot. I had the strangest dream—that Carmen and I were on Om and we had to cross a perilous river and then we came to a giant Dab and we were playing pov pob when a flock of those flying bat-like things with flames coming out of their behinds flew down to us and admired our skill. They asked us to show them how to play, and at first, we said no because we were afraid, but they assured us that there was nothing to fear. We had to follow them down into the dark and when we got to the bottom, we found a huge field and there were two mannequins dressed to look like Omites. We said hello to them and then the fire birds invited us to rest on a bench nearby before we started the game. We tried to sit down, but it was really a red-hot griddle. We jumped up, but our butts were burned and all the firebirds laughed. They told us that we'd have to wait a while to play the game, so we should rest in the Dark House. We knew then that we were really their prisoners. Inside the Dark House, they gave us lighted cigars and said to be sure and not let them go out. But we fell asleep, and when we woke, the cigars had gone out.

"After a long time passed, we were called out of the Dark House and outside, everything now had frozen over like one huge iceberg. A voice came out of the middle of this wall of ice and said that because we had let the cigars go out, we were going to be frozen solid and then broken into pieces like popsicles. And then—" Chia stopped.

"What? What, ese?"

Chia shrugged. "I woke up."

Everyone looked at Tia, whose usual buttoned up face gaped with an awe she couldn't hide. "You had a sacred dream, Chia."

"What does that mean?"

"Well—" Tia hesitated. "Your dream mirrors the story of creation in the Popul Vu, the book of sacred writings for the Mayans. This kind of dream usually means that one has been chosen for sacred work."

"But she's not—" Carmen stopped.

"Yes," Tia said. "Usually it is our people who have these dreams."

"You did say, Tia, that we have to think differently now," Carmen said. "These are different times."

"Is true. Times have changed, and we have to change also. This means that you can be brought in on many of our secret rituals and you can help with much of our work. It also means that we have even more power to tap into. And I think we can use this right now. Let's go over to those trees and we'll review the shape shifting lessons, Chia."

Carmen jumped out of the car after them and gave Chia a hug. "Whoopee!" She pumped her fist in the air then climbed back into the car to take her turn with the binoculars. As she adjusted them, it occurred to her that she might be winning the battle with her inner imp who, in the past, would have slimed her with the green goo of jealousy, despite her resistance.

Choppo leaned his head on the seat back and fell asleep. Carmen and True reviewed the steps for shape shifting and then Carmen picked up the binoculars.

Carmen's eyes began to water from staring. Then her eyelids fluttered sleepily, when suddenly, she saw someone moving around in front of the building. Snapping herself upright, she gasped.

CHAPTER 36

"This is it—the place where they've got Tomas! I just saw Fernando!" Carmen squealed as Tia and Chia rushed back to the car.

They were ready to go now. After they all gathered together, Tia went over the plan she had hatched the previous night. "You have all done well with your shape shifting lessons. Let's cross our fingers and eyes and hope that this new research works. These mutated fleas can help us if the shape shifting works the way it did in our trial runs. I had to make a few adjustments, but first we'll send in our new pet—"

"Don't say Chia Pet. She hates that."

"Okay. We'll send our new cat, K'in Chaac, named after a famous Mayan artist, into the building to find where Tomas is being kept and how many men are there. Then everyone else except Choppo will take our new form, and we'll enter."

Carmen was hopping from one foot to the other. "Tia, Tia. This cat looks like one we had when we were little—Chino—because we thought she had Chinese eyes. It has the same markings, that little white heart above the nose. Tomas loved that cat. And look, there's a pink streak along her flanks, just like in your dream."

Tia set Chia, in her new cat form, on the ground and stroked her tenderly. "You will do well, K'in Chaac. Now go!"

They watched the cat slink across the road, through the weeds and dead crab grass to the door. It sat on the stoop, mewling. As they expected, nothing happened, so Choppo carefully raced across the road, picked up a rock, and took up a position behind a parked truck off to the side. He stood up, threw his rock at the door, then ducked back down.

The gorilla stuck his head out the door then looked down at K'in Chaac, who set up a storm of meows. The man struck his boot toward her, but K'in Chaac split through the opened door in a flash.

"Hey, you damned critter!"

Carmen, Tia, and True now stood by the car on the side away from the road. Tia watched the building through the binoculars. All she saw was Choppo, who had stood up and was heading down the road toward the gas station, she guessed to use the toilet. A good ten minutes passed before the door opened and the big gorilla man tossed K'in Chaac out like a discarded sack of beans.

The next thing Carmen knew, Chia was standing before her, crying. "I saw Tomas. I saw him. They have him in a room way at the back of the building. That place is filled with rooms full of statues, antiques, pottery, bones, even an old saddle. Tomas was sleeping, and I saw another man, a creepy-looking man with lots of tattoos, come into the room and give him a shot. There's about ten guys in the house. They're all inside working in different rooms. Some work at computers, and some are like guards, cuz there's other rooms like the one Tomas is in, but no other prisoners that I could see. And you are right, Carmen. That's Fernando in there. He seems to be working for them."

"I thought Fernando was in jail or juvy. What do you think—"

"Never mind for now," Tia snapped. "Good work, K'in Chaac. Now it's our turn to go in. Is everybody ready?"

"We better hurry," Chia said. "I heard them talking about moving Tomas somewhere else today. One said that the big boss is getting nervous cuz Silver is still in the hospital and they can't keep drugging the kid forever. Then he said maybe they need to just get rid of the kid."

Carmen's eyes popped. "Okay. We have to get Tomas out of there for sure. But that's good news—that Silver's still not well enough to cause us trouble. Okay. Let's go, *companeras*."

"Remember, girls, in your new states, it is not natural to speak. So we'll have to communicate with our minds. It will be like speaking, but not out loud. Chia, you'll stay here and keep your eyes on the front. When you see Tomas coming out of the building, you run across the street and help him. He will be pretty drugged, most likely. Now where has that Choppo gone?"

Carmen pointed to the station. "He went down there, maybe to pee."

Tia shook her head while Chia took over the binoculars and the rest of them held hands, chanting. Tia had lit the candles and placed them in a circle. "This will be difficult, since we are not in an ideal place to shape shift. But we can do it. Follow the instructions I gave you exactly. Don't—"

"Um, we've got company, Tia."

Out of nowhere, it seemed, a highway patrol car pulled up behind them. "Buenas dias," a tall red headed officer said, through a wad of gum, as he climbed from his patrol car. "Y'all got some ID...*papeles*?"

"Of course, and we speak English. Just let me get my bag from the car." Tia made a move toward the car, but he held up a leather gloved hand.

"What the heck's all them candles for?"

"We are making an *offrenda*, an offering—a small shrine here where our dear friend was killed in a car accident just the other—"

"Oh yea. Heard 'bout that. Wasn't on duty that night, but sure was terrible thing. Them bastard—scuze me ladies, them dang drunk drivers."

Carmen's eyes almost popped out of her head. How could Tia have known that? Or was it just a lucky guess?

The patrolman had his back to the road and didn't see what Carmen now saw, that the door to the building had swung open. One of the men had exited with a duffel bag and was heading to the van parked on the other side by the ditch. There wasn't much time. Her heart jolted.

Busy with the patrolman, no one had noticed Choppo coming up from behind a row of oleanders just past where he'd parked the cab.

"Ho, there—whas goin' on?" Choppo stumbled and almost fell right in front of the cop's leather boots. He caught himself, however, and lurched upward, his bloodshot eyes wobbling.

"You been drinkin', Mister?" the patrolman asked, extending his hand. "How 'bout I have a look at yer license."

Carmen saw another man come out of the building, and the two stood talking, watching the scene across the street from them.

They could all smell the booze wafting off of Choppo now and his silly grin did nothing to help his case.

"Chure, chure. I gotta licensh." Choppo's moved his silly-putty lips with an effort. "I just had one beer, Mishter Gold Star."

Tia clapped her hands to the sides of her head and rained a confetti of angry Spanish down on Choppo. She turned to the cop. "He drives us here, and now look how he is. You can throw him in jail, with my blessing."

The patrol officer seemed only too happy to arrest Choppo, and Choppo did not protest. Turning to face the cab with his legs spread, he was searched and then cuffed. As they watched, Choppo was marched to the patrol car and then driven away.

Seeing the alarm on the girls' faces, Tia shook her head. "I'm sorry to have to do that, but it was the fastest way to get rid of the cops. We'll get him out later."

Carmen dropped the binoculars. "Oaky. We've got to hurry. They're getting things ready to go, I think. Is there a faster way, Tia, for us to shape shift?"

"No. Take your time, Carmen. Do not panic, whatever you do."

Tia began to chant and Carmen and True joined in. Chia took up the binoculars now. Another man had exited the building with a box the size of a laundry basket, which he stuffed in the back of the van. She saw him step down from the back end, holding a pile of something shiny. Blinking, she saw that it was shackles and cuffs. Her hands grew slippery with sweat, and she almost dropped the binoculars.

She was alone now and couldn't see her sister, Carmen, and Tia in their new flea form, so all she could do was stretch her eyes looking. Then she began her own chant, a Hmong prayer she had learned from her grandmother in Laos.

Minutes ticked by, and only a few cars passed. Caw Caw had returned and settled down on the headrest, also waiting. In the distance, Chia heard a siren, but after its wail drew closer, it veered away, back into the distance, and vanished. The metal door buckled and waved when her eyes watered. The whole day seemed unreal, like a movie she hoped would not end badly. She was excited at the possibility of seeing Tomas again but also a bit scared.

Her feelings for Tomas had grown while they'd been apart, and the one time she'd seen him on Om, she'd had that same old happy-sick feeling she'd felt when he used to walk her home from school before all the trouble began. She remembered the one time he had kissed her.

She'd been teasing him about Muncea, and he acted really mad. Then he'd stopped in the middle of the street, before the whole world, pulled her to him, and kissed her right on the lips. Many times after that, she'd recreated that moment in her day-dreams. What if he felt different now? What if—she had never thought of it before—but what if, he had a girl on Om?

Stop it! she scolded herself. She thought instead about how she was being depended upon to watch the doors and how she'd better pay attention.

When the door opened finally, she did not see Tomas. Instead, she saw Fernando scanning the street. He seemed to look directly at her, but she couldn't tell if he had seen her or not before he turned back and shut the door.

CHAPTER 37

C aw Caw sailed smoothly over the road, with her cargo tucked under her wings, and landed on the winter barren limb of a magnolia tree. The three fleas, Tia, Carmen, and True, crawled out and launched themselves into the air, landing on the ledge above the doorway, waiting. Caw Caw set up a noisy racket, cawing, screeching, and even diving at the metal door.

"What's goin' on here today?" Fernando demanded. "Hey, what the hell? We got some kind of gang banger bird out here? He a crip or a blood?"

Well, he black so he be a blood, less he a buster and spyin' on us." His grin was only half serious. Manny had followed Fernando out the door, shaking his head.

"*Cerrado, hombre.* Hey, where's that bag?"

"You had it, *cabron.*"

They turned to enter the building, with no knowledge of the three, tiny intruders who had slipped inside the building.

Tia, in her flea form, led the group to a coffee pot, behind which they huddled briefly. There was no time to waste. Fernando had just called to Manny to hand over the credit card so he could get some gas for the trip.

Tia went down first, dipping, then settling onto Manny's knit hat. From there, she crawled down past his ear, on down his neck, to the best spot to inject her tranquilizing nectar, the vein that stood out on his neck.

"Ouch" he squalled and narrowly missed smashing Tia flat as he swiped at his neck.

In a matter of seconds, though, he was weaving down the hallway. Then he slumped to the floor.

"Manny! Get me that freakin' card, man."

Carmen had touched down on Fernando's collar and now teetered there, unused to her skinny, new legs. Just as she was ready to plunge into his neck, he jumped up. She lost her balance, sliding downward, landing in a tuft of hairs at the base of his throat.

True hopped into one of the back rooms. Tia had said to strike hard and fast, since there were at least eight or nine of the bad guys and only three of them. True found two men swigging beer, with their feet propped up on a desk where two computers hummed, one screen full of names and numbers. One of the men punched the other with a soft fist and then they were both scuffling like snarling street kids. Just as True would almost hit one target, it moved then flew in the other direction. They were now down on the floor, one clamped in a wrestling hold, screaming out a chain of cuss words.

True zoomed in and bit right into the neck of the one being held down, his shriek blending with his cuss words. When he went limp, the other one sat up laughing. "Got ya a good one, *Tonto.*"

There was no response.

"Hey, Tonto, whas up? " He slapped Tonto's face lightly then felt a sting on his own neck. In a matter of seconds, he slid down on top of his sparring partner, like two marionettes whose strings had been abruptly cut.

Tia had taken care of the ones who seemed to do most of the manual labor. They had been busy packing up boxes of what she suspected were confiscated artifacts in one of the back rooms. One had stopped working for a moment, stretched his arms out from either side of his body, and yawned widely, almost an invitation for Tia's bite, which she obligingly gave him. *That was too easy*, she thought.

She hoped that the next one would be as easy, but when she hopped into the room where he sat on guard with Tomas, she saw him puffing away on a cigarette, bad news for a flea. Gingerly, she picked her way over his body, trekking upward from his thigh on the chair where he sat, staring into space and flicking ash into the base of a sickly, washed-out rubber plant between him and the metal bed where Tomas lay sleeping. As she worked her way across his belly, hopping from one roll of fat to another, kind of like riding a beach buggy at the sand dunes, she fought nausea from his cigarette smoke. She paused, almost retching when the man, who had been scratching and cussing, let out a yelp. He brought his big, beefy hand down and smacked Tia, rolling her over like a log heaved over the edge of a cliff. She was almost flattened and, struggling for air, collapsed in his arm hairs.

Meanwhile, True had disposed of two more workers in one of the back rooms. She met up with Carmen on the sill over the doorway.

'*Good going,*' Carmen told her telepathically. '*We've got them all but Fernando and the one who guards Tomas.*'

True nodded her tiny head so Carmen would know she understood. '*I got a funny feeling about Tia,*' she replied. '*Let's go find her.*'

They hopped into the room, Carmen leading the way, and found Tia laid out, as if lifeless, next to a mole on the man's arm. She was shaking up and down as if on a ride at the fair, when the man hacked and coughed in a dirty cloud of his own smoke. He was also clawing at his arm where Tia lay.

'*I'll hop around on his other arm while you get Tia,*' True said as she squatted into position to leap.

That would make it easy for Carmen. But she also knew that True was taking all the risks. Carmen felt her skinny little flea knees weaken. She took a deep breath. '*No True. I have to do this. I'm the oldest. I'll keep him busy—*'

'*But I'm faster—*'

'*No! There's no time to argue.*'

And saying this, Carmen leaped at the man's nose, which he promptly swatted, coming so close to her that she lost her balance and tumbled into another ring of smoke that smothered her tiny body. Shaking her head, she picked herself back up and darted at his face, this time grazing his cheek. While she danced, dipped, and skipped just out of his reach, she was reminded of the crop dusters they used to watch diving under the wires in dare devil acrobatics.

True had reached Tia and was trying to revive her. After she had dragged Tia off his arm and onto the floor, she raced back to help Carmen, just in time to see Carmen looping the loop in the air and circling back right into the jaws of danger.

Carmen took a wild leap at the man's upper lip and dug in. As the cigarette flew through the air, the man opened his mouth in an ear-splitting scream. The cigarette had flipped onto his arm, narrowly missing True, but burning him.

In the middle of a storm of cuss words, he slumped over and hit the floor with a thud. Carmen and True touched high fives in the air, but their celebration was short lived. The man had fallen over onto the spot where Tia lay on the floor, trapping her under him.

True looked at Carmen, with her slanted bug eyes. '*Now what?*'

Carmen had no idea what to do, but as she pondered, she felt a shadow closing over her. She looked up at Tomas who had been unchained, probably for relocation. He was now bending over the fallen man, looking puzzled.

Stumbling, he worked his way to the doorway and turned. He looked back as if not sure he trusted his eyes and then disappeared through the door into the next room.

True rubbed her two front pincers together. '*We got to do something to get Tia out.*'

Carmen went blank. With no clear ideas coming through, she made a split second decision. '*Okay. Here's what we'll do. You crawl up into his ear and rub ear wax all over yourself. Then you can slide under his arm where he's trapping Tia.*'

True shivered. '*Ick!*'

'*Got a better idea?*'

'*Yea. You cover yourself in ear wax.*' True was not so eager for heroics now. This was just dirty, stinky work.

'*Okay, I'll do it*,' Carmen said, hoping that True would still volunteer, but she didn't.

At the rim of his ear, Carmen spun her elongated flea's head around, but True wasn't budging. So she paused, took a deep breath, and dived into the fleshy cave. It twisted around like an old time fire escape or a twisty barrel slide at the park. Carmen swung from the ear hairs, slowly descending. She saw a soft bone covered with skin that looked like a drum and was tempted to give it a few thumps, but she didn't want to risk prodding the man. His ear was pretty clean. There wasn't a lot of wax. But as she lowered herself into the depths, she finally saw a puddle of gooey wax.

Here goes, she thought and stuck one pincher in. It was horrible, like climbing into a vat of rancid grease, but this was, ugh, ear wax. And the smell wasn't so great either, kind of like a grimy candle and dirty soap scum. Carmen crept downward and rubbed her body into the wax, finally rolling into it fully. She almost gagged. But when she was finally coated, she started her climb back up and out of the ear, a much more slippery trek than going down. Several times, she slipped backward. But finally, she reached the lip of the ear.

When she emerged, True was there waiting. '*Wow*! *You did it*! *I've been thinking. Rub some on me. We'll go under his arm together. It may take both of us to pull her out.*'

ᕱᕲᕱ

Tomas was now leaning against the wall in the hallway. He felt so weak that he could hardly walk more than a few steps at a time. And his head felt like it was stuffed with cotton. Blinking his eyes again and again, he tried to focus, but he couldn't bring the pieces together. Just as he reached the door of the outer room, he fell forward and landed on the floor in a heap.

When he opened his eyes, Fernando was clutching a back-pack and bending over him. "What's goin' on here? It's like all these dudes here tweakin' on somethin'. You okay, homeboy?"

"Don't know. They all knocked out—but you with them, ain't you?"

"Naw. Dr. Sicko, he's my P.O. tole me to work for them—
he sprung me outa juvy. They say they own me then, but don't
nobody own Fernando, man. Then I find out they knockin' you
down, and they go after that Meeow kid. I don't go for that—
ain't right—hurtin' kids. I say okay, okay, I help you, but all the
time I'm thinkin', *How can I get my homeboy Tomas outa here*?
And today I'm gonna help you with that other thing and then I
was goin' to get them to let me go in the van to move you and
we goin' to—"

But Fernando didn't finish his sentence. Instead, he
grabbed his neck, gave one loud yelp, and, still holding the
backpack, pitched forward.

Tomas saw nothing, but he felt a tickling on his arm, which
he shook before taking a deep breath. He had to pull himself
together enough to find the van keys. They had to be here
somewhere. He had to find them quickly before someone else
came. As he searched the office, the tickle traveled up his arm,
over his shoulder, and up the back of his neck. Must be cats or
dogs around here, he thought, with their party crasher fleas.

He shook his head again, as if to clear it of spider webs, but
now a splitting headache added to his discomfort. Then he heard
footsteps coming from outside.

CHAPTER 38

T rue and Carmen had now hopped down to the floor where the arm lay like a felled Redwood tree over Tia. Carmen hoped that she could breathe beneath him. *'Go ahead kid. You're the smallest. See if you can wiggle under there.'*

True paced back and forth around the spot where she thought Tia was. The arm was flat on the floor, an immovable trunk of flesh. Carmen joined her, looking up at the wall of dark skin with its carpet of spiky hairs. His cigarette box lay beside them, open with two white cones extended.

'Hey, we can use these!' Carmen said. *'Help me get them out and we can push them underneath and open up a space under his arm.'*

Together, they lugged the cigarettes out from the box and, panting, shoved them under his arm about two inches apart. This made a very small cave. They both pushed, wriggled, and squirmed into it.

Finally, True pulled out. *'I think I've got ahold of her foot. Let's keep going.'*

Carmen crawled back out, shoved the cigarettes farther under the arm, then rejoined True. Together they pulled on what they hoped was Tia's leg. Little by little, more and more of Tia's flea body was revealed as they pulled with all their might. Finally, they had her out. They sprawled beside her where she lay limp and still.

'*Does she breathe?*' True asked in a whisper. She was almost afraid to ask, afraid of the answer.

'*I think so, but it's very faint.*' Carmen put her own flea's head close to Tia's. '*We need to get her out of here.*'

'*We need to shape shift back now, do we?*' True looked at Carmen with her baby flea eyes.

Carmen's stomach sank in the same way it had when she had spent all day writing an essay on pirates, only to find out her topic was supposed to be on pyrite and its use in iron ore production. She had been so busy trying to climb the hill that she hadn't bothered to look for the road around it. They could have shape shifted back to themselves before and easily have moved the man's arm. *Good thing True is too little to think of that also*, she thought. But when she snuck a look at True, she saw the same thought dancing in True's eyes.

'*Yea, let's shape shift. Better late than never. And, uh...*'

When they had both successfully shape shifted back to themselves, True hunched her shoulders, grinned, and stuck her pudgy finger up to her lips. "No worry, our secret."

"Yea. Maybe Tia has lessons on making better panic decisions."

❧❧❧

Tomas grabbed the first thing he saw, a staple gun off of the desk nearby, and hid behind the door, waiting for it to open. He hoped he had the strength to use it if he needed to. Poised at the door, he listened and heard the faint movement of someone outside. Still holding the staple gun, he moved around to where he could open the door, which he did very slowly. And there stood Chia, looking as frightened as he did.

Chia gasped then threw her arms around him, her face smeared with a happy wetness. "I can't believe it's you, Tomas. We've been so worried."

Tomas couldn't hide the silly grin that stretched so far across his face, it almost hurt. "You need anything stapled?" he said, as he unwound himself awkwardly from Chia's embrace.

Chia burst into nervous laughter then threw her hands up, "Careful with that gun, it could be loaded."

"Only blanks, *dulcita*. Hey, help me find the keys so we can get out of here before these hombres wake up."

Chia felt a warm glow flooding over her with Tomas' "*dulcita*," a word she knew meant sweetie.

Before they could move, the other door opened to reveal True and then Carmen, who leaped onto Tomas, her legs circled around him, screaming, "Tomas! Tomas! I can't believe it. Mami will be so happy." She laid her head on his shoulder, and now everyone was crying at once, even True.

"Why we cry?" she asked Chia finally.

"So why did you cry, if you didn't know why, little sister?"

True shrugged. "I want to be in the party, too."

"Yes!" Carmen squealed. "We will have a party tonight for sure."

"Wait, where's Tia?" Chia's happy smile faded to a sudden look of alarm.

Carmen also sobered. "We need to get her home pronto. Show them, True."

True held out a matchbox nestled in her hand, around which they all gathered now. In the middle, lay a tiny unmoving speck.

Tomas frowned and looked from Carmen to Chia. "What the—"

Chia hurried to answer. "We shape shifted into poisonous fleas. That's how we took out all these…"

"*Malcriados*" Tomas finished for her. "*Chevere*. Okay Let's find the keys and get moving. The sooner we get out of here, the sooner we can help her." As he said the words, he seesawed back and forth on his feet, barely able to stand.

Carmen had already started moving. "We have a car, T. And Chia's got the keys with her. *Vamanos*."

But Tomas almost fell over when he started to move his feet. Carmen and Chia ran to hold him up.

"We gotta take Fernando with us," he said and he used what little strength he had left to convince them that Fernando had been trying to help him escape.

So they just dragged Fernando, looping his backpack over his shoulder.

Finally, when they were all settled in the car, with Tomas' head resting on Chia's lap in the back seat, and Fernando squished beside Tomas against the back door, Tomas raised his head weakly. "Who's gonna drive this crate?"

"I am." Carmen turned to smile weakly at Tomas, repeating what her father used to say when they traveled the winding roads to the migrant camps. "Close your eyes and open your Bibles, *mi familia*."

CHAPTER 39

There was a great celebration that night at the encampment where they had taken Tomas to surprise Mami.

But first, they had put Tia in her matchbox in the tent. Chia, Carmen, and Flora Linda had lit candles, chanted, and said prayers. True had done a soul calling ceremony, burning joss sticks and paper money in a flat, brass bowl, while Chia banged on the gong. True had galloped around the tent on a stick that Flora Linda found for her, throwing her water buffalo horns and rattle on the floor again and again.

Finally, they had all left the room, making sure to open the door between the two rooms and also the flap that led to the outside. While everyone else began the preparations for the celebration, True sat outside the tent chanting.

"Where are you our Tia?
"Where have you gone so far away from us?
"Are you wading in the river?
"Are you climbing over the distant hills?
"Do you wander among the stars?
"Come back to us our Tia.
"Come back and sing with us and teach us again.
"We call you home to us.
"We call your arms, your legs, your eyes
"We call your mouth, your nose and your toes

"We call your heart
"Come home and join the celebration.
"Come home and bring us your wisdom."

"We are calling your love for us
"to come back into our hearts and sing
"to join us on our journey here on earth
"come back to the ones who need you.
"We call you now to us.
"Let your spirit sing and fly to us
"over the distant trees and let the wind
"bring you back. Let the sun shine
"the beauty of your soul down on us.
"Come back to us.
"Come back to us and show us your love and magic."

Then she was singing and chanting in Hmong with Chia joining in. It began to grow dark. The air was filled with the delicious aroma of the barbeques fired up for chicken, hot dogs, slabs of pork, and pots of beans. Word had gone round the encampment of the return of the missing boy, and everyone was ready to join in the celebration.

Carmen was pleased with herself for getting them home safely in Choppo's cab, but she was still worried about Choppo and not sure what to do about it without Tia's help.

She and Chia had been discussing the problem, when Chia's face suddenly lit up. "Look, Carmen, over there." She pointed through the smoke and failing light to a cocky-looking Choppo headed their way.

Both girls rushed toward him. "How'd you get out of jail? We were just trying to figure out how—what to do." Carmen's words were tumbling together. And she caught the faintest odor of alcohol when Choppo waved his arms.

"They can't keep old Choppo in jail, y' know. Two cops, big guys, I wrestled 'em down and took their guns. Yea. I broke outa there pronto. Takes more than a few steel bars to keep me down."

Carmen and Chia exchanged skeptical looks.

Chia couldn't help but say, "C'mon, Choppo. What really happened?"

"You don't believe that I could break out?"

"Okay, I believe that you could, but not that it happened that way."

Choppo smoothed his hair and grinned. "Okay. They booked me, but I got friends who bailed me out, and I knew they couldn't keep me cuz they didn't have no proof that I been drinking that beer while driving. And they didn't give me no breath test. And I knew Tia wouldn't testify against me, so I wasn't worried. But hey, Tomas was pretty tore up, and where's Tia?"

Despite herself, Carmen burst into tears. "Tomas'll be okay." Her tears were streaming now. "But Tia, she's—she shape shifted and got injured, and now—"

Choppo's face betrayed his alarm. "She's not—"

"She's alive. True and Uncle Blong are working on a soul retrieval," Chia said. "We're trying to stay positive. Everyone in camp is making a feast to celebrate Tomas' return." She waved at the clumps of people grouped around their fires.

Around Flora Linda's fire gathered faces of all colors. Connie was there with a tall black man with a tiger sweat shirt and a small group chattering in Spanish. Flora Linda brought out her flute and played a somber tune. Everyone was waiting for the sign. They didn't know what it would be or why they waited, but they held their communal breath and sang softly, sipping slowly at cans and bottles and paper cups.

The air filled with smoke, pink-candled light, and expectation. Suddenly, Flora Linda's tune swung from the solemnity of wet umbrellas to the delight of thrown confetti.

There in the doorway of the tent stood Tia, looking somewhat dazed and pale, but smiling. "Quickly, Choppo," she said, her voice thin and faltering, "There's no time to lose. I must make that phone call to alert the hospital about the poisonous flea stings."

"You are weak, Tia. Let me make the call," Carmen stepped forward.

Tia swayed and then nodded to Choppo. "Get my bag. I have the information inside that you need to tell them. Here's the phone number of the hospital with a poison control department." Tia then turned to the gathered crowd. "Let's get this party started."

A loud whoop came up from somewhere in the midst of the camp, and soon everyone was singing, dancing, and buzzing happily. A thin man with shaggy hair brought out a guitar. He and Flora Linda played tunes together, joined by Choppo on his harmonica when he returned to camp with Carmen. As the fire crackled and the music and barbeque scents filled the air, Tomas looked from Mami's to Chia's to Carmen's faces, all glowing with happiness in the campfire. He threw back his head like a coyote, howling its delight up to the moon and stars.

CHAPTER 40

Chia woke, shivering, tucked between Carmen and True inside the tent. The rhythmic bark of a dog could be heard outside in the encampment. Basking in the glow of remembered music and laughter, she hugged herself happily.

An old man named Juggler had juggled cans of soup and then tennis shoes. Connie had told jokes and Flora Linda had pulled flowers out of people's ears. Even Mami, glowing with happiness, had sung and joined in the festivities.

When Tomas had put his arm around Chia, she felt a warm glow work up from her toes to her head. To draw attention away from her blazing face, she had blurted, "Hey, what happened to Fernando? Last I saw, they put him down in Flora Linda's tent to recover, and then he was gone."

"Dunno. Ferni's got a lot of heat on him. He'll get in touch, I hope. There's something Fernie said, but I can't remember. That time's still fuzzy."

"Hey, wanna dance?" Chia asked, trying for an uncaring tone.

Chia and Tomas then danced until he grew too weak and had to lie down in the tent. But Chia had continued dancing and singing with Carmen and True until early in the morning.

☙☙☙

One week later:

Carmen was sitting in Tia's backyard, shelling peas, wrapped in a heavy, woven Indian blanket. Chia's people seemed to have an endless supply of fresh vegetables all year long. Carmen was helping to prepare food for a dinner that night for True and Chia, and her own family that now included Tia and Mami. Thinking about her new "stretched family," as Chia had called it, sent fingers of warmth up and down Carmen's spine. In the little window on Tia's back porch, she caught glimpses of Mami moving about the kitchen, preparing her special chicken mole.

Tia had many devoted clients who came to her for healing and help with a wide range of problems. They now were also buying Mami's burritos and tamales, putting money in Rosa's pocket, which seemed to bolster her new health and vigor as much as any of the *limpias*.

There had also been *limpias* for Tomas and for Tia, who was still regaining her strength.

A flash of white in the window interrupted Carmen's thoughts. Good. The mail was here. She was anxiously waiting for her report card to come, hoping to get to it first, afraid of what it contained.

But Tia was too fast for her and grabbed the mail before Carmen could reach it. Tia shuffled through the mail slowly, deliberately. Some bills, advertisements, other business, and a letter with colorful stamps from Mexico.

Carmen couldn't contain herself and blurted, "That looks really important, Tia. It's from Mexico, isn't it?"

Tia's face lit up. "Ah, I have been waiting for this." She tucked it into her skirts.

Carmen frowned. "Don't tell me, more waiting for me, too?"

"You can join Rosa in the waiting room and cry on each other's shoulders. I'll read this to everyone after we eat."

Carmen just rolled her eyes and left, knowing it was futile to press Tia on this.

e∕ɔe∕ɔ

When Chia and True arrived, Carmen smiled to herself, noticing Chia's not so subtle glances around the room, looking for Tomas, she guessed.

"Your novio can't join us, I'm afraid." But when she saw Chia's crestfallen look, Carmen softened her tone. "He's been spending as much time on Om as he can and he's also been talking to the FBI. They want to build a case against Silver, but they need more evidence. All that has exhausted him and he's resting right now in Tia's trance room."

Chia couldn't hide her disappointment but said, "I just hope things aren't too bad on Om right now."

Tia clapped her hands, "Let's eat, everyone, before the food gets deported."

So they ate, stuffing themselves with Mami's chicken mole; frijoles; salsa made from freshly ground chilies, braised peas, and mustard greens; chicken prepared Hmong style, with sticky rice; spring rolls; and pepper dipping sauce. When they were all done, they gathered around the fire pit outside with the first evening stars sparkling low on the horizon.

Tia looked solemnly around the group. "Just to fill you all in, Tomas and I are still trying to find the plato. It can be of great help on Om, but Tomas has to conserve his strength and he can only do so much. We don't think that Silver has the plato because I have had several dreams that lead me to think this. Please plant thoughts of finding the plato into your mind before you fall asleep to let your dreams work for you. We also have news that Silver is out of the hospital. My spies have been watching him and his men. You must all be very careful. Do not take any risks and make sure you aren't being followed. "

Carmen was rocking impatiently back and forth in her folding chair. "Tia, Don't forget about the letter from Mexico."

"*Si. Si.* It is a bit long, so I'll just tell you what's in it. It's from a cousin in Mexico I had lost touch with. But she lives in Guadalajara which is close to the village where Septima is visiting other relatives. She tells me that when Septima got to Mexico, she was so ill, they had to take her to a clinic, but the doctors couldn't find the problem. So Septima has been seeing a *curendera*, and finally, her condition is starting to improve."

Tia paused, just as Carmen jumped up. "Holy Guano! After all her lectures to us about witches and sacrilegious magic."

Tia frowned. "But we are glad she is better, no?"

Carmen opened her mouth to speak, but Rosa piped up. "*Gracias de los santos para las curenderas.*"

Carmen grinned. "That's right Mami. It's good to mix magic."

Then Tia stood up, her serape hanging down in a tent around her. "I know you have lots of questions that need answers. Tomas thinks there is a connection between the plato and Fernando. He has a vague memory from the warehouse, but it's still fuzzy. I know you girls might be ready to light out tomorrow, if not sooner, in search of Fernando. I must, however, veto this. I don't think it's a good idea. I don't want you getting mixed up with the gang bangers. And our time would be better spent in lessons and healing right now. You all have much to learn, and we're just getting back to normal. I feel stronger than ever, but if Fernando has information about the plato, I think he'll contact us. *Haberle visto las orejas al lobo.*" Tia paused. "I guess I have a few sayings of my own. We have seen the wolf's ears—in other words, we've had a few narrow escapes lately, and I think we need to lay low. I have a feeling about the plato—that it's safe. So, tomorrow, come here and we'll begin some advanced lessons in *curandisma* and other skills that you'll need for future visits to Om. And don't forget your dreams."

Carmen looked at Chia. "What do you say, *hermana*?"

"Okay." Chia moved her head up and down but her heart was moving back and forth.

"Now, for *la musica*," Tia continued. "Flora Linda has brought her special instrument, and she's written a tune for us. It's called, 'When the Ice Melts.'"

Flora Linda bowed low and everyone stomped their feet and clapped.

CHAPTER 41

The next day, Saturday Carmen and Chia had agreed to meet at the Pho.

Chia arrived without True, looking tired, "All this stuff has got me worn out. True has the skittles today, so she's at home."

Carmen was puzzled. "Skittles? What's that?"

"No, not skittles. I always get that word mixed up. I think I mean sniff...sniff..."

"You mean sniffles."

"Yea. that's it."

Carmen gave Chia a long look then finally said, "I know you're not happy about Tia's decision, Chia."

"No, but she's probably right, don't you think?"

"Yea, probably, about Fernando. But that doesn't mean we can't do something else. Look, I have an idea. I've been wishing I could talk to Uncle Teo and ask him some questions. He's involved in this, we know, and I've got my suspicions. We know he's back at the house, so let's go over there. I'll just knock on the door and talk to him, mention the plato and see how he reacts. Maybe I can find out something." She winked. "I have a feeling."

Chia frowned. "Uh-oh, not you too. But, I don't know, Carmen. I don't trust him. And maybe he's dangerous."

Carmen gave a horsey, blubbering snort. "Uncle Teo? I'm not afraid of him. He's a big ox with marshmallows for guts."

"I don't know, Carmen, it sounds like a crazy idea—let's do it!"

So they headed out to Immaculate Motors on foot. The Mongoose was long gone.

❧❧❧

Immaculate Motors looked the same, but deserted, with the weeds several inches taller. And there in the driveway was Teofilo's truck.

Carmen knocked loudly. "Oh hi, Uncle Teo," Carmen said, trying for a chatty tone. "How was Mexico? How's Tia Septima?"

Teofilo looked like a water-logged buffalo, his jowls hanging spongy, his whole face inflated with a huge question mark. "Umm...look, I had to sell this place. We needed the dough. It sold after we left, so I don't get a chance to tell you."

Carmen knew that was a lie.

"But I might get a chance to get it back. Deal's uh...going kinda sour."

Carmen smiled her fake, cheery smile. "We got a place to stay. Don't worry. But I would like to know how you sold this place without Tia Septima's consent."

Teo looked down at the floor sheepishly. "Uh—I sign for her."

Carmen tried to peek behind his hulking frame, but all she could see was a mess of things thrown everywhere. "What you mean is that you forged her signature." She glared at him then continued. "But I would like to ask you some questions, Teo. Can I come in?"

"Now's not a good time. How 'bout you come back tomorrow?"

"Okay. Just tell me this, Uncle, did you ever know anything about a plato? It belonged to my family. It's not worth much, I don't think, but it has sentimental value to us."

Teo's eyes widened as he fought to keep his face neutral. "Noooo, *nada*. Not no plato. If I find one though, I call you, pronto."

He tried to shut the door, but Carmen had anticipated this and shoved her foot with lightning speed into the door frame. "Look here, we know you worked with Silver, and that's why Tomas was grabbed. But I don't know if you know that he was crooked, taking people's stuff and working with the ICE to deport them. Tomas is testifying against him—he's with the FBI right now."

Tomas was planning to testify, but only if they could build a case. But Carmen let it sink in anyway. Even dull Teofilo should be able to see that he might be implicated. His face now was a map she had seen many a time when he'd been threatened by Septima—a map of confusion and imminent flight.

"*Mira*, Carmen, I don't know about Mr. Silver doing stuff like that. I know him from long time ago. I fixed some vans for him. Your father—he worked for him—he was getting people across *La Frontera*, you know."

Carmen gasped. "My father would never work for someone like that. But wait—" Her hand flew up to her mouth. The wheels in her brain spun into blurs as puzzle pieces fell into place. If Teo had been doing work for Silver, it would only make sense that he might have blabbed about the plato to him.

Teofilo couldn't hide the combination of fear and sheepishness that fought for his face as he rubbed his chin nervously.

Chia, who had said nothing up until then, now spoke. "You should know that Silver and his men are dangerous. They kidnapped my sister and also Carmen's mother."

"Not to mention grabbing Tomas," Carmen hurried to add.

Teo's voice now shook as terror hijacked his face. "Jesus y Maria, I know Mr. Silver not so nice, but not so bad as that. I swear to los santos, I never would help Mr. Silver do nothing that bad. I need the dinero, and he give me some when I am broke and he say at first that he will pay a lot for the business, but when I sign the papers, it's all different." Teo looked almost as if he would cry.

"So did Silver ask you about the plato?" Carmen persisted. "The FBI may be asking about that."

"Maybe, I'm not sure. Mr. Silver he asked me about a plato before I went to Mexico. I can't remember what I told him."

Teo was a terrible liar, Carmen thought as she gave him her best version of Tia's stink eye. "So that's how Silver found out about the plato. He stole it from us, you know."

Teo looked genuinely surprised. "But he is asking me about it again."

Carmen did her best to keep her mouth from gaping open. "When was that, Uncle Teo?"

"Uh…" Teo rocked unsteadily on his big, floppy feet. "This morning he come by to bring papers. Our deal is no good now, he says. And then he asks me about the plato. But I don't know nothing."

Carmen snuck a look at Chia but didn't need the BSC to read her thoughts—Silver did not have the plato.

⌘⌘⌘

Carmen unwrapped a granola bar and washed it down with cinnamon, orange tea that Flora Linda had handed to her in an old stone mug. They were at the encampment, where Teo had dropped them off from Immaculate Motors.

"Guano, Chia," Carmen said. "Did you see Teofilo's face? I had him on the run with my questions. If the FBI ever gets ahold of him, they'll have a party. He can't answer questions at all. He gets all confused. And it doesn't take much to scare the truth out of him."

"Or at least part of the truth." said Chia. "But hey, you were pretty good, Miss Jr. FBI."

"Well, what could he do? I already had him cornered. But that business about my dad working for Silver. I know my dad wouldn't have worked for bad guys like that. I think that he was trying to use them so he could get information about people who needed help to keep them from being deported. But they double crossed my dad and had the ICE go after him. They said my dad pulled a gun on them, and that's why they shot him, but Pops never had a gun. I know for sure. I bet Dad trusted Teo, though, and told him stuff which Teo then told Silver."

Chia grinned. "Good work Sherlock. Hey, Flora Linda, got any more of those granola bars? Grilling suspects makes me hungry."

Flora Linda nodded, dug into her pocket, and handed Chia a granola bar.

"Thanks," Chia said. Then she turned to Carmen. "We need to let Tia know about Silver not having the plato."

Carmen nodded thoughtfully, then caught Flora Linda's eye. "We've got some work to do here. Can you make sure no one disturbs us?"

Flora Linda nodded, winked, and left them.

Since the sun had disappeared, leaving the day chilly and damp, they were inside the tent where Tia sometimes did her trance work. "I'll try to reach her on the BSC," said Carmen, leaning back against a stack of blankets. "I thought she was going to be here today. That's why I had Teo drop us here."

Minutes later, Carmen opened her eyes. "She's not answering and neither is Tomas. What do we do now?"

"You know what, Carmen? I don't think we are applying the lessons Tia has taught us. Let's sit still here in the trance room and wait."

Waiting was not exactly Carmen's style. "Can't we at least chant?"

"Okay, I'll chant in Hmong and you chant some of the words Tia taught you."

They sat down on the spread out sleeping bags across from each other and began to chant. Carmen felt herself growing very sleepy and had to snap her eyes open several times. Then she noticed a strange purple glow filling the tent. She looked at Chia to see if she saw it, also. But before she could speak, she heard a buzzing and then they both saw a fat bumblebee whining around a pile of quilts where it landed and sat very still.

Both of them dived for the spot where the bee sat. But as they did so, it jerked away with one last quick buzz. Hurriedly, they pulled the stack apart to find a crate buried underneath. Under the crate was a plank that they shoved aside to reveal a dirty, khaki green backpack with orange spray painted letters and the same thunderbolt through a big 13 just like Fernando had inked on his neck.

Inside Fernando's backpack was the plato, wrapped in velvet. Carmen pulled it out and cradled it, smiling at Chia. "Tia was right. No need to go chasing down Fernando to find this. It came back to us, Cousin Chia."

❧❧❧

Choppo turned to look at them in the back seat. "What's up with the taimado twins? Crafty ones," he explained at their puzzled looks. "You two look like the fat cats who ate all the chicharrones."

"We have a surprise, Choppo. We found the plato!" Carmen could not contain her excitement.

But when they entered the trance room, Tia was sporting a smile as wide as the Milky Way. "I know what you have there. Let me see it, my *brujaitas*."

Carmen handed the backpack to Tia. "It's not fair, Tia. We can never surprise you."

"Surprises are over-rated. They only last a few seconds, after all. Now leave me alone for a minute while I prepare this beauty for viewing."

"Okay" said Carmen, her voice betraying her impatience. "We were waiting for you at the encampment. What happened to you?"

"I was doing dream work and my dreams told me to stay here and wait for you."

The few minutes it took Tia to set up the plato seemed like hours to Carmen and Chia. Finally Tia emerged from the trance room and immediately threw up her hand, as if to hold them off. "I'm sorry, but I think we need everyone here for the unveiling. Chia, can you bring True back tonight after dinner?"

Chia frowned. "Oh, yea, I guess so. But—"

"Can't we take a peek? After all, we found it and we brought it back to you. We could have looked at it on our own, you know," Carmen said, feeling like a little kid begging for a treat.

But Tia would not be swayed, and they made preparations for everyone to come together that night, She arranged for Choppo to pick everyone up in the cab after he had run several errands for her.

Carmen rushed through dinner and was helping Mami grind chilies in the molcajete for more salsa when the doorbell rang and she raced to let Chia and True in, with Choppo just behind them. Chia held up a bag of more chilies from their garden for Rosa. Tomas gave Chia a big hug and ruffled True's shiny hair. Flora Linda followed the girls in, dressed in a long velvet dress, army jacket and her usual pink boa.

"Where's Connie?" Carmen asked Flora Linda.

Before she could answer, Choppo, who wasn't looking very well, stammered, "She said to tell you she'd catch you later. She had to do some recycling tonight." He coughed and popped another mint into his mouth. Carmen wondered if he'd been drinking again.

Tia was sitting hunched over the plato in the trance room, wrapped in an Indian blanket, her face painted with an elaborate design of colors that made her look like a butterfly upside down, wreathed in sage smoke, the room blooming with its familiar, burned funk. She said nothing to them, so they gathered around her, waiting.

The plato was arranged in a bed of dark purple velvet. It was only about ten inches across, with elaborate scenes that circled around the borders. Raising her head slowly, Tia nodded to True and glanced at a set of drums in the corner. True went to them and began to drum softly, catching the beat of candle light flickers that swept over the walls. They all settled on cushions. Flora Linda moaned softly in sync with the hypnotic rhythms.

Carmen closed her eyes and felt herself drifting into a dizzy, dreamy spell, much like being inside Parajaflor, but not swaddled down. Instead, she felt untethered. At first she was frightened, afraid if she let go, she'd drift away into a black hole and never be heard from again. But little by little, she gave in and a warm glow filled her. After what seemed like hours or seconds—she couldn't tell—she opened her eyes to see Tia holding the plato out to them, offering them a pile of dark black chips. They were Mami's special chips that she made from purple cornmeal, seaweed, ground seeds, cilantro, galangal, hot Thai peppers, and herbs that she and Chia had experimented with. They had wanted to make a snack chip that combined the flavors of their two cultures and they called them Mex-mong chips. Earlier, Mami had made a special salsa to go with them and was now sitting in the corner grinding chilies again. Carmen thought this had become Mami's own personal therapy. Cups of green tea were passed around and, as everyone ate, Tia began to talk.

"We are using this plato to serve food because this is part of our new journey—combining our energies, our gifts from the separate cultures for a higher purpose always. We will all take a vow today to help our people in ways that are uplifting and empowering. We can never use the powers that have come to us for bad because they are entrusted to us to use for good and not to bring harm to others." Tia stopped and looked around the room. "This is a blessing and a burden. Do you know what I mean?"

No one spoke, but a voice came into the room, seeming to enter from above. "Yea. Means we gotta do different now. No cappin', no merkin', no more killin'. Gotta go wit a new way, T says. Das cool." Seemingly from nowhere, Fernando entered the room as he spoke and plopped down on the floor beside Tomas, his hoodie pulled up over his head.

Tia waved her upturned palm at Fernando. "We need to thank Fernando for the plato. Without his help, we would not have gotten it back. He risked his life to help Tomas and to retrieve the plato for us, and we are forever in his debt. And you are right, Fernando. We hope that a new way of living means no more violence and killing. And we can all live in peace together." She lifted a ball of thick red string and handed it to True, who unwound it and handed an end back to Tia, which she cut with a tiny pair of swan shaped scissors. She did the same for everyone and then moved them into a circle around Fernando, with the strings radiating outward. Tia, True, and Flora Linda began the chant, then everyone else joined in.

Finally Carmen spoke. "Tia, there's lots of things I still don't understand. For one thing, how did Fernando get the plato?"

Then everyone was talking at once. In the muddle of voices, Fernando leaped up from his spot, gave them all a strange twisted finger salute, and bolted from the room.

Chia had grabbed True, protectively. "What's wrong?"

"No tension...don't worry. Fernando will be back. *El es inconstante*...what's the word?"

"Skittish?" Carmen said, coming back in the room. She had run after Fernando to see where he might go, but he had just seemed to disappear.

"He's got a lot of heat on him," Tomas said. "But he's got good reasons to be afraid. I think Silver's been tailing him. And the gang bangers are after him also. I want to help Fernie jump outa the gang, if we can find a way to bring charges against Silver. Fernie contacted me about an hour ago and told me where the plato was and what had happened with it. Of course, by then, you two had already found it. "

Chia sighed. "I'm sorry he ran. I wanted to thank him myself for helping Tomas."

"Si, I too," said Mami.

"But really, all of you helped with returning our treasures—both Tomas and the plato," Tia said. "I think now is the time perhaps to tell you the story of the plato. Get yourselves comfortable. Our part of the story began in Mexico many years ago."

Before Tia could continue, the door banged open and two large men in black t-shirts with the words ICE on them burst into the room. One of them, the man Carmen recognized as Dr. Sicko pointed a huge, ugly gun around the room. "Hands up everyone! Grab those two." Dr. Sicko motioned the other man toward Choppo and Tomas. Quickly, he pulled out handcuffs, cuffed them both together and sat them on the floor back to back like helpless Siamese twins.

They heard him before they saw his snaky silver smile, an angry, metallic zing as Silver flicked out his tape measure, entering the room. "Up against that wall, everyone and put your hands over your head! This time we're taking the plato for good."

Tia made a sudden move and Tonto, who had followed Silver into the room, grabbed her from behind. "I got this one. She's some kinda witch, but we got the magic of the Glock on our side." His laugh was low and surly. After tying up Tia, he grabbed both Chia and Carmen and roughly shoved them against the wall where everyone else now cowered.

The other Ice man began to tie up Flora Linda next. Mami was crying softly huddled against the wall, cradling her molcajete. Chia had faced True away from them and stood wrapped protectively around her.

When Carmen saw Mami crying, red hot, unbridled anger exploded inside, but remembering her rash actions of before, she shoved her fury down and spoke, trying to keep the shaking out of her voice. Maybe she could at least slow things down.

"We know you're not real ICE," she said, struggling to keep the quaver out of her voice.

"At least we're real Americans, not wetbacks like you. Sicko, get the plato. We got to get ready for our trip."

"Trip?" Carmen's eyes bugged out despite herself.

"Yea. Don't play dumb. We found out about the vacation benefits of this plato, thanks to your gabby cab driver there." Silver snapped out his tape measure at Choppo.

Choppo turned red as the chilies in Rosa's salsa. "That guy," he inclined his head toward Dr. Sicko, "calls himself a parole officer. What kinda cop gets people drunk when he knows they got a problem and..." Choppo trailed off, letting his head droop to his chest.

Silver snorted then stooped to grab the plato. "One of our...uh business partners already had suspicions about it anyway."

But just as Tonto reached to tie Rosa's hands, she whirled and with one smooth motion, flung her mortar full of ground chilies in Silver's face. With a gasp, he fell to the floor screaming. Almost at the same moment, Caw Caw swooped down from the upper shelf where she had perched and flapped into Dr. Sicko's face. Both startled and thrown off balance, he dropped his gun. Carmen, swiftly and surely, grabbed the gun and stepped in front of Rosa. Caw Caw then hurled herself at Tonto, clawing and pecking at his eyes. Rosa quickly untied Tia, who grabbed the gun from Carmen and pointed it at Silver, writhing on the floor.

"Call your men off, Silver, or I'll shoot. I know how to use this thing, I assure you."

Silver sat up, moaning and rubbing his eyes, tears streaming down his face.

"Don't rub your eyes. It only makes it worse," Tia said calmly. "Now, unlock them," She motioned toward Tomas and Choppo.

"Boss—" Dr. Sicko started, but Silver, still clawing at his face, yelled, "Just do it, you fool." He gasped for breath. "I—I can't breathe."

"It only feels that way, "Tia said. "Someone get me a wet cloth from the kitchen and put some of my salve on it."

Choppo, who was now free, untied Flora Linda who went to get the cloth.

After he was unlocked, Tomas whispered something to Tia and left the room. No one moved or spoke. Returning to the room, Choppo spoke to Tia. "I'm sorry, Tia, I know I was—"

Tia didn't move or look his way, keeping the gun trained on Silver. "We'll deal with that later, Choppo. Take those cuffs and hook Silver and Dr. Sicko to that table."

"Carmen, look outside and make sure there aren't any more in their van."

Carmen ran to follow her orders and then returned. "Van looks empty from what I could see. Unless they're hiding inside."

When the door opened again, Carmen's heart nearly leapt out of her chest, but there to her relief, filling the doorway, were the FBI men she had seen Tomas talking to before, with their guns drawn. "Read 'em their rights," one of the men yelled.

Tomas came in the door behind the men. "They were waiting for my phone call. I think we've got a good case now. And we can add impersonating an ICE to their charges also. Course that big one was a real ICE. They've had their eye on him for a while, just didn't have any hard evidence."

"Wait." Tia took the cloth Flora Linda handed her and bent down to pat the skin around Silver's eyes. "This is my special cream to help with the burning. We want you in good shape to stand trial, Mr. Silver." She winked up at Carmen and Chia.

By now everyone had been untied and watched solemnly as the FBI cuffed Silver, Dr. Sicko, Tonto and the other big one with the ICE T-shirt.

"There's also Briggs, who co-owns the real estate company," said Tomas, rubbing his sore wrists. "And there's some others too who worked for Silver."

"You're going to have to come with us down to headquarters then, to help us identify them. Let's get going." The room was now filled to bursting with all the FBI men and women added in.

Because of its heavy weight, Tia almost dropped the big gun she still held. She handed it over to the agent closest to her. "Here, you can have this. I'm allergic to these things."

"Do you really know how to use it?" Carmen asked her aunt as she watched the agent take the wicked looking weapon.

Tia winked. "I could use it to pound chilies with I suppose. As you saw, chilies are a very potent weapon."

After the FBI agents and their suspects had all left, Tia suggested they all do a short meditation to try and relax and get rid of the tension of the evening. With Tia chanting, everyone lay back on the pillows and followed her instructions.

Minutes later, after a period of stillness, Tia spoke again. "I was telling you the story of the plato, and I think it would be good to finish it now. Unless you would like to wait for another time."

"No. Tell it now." Carmen bounced on her haunches. "Can you stay a little while longer, Chia?"

"Let me go phone." She returned with a sigh. "Can you tell it in a half hour? That's how much longer we have."

"I'll tell the fast version." Tia gathered everyone around the plato. "As I was saying, before we were almost so rudely killed—" She winked. "—this story begins in Mexico, long ago.

Bear with me if I repeat some things, but not everyone here knows all the details of the story. We have always had *curenderas* in our family, and since they do not accept money for their services, your Great Aunt Yoruba accepted a beautiful plato as a gift from a family whose daughter she had cured of soul loss. The poor girl had been depressed and not eating for months. Yoruba preformed a number of *limpias* and the girl completely recovered. Yourba had a series of dreams where she received the information about the plato's magical powers. One day an old man came to her house to buy herbs and when he saw the plato, he gasped. He told Yoruba that it was a very old Mayan artifact that the Mayans had used to travel to another world. Shortly after that, the old man disappeared, but Yoruba kept the plato safe.

"When your father began to help people across the border, he contacted Yoruba and she made her house available to him. They only helped those who needed to be united with family members or needed medical help or other emergencies. Yourba had contacted me and told me about the plato, and we decided that I should take it and try to use its special powers in my work, so Veloz, Carmen, and Tomas' father, was entrusted to bring it to the U.S. for me. About the same time, I had to leave town to take care of a personal problem. So Veloz decided to hide the plato at Immaculate Motors. He told Teo, who had been helping him in his work where he was hiding the plato. But he only told him that it was a very old, valuable artifact. Teo did not know of its magical properties."

Carmen squirmed in her spot on the floor. "How did you find all this out, Tia?"

"That's another story in itself. But, let me just say that Teo is like a rusty box, easily pried open. And some of this I translated from the letters you found, Carmen. In one of the letters, Yoruba wrote to tell Veloz that Teofilo couldn't be trusted. So your father hid the plato again, without telling Teo. That was right before he was killed. Now, I will turn the story over to Rosa. She was important in helping me to put together the pieces of this plato puzzle. Speak slowly, Rosa, and I'll translate."

Rosa spoke rapidly, despite Tia's request, and when she was done, Tia chuckled. "Rosa says, 'A wolf must die in its own skin.' We make our own little sneak attack on Teofilo. First we flattered him, then we frightened him. We told him the FBI wants to talk to him. Of course, we didn't know you girls had just been there with the same story. He cracked like a rotten walnut and told us how he had been fixing up Silver's vans, doing some upholstery work, when Silver asked him about a plato. Of course, Teo said that Silver threatened him, and he told him he would look for it. Of course, it wasn't where Teo thought it would be.

"Silver didn't believe Teo when he said he couldn't find it and set about trying to buy Immaculate Motors. Teo says he was scared, and he was also hoping to make some money on the deal. Fear and greed, always a bad combination. And he and Septima were not getting along so well, anyway. So he forged Septima's signature on the sale papers. All this happened later, though. He had left Septima in Mexico and come back here to deal with Silver. So Septima didn't know anything about all this. Of course, when Carmen gave me the letters from Yoruba, I knew the plato was still there.

"Christmas day night, Choppo and I went to Immaculate Motors to look. I knew there was no attic, but I remembered a crawl space above Teo's workshop, that was now covered in vines. You wouldn't see it, if you didn't know it was there. We got the ladder, chopped away the vines, and there inside the space, wrapped in old, dirty burlap and shoved way in the back, we found the plato. You know what happened after that."

"Except, we still don't know how Fernando got the plato, Tia."

"After Silver took the plato from us on the road that night, he hid it in the warehouse where they were keeping Tomas. Fernando was supposed to be helping Silver and his men. He agreed to that with his probation officer, who is Dr. Sicko. But Fernando was planning to try and help Tomas escape. Tomas had told Fernando about the plato when Fernando snuck into his room in the warehouse one night. And when Fernando saw it there that day we rescued Tomas, he snuck it into his backpack.

"He took off that day at the encampments and left it in the tent because after the effects of the flea poison wore off, he became paranoid, and he just ran. Tomas had only hazy memories of the day of the rescue and didn't even know Fernando had found the plato or hid it or anything until about an hour ago, when Fernando contacted him and told him the story and Tomas told me. The gang that Fernando is trying to get out of has been after him so he doesn't stay anywhere too long. I hope we can help him with a *limpia* or a *platica* one of these days." Tia paused and mopped her brow, smearing some of the painted on colors.

"So that's the story, my friends. I just want to add that all of you should be very proud of your part in our rescue of Tomas and in finding the plato. No one of us could have done it alone. I am very hopeful that we can all continue our work together and make good progress both here and on Om. They are experiencing another lull right now, perhaps because we have the plato back, but we still have much work to do there. I am so proud of you girls. You have all faced your fears with courage and learned many new skills. Also, Flora Linda, take a bow."

Flora Linda stood up, twirled on her toes, and bowed low as a shower of sparkle dust rose up around her.

Afraid that Tia was forgetting Rosa, Carmen held up her palm, trying to hide her finger, pointing to her mother.

Tia turned to Rosa. "There is one person, however, who showed more courage tonight than all of us put together." She bowed to Rosa, slowing pointing the jaguar stick her way.

Rosa beamed. "I—I so happy—so much *gratitud*. Tomas is back." She stopped, full of tears she tried to suppress. Finally, she continued. "I want to stay here now. I have a casa...a home and *mucho amour. Gracias, muchas gracias. Los santos tienan novenas ahora.*"

"She's saying 'the saints have novenas, which means our time has come now,'" Tia translated for everyone.

"Choppo." Tia waved her jaguar pipe at him.

"I'm not worthy of—" Choppo cleared his throat, then continued. "I messed up real bad, I know. But I won't make excuses."

"I'm glad to hear it. That is the first step in making a change—taking responsibility for your actions. But you have helped us much and I know you are truly loyal. We will give you another chance, only if you make one promise."

Choppo saluted. "At your service."

Tia smiled. "You will not be afraid to ask for help when you need it."

Choppo nodded and bent his head, his shoulders shaking with a sudden burst of tears. From Tia's shoulder now, Caw Caw squawked loudly.

True's big eyes grew even bigger. "We must thank her, too."

"Of course, she is my trusty sidekick, my shadow, my—" Tia paused, searching for words. "My soul candy." Everyone laughed at this. "Bring her a gift of thanks next time you come. You know what she likes."

True's eyes lit up. "Gummy worms!"

Chia's grin turned to a worried frown. "Tia, maybe I shouldn't be asking this. But I'm wondering where you'll keep the plato. It needs to be in a safe place, and perhaps only you should know where."

Tia frowned. But before she could speak, they heard a loud banging on the front door. Mami moved to get up, but Tia signaled her to stay. "I'll get it. I think our ceremonies are over. Perhaps we had better straighten up. Choppo, can you take Chia and True home now?"

After the girls left with Choppo, Tia stayed at the door for several minutes. As Carmen began to gather up the red strings, she heard an anxious woman's voice rising in volume. "I don't know what to do. Can't you please help me? I need someone to…"

Carmen could hear Tia shushing the woman now, and their voices dropping to a combined mumble.

"Carmen, *mira*," Mami waved from the doorway. "Look—I find in the porch back *ahora*." Mami was holding up a small basket of grapes with a note attached.

Carmen took the note and read, "Thank you Mrs. Estrella for helping *mi hermano*. He much better now." It was signed Rosa Pelig. "Rosa Pelgi, Rosa Pelig…Rosapeligrosapelig…"

Suddenly she stopped, ran outside with the basket, and threw it down on the ground, scattering the grapes. As Rosa looked on in shock, a huge black widow spider crawled out from the overturned basket.

Without stopping to think, Carmen tried to stomp on it, just as Tia returned. The spider, however, scurried off into the darkness.

"Someone sent a basket with this note." Carmen handed the retrieved note to Tia. "A thank you fruit basket, with an extra little surprise—a black widow."

Tia's dark eyes popped. "That was quick thinking, Carmen. What gave it away?"

Mami looked shaken and pale. "*Si*. And you are so afraid of spiders, *mija*."

Carmen blushed. "I just kept repeating the name and when it blended, Rosa and Pelig made peligrosa, which means danger. Maybe a little bit of intuition kicked in, too."

"We still have enemies, and I think I know who this comes from." Tia's eyes took them all in. "The *mal bruja*. I asked around the neighborhood and they thought she had gone to Mexico. But this is not the first gift she's left me. I'm quite sure now that she's tied in with Silver. The night they broke into my place, I saw a large, dark woman roll down the window, just as they jumped into the van before taking off. She must also want the plato. We will have to remain vigilant."

"And remember that Silver said they had a business partner who suspected the plato had magical powers. I bet it was the bruja and she was working with them. But, who was at the door, Tia?"

"A poor woman who went to a *mal bruja* to get her husband to come back to her. The *bruja* got over five hundred dollars out of her and now things are even worse. Mrs. Soto's being deported and the husband will have the house and all their stuff to himself. And his girlfriend's moving in. I told her I'd look into it, but I have my suspicions."

Carmen shook her head in disgust. "You think the *mal bruja* took her money and tipped off the ICE that she wasn't legal?"

Tia just tapped her foot and fiddled with the feathers on her cane. Finally, she said, "*Si*. And she probably got some money out of the husband too. But she is a crafty one and especially evil. Unfortunately, we have no evidence on her at all."

CHAPTER 42

After they had cleaned up the trance room, Tia turned to Carmen. "I'm very proud of you girls, but you took a risk going to Teofilo's alone, you know."

"Oh Teo—he tries to sound tough, but he's just a big bag of...of feathers." Carmen fluttered her fingers. "What do you think will happen to Teo, Tia?"

"Well, I don't think Septima will divorce him because of her religion. And it looks like he will get to keep Immaculate Motors. I suspect that Septima will come back one day when she's fully recovered. Teo's big mistake was trusting the bad guys. And greed, too. But greed isn't something people often recover from."

Just then Carmen sucked in her breath. "Guano! I bet it was the *mal bruja* who put a spell on Septima and made her ill."

"I suspected that before, Carmen. But now I'm almost certain. We've done a lot—Silver and his men are well on their way to prison—Tomas is back, Mami is well, and we have the plato. But Tomas and I talked last night about Om. Sometime in the near future, you will have to go back and take the plato with you. That will be a big job. I want you to be ready."

Carmen jumped up and saluted. "Ai ai, commander. Carmen Luna at your service."

"But you are *not* ready." Tia's face was contorted with the bright colors slashing her face with angry Vs.

Carmen was shocked to see her aunt looking so harsh. "What do you mean?"

"This!" Tia held out a slip of paper.

Carmen knew what it was. "Oh yea, I was going to talk to—"

"No excuses. What is this? You got a D in Math? An F in P.E.? We'll have to cut your other lessons out until you bring these grades up."

"No! Please, Tia. I won't be able to concentrate on school at all if I can't do my *curendera* and *bruja* studies. Anyway, if I'm going to be a *bruja*, what do I need with school? You didn't go—"

"And every day I find another thing that is hard for me because I can't write and I can't talk to authorities the way I should be able to. That woman I just told you about, Mrs. Soto, what she needs right now is a lawyer. I will send her to someone, but he is very busy. He can't keep up with all the work that comes his way. We have battles to fight on Om and here on Earth, Carmen. I will continue your training for the *curendera*, but you must do better in school, or we won't go on with it. You could be of much help to people like Mrs. Soto, if you got a law degree." Tia was silent, watching Carmen. Then she said, a bit more softly, "What did you see yourself doing for a job later on?"

Carmen shook her head. "I didn't see myself doing anything. Mrs. Lasky told me I should go to beauty school. And Miss Goff said I'm not college material—she hates me."

Tia arched her eyebrows disapprovingly. "Come on now, Carmen. What makes you think that?"

"'Cuz she only likes white girls. She got Melissa Sanchez expelled because she said she smelled pot on her, and I know Melissa doesn't do that. But after that, her dad got deported back to Mexico. Goff says I'm a lazy *pachuca* 'cuz I cut one corner of the field off when she told me to run laps. She said I was talking, but I wasn't. She gets me mixed up with Lupe all the time. We don't even look that much alike. And then she flunked me after I cut off the lap—one lousy lap."

Tia shook her head. "That sounds unfair. But you know what? It's not fair what's happening to Mrs. Soto either. You need to put yourself in a position so that people can't get away with unfair treatment. That's what I want to see for you." Tia picked up the plato and handed it to Carmen. "Go ahead. Hold it. It only bites if it doesn't like you."

Carmen took the plate in her hand and looked deep into the washy colors and the figures etched into the clay. She saw feathered serpents; dragons; a bird monster; a fish monster; figures dancing, singing, cooking; some half human, half jaguar, or fish. She saw people in masks and plumed headdresses, carrying fire and water, playing flutes and playing ball around the tree of life, twined with serpents, branching up into the heavens above and the underworld below. Carmen began to feel woozy. Her arms and legs went mushy and loose. She closed her eyes.

Holding the plato to her heart, she saw a young woman's face smiling. The woman turned and, carrying a brief case, walked into a large room filled with people on benches. A woman sat in at the front of the room with her right hand raised, palm up, and a man asked her to swear to tell the truth, the whole truth, so help her God.

Carmen looked closer. It was Miss Goff and she was on trial for discrimination and unfairness. If convicted, she'd have to run laps around the courthouse until she had no breath left to call out detention or discredit anyone ever again.

Carmen clutched the plato tightly, finding that she could not let go of it, almost as if it anchored her to the ground. Or as if it were a steering wheel and any turn would take her down a distant, beckoning path. She gripped it so hard her fingers numbed, but then they began to tingle in soft flutters of electricity.

A face swam into view, at first blurred and washy, then slowly, Great Aunt Yoruba took shape. Black opal eyes sparkled through the fog of years, unsmiling, but exuding a sense of comfort and peace. As she extended her hand, other shadowy forms floated nearby, ghostlike, bumping and blending together.

Then the lilting notes of a flute could be heard, bits and pieces of a song, its familiarity floating just out of reach as Carmen was filled with sadness and love, seemingly without a source. Although her mouth did not move, a man's voice came somewhere from within Yoruba's center.

"Carmen my love for you and my family has always been nearby. But my soul has wandered restlessly since the day I left you, never at peace. Now that you have the plato and my family is back together, I can cross the bridge I've been stopped at so long. I am filled with contentment for the first time. And you have all done good work, continuing what I began. It's because, as Tia has taught you, you have worked together. Remember, though, I'll always be there beside you."

Carmen felt a jolt then, as if she'd had the air knocked out of her. She gasped for breath and looked down at the plato to where something shimmered like a large plum, glowing an intense purple-blue.

Tia spoke from behind her. "Now we can get down to real work. It's only the beginning, *mija*."

END OF BOOK 1

Study Guide for Carmen & Chia Mix Magic

1. What does the color silver symbolize in the story?

2. What does ICE stand for? How does the author use ice in the story as a symbol and a metaphor?

3. Give specific examples from the story of situations where characters only succeed by working together.

4. Give specific examples of racism in the story. How is the girl's encounter with the policemen downtown an example of attitudinal racism?

5. Carmen adopts the word "meso" (meaning middle or in-between) as one of her magic words. If you think of this word symbolically, how does it relate to the story?

6. Why does Carmen fear being like her mother?

7. How does Rosa change in the story?

8. Discuss how Carmen and Rosa's relationship changes in the story.

9. What other characters in the story change? How do they change?

10. Irony means "an event or language that is contrary to what is expected, sometimes with humorous results." What is ironic about Septima's attitude toward curanderas?

11. How are the different senses used to show danger in the story?

12. What is the importance of the color purple in the story? Give specific examples from the story that show its significance.

13. What clues foreshadow True's being revealed as the secret shaman?

14. Name the particular fears of Carmen, Chia and Mami.

15. Explain how each person's fears are illustrated by a story they recount from the past.

16. What role do animals play in the story?

17. Give an example of a Hmong folk tale from the story.

18. Give an example of a Mexican folk tale from the story.

19. What is the Popol Vu and how is it important to the story?

20. What do you learn about the Mayan culture from the story?

21. What do you learn about the Hmong culture from the story?

22. What role do lawyers play in the story? Why are they important?

23. This story is told from many different points of view. Why is this important?

24. One major theme of the story is cooperation. What are some others?

24. What important issues about immigration are brought out in the story?

24. Do you feel differently about homeless people after reading this story?

25. What theories or attitudes are suggested by the author as guides for new ways of interacting that will promote understanding and peace in the world?

26. In Chapter 35, Carmen says she doesn't think that people can change. Do you agree with this or disagree? Do you think the author agrees or disagrees with this?

27. Are fighting, violence and war inevitable in the modern world?

28. What new attitudes toward conflict does the story promote?

29. Which character on Om gives a speech directly related to questions 27 and 28?

30. What are the values considered important on Om? How would these values change the world you live in?

31. How is the plot of this story different from other fantasy books you might have read? What is the author's purpose in departing from the traditional plot features of most fantasy stories?

About the Author

Award-winning author Dixie Salazar has published five books of poetry: *Hotel Fresno* by Blue Moon Press in 1988, *Reincarnation of the Commonplace* (national poetry award winner) by Salmon Run Press in 1999, *Blood Mysteries* by University of Arizona in 2003, and *Flamenco Hips and Red Mud Feet* also by University of Arizona in 2010. *Limbo*, her novel, was published by White Pine Press in 1995. Her newest collection, *Altar for Escaped Voices*, was published by Tebot Bach in February of 2013. Salazar is also a visual artist, working mostly in oils, with an extensive showing record in the Central Valley of California, Merced, Sacramento, San Francisco, Las Vegas, Nevada, and New York.